BLOOD
AND SOIL

by Vinny Cusenza

PEN & PENCIL PRESS

Ebook ISBN: 979-8-218-61848-3

Print ISBN: 979-8-218-61847-6

Cover design by: Minnie Cho, FUSELOFT, fuseloft.com

Interior design and typesetting by: Christine Baker, Labrador Publishing, www.labradorpublishing.com

Published by: Pen & Pencil Press, Brooklyn, New York

Printed in the United States of America

PRAISE FOR BLOOD AND SOIL

A tale of two vastly dissimilar young men struggling for acceptance, love, and justice in a time of intolerance...a page-turner packed with suspense, murder, heartbreak, and healing, and an allegory of the search for our authentic selves.

> – Getty Ambau, author of the award-winning Desta adventure series

Blood and Soil is a twisty, atmospheric murder mystery that pulses with violence and shimmers with tenderness.

> – Beth Ann Bauman, author of *Rosie and Skate* and *Jersey Angel*

Cusenza's novel makes for an admirably ambitious debut, blending choice facets of American and regional history with a star-crossed romance. Both blood, in this often violent action-adventure, and soil, in vivid descriptions of a certain corner of New York State, can be found in abundance – and the title's allusion to an infamous Nazi slogan proves far from coincidental.

> – Lance Ringel, award-winning author of *Flower of Iowa* and *Floridian Nights*

To Mom and Dad, children of immigrants,
who overcame intolerance to achieve their American dream

We are all formed of frailty and error; let us pardon reciprocally each other's folly. — *Voltaire*

1

Saturday August 27th, 1960
AFTERNOON: TONY

He steered out of the woods to the county road and scanned the rearview mirror obsessively, as if desperate to outrun this disastrous day.

Familiar signposts shot by; the turnoff for town, the bend where the road skirted the Old Rhinelander cove. In the blur of bungalows and tackle shops, images flickered from the backwoods with Jake.

Tony's eyes left the road as he approached a shirtless, well-built man in dungarees and work boots on the right shoulder, leaning on a shovel. His wide-open stare captured Tony's gaze at the moment a big panel truck crested the pavement ahead.

Almost too late, he saw that he'd strayed over the yellow line, and cut the wheel hard right. The truck narrowly missed him, the angry blast of its horn bending around the Falcon as he grappled the wheel, still straining for one last glimpse of the shirtless man in his rearview mirror.

Tony's chest thudded at his recklessness. Jake had set loose a wild force in him that he couldn't control, and now he'd ruined his chances with him. Tony clamped a palm over his mouth and let out a strangled cry.

Jake had thrown down the gauntlet. *We can't be anything until you know what you want.* Camping hadn't helped; if anything, it had exposed Tony's bone-deep ambivalence about Jake. And himself. Where did that leave him? Them?

Who was he? Columbia man, his parents' pride? A perv on a police blotter? What was the way forward, when all of his choices meant exiling a piece of his heart?

EVENING: EDDIE

Eddie held his breath for the awful sound that meant it was done. His head throbbed with the incomprehensible: his best buddy Stefan was dead, and Eddie had just avenged him.

He careened through the woods to the clearing where Stefan's sister knelt, rocking and moaning. He grabbed her long flaxen hair and slapped her hard with the back of his hand.

"You two-faced whore! Look what you've done!"

"Animal! Murderer!" Karla growled and clawed at him, but he grabbed her outstretched arm and twisted it behind her back before dragging her off, bare heels plowing lines of resistance in the loamy earth.

Eddie shoved Karla into the El Camino, slammed the door, and landed hard on the driver's seat. The mixblood's sickening stench of sweat and lust filled the cab of the truck, the one that Silas had taken her up the mountain in tonight. *Taken what wasn't his.*

He pawed the unfamiliar dash for the keys, started the engine, and plunged them headlong through squealing brush. Heart hammering, Eddie's eyes bounced from the rushing forest to Karla, pressed against the door, her splayed, bloody fingers smearing the glass, painting over the pallid moon.

His stomach lurched. He'd tried to stick to the plan, goddammit, but everything had gone wrong. How was he supposed to keep a cool head, face-to-face with the scum who'd screwed his girl?

This was worse than all of his other fuckups put together, and he was terrified that Uncle Otto would find out and make his life hell. But Uncle was the sheriff, and this was campaign season; maybe he could make it all just go away, like he'd bailed out Eddie before.

Uncle had said that his half-breed opponent was giving him a run for his money this election. Maybe he *had* to bury Eddie's big problem, if he wanted to stay sheriff.

Eddie's sweaty hands slipped on the wheel and the chassis shimmied, wrestling him for control. A sudden click and rush of air snapped Eddie's eyes back to Karla, shouldering the open door, and he lunged for her just as a sharp impact slammed it shut and threw her against him.

Karla squalled and thrashed him with her fists, wailing "*Silas!*" again and again, each cry a knife to Eddie's heart.

Eddie hooked his arm around her neck and squeezed with a force that lifted him from his seat. After she stopped struggling, he choked out the words that had always lodged in his throat like hard stones, the ones she'd come here tonight to hear from someone else's lips.

"*I love you, Karla.*"

MIDNIGHT: JAKE

Jake steadied himself against the door of his pickup as the mountain spun around him. He probably hadn't needed all that drink in town, but he'd been in a mess of confusion about Tony after breaking camp. At least now the roar in his head had quieted.

He scythed his way through weeds to the barn door and wrenched it open. He glanced sideways toward the new project on his workbench. Digging into his satchel, he pulled out the new woodworking gouge; sleek, Swiss, expensive.

He held it in the half-light, but his vision wouldn't focus, and then his whole body collapsed in on itself. He flung the tool to the dirt and strode to a basin and pitcher on a stand under a dangling mirror. Filling the basin, he dipped his hands and splashed his face repeatedly until he was dripping wet.

He toweled with frenzied strokes, stopping only when his skin grew hot and raw. He stared into the glass at the blue-gray eyes, chestnut cheeks, and dark hair, and made a sound like a wounded animal.

Mountain monkey.

He knocked the pitcher and basin to the ground, and stumbled to a shelf thick with sawdust. He grabbed an open bottle, wiped its lip against his shirt, and took honey-colored gulps, fire sluicing his chest, pulling him down.

"Goddamn me," he muttered.

He must have dozed. He pushed up from the packed dirt and wobbled outside. The sudden flood of moonlight made him wince. He scanned the front yard; no El Camino. Fear razored through him. It had to be three a.m.: where the hell was Silas?

His brother had been courting trouble since spring. He'd ignored all the KEEP OUT signs and gone where he had no business being, where any fool from the mountain knew not to trespass.

Jake staggered to the house and up the sagging porch steps, where he left his boots and went inside. He tiptoed upstairs and climbed into his bunk. His brothers' snores soon delivered him to sleep.

Too soon, his eyes opened to a wan glow edging the curtains. Temples throbbing, Jake dropped to the rug soundlessly, grabbed a clean T-shirt, and pulled on dungarees and socks. He scanned the room; his two eldest brothers lay sprawled in their bunks. Silas's sheets were untouched.

Jake sidestepped a loose floorboard, padded downstairs to the kitchen sink, and splashed his face and neck with icy water. He toweled dry, slipped on the T-shirt, and strode to the door. He stepped out and set it softly in its frame.

His gaze shot to where Silas's flatbed should be. His brother had slept off plenty of benders in the barn or the old miners' ruins to dodge Mama's lambastings, but something was off this time. Ugly scenes flickered behind Jake's eyes, and his stomach tightened.

The forest rattled and clicked last call of the night. Jake scooped up his boots and sat in a weathered rocker, tying the laces with quick, spiderlike movements. He felt something wet nuzzle his hand. "Maisie." The coonhound beat her tail against the rocker. Jake rose and sprinted across the lawn to his pickup, Maisie at his heels.

They rode for some time on rutted dirt roads hemmed with late-summer brush, finally rocking to a stop at Sky Notch. Jake headed on foot down a hillside to level ground strewn with mason's stones and moldering shacks.

He approached a weathered manse with a large porch, frame out of plumb. His sights snagged on a freshly splintered step, large whorls dug in the dirt before it, the forest floor spattered rust brown.

He hopped a missing board and entered. In the main room, a knotted heap of blankets and clothing lay near an empty duffel bag. Wax speckled the floor alongside upended candles and cigarette butts.

Jake paced, lungs heaving, feet scraping grit and leaves. He strained to make the picture mean anything but what his thoughts screamed.

Maisie's insistent, staccato calls cut through his spiraling panic, and he ran out toward the light. She squealed and paced the outcropping. He brushed aside branches, crept to the edge, and peered into a bright void.

Jake spotted a shadow fifty feet below. He jumped and slid his way down the scree, Maisie at his heels. Skidding to a stop, he grappled Silas's broken body, and his lungs burst with a ragged, keening cry.

2

Nineteen days earlier, Monday August 8th

Tony had overslept and rushed to the safari park for his 8:30 orientation. He slunk his way to a folding chair toward the back of the trailer, feeling the room's attention.

His old Brooklyn Dodgers cap hid unbrushed curls, and he nervously tugged it tighter. The man at the lectern in a suit several sizes too tight turned toward him and frowned, and Tony batted off the hat.

He'd been lucky to nab a job at Wild'n'Wooly so late in the summer. He certainly hadn't expected there to be this many new recruits three months into the park's summer season. It seemed like a bad omen for what was in store for him.

After spending the first two months of college break backpacking around Europe, he'd felt he owed it to his parents to earn back a fraction of what they had spent on his trip. Maybe make some spending money for junior year, so he could pay his way for the weekend carousing his Columbia classmates were always dragging him off to.

He scanned the pale faces crowned with sun-bleached crewcuts, and wondered how much his Mediterranean complexion stuck out. It certainly had made him a curiosity at Columbia's freshman orientation.

That week, he'd made the mistake of volunteering his Italian heritage, and had then endured a year of Mafia jokes from the other students, most of whom looked like they'd stepped out of the pages of *The Great Gatsby*.

Tony's gaze paused at an unexpected smudge in the sea of white—a guy about Tony's age with piled-up black hair, earthy skin, and a long, straight nose. Was he one of those Jackson Whites, the backwoods people his neighbors at the lake sniggered about? In the packed room, the seats bracketing his were empty. His sights crossed Tony's, and he startled.

Tony trained his attention on the handouts, while the podium man, suit now threatening a blowout, wheezed on about uniforms, punctuality, and security. But Tony's eyes kept drifting across the room to the outsider.

At the break, Tony made his way to a long table laid with refreshments. Through a gap in the grasping arms, he grabbed a soda, and as he extricated the paper cup, soft fur brushed his skin and his muscles spasmed, the cup spilling onto a dark forearm.

Tony looked up into the stranger's eyes, like a bright winter sky over Lake Mennepequa. "*Oh!* Sorry." He grabbed half a stack of napkins, knocked over another soda, mopped up the mess, and apologized again. Mortified, he buried his face in a new cup to steady himself.

The man studied Tony with a firm gaze, which didn't help. "You ain't from these parts, are you?" he said, whittling the ends of his words.

"Who—me?" Tony said stupidly. "I come here every summer." He attempted a casual smile. "You?"

The man took a long swallow. "Live here." Tony's eyes lingered on a swell of broad shoulders, the cleft chin, his coiled bearing.

Tony stretched his slight frame to break a straitjacket of nerves. "So how did you hear they were hiring?"

The stranger dipped an eyebrow. "They're always hiring."

Tony nodded thoughtfully and wet his lips with his tongue. "When I returned from Italy last week, my folks mentioned this job, and I thought it would be good to go back to Columbia with some cash in my pocket, instead of mooching off my old man all year." Tony flashed a sheepish grin.

The man pursed his lips and nodded appraisingly; good or bad, Tony couldn't tell. "Mm-hmm, makes sense," he deadpanned, keeping a bead on Tony.

Tony felt pinned like a bug in a specimen box. "What does?"

The man cocked his head, then swept his eyes over Tony. "All of it," he said, cheek dimpling.

Tony instantly felt freakish for his polo shirt and khakis and chatter. The man tossed his cup in the trash and turned toward the bank of seats. Tony thrust a hand across his path. "Tony Marsala."

The man rocked on the balls of his feet, considered the offer, and then Tony. The room seemed suddenly airless. Tony stuffed the dangling hand in his pants pocket.

"Jake." The man pointed with his chin toward the middle of the room. "Got empty seats by me, if you like."

Tony retrieved his things and followed Jake. They sat through a talk about team spirit and the privilege of making memories of a lifetime for visitors. Tony got distracted by the funny portraits of the other recruits Jake was sketching in the margins of his handouts.

Tony grabbed his own pen and began scribbling his own, while they sat through a jumpy film about the park, filled with smiling staff, carloads of visitors, and animals fit for a Disney movie.

After that, podium man had everyone call off numbers and gather in groups. When Jake rose to join his, Tony bolted upright, pen and scribbled pages spilling at his feet. He squatted to gather them, then looked up to see a bemused Jake watching him.

"You missed something under your chair."

"Oh! Thanks," Tony said, ducked down to grab the pen, and banged his head on the way up.

Jake sucked in air. "You okay?"

Tony's head throbbed and heat filled his cheeks. "Doing great!" He bobbed his head like a dashboard hula girl, and hurried off.

Tuesday August 9th

The door of the Ford Falcon growled as Tony stepped onto the gravel lot. It was his first day guiding city gawkers on their drive-through safaris. Before him stood a squat, sheet-metal trailer on cinder blocks that doubled as staff headquarters and a crew locker room.

Shrill cries pierced the air, and he turned to see several peacocks prance and preen for a group of hens pecking the crushed stone. One eye locked on the scene before him, Tony unzipped his bag, grabbed his camera, and shot frame after frame. *I have to buy color film.*

The parking lot began to fill, and he stowed his camera and hustled inside. He put his gear in a locker, scanned the schedule for his first assignment, and swore under his breath. *Rhino barn.*

The park tour leader yesterday had said that shit-shoveling was a regular part of the job, and that rhinos were the worst. Their barn got cleaned out just twice a week, which meant that the floor of matted straw and their spoor had time to cure to the consistency of damp adobe.

Tony checked his watch: 7:57. The rhinos were already gone to their viewing pen, and the barn was a hundred yards back of the locker room. No matter how slowly he dragged his boots, he was at the gate before eight o'clock. He wrinkled his nose and tried breathing through his mouth to tamp down the stench, but his throat clenched in a coughing fit.

He heaved the shovel straight down and jumped on the heel of the blade, which entered the stinking muck like a sword in a stone. As Tony's boots slipped to the ground, he rammed his chin on the shovel handle. He staggered backward and cursed the tool, standing ramrod straight, mocking him.

After two hours, he had filled a dumpster halfway with filth. Straw danced in the air like gnats. His shirt was soaked, his body one big ache. He was sure he wouldn't make it to the end of his first shift.

When he'd learned of the job last week, working with wild animals had seemed like a great idea, maybe even grant him bragging rights back on campus this fall with the country-club class of '62. And take his mind off why he was so unhappy there.

Columbia had plunged Tony into a world of self-assured boys from Park Avenue and Oyster Bay and Greenwich whose priorities were girls, sports, and school, in that order. Strange as Ivy culture was, Tony had quickly adapted to its trappings.

But then blending in was something he'd worked hard at his whole life. To be the good son, model student, agreeable classmate. By high school, he was juggling his public persona with a fantasy world of pinup boys stashed under his mattress.

Segregating his two selves hadn't worked well at his all-male college, where he was in the constant company of men in dorm rooms and showers, at lectures and meals and library carrels.

And after hours in his residence hall, when rep ties and blazers came off, Tony was all at sea with classmates who casually bared body and soul. The unceasing intimacy left Tony struggling with his feelings.

On his first winter break back home, he'd holed up in his room and slept ten hours a day, avoiding family and friends. His mother had confronted him with his manifest misery, insisting he see a psychiatrist. He'd been horrified that she'd worked out his terrible secret.

And he knew all too well how risky it could be to cross her. She'd made it terrifyingly clear to Tony from an early age that madness ran in the family, and anything short of his abject obedience in the smallest of things could push her over the edge. *I slave all day in this house, and you won't even make your bed? You'll give me a nervous breakdown!*

Tony's immigrant clan had shown that America could break you. His dissolute Zio Rocco had tried to enlist his way into his country's esteem in December 1941, only to come home from the war *funny in the head*, Nonna had said. Zio Calogero, the brilliant elder brother, had worked his way from the tenements to medical school, only to buckle under the weight of respectability, losing his wits and his practice.

Tony had sometimes wondered if his desires were just another form of the family illness. The idea that he would wind up broken like his uncles frightened him even more than the prospect of psychoanalysis, and in the end, he'd agreed to treatment, hoping that it might keep his mother from probing his unhappiness any further.

Tony's talent for pleasing others had easily transferred to the therapy room. Tony would be the doctor's best patient, work as hard on his psyche as his studies. Come fall, Saturday mornings he'd slip away from his dorm, take the subway to the West Seventies, and submit to Dr. Clara Goodwell's horn-rimmed gaze.

A few sessions about his social life had ballooned into long-term analysis. From behind her mahogany desk, the steely-haired doctor had dissected, labeled, and catalogued his every utterance.

She'd been most interested in Tony's troubled relations with his mother, and prescribed an aggressive course of treatment for latent homosexuality, neurotic anxiety, and gynophobia. Under doctor's orders, he had been making awkward overtures to Barnard coeds for the past eighteen months, and faithfully reporting back the same failed results every week. Worse, therapy had so far had no effect on Tony's pathological desires for his uptown men. *Not productive*, Dr. Goodwell would cluck.

And now those same feelings were coming hard and fast for the guy he'd spilled his soda on yesterday.

Tony walked into HQ at quitting time completely spent and stared dully at his locker. One bench over, Jake unbuttoned his ranger shirt and gave Tony a long look. "Hard day in the shitkickers, man?"

Tony's eyes widened. "Shit just about sums it up."

Jake gave a knowing nod. "Did you hear 'bout the baby elephant at the petting zoo? Tried to stuff an old lady in its mouth. Thought she was lunch." He snorted a laugh.

Tony burst out laughing and bucked against his locker. "This place is nuts."

Jake stripped off the shirt, exposing a sheath of downy muscle from collarbone to waist.

Time slowed. Tony watched himself reach into his bag for the camera, lift it to his eye, finger the silver button...

He started, unsure how long he'd been staring. *Not productive.*

Jake aimed his sights at Tony. "Wrong button," Jake said.

Tony looked at Jake in confusion. He nodded toward Tony's shirt with his chin, and Tony reddened. He puffed his cheeks, unbuttoned his misaligned shirt, and started over. "I'm glad this job's just till Labor Day."

"For you," Jake snorted, wrestling a clean shirt over powerful shoulders. He gave Tony a wry smile, and held Tony's eyes a tad longer than he needed to. Then he slung his bag over one arm and walked out.

Wednesday August 10th

Jake circled the block of Broadway nearest the hardware store in Iron Run for the third time, swearing under his breath. He could've waited for his next morning off, but he'd come straight from work instead, eager to get his hands on a new tool he'd ordered.

The roadwork on Broadway wasn't helping. He finally parked in a leafy lane of big houses two blocks away in an unfamiliar neighborhood. Turrets and gables rose above broad, landscaped lawns and crushed-stone driveways. Eyebrow lintels seemed raised in alarm, and slate shingles glinted coldly. His neck prickled.

Jake headed down the block, buoyed to think that the fine veiner might take his carving to a whole new level. Maybe even make the walking stick he was whittling worthy of Grampa.

He slowed to admire a finned white Caddy with red upholstery, top down, parked in a circular drive. A man raking the opposite lawn halted to watch him, hand on hip, and Jake quickened his pace.

Faces emerged from parted drapes as he passed each house. A woman walked to her mailbox, eyes never leaving him; a man polished his car, frowning. Children with baseball gloves and Hula-Hoops stopped and stared.

Jake turned the corner and strode up Broadway, eyes on the pavement, heat under his skin. At the curb, his sights snagged on muscled calves, attached to a built blond boy unloading bags of crushed stone and mulch from a truck. A cold, rude stare met his eye.

In the street, he sensed a vehicle pacing him. Jake glanced sideways at an Algonquin County squad car, and in it, two burly uniformed men.

"Stop right there, boy."

Jake halted and eyed them warily.

"Got a call about suspicious activity by a man fitting your description."

"Officer?" Jake said.

"Don't play dumb, boy. Been a string of break-ins in town. Every summer brings the riffraff. What business do you have in the blocks back of Broadway?"

"Just parking, sir."

"C'mon, boy, you can do better than that."

"Sir, I come to shop at the hardware store."

The cop in the passenger seat stared intently at Jake, then his satchel, and stepped out. "Give me the bag."

The officer got a hand on it, Jake still holding on. With

barely contained anger, he pushed his bag at the cop. In a flash, Jake was face-first against the roof of the cruiser, the cop forcing Jake's legs wide and roughly frisking him.

Jake sputtered "What are you—"

"Shut up before I cuff you."

"I have rights!"

The officer sniggered and got into Jake's face. He could smell the man's sour breath. "You'll do what I say and thank me for it."

The man emptied Jake's bag onto the sidewalk and pawed through keys, cash, ID, rags, work gloves, and a carving knife. "I'm gonna have to keep this," he said, waggling the tool. "You could hurt someone, boy." The officer sprang to his feet and spun Jake around.

"Now, you go straight to the store, do your business, march to your vehicle, and get out of here. Because next time we come for you, we'll be talking down at the station. Understood?"

Jake swallowed his rage. "Yes."

"What was that, boy?"

"Yes, sir."

"Now run along."

As Jake raked his belongings into his bag, a gob of spit landed inches from his shoe.

Thursday August 11th

Tony told the adults driving a boisterous wagonful of kids to keep doors locked and windows shut in the baboon compound, then closed the electrified entrance gate behind them. He turned toward the next car in the queue, and the sound registered: a faint, phlegmatic hiss.

He caught movement at the edge of sight, and there was the beast emerging from a stand of trees, neck erect, rage in its monstrous eyes.

Buzzard was the meanest ostrich in the park, and it was mating season. Park management had determined that ostriches, unlike their many ferocious neighbors, weren't dangerous enough to fence in, and so they roamed freely through the park.

Tony had been warned that you only knew a cock's territory by stumbling into it. That season, Buzzard already had sent a ranger who'd made that mistake to the hospital with two broken ribs.

And now, four hundred pounds of fury was sprinting Tony's way. He figured he had maybe fifteen seconds before a big pink leg launched him over the fence and delivered him to a dozen baboons.

Tony pounded the entry gate's release button. Dead! His gaze shot across the compound to find the reason: a VW bug had stopped halfway through the exit gate so the hominids could ogle the monkeys. Tony knew that both gates couldn't unlock in concert for security reasons, which left him standing on open ground with nothing between him and catastrophe.

Buzzard closed the gap to two car lengths. In desperation, Tony grabbed a highway cone and hoisted it in a set shot, aiming for his assailant's head. The cone wobbled and arced, finally thudding uselessly at the ostrich's feet. Blood pounded in Tony's ears. The nine-foot bird bucked back and forth, wings beating the air into whorls, and nipped at the air above Tony's head.

Tony stumbled backward until his head hit the fence. Time slowed as he watched Buzzard lift one massive shin toward him, just as a branch flew into view and thumped the bird's chest.

Buzzard was briefly stunned, but quickly recovered. All at once, the gate clicked open, someone yanked Tony by his shirt, and metal clanged behind them. The bird repeatedly kicked the fence, and it shuddered like a shock wave.

Inside the animal pen, Tony's rescuer threw a protective arm across Tony's heaving chest, pinning him to the fence. Like doomed gladiators, the two rangers lifted their sights to appraise their new adversaries, and stared in wonder. The baboons, spooked by the man-bird battle, clutched one another at the far end of their pen.

"DenBleyker's Ostrich Wackers at your service!" Tony turned to find Jake, a puckish grin on his face, and Tony smiled, too.

The berserk bird was still rocking the fence when the two men heard tires squeal midst a fanfare of horn blasts and Aussie curses. George, the park's ringmaster and chief animal handler, threw his Jeep between fence and ostrich, which fled in a zigzag sprint, neck whipping side to side.

"Looks like you showed the old bastard who's alpha bird here!" George had the complexion of seared beef, and his bulging forearms wore wild patches of ginger fur.

Two fresh workers tumbled out of the Jeep to relieve Tony and Jake. Tony put weight on one foot, started to fall forward, and Jake caught him by the arm. They both froze for a beat.

"I think I sprained an ankle," Tony said, stomach fluttering.

"Lean on me," Jake ordered. They hobbled over to the Jeep and flopped into the back seat. Tony was drenched from heat and panic, and Jake blew out a stream of air.

George loped an arm around his seatback and regarded his charges. "Rough hour in the saddle, mates?" George cackled like a hyena, and threw the Jeep into reverse.

Tony wrinkled his nose at the acrid smell coming from

behind. He turned and gasped to find a long-toothed tiger staring at him across a metal grate.

"That's Baby," Jake whispered. "George goes nowhere without him."

"You talk like you know this park."

"Not my first rodeo here," Jake sighed. "Must be the excitement keeps me coming back." Tony scanned Jake's face to be sure he wasn't serious.

The peacocks were in a frenzy of calls and displays as George lurched to a stop at park headquarters in the blazing midday sun. He propelled himself from the cab toward the trailer at a martial gait. Tony leaned on Jake as he got his footing.

They stumbled on three legs to a railroad tie at the lot's edge, and dropped onto it. Tony felt Jake's attention on him.

"Thanks for saving my neck," Tony said.

"You'd do the same if I got attacked by a big goon with feathers...wouldn't ya?" Jake smiled all the way up to those blue-gray eyes, briefly blinding Tony.

"Um...I think you'd be better off calling the cavalry."

Jake chuckled. "I wouldn't blame you. I was scared as shit out there."

"You could've fooled me."

They locked eyes a long moment. Tony broke his gaze, then rose and gingerly put weight on the hurt ankle. The throbbing had abated somewhat, and standing wasn't worsening things.

"Better?"

"I think it'll be okay," Tony said with more confidence than he felt. Jake nodded, stood, and dusted off his pants. Tony groped for the courage to ask what had been on his mind until Buzzard emptied it.

"Hey, um...do you want to grab a bite after work?"

Jake seemed dubious. "I got to pick up a load of feed and get it back home. Maybe catch you some other ti—"

"Tomorrow then?" Tony blurted.

Jake seemed to weigh the offer, then nodded. "I like the pizza joint on Main in Iron Run."

Tony worked his ankle, walking in widening circles, which gave him a moment to corral his inner turmoil. "Then you wouldn't mind company?" he asked.

Jake chuckled. "Thought I just made that clear. How's five thirty?"

"Okay!" Tony trumpeted.

"And bring your drawings." Jake winked. Tony's cheeks torched hot.

Friday August 12th

Four middle-aged women in print dresses sat at a large folding table in a cramped corner of the Algonquin County sheriff's office, ears pressed to telephones, and spoke brightly from identical scripts.

"Sheriff Otto Schmidt will stop the invasion..."

"...take back the Highlands..."

"...protect our way of life..."

The fourth canvasser ran her finger down a long list of names on a separate sheet, and tapped the entry she sought. "Thank you for your support, Mr. Grunnwald. Sheriff would like a word with you. Please hold the line while I transfer you."

Down the hall, a bull-necked man in blue rocked in his chair, pecking a cigarette case with a pen. Clipped hair bristled above a doughy face. He pressed the blinking button on his phone and drew the receiver to him like a gun from its holster.

"Manfred! I'm sure you've heard...Yes, the coroner is running for my job. A traitor...in more ways than one. He appeals to the wrong element in this county...no wonder why, really. He's been passing for one of us all these years. His mother was a mixblood from the mountains, didn't you know? Now, what kind of example does that set for our youngsters?

"Listen, Manny, I called to see if you would host a little fundraiser...The Old Rhinelander has the right atmosphere. Beer and brats and old German songs...just like Fesel's Pavilion in the thirties. Ah, the Bund...those were the days.

"I know it's short notice, but I'm thinking Saturday. Yes, Manny, *this* Saturday. I wouldn't ask you to donate a prime summer night if I didn't think that a Sheriff Brandt would spell disaster for all of us. If we let him overrun the Highlands with his kind, it'll kill your business. Think of Saturday as an invest-ment in your future!

"Now, Manny...you know I've stood by you all these years, made sure that the past stays buried...Yes, yes, nothing to worry about. Your reputation is safe with me. I always look out for my friends...I'm sure I can count on you, right?...Manny?

"Good, then. I'll have Margarete work on the details. We should all wear our uniforms. Looking forward to it!"

Otto Schmidt tossed the receiver in its cradle like a winning shot, and spun his chair to the window. He looked out on the cleft in the rock where Iron Run wedged itself between two flanks of the Munsee Mountains, and nodded. He was feeling good about the election.

As for those whose loyalty needed prompting, he'd been sure to remind them, not so subtly, that he still controlled all the evidence needed to destroy them. He hadn't endured America's witch hunt against the "Huns" in the twenties only to hand over power to a mongrel like Brandt.

He remembered gray clouds scudding across a bright

Manhattan sky that November day in 1923 when he and brother Franz stepped off the Battery wharf. How the settlement house matrons had greeted them with warm cider and train fare to Yorkville.

The streets had been a carnival of hawkers, pushcarts, trolleys, and motorcars. The two of them had made their way to South Ferry for the Third Avenue Elevated, chattering with excitement and the cold.

At the clerk's booth, a tattered poster had advertised liberty bonds. On it, a white-bearded man in top hat drew back an American flag to reveal a snake wearing the *Pickelhaube*. Otto's imperial helmet. He'd ridden uptown in silence, eyes scanning the crowded car for trouble.

In the beer gardens of East Eighty-Sixth Street, Otto had soon learned of the wartime terror of America's Germans: newspapers shuttered, property burned, people jailed, even tarred and feathered, for the Kaiser's sins. How people had purged all signs of *Deutschtum* to survive.

And five years after the Armistice, his kind was still being heckled, spat on, threatened. Otto's grievances against his adopted country had only grown as he followed Germany's worsening turmoil at the hands of America and the Allies.

He had quickly climbed the ranks of *Deutschamerikaner* New York, rubbed shoulders with its many sellouts and appeasers, allying with anyone, trusting no one, trading favors for power—until the ladder had been kicked out from under him by that *Verräter* Griebl.

In the hell of Crystal City, he'd begun his resurrection. And he'd persevered in this little bit of the *Schwarzwald* in the Highlands, a place where he had beaten these dissolute Americans at the only game that mattered: power. He fingered his sheriff's badge, gazed upon his domain, and lifted his chin.

Die Fahne hoch! Die Reihen fest geschlossen!

He had the whole damn county by the balls.

Jake looked up from the menu to find a lens pointed his way, and raised his arms in mock surrender. *Click.* Tony fingered the film advance under the chrome-and-black box, then slid into the booth, opposite Jake.

Jake forced a grin. "Give fair warning next time you put me in your crosshairs."

"Sorry. I've been obsessed with this camera since I got it this spring." Tony lifted the leather strap over his head and set the camera next to his placemat.

Jake studied it. "Looks pretty fancy."

"My classics professor gave it to me. He's always on to the latest gear, and when he traded up for a Nikon F, he 'lent' me his Kodak Retina," Tony said, eying it reverently.

Jake rolled his eyes. "Nice to have friends like that. Time to fix our retinas on the menu." He lifted two vinyl folders from a metal stand and handed one to Tony.

"Sorry. Sometimes I get carried away with this stuff." Tony swept the camera off the table and onto his seat.

They plundered a large pie and compared yesterday's sketches, sputtering root beer over their lampoons of the big girl with the poodle cut, a tattooed muscleman, and the park official with a bad comb-over.

"You're pretty good with a pen," Jake said.

Warmth climbed Tony's chest. "Oh, I just doodle when I'm bored. At lecture classes, I'm always embellishing my notebook until it looks like an illuminated manuscript."

Jake squinted. "A what?"

"Uh...nothing." Tony blotted his face with a paper napkin,

then smoothed it out on his placemat. He shot Jake a glance. "I guess you inspired me."

Jake crunched a bit of crust. "More like Monday's orientation drove you to draw."

Tony smiled. "But you're a natural," he said, a bit too brightly.

Jake shrugged. "My hands are always busy."

"What with?"

"Guess college boys don't have chores."

"School breaks, I'm on trash duty," Tony said assuredly. "Believe me, it's a constant battle between man and racoon," he said, and instantly felt foolish.

Jake chuckled. "I reckon college beats working."

Tony's eyebrows pinched. "Most weeks, I've got three or four papers to write and a half dozen books to read. I have to pull at least one all-nighter just to keep up!"

"I've done a few of those myself." Jake's leer set off tiny temblors in Tony's gut.

"So you said yesterday that this wasn't your first rodeo at Wild'n'Wooly."

"Yeah, I started two summers ago. I didn't expect them to hire the likes of me, but then I found out why they were so desperate."

Tony gave him a puzzled look.

"No work November to April, and a long drive home for most people. And you gotta be real hungry to shovel shit for crap pay."

"Then why did you come back?"

"Didn't have no choice."

"Any choice." The words were out of his mouth before Tony could stop them. "Sorry," he mumbled.

Jake arched an eyebrow and continued. "Had a decent job at a lumberyard until early this year. When business slowed, they laid off the three mountaineers, and kept the good ol' boys."

Tony gave Jake a puzzled look. "'Mountaineers'?"

"People like me." Jake's tone was prickly.

Tony wondered why no one he knew at Lake Mennepequa had ever called the people in the mountains by that name, but thought it best not to ask Jake just now.

"Well, what happened at your job wasn't fair." Tony huffed.

"*Fair* ain't how it works around here. 'Specially just now with the sheriff running for re-election, hollerin' about people like me."

"Why didn't you complain to the authorities?"

Jake laughed darkly. "That would be the sheriff."

"But there are laws—"

Jake cut him off. "Otto Schmidt *is* the law."

The entry door jingled, and Jake's sights shot to the cause, his expression darkening. Tony followed his gaze to two ordinary cops getting coffee to go. Why was this more compelling than Tony's conversation?

Tony slapped the table. "You are *such* a talented artist!" he cried.

Jake finally noticed the spectacle of Tony, and suppressed a laugh. "You're a funny guy."

"You too." Tony blushed. "I mean, not funny-different. Just, you know, funny."

"Oh, I'm different, all right." The entry bell chimed again, and Jake's eyes followed a crew-cut man in T-shirt and denim, cigarette pack rolled in his sleeve, to an empty counter stool. Tony watched Jake study the man as he seated himself, and then loudly hocked his throat. Jake's continued preoccupation with the clientele made Tony peevish.

"Why are you staring at that man?" Tony asked. "He looks like half the guys in this town."

"Exactly my problem," Jake said.

"Why would you say that about someone you've never met?" Tony asked, his tone accusatory.

Jake gave Tony a weary look. "You really have to ask?"

Jake threw down his money and strode to the door, leaving Tony unsettled. He didn't know just how, but he had made a mess of this...not-a-date. He hurried to catch up with Jake outside in the thick summer air.

Jake stretched his arms over his head, Tony's eyes snapping to his bared belly and a line of fur that disappeared under his belt.

"D'ya mind?" A woman with groceries halted inches from Tony.

"Sorry," he said, turning sideways to let her pass, almost toppling from the curb. Jake's eyes creased in amusement.

"What do I owe you?" Tony asked Jake.

Jake smiled. "Next time, your treat. See you at the park sometime," Jake said evenly, then smiled, all teeth and bright eyes.

Tony felt suddenly lighter, nodded, and sprinted away.

Monday August 15th

By Tony's fifth day at work, he'd begun to see the humor in his customers' antics, like the knucklehead this morning in a Buick Electra who drove into Tony's compound, set a sandwich on the hood, and exited with a big bear butt imprinted on their car.

He'd found himself consumed with what he would say to

Jake at quitting time. Tony had rehearsed the idea in his head all weekend, and now he stood at his locker six feet from Jake, mind a blank, studying Jake's strong neck as he dressed.

"How's it going?" he said, stretching his mouth in what he hoped was a smile.

"Let's see...fifth day in a row at the park; cut a cord of wood, fixed a porch post, brought down two deer, tended vegetables, hauled in grain for the chickens." Jake stared at Tony with pursed lips, as if to say *go enjoy that.*

Tony tucked in his shirt and zipped up in silence, scouring his mind for that elusive speech. Jake cinched his belt and balled up his work clothes, and Tony, desperate to hold Jake's attention, blurted out the first thing that came to him.

"So what'll you do when the park shuts down in the fall?"

Jake chuckled to himself. "I got enough to see about between now and Saturday," he said, grabbing his bag.

"I'll be studying five dead languages for my Classics major," Tony said pointlessly.

"And I'll be here chopping and fixing and hunting and hauling, like always," Jake deadpanned, and headed for the parking lot.

Tony hurried after, desperate to revive this dying conversation.

He caught up with Jake as he swung himself into the cab. "Um...you ever come down to the lake?"

"Not really my kind," Jake said.

Sweat popped from Tony's temples, like the tempest in his head was raining inside out. "So I guess that means you wouldn't wanna come over to my house for a swim anyway." Tony heard himself, and cringed.

Jake seemed to weigh Tony's words, and then gave a short shake of his head. "I picked up some extra shifts, so's I gotta work straight through Friday."

"But, maybe you could come after work, and...stay for dinner?"

Jake's brow furrowed. "You really think that's a good idea?"

"Why not?"

"Your folks, for one."

"Oh, they're fine with me bringing home friends."

"Any of them like me?"

"It—it'll be okay." Tony quickly appended, "I *promise*."

After a moment, the absurdity of unkeepable promises made them both smile.

"Well, I guess we'll see, won't we?"

Warmth flooded Tony. "Tomorrow at six?"

Jake wet his lips. "I got an early shift Wednesday, so I can't stay late," he said, and shut the cab door.

"Great! The turnoff's a mile after Sharkey's. Take the lower road, and we're two houses up from the private beach, waterside."

"Private beach." Jake nodded to himself.

Tony leaned in. "Sorry?"

"Nothing. See you then." Jake started the pickup.

"See you!" Tony sang, squinting at Jake's sun-drenched afterimage as he backed up his truck. *Wrong f-stop, bad light.* Several better versions of the scene flashed in his head, all with Jake's arm around Tony in the passenger seat. He blinked into the brightness.

What was he doing?

3

Tuesday August 16th

Tony slapped the squalling alarm clock into silence. He rolled across the oversized bed and glanced unfocused toward the light. A breeze ballooned the curtains and carried the drone of motorboats. He sat up and looked out on Lake Mennepequa, his gaze distancing to the far shore.

Fuzzy bands of white and green resolved into the boat berths and sweeping lawns of the summer colony. He linked forefingers and thumbs at right angles before his sights, adjusting the view to get equal parts blue-white-green in the frame, then clicked a phantom shot. *The rule of thirds.*

He slipped into swim trunks and flip-flops and stepped onto the porch. Cranking open the jalousie windows, he inhaled pine and seaweed mixed with motor fuel. Scenes of summers past flickered: boys with sun-bleached hair in tight bathing suits, swimming, skiing, sunning themselves on tethered rafts.

Tony jogged to the dock, feet slapping wooden planks, and dove headfirst into clear waters, his breath bubbling past him as he swam. Startled sunfish wriggled through a field of green, and motorboats hissed like a hot kettle. Flexing arms and legs, Tony broke the surface, blew mist in the air, and swam to the dock.

He launched himself onto the boards and sat, legs dangling, while water coursed his body and pooled under him. He stared into the grainy green and his chest pounded.

Jake was coming today. In the light of morning, the whole idea seemed crazy. He and Jake, testing the waters of who-knows-what in this fishbowl of gossip?

As it was, he could barely speak two sentences to the man without putting his foot in his mouth. He could just see the two of them at the lakefront on loungers, Tony tacking from tongue-tied to too much talk; Jake reticent, dubious, while from the gallery above, church matrons followed along through opera glasses.

As a reprieve from prying eyes, he'd planned a ride up the shore in the family outboard boat to his hidden cove, where a sheer mountain face plunged to the water, offering little unwanted attention. He'd have Jake to himself, stripped down and dripping wet.

Despite his assurances to Jake, Tony expected his parents to grill him at the dinner table. In the twenties and thirties, they had struggled to overcome the pervasive libel that Italians were criminals, and to prove they were a credit to America. And that proof included the company they kept.

Tony recalled the many nights he'd heard his parents bicker about public behavior and appearance. *Not that suit, that's what the gangsters wear. All that makeup, you look like a* puttana*! Mamma mia, I can smell the garlic on you from the hall. Stop with the hands when you're talking!*

By bringing Jake home, would Tony jeopardize his family's standing among these summer colonists, with their banks of wide windows surveilling the social order?

Last summer, Tony had gone for a swim and picnic at the whirlpool with his brainy friend Karla, two years his junior, who'd grown up here and seemed to know everything about the Highlands. They'd stretched out on a sun-warmed rock, and Tony had prodded her to explain her world to him.

She'd described how the people who ran it were still stuck in a great imagined past, how before the war they'd paraded down Main Street with swastikas. *Things are getting worse now between us and the mountain people,* she'd said.

Where once her parents and neighbors might have had little to say about the "mixbloods," lately even their pastor had spoken out—from the pulpit—about the threats to traditional American values in the Highlands, and to remember that when they voted. And the county sheriff had harnessed their fears for political profit.

As he walked back from the dock, the memory filled Tony with unease. Was he about to put his family on the losing side of a war they didn't want?

Tony's mind filled with all of the reasons why today would be a disaster. Did he even know what he wanted from Jake, or what Jake thought of him? All he knew for certain was that Jake filled him with a hot urgency, like he had to get out of a burning house.

Would Dr. Goodwell's cure go up in flames too?

***

Jake squeezed the pillow tight to his chest and whimpered. He ran a hand down his face, and opened his eyes to the feeble glow at the window. Slipping from the upper bunk to his feet, he stepped into pants and moved silently downstairs.

He took in the snug parlor, the dinner table squeezed under a cracked window, the passage that led to the ample kitchen, and beyond the stove, the bathroom his father had built from an old laundry basin.

Jake savored these moments of stillness, before his mother and brothers clattered downstairs and duty claimed him. He whispered a light call to Maisie, who seemed to leap directly from sleep to her feet, and they both went out to the porch.

The mountain smelled fresh and dewy, restored from yesterday's withering heat, and it filled Jake with hope that the day might renew him, too. He breathed in the forest, and a current ran from belly to chest, like the feeling he'd had in his youth exploring the high country with his brothers.

They'd move silently from ridge to saddle, eluding catamounts, hunting squirrel, deer, and bear by their wits, like their Ramapough native ancestors. Jake had loved exploring the mountain's voids, squirming through cut-stone maws into underground channels.

Grampa had told of their people guiding the new settlers to the black rock that brought fortune, how the ironmasters and patroons had pushed the Ramapoughs from the best land in the valleys and foothills, and indentured, even owned their men and women.

From Wawayanda to Anthony's Nose, Jake's people had worked the high country's mines with powder and pickaxes, cleared roads, dammed streams, raised workers' villages. At Cat Swamp and Jenny Jump, they built stone bloomeries and blast furnaces.

And the Ramapoughs had forged the implements of war—most proudly, Grampa said, Townsend's great iron chain, strung across the Hudson to block British warships and hasten American independence.

For a hundred years after, there'd been enough work, until deep mining lost out to the open iron pits of the Midwest, and the shafts and forges went silent. After that, Grampa said, what kept their clan going was the sacred land and its life-giving spirit.

Jake left Maisie contentedly chewing a hambone and strolled toward the creek, past the muffled *tuk-tuk-tuk*ing of the chicken coop. He thought about the waves of colonists, milking the Highlands and moving on, leaving his kind to pick up the pieces of their shrunken lives.

Now new settlers were pushing in, filling the land with bungalows, boats, and barbecues, and like all the ones before, putting a fence around the Munsee Mountains and calling them theirs. Making him a trespasser on the land the Creator had provided his people.

Jake strode across the yard and entered the barn. On his worktable, two vises clasped a rod, a snake's shadow just emerging from the pliable hickory. Its form twisted around the wood and dissolved into the raw shaft where he'd left his carving the previous night.

He tried invoking the Spirit's power, but was too antsy to resume work. He left the barn and crossed the wide field, sunrise raking the damp grass. Then he hopped the fence from the slope that dropped to the stream.

He felt the day's heat gather. He pulled off boots and socks and stripped, then banked his way down, letting the low sassafras and viburnum brake his descent.

He hopped into the creek with a splash and a whoop, dispatching two turtles from their perch, and sank to his waist. He lay back and peered at a blue chink in the roof of oak and ash.

He thought of the boy at work who disarmed and alarmed him all at once. The wavy hair and olive-tinged skin. Guileless, earnest, a bit naïve, but interested in what Jake had to say. Eyes restless, as if Tony, like Jake, sat uneasily at the center of his life.

At the Garden State Club and Doc's Tavern in Paterson, he'd cruised plenty of town boys at war with themselves. He'd tried to please them, to fit into their world, but always, after the press of bodies, the loathing was palpable in their averted gazes and mumbled excuses. Which had convinced him that what happened to his friend Elias had been all but inevitable.

Jake thrashed his head from side to side in the stream, sending plumes of water skyward, shaking off the memory. Could things with Tony end just as badly?

Tony heard the horn and hurried to the gate. Jake's pickup idled next to the hemlock hedges that walled in the Marsala bungalow. He motioned to Jake where to park, then found himself pinned where he stood by the wild eyes of a wiry, gray-haired woman in a pink-and-blue housedress.

"They're in the house again." She seized Tony's arm with one bony hand.

Tony mirrored her gravity. "Who is, Mrs. VerHogen?"

"The Luftwaffe. I told them there wasn't room inside for their Messerschmitt, so they put it *under* the house, without even *asking*. Don't you think that's rude?" she asked.

Tony rubbed his forehead. "Yes, very rude." He looked with alarm at Jake, leaning on his truck, eyebrows pinched.

"Would you go talk to them, please? I'm at my wits' end!" The woman yanked Tony's wrist with both hands. The momentary tug-of-war ended in a standoff.

"You didn't get your newspaper again, did you, Mrs. VerHogen?" Tony asked, stepping just out of reach.

"They've been stealing them." She rubbed her hands distractedly.

"Because if you had, then you'd know that Germany surrendered." He'd been reminding her for two weeks now, and each time she'd reacted like it was today's breaking story.

Mrs. VerHogen narrowed her eyes. "Don't believe it. You should check under your house, too. Those people hide their secrets underground."

Tony shot a glance at Jake, hand clamped on his mouth to keep from laughing. Tony studied the footpath to keep his composure. "Well, I'm sure they'll keep until morning."

Mrs. VerHogen threw up her hands and walked off, muttering.

Jake exploded in laughter. "What was *that?*" he asked.

Tony sighed heavily. "She lives three doors down. Been like this on and off for years."

"So...she just roams the land accosting her neighbors, with no one looking after her?"

Tony shrugged. "Mr. VerHogen is a drunk, so he isn't much help. But you know, she's entitled to her paranoia; the neighbors will have nothing to do with either of them. They're Christian Scientists, which around here is practically heathen."

"So much for Christian charity," Jake muttered.

"Just like you said yesterday, the folks here are really not my kind."

"How you figure that?" Jake swept his gaze along the hedges and gables and lawn jockeys that repeated to the end of Tony's street and said, "What I see, you doin' just fine."

"People around here are pretty clannish. To them, I'm a curiosity."

Jake frowned. "What's curious about another paleface in the neighborhood?"

"Well, I'm an Italian Catholic from New York City: that's three strikes against me."

"Thanks for explaining your hardships," Jake said flatly.

"I only meant that we both know what it's like not to fit in." He looked at Jake, who seemed uninclined to weigh in. Tony ran his hands up and down the sides of his shorts. "So, what do you say we go for a spin?" Jake stared blankly.

"In the boat," Tony clarified.

Jake smiled at his shoes. "'Course you got a boat."

"Brought your bathing suit?"

Jake patted his knapsack.

Tony led them to the house, where the smell of tomatoes and garlic met them at the door. "Ma, we're going for a ride and a swim," Tony called as they passed the kitchen.

Antoinette Marsala leaned over the stove, stirring a pot with a wooden spoon. Without turning toward her son, she shouted over the exhaust fan's din. "Okay, dear, just be back by seven."

They went into Tony's room to change. They stood on opposite sides of the bed to doff shirts and shorts, then turned away from each other to finish undressing. As Tony slipped thumbs under his briefs, his eye snagged on Jake, framed sideways in the wall mirror.

Their sights collided briefly in the glass, then bounced apart. Tony busied himself with the drawstring of his swimsuit.

"Ready!" Tony reached for his sunglasses on the dresser, and they skittered away. He pounced on them, then looked sheepishly at Jake's reflection.

Hands on hips, Jake gave mirror-Tony a cockeyed smile. "So, you gonna show me this swimming hole, or what?"

From the porch, they followed a footpath flanked by white birches down to the water. All along the shoreline, the same summer cottages that hid themselves from the street behind palisades of greenery and fencing showed their welcoming faces to the lake. Flowers framed picture windows, pinwheels spun from porches, and flags snapped in the wind.

Tony hopped across the hull of the boat and unfastened its cover, Jake following suit. Then Tony methodically folded the heavy green canvas and deposited it into a large wooden bin on the dockside patio. He hopped into the driver's seat next to Jake, turned the key, and let the engine idle.

Tony busied himself tossing ropes from eye hooks onto the dock. Back in his seat, he grasped the throttle and started to relax, like with every boat he'd steered since his first dinghy at age twelve. Each time he'd pulled away from shore on his own, he'd felt the same exhilarating freedom to do as he pleased.

Now, with Jake on board, ease was fleeting. Distracted, he shifted into reverse with the engine still revving, and the boat jerked backward from the dock, sending them both into the dashboard.

"Sorry," Tony said, feeling like an idiot.

Jake clutched the gunwale dramatically. "Just give fair warning before you throw me overboard."

They picked up speed and rode along the far shore, past log mansions, stone castles, and Adirondack chalets. Tony thought Lake Mennepequa must seem like a floating country club to Jake.

Jake regarded the lakeside compounds without expression, arms folded. His gaze panned across the pulsing green vista. "This lake looks real different when you're actually on it."

"You've never been?" Tony asked in disbelief.

Jake shook his head.

"But you're just up the mountain."

"Why would I come here, when there's KEEP OUT and PRIVATE PROPERTY signs nailed to every third tree?"

"Oh, no one pays those any attention," Tony said.

"You do if you look like me and you don't want trouble," Jake shot back.

"What about high school parties? Cookouts? Fourth of July fireworks?"

Jake chuckled mirthlessly. "Can't RSVP without an invite." He let his arm trail off the side of the boat.

Tony was still unconvinced. "Are you saying you've never been to Sharkey's Pier? Anyone can swim or rent a boat there."

"Tony, I don't go where I'm not wanted," Jake admonished, ending the interrogation.

Tony volleyed Jake's rebuke. "I get that. I feel the same way, really."

"I'm sure you think so," Jake said, voice rising in irritation.

Tony steered through wakes cut by the big racers, prows like sharks swallowing the rush of water. Mercifully, the roar of their engines gave him reprieve from more talk. He relaxed his grip on the wheel and let the boat's spray calm him.

Soon they slipped beyond a hook of land and came to a deserted stretch of shoreline where steep, wooded hills edged the water. Tony cut the engine, and the boat planed to a stop. Shadows washed the western ridges, and the air was almost granular, rendering the far shore in pinpoints of light and shade.

Tony tossed over the anchor and swept his gaze all around. "This is my favorite spot to hang out."

Jake nodded. "I can see why." His mood seemed to lighten, and with it, Tony's. Tony shed his T-shirt, stepped onto the gunwale, and pushed off crying, "Man overboard!" as he disappeared feetfirst. Tony held his breath underwater for a good minute.

"Tony? Where are you?" Jake's voice sounded miles away. Tony felt a wave of pressure as Jake dove headlong into the lake and thrashed about. He heard Jake shout his name twice, and then sensed his body breaking the surface. Tony took that moment to pop up directly in front of him.

"Fooled you," Tony said, spraying Jake with a mouthful of water.

Jake dodged it. "Nah, I figured you didn't drag me out here for your funeral," he said with mannered indifference, and then chopped the surface with his hand, splattering Tony.

They drifted awhile as the breeze prickled their skin, filaments of seaweed tickling from below. Jake expelled a satisfied sigh. Tony felt his stomach unclench.

Suddenly, Jake eyed Tony with mischief. "Last one to the boat's a rotten egg!" He broke into a frenzied crawl, showering Tony. Tony sputtered and splashed, finally pulling himself onto the boat's stern. He found Jake sprawled face up on the deck, eyes closed, as if to say, *What took you?*

"For someone who never comes to the lake, you're a strong swimmer," Tony gasped.

Jake opened his eyes. "Never said I don't swim. Just not here."

"This is pretty great, though, huh?" Tony spread his arms wide, inviting Jake to concur.

Jake shielded his face from the sun with his arm and studied Tony through one squinted eye. "If you belong here."

Tony couldn't understand why Jake would play killjoy at this perfect moment in his special place. "No one cares who you are in the middle of the lake," he said with some annoyance.

Jake dropped his arm and let his head loll to one side, as if to say, *I give up.*

Tony filled the silence with more talk. "So tell me about all the cool places you swim."

"Creeks. Small lakes and ponds in the backcountry. No one to bother or be bothered by." Jake narrowed his eyes and leaned toward Tony. "Nothing like this snooty swimming pool of yours."

Tony matched Jake's squint, grabbed a gob of seaweed from the floor, and threw it in Jake's face. Jake sprang up and spat theatrically before wrestling and pinning Tony to the floor. He tensed, eyes on Jake, who grabbed the seaweed and stuffed it down Tony's swimsuit. They locked arms, and fell silent for a moment, ruddy with effort.

Then Jake loosened his hold, and Tony stopped resisting. Light prismed Jake's slick skin, and his eyes bored into Tony's. The only sound was the *slop slop slop* of the hull.

Tony felt his chest exploding, and yanked himself out from under Jake, who jerked to his feet and brushed the seaweed from his hands. Tony pushed himself up, all goosebumps, suddenly spent. He grabbed a towel and wrapped it around his shoulders.

"I could use a hot shower," he said, and swung behind the steering wheel.

Jake stood motionless, facing the stern.

Tony pulled up anchor and they set course in silence, wind whipping the lake into foam. Tony drove in a trance, everything around him suddenly too bright, like a wide-open lens.

All at once the dock loomed. He slammed the gear into reverse, and the boat bounced off the padded wood with a squeal.

Jake righted himself on his seat. "You sure can give a guy a thrill," he said, rapping his fingers on the boat's hull.

"Sorry. I'm normally very good at this," Tony said wanly.

They secured the boat and cover, and climbed single file up

the slope to the house, clutching their beach towels against the breeze.

Jake grabbed his clothes from Tony's bed and marched to the bathroom. Tony closed the bedroom door and peered in the mirror at the flecks of green in his snarled hair.

Moist heat pushed against his eyes, and he turned away. Something powerful had passed between them in the boat that Jake now wanted no part of. Could he blame Jake, when Tony was the one who'd pulled the plug?

Nerves whittling his insides, Tony listened to the rushing water across the bedroom wall until it stopped with a metallic squeal. He dropped out of his suit to find a mess of seaweed at his feet; strands of it still clung to him.

Jake reentered fully dressed and paused at the sight of a naked Tony raking seaweed from himself and the rug. Tony snatched up his towel and fled. He ran the shower cold for a long time.

They met up again in the kitchen and stood at arm's length, watching Mrs. Marsala set the large Formica-and-chrome table. At its head, Salvatore Marsala tucked a napkin into his collar.

"Ma, Dad, this is my friend Jake," Tony announced.

Antoinette Marsala glanced from her son to his friend and shot a look at her husband. Everyone seemed to snap to attention. Tony's mom commenced serving the meal with the vigor of a steam shovel, digging spoons into platters and heaping four plates with escarole and beans and lasagna.

Tony and Jake sat down under her eye. Their shoulders brushed, and instantly they shimmied their chairs farther apart. Antoinette stiffly lowered herself into her seat.

Sal Marsala poured red wine from an unmarked bottle into small juice glasses and said grace. Everyone picked up a fork in silence.

Tony's mother dotted pursed lips with a napkin, eyes down. "Did you have a good swim?" she asked.

Tony looked at her, then his father, then her again. "Yes, Ma."

"That's nice," she said absently.

Everyone chewed.

"Well now, how is that animal park, son?" Sal asked, flashing a mouthful of food.

Tony took a moment to summon cheer. "It's like they crossed Freedomland with the Bronx Zoo," he said brightly.

"They say Freedomland's bigger than Disneyland," his dad said. He lifted a forkful of escarole and beans and slowly munched. The minute hand on the wall clock clicked a notch.

Mrs. Marsala suddenly erupted with enthusiasm. "Why, we all should go sometime!" she exclaimed. She looked across the table at her son, and her smile wavered. "Wouldn't you like to, Tony?"

Tony folded his napkin. She crumpled her own before turning to her husband. "And I haven't been to the zoo in ages! Wouldn't that be fun, Sal?"

His eyebrows joined in confusion. "Nettie, you never said boo about any zoo since the day we met."

Stepping on his line, she jerked to her feet. "Who's having more?" she trilled. Each boy protected his plate with a hand. Tony's mom refilled her husband's dish and everyone's glass.

"What do they have you doing at work, Tony?" Sal asked.

Tony covered his full mouth and nodded toward Jake. "Why don't you ask him?"

His parents both blinked at Jake, who was stabbing an evasive bean. Antoinette fussed with her summer bob. Sal ground food between his teeth. The boys regarded the unscalable wall of food on their plates.

"Ma, Dad, is something wrong?"

Antoinette sprang from her seat again. "Why would there be?" she tittered, as she collected the boys' half-full dishes, and set them on the kitchen counter.

Tony's dad drained his wine, and his mother returned to the table for the platters and spoons. Jake cleared his throat; Tony eyed him apprehensively.

"Mrs. Marsala, everything was great," Jake said.

"Oh, I'm glad you liked it," she sang in a girlish arpeggio. Suddenly her face knotted, and she half screamed a sneeze into her apron. "Oh, *Dio,* excuse me. All this country air." Jake's eyes widened.

"Is your friend here for the summer?" Sal asked. Jake opened his mouth to speak and thought better of it. Somewhere a speedboat growled.

Tony firmly set his glass on the table. "Jake lives here."

"So he's home from school. Good to see the family, isn't it?" Tony watched Jake, who studied the floral tablecloth, his jaw shifting.

"Dad..."

"Where exactly does your friend live?" Sal asked, head cocked, still working his lasagna. Tony squirmed.

"Up the mountain, by Blackman's Ridge," Jake said, his sights leaving the room.

Sal glanced at his son. "What, with the hillbillies?"

"Dad."

Mr. Marsala pressed a thumb to four gathered fingertips and shook his hand from the wrist. "When did *hillbilly* become a dirty word?" He winked at Jake, who stared poker-faced. "You used to beg me to read you *Li'l Abner* in the funny papers."

Tony rolled his eyes. "I was *very* little."

Jake held up a hand to Tony and softly said, "It's okay." He turned his attention to Mr. Marsala. "My family's lived in this county a long time," he said.

"Sal, maybe that's enough questions," Antoinette ordered.

Sal opened his arms wide. "Nettie, I'm just curious about the boy. Nobody comes *from* here. Unless you count the Injuns. So where is your family from, son?"

Jake's chest rose and fell. "It's a long story." He fingered his fork.

Nettie Marsala marched to the table and whisked away her husband's unfinished second helping. She met his grunt of protest with fierce eyes, then pivoted to her son. "Tony, why don't you and Jack go out and enjoy the sunset?" Her tone brooked no protests.

"It's *Jake*, Ma," Tony said. He glared at his parents, and pushed back from the table. "C'mon, Jake, let's go."

The lake's surface shuddered in shifting patterns. Jake and Tony sat at a picnic table under an oak near the water's edge. Swallows corkscrewed through the branches as the sun slipped behind a line of pines on the far ridge, throwing bolts of color from the treetops. Tony squinted, clicked his tongue, and blinked at the extravagant sky. *A perfect shot.*

The silence enveloped them, and Tony's gaze strayed to Jake.

"So what's it like living on Blackman's Ridge?"

"With the hillbillies?" Jake leered, and shot an acorn into the shallows.

Tony sucked in air. "God, my dad...he didn't mean—"

"Yes he did. And it's nothing I ain't heard a hundred times," Jake said.

After a beat of silence, Jake chuckled, and gave Tony a crooked smile. "So you were into *Li'l Abner*, huh?"

Tony's ears got hot. "I didn't know any better."

"What's better than a hunky hillbilly busting out of his shirt?" Jake winked.

The quip didn't ease Tony's remorse. "My folks aren't usually like this. I didn't think…this would be a big deal." Tony said.

"No, you didn't. But *I* did," Jake said, eyes flashing.

"My parents are just curious about you," Tony protested.

Jake harrumphed. "When people say that, it never leads no place friendly."

"Believe me, they know a thing or two about being outsiders."

Jake stiffened. "Who's the outsider? My people was here long before—" Jake stopped himself from saying what Tony knew was on his tongue. *Before any of your kind.* Tony sighed. He was making everything worse. As usual.

Jake's tone softened. "Look, I know you mean no harm, but you really don't know what life is like here, outside of your pretty lake." He swept his arm across the shimmering view. "People in town always talking to me like I'm dense, or some kind of savage, and then behind my back they call me a *Jackson White*." He heaved the words like a bad meal.

Tony looked blankly at Jake. "But that's what everyone calls the mountain people. Isn't that…what you are?"

"Are you a *wop*?" Jake shot back.

The word burned in Tony's chest. "That is *not* the same thing—"

"Oh really?" Jake said acidly.

"That's a slur! *Jackson*—that's just a name, and *White* is a—a color."

Jake reddened. "Tony, it's the same gut punch for you and me."

Tony audibly sighed. "You must think I'm prejudiced."

Jake shrugged and looked away. "There's something 'bout

being human that wants to put down what's different in people. Don't take it personal."

"How else should I take it?" Tony said hotly. "And it's per-son-al-*ly*, not person*al*," he said haughtily, not sure why Jake's syntax bugged him just now.

"Cool down, pardner. Look: some of the mountaineers on my side of the state line don't trust their own kind on the other. My clan will tell you all about the Indian and the Dutch in us, but don't you bring up our slave blood, or call us Negro! Everyone hates *somebody*, Tony. That's just the way it is."

Everyone? That was too much. "My family knows what it's like to be hated! My grandparents came to New York in steerage. They got no handouts, worked hard, fought for their country, and still had doors shut in their faces. They got treated the same as if *they* were Negroes." Tony's voice was brittle.

"Difference is, it took your family two generations to become American, and we've been waiting three hundred years."

"*I am not a bigot.*" Tony's voice shook.

Jake eyed Tony with concern, and quieted. "I ain't sayin' you are. But you want to make our troubles the same, and they're not." He lowered his voice. "When something bad happens, you call the police, right? I got to police myself so the cops don't make trouble for me. Tony, look at me. Look at *me*."

Tony's eyes met Jake's, twin pools of quicksilver moonlight. The urge to let go and to hold back warred inside of him. He wobbled to his feet and stepped to the water's edge, hugging himself.

After a moment, he turned to Jake, tipped his head toward the private beach, and started walking. After a sandy expanse, they threaded their way along outcroppings that plunged to the shoreline. Angled wings banked through blooms of insects as the first stars pierced the night.

"If I made you feel uncomfortable, I apologize," Tony managed.

"But...you don't know why you're apologizing, do you?"

Tony was too embarrassed to admit it. Jake clucked his tongue.

"You know...I had to do a paper in high school about Manifest Destiny. So I wrote about the Trail of Tears, where the Indians got marched to their death. Teacher gave me a *D*. Why? Said it wasn't in our textbook."

"Well, I never heard about it," Tony said doubtfully.

"You really think they want you to know that the guy on the twenty-dollar bill was a murderer?" Jake clicked his tongue.

"How do you know that's true?"

Jake tapped his temple. "My elders hand down the stories."

Tony shook his head. "Stories aren't history," he said flatly.

"And some people make up stories and call it history, 'cause the truth don't make them look so good. My kind's living our history every day, no matter that the world pretends we don't have a story to tell."

Tony didn't understand exactly how he'd gotten this far out on a limb, but he was eager to climb back before things got any worse. "There's a nice spot up ahead where we can sit," Tony said, and they moved on, both seemingly glad for a moment of quiet.

Finally, Tony spoke. "Okay, then, tell me about your life."

Jake took his time responding. "Well. It's...a whole 'nother world from yours. I could travel these mountains acrost four counties and never see your kind. The land provides, and we do for ourselves. Folks are connected by name and kin and tradition. We hunt and farm together, look out for each other."

"Like the hill towns my grandparents came from," Tony said earnestly.

Jake sighed. "My kind didn't just *come from*. We been here. And like Grampa says, roots grow where the seed falls."

"I've got roots, but my family didn't stay put," Tony said with some pride.

"Some folks don't get that choice."

Tony had been raised to believe that everyone made their own opportunities, and Jake's circumstances seemed like knuckling under to defeat. Tony shook his head, but said nothing.

That seemed to animate Jake even more. "Okay, here's *my* family: my ma died in childbirth havin' me. My pa's brother married his first cousin. Then Uncle died, and Pa an' Auntie raised me as a brother to her three boys.

"Now you tell me how I explain to your parents that I got three cousins for brothers and a mom who's also my aunt. Your neighbors be telling a thousand jokes about inbred retards, and they'd come for us with pitchforks if we tried to move in next door to one of them."

An unbidden cartoon reel of head-scratching, bucktoothed hillbillies played in Tony's head. Tony struggled to take Jake's part. "People shouldn't judge you for who you are," he said stiffly.

"Hasn't stopped them yet," Jake said.

They came to a knoll surrounded by pines, strewn with filaments of moonlight. They sat in silence, close but not touching. Tony's neck pulsed. He felt rooted where he sat.

"Jake...I just want to say that I'm glad you're here."

Jake studied Tony in the pale light, then lowered his gaze. "I got to apologize for talking so harsh, Tony. The world's troubles are bigger than both of us."

The hum of a motorboat reached them from somewhere far across the lake. Below in the dimness, seaweed swayed in the waves rolling to shore.

Tony cocked his head. "I guess you think I'm pretty naïve, huh?"

Jake shook his head. "Maybe just...too optimistic sometimes."

Tony drew in the night air and let it out slowly. "Sometimes I daydream about a place where I can just be myself, instead of who people want me to be."

Jake inclined his head. "And who are you?"

Jake's bluntness briefly flummoxed Tony. "A loner, I guess. I worry that if I show someone the real me, they won't like what they see."

Jake nodded. "I have a hard time getting close to people, too."

Jake raked the grass with his fingers, and his arm brushed Tony's thigh. Tony flinched, and his eyes darted to Jake. The set of Jake's jaw made his insides flutter. The air seemed charged.

And now came the old, panicky feeling. Tony raised his wrist toward the moonlight, and worked out the time. "God, it's almost eleven, and you've got an early shift tomorrow," Tony said, more stridently than he'd intended.

Jake took the hint and shot to his feet. "Guess I'd better head out. Long drive." Crestfallen and relieved, Tony rose too. Jake looked to him for his reaction.

Tony pushed out the words. "Why don't you stay over? It's only ten minutes from here to work, and you'll save yourself time and sleep." Tony's heart banged his ribs. Jake pursed his lips and studied Tony.

"Well...okay, sure," Jake said.

Tony felt dizzy. What had he done? He instantly backtracked. "But my dad's got all his junk crammed in the spare room, so you'd have to share mine, and it's only one bed, and I snore. And there's just one bathroom, which my father monopolizes in the morning—"

Jake waved his hands before Tony sights. "Hold up! We're five in a four-room house. I'll be fine," he said, chuckling.

They took an unpaved footpath in moon shadow, the crunch of gravel underfoot. At the intersection with the upper road, Tony saw cats'-eye taillights next to the Van Hoek's overgrown yard. A lone figure emerged from the vehicle and dashed into a cone of light: Karla. Just as swiftly, darkness swallowed her, and the car rolled away.

They entered the Marsala house through the back door and tiptoed past his parents' room.

Tony's nerves were on a tripwire, and he closed his bedroom door behind them with a *whump*. He gasped and put finger to lips. Tony waited to hear his parents' sawing and wheezing, and mouthed, *Whew*.

Jake knit his brow. "You sure I should stay?" he asked in a whisper. Tony flipped on the nightlight and patted the big bed. Jake circled it, pulled his T-shirt over his head, and dropped out of his shorts. In the dimness, Jake's briefs held their weight softly, gracefully. Lightheaded, Tony turned into the corner before stripping down.

They both slipped under the covers and lay back to back, as far apart as the mattress allowed. The room grew unnaturally still. Tony's senses hummed. He swallowed with great effort, wanting to speak, afraid of what he might say.

"What are you thinking now?" he whispered.

Jake's breath quickened, and he rolled over, pressing Tony from behind. His arm snaked across Tony's side, fingers digging into his briefs. At Jake's touch, Tony's body exploded in spasms, and he pulled away. Stumbling from the room, he locked himself in the bathroom and sat on the toilet lid, his veins ice, body racking, for what seemed like hours.

When he felt steady enough to stand, he crept back to his room. From the doorway, he studied the upfolds of Jake's sprawled form beneath the sheets, listened to his nasal breathing. Then Tony lowered himself gently to the bed, straitjacketing himself with his arms.

Before dawn, Tony awoke to an empty bed. He remembered fragments of the night: the fullness of Jake's body, the sense that he was splitting apart. The grind of gravel and rubber, an engine's whine.

In frequent night terrors of childhood, he'd awaken in the dark and feel a heaviness fill the room, pressing down, smothering him, and he'd cry out for his mother. Now he shut his eyes against that unbearable weight to find Dr. Goodwell's flinty visage behind them. Why did he always look to others to be saved?

He recalled his seventh-grade class on Greek mythology, and the strange heat under his skin learning the story of Ganymede and Zeus, the eagle uplifting the shepherd boy to Mount Olympus. Then the dreams had started, saviors on soaring steeds bringing bliss and wet sheets.

And lately, the midnight chimeras were back. In a dream just two nights ago, he held tight to Herakles on Arion's back, and when the hero turned to him, his eyes were Jake's. Tony had awakened with the old, familiar anguish.

Just like he felt right now, lying in a fetal curl.

4

Wednesday August 17th

The wire service thundered in the *Mountain Observer*'s cramped offices. Dan Schreier dropped the phone receiver into its cradle and scribbled notes in a spiral book. He looked across the room at a balding man hunched over a desk, poring through news dispatches on torn sheets of paper.

"Hey, Emil, give baseball a rest! Tell me, whadya know about a summer camp in the Highlands before the war?"

Emil started. "What?"

"Chuh-man camp," he said, in mad-scientist voice. "Called *Hochland*. You grew up around here, what can you tell me?"

Emil turned his head and grimaced. "I plead the fifth."

Schreier rolled his eyes and swung back to his typewriter. For most of the summer, he'd been on to a story about the county election that none of his colleagues seemed interested in. Like a gumshoe, he'd been sniffing out rumors that swirled around Sheriff Otto Schmidt.

With the help of a few timorous locals and a contact at the FBI, he had assembled a thick dossier on Schmidt's American life. He'd pored over Bureau reports and memoranda on the German-American Bund from 1939 to '41.

Schreier had formed a clear picture of these immigrant fascists and their efforts to make the United States fertile soil for Nazi dominion. They'd started summer camps, modeled on Hitler Youth, to groom the shock troops and future leaders of Hitler's American Reich.

Schreier had Schmidt's story all sketched out: In 1920s New York, a German émigré finds *Vaterlandsliebe* at the Steuben Society. By '34, he's embraced the Friends of New Germany and their call to defend Aryan America and the Hitler revolution against Bolshevism.

At the FNG, Schmidt meets Ignatz Griebl: Yorkville obstetrician, US Army medical officer, and head of Hitler's American spy network. Griebl recruits Schmidt to report on the accelerating American naval buildup.

He gets hired as a machinist at the New York Navy Yard in Brooklyn, installing bolts, gauges, and bearings, notably for the USS *North Carolina*, the first of America's new class of battleships, bigger and faster than anything afloat. He keeps a low profile among ten thousand laborers; on breaks, he strolls Wallabout Bay with camera and notepad stuffed in his coat.

Then Congress labels the FNG an arm of the German Reich's Nazi Party, and the group expels its German nationals and shape-shifts into the German-American Bund.

Sensing an opening, a naturalized Schmidt rises through the ranks to become personal bodyguard to GAB *Bundesfuehrer* Fritz Kuhn. But in '38, a cornered spy tips off the FBI about Griebl and he sings, then slips away on a Hamburg-bound boat.

The Bund smuggles Schmidt to Algonquin County while

the heat dies down, appointing him *Vorsteher* of their new summer camp. In sight of New York, Camp Hochland was to be the GAB's most ambitious proving ground for a cadre of Roosevelt-hating Aryan Americans, a beachhead for the thousand-year Reich.

But Schmidt refuses to lie low in the Highlands. He founds a new Bund chapter, entrenches himself as de facto president for life, and amasses a following from Paterson to Newburgh.

After Pearl Harbor, all his horn tooting makes him easy pickings for the FBI, which hustles him off for the duration of the war to Crystal City, a Texas internment camp for Americans suspected of Axis sympathies.

And now, eighteen years after the FBI shuttered Camp Hochland, there it sat, moldering in Otto Schmidt's backyard. Schreier intended to remind voters of its history. He reviewed his research, rehearsed his pitch one last time, and walked down the hall to meet with his editor in chief.

Tom Langer was a no-nonsense Highlands native, jowly and bristle browed. He listened to Schreier over black-rimmed glasses, forehead wrinkled, lips tight.

"A story this incendiary needs ironclad evidence," he said.

"I've got my contacts at the FBI," Schreier replied with a wink.

Langer stiffened. "You do understand why no one else in the county will touch this story." His tone carried a warning.

Schreier shrugged. "No one wants to pick a fight with the local bully."

"One word: fear. There are reasons why Schmidt has had little opposition until now. *That* story goes deeper than this electorate has the stomach for." Langer's thumb swept back and forth across his watchband.

Schreier tossed him off with a grin. "Not after they hear what I'm digging up. You've heard of the Bund, right?"

Langer's gaze briefly flickered. "I've got a source confirming that Schmidt wasn't just a flag-waver, he was its standard-bearer."

Langer squirmed in his shirt as if it had suddenly shrunk two sizes. "You'll need to go much further than that to prove what you're alleging."

Schreier arched an eyebrow. "No one could just gloss over a Nazi bigwig in their midst."

"Unless they'd rather forget," Langer shot back.

Schreier leaned in, elbows on knees. "Since Israel nabbed Eichmann, the wire's been buzzing with Nazi stories. It sells papers!"

"There are other considerations here beyond your understanding," Langer warned.

Schreier raised his arms in surrender and made his final pitch. "Okay, okay, boss. Just let me go to Schmidt's rally at the Old Rhinelander on Saturday. No interviews, only a little undercover research. For one night, I'll be just another German for the cause. End of story."

Langer's face held like granite. "Dan, tread carefully here. People could get hurt. And a Jew should know that better than most."

He winked. "Don't worry, boss, I've got it under control. Remember, I lived in Berlin with these goose steppers. What do you say?"

Langer hesitated, then smiled under steely eyes. "Okay, Dan. But don't say I didn't warn you. Schmidt's got a formidable machine in these parts. Your last name might not be Ben Gurion, but they've got a good sniffer when it comes to the Hebrew race, if you catch my drift." He rose and extended his hand.

Schreier took it. "Sure, boss, I'll be careful. And thanks for your support." Schreier strode out of the office, and Langer's grin vanished. He closed the door, swept up the phone, and dialed.

Friday August 19th

Tony scanned the wall of metal doors, approached Jake's locker, and slipped an envelope through the grill. He hurried to the time clock and stabbed his punch card in the slot. Tony glanced at the bulletin board, where a bold yellow sign admonished SECURITY IS UP TO YOU! Tacked just below it, a *Mountain Observer* headline screamed, "Baboons Feast at Backyard BBQ."

Tony checked his schedule. First hour: rhino release. Elephants would have been better, but at least no shoveling today. He scanned the chart for Jake; their schedules aligned for first hour and lunch. His breath hitched.

Tony joined Jake and three other rangers waiting for instructions at the barn. The rhino herd stared stupidly at the open gate, like they'd forgotten that their meal was waiting as usual at their viewing pen.

A Jeep bucked to a halt, and George threw his bulk over the driver's door.

"Marsala, you're on Jeep duty." Tony froze. "Well come on mate, get them fat arses up the road!" George gestured toward his vehicle.

Him, drive George's personal wheels? Tony had never herded anything, and the trail ahead looked like an axle breaker. But that wasn't why he was panicked.

He'd never driven a clutch.

"Um, George, I really don't think I—"

"Come on, now, get it in gear, before I put you on shit shoveling!"

Suddenly, humiliation at the wheel seemed attractive. Tony hurried over, yanked open the driver's door, and gingerly sat. His eyes sought out Jake, who gave him a nod of encouragement. He looked down at three pedals. *They must all be there for a reason.*

He put the key in the ignition, shuffled his feet, and pressed two pedals with the ball and heel of his left foot, the third with his right. He closed his eyes, turned the key, and the engine sputtered and died.

His gaze shot from George's sour expression to Jake, who was slowly mouthing what looked like *ca-la-ch*. Clutch! He studied the floor again, decided the oddly shaped pedal must be the clutch, and pressed down on it. He turned the key, let up the clutch, and forgot his other foot. The engine quit and the chassis lurched, throwing Tony's hat into his lap.

A beet-faced George watched from the top of the hill, spewing curses. "Left foot off the bloody clutch, right foot on the bleedin' gas!"

Jake said something to George, and then headed toward Tony. He hopped over the low passenger door, and positioned himself right up against him.

"What are you—" Tony could barely catch his breath.

"Just relax your legs."

"But I don't know how to—"

"That's obvious. Let me guide you," Jake said softly.

Like a puppeteer, Jake moved Tony's shins in a three-step dance across the pedals three times, explaining what to do with the stick with each footstep. After three goes, Jake watched Tony pantomime each move on his own. He nodded brightly at Tony. "You've got this."

Tony puffed his cheeks. He prayed that God keep him from

destroying the engine. A shriek of grinding metal sent three rhinos charging off in the direction of their pen, while the rest of the pack stared after them. The other rangers tittered and shook their heads.

Tony gave it gas, and the Jeep crept forward as if something were holding it back.

"Emergency brake," Jake whispered, and hopped out of the cab.

Tony nodded, released the brake handle, and shot off like a rocket.

"Now make it snappy, and try not to run down them Vegemite-brains!" George screeched.

Despite orders, Tony crept along, stalling twice, dodging boulders and craters, while Jake and the rest of his foot guard thumped the stragglers' thick hindquarters with sticks and stones.

When one bull got all turned around and started jogging straight at the Jeep, Jake threw away caution and raced in front of the beast's deadly horn, shouting and thumping to steer it away from Tony. Just as Jake regained the upper hand, he turned toward Tony and gave him a heart-melting smile.

Three hours later, Tony caught up with Jake on the cafeteria line. He had thought of almost nothing but lunch since rhino duty, and still had no idea how it would play out.

"Hi," he said. "Can we sit somewhere private?"

They took their burgers and fries to an empty picnic table in the shade. Tony shuffled his cutlery around his tray and looked up from his plate. "Thanks for saving my neck first hour today," he said.

"You owe me two now," Jake said, seeming distracted. He

cleared his throat, pulled a sealed envelope from his shirt pocket, and tossed it onto the table.

"What's this, man?" Jake said.

Tony's eyes flitted from paper to Jake. "Guess you better open it."

Jake tapped the envelope twice and ripped off the short end. Out slipped a postcard of Lake Mennepequa. He turned it over and studied the handwritten message, his mouth a hard line.

"Jake, I'm sorry about Tuesday. I like you a lot, but...this is scary for me."

Jake looked pained. "Listen, I appreciate the note—"

Tony flinched. "But."

Jake leaned back and studied Tony. "We barely know each other, and our lives are real different."

"I don't care that you're different!" Tony burst out.

"But I am. And you should." Jake stared at Tony until he blinked.

"But we have so much in common—" Tony protested weakly.

Jake peered through pressed brows. "Tony...let's get real here."

"Real?" A firehose of words burst from Tony. "Can I tell you what's real? I wake up and my first thought is if I'll see you at work, and then I look for you every hour of my shift. And when I'm with you, I can barely function!"

Jake shushed him, eyes sweeping the picnic area. "Tony, it's okay, it's okay," he said, his bobbing Adam's apple belying his words.

Tony lowered his head onto crossed arms. "But I'm not supposed to feel this way!" he moaned.

Jake's eyebrow shot up. "*Supposed* to? Says who?"

"My...psychiatrist." Tony lifted his head and peered at Jake uncertainly.

Jake flushed. "Your *psychiatrist?*"

"She thinks this"—Tony swept his hands between them—"is a mistake." His chest pounded.

"And you want her to *cure* you?"

Tony began to nod and then shook his head sharply. His mouth quivered, and he shrugged.

Jake smacked his hands on the planking. "Then just why exactly are you in therapy?"

Tony steadied himself. "Sometimes, I—I think I go just to keep everyone happy."

Jake stiffened. "Tell me, Tony, what makes *you* happy?"

Tony slid forward on his bench and pressed a leg against Jake's. Jake hung his head and slowly moved it from side to side. "Tony, what happened last week? You've been avoiding me for five days."

Tony's mouth moved like a fish out of water. "I needed time. And I thought you'd be mad at me."

"I'm not mad. Frustrated, yeah. But I was worried about you."

"I couldn't stop shaking. It was scary."

"Because I touched you." It wasn't a question.

Tony shook his head vigorously. "It wasn't you."

"Wasn't nobody else in the room."

"I—I've never been with a guy before," Tony blurted. He stared at the grass under his bench.

Jake mulled that a moment. "You're saying you've never..."

"Never." Tony wanted to crawl under the table.

"Let your hands go where they wanted? Let your body be in charge?" Jake stared in disbelief.

Tony covered his face with his hands. "How do I explain what happened Tuesday?"

Jake folded his arms. "Try."

"It's like there's a wall three feet thick around me, and you took a sledgehammer to it."

Jake darkened. "I did no such thing."

"Well, I know, but—"

"But it felt that way. You said this is scary, but what you really mean is *I'm* scary. Because I'm not like your college boys."

"No! I'm afraid because you're the first guy who ever saw who I really am and didn't push me away!" Tony almost shouted. The buzz in the lunch grove seemed to pause.

Jake quieted. "Look, Tony. You stay here another two, three weeks, and you're off to school. And then what?"

"I don't know. I don't *care*. It doesn't change how I feel right now," Tony said, blinking hard.

"Unless your shrink says otherwise." Jake glared at him.

"No," Tony said weakly.

"Tony, you come and go, but I got nowhere else but here. What does it cost you if things don't work out? Oh well, just a summer fling, then back to *real* life." Jake shook his head. "I don't get that choice."

Tony felt his eyes welling and tipped up his head. He stared at the ridge that separated the park from the lake, that walled off Jake's world from his.

"You don't know what it's like to live in one place your whole life and...have people leave you." Jake's voice faltered.

The intimation stung Tony. "I would never do that. Just because I'm in college, that doesn't mean I couldn't see you, or you could come see me, and anyway, I get winter and spring breaks, and three months of summer vacation—"

"Tony, you're getting way ahead of yourself." Jake threw Tony's postcard on the table. *"What do you want right now?"*

To stop pretending. "Um...I don't have an answer yet," Tony mumbled.

Jake slumped on his bench. "Well then, I don't know what to say."

"I just need to think this through." Tony rubbed his throbbing temples.

Jake slowly blew out a breath. "You need to figure yourself out, and I got to think on what I get out of this."

"Maybe we could do that...together. Away from everything, somewhere in the mountains."

"You mean go camping?" Jake looked down at the card on the table. He rubbed his neck, puckered one cheek, and searched Tony's face.

"Just the two of us, without all of the...distractions around here."

"You mean without reality getting in the way," Jake said. He shot a glance at Tony, and the corners of his frown crept upward. "Ah, I could use the break. I haven't been away from home for two sunrises since right after the lumberyard fired me."

He looked in Tony's puppy-dog eyes, and sighed. "Well, okay, then. As long as one thing's clear: *we* can't decide anything until *you* know what you want."

"Great! Let's try to trade off our shifts for next week. Say, Friday and Saturday?"

Jake nodded. "And I know some parts around here where my brothers and me used to hunt deer and turkey and never saw a soul."

Tony pointed to his watch and stood up. "We could go for burgers at Sharkey's next Wednesday and firm things up."

"I told you, I don't mix with the hoods who hang around there." Jake grabbed his tray and followed Tony.

Tony dropped his lunch trash in a big black drum. "Someplace in Iron Run, then?"

"Nah…I got a better idea. Come over for dinner so I can return proper your parents' favor," Jake said.

Tony's eyes widened. "Oh, I wouldn't want to put your aunt to any trouble."

"Mother," Jake corrected. "And it's cool with her."

Tony checked his watch again and shifted his weight uneasily. "But how'll I find you? I've never driven up to Blackman's Ridge."

"Calm down, Miss Worrywart. Just meet me here in the lot at quitting time and follow me home," Jake said, a smile creasing his cheek. He headed up the hill to his next shift.

Tony trailed him like a lost duckling. "But nothing's paved, and there aren't any streetlights, and I don't really ever drive in the dark…"

Jake turned and smiled at Tony. "Are you done? It'll be fine. And just so you know: mountain folk don't bite." He gave Tony a reassuring squeeze of the shoulder and marched off.

Tony felt his gut twist. The sounds of the lunch mess faded and he was ten again, cowering before a scowling man with a shotgun.

Saturday August 20th

The Old Rhinelander Inn dominated the northern end of Lake Mennepequa. It sat on a tall finger of land whose south side dropped abruptly to a sweep of blue-green water. To the north, a drive lined with Linden trees led to the inn's entrance facing a sheltered cove.

Here, the land formed a wide apron, with lush plantings and a small car lot. Stairs of hewn rock descended to mooring berths, where patrons handed the reins of their floating chariots to valets in lederhosen.

Dan Schreier whizzed past a cluster of waiting attendants and parked his beat-up Rambler American among the large luxury sedans. As he hurried off to join Schmidt's adoring fans, he noticed one of the parking attendants study his license plate, and scribble on a pad. *Ah, the Gestapo lives on.*

Schreier approached the sprawling inn, roof cloaking the half-timber-and-stucco facade like a cowl. Below two flags on inclined poles, a banner for the Schmidt campaign swagged the double doors.

Alongside the American flag, a standard familiar to tonight's patrons supplanted the Rhenish heraldry. In a navy field, a large black sprocket circled in white contained a red *D* for *Deutschland* in Gothic script.

Arriving guests slowed to admire the pennant. A woman stood, hand to mouth, while two men with matching yellow lapel pins gave a quick upward flick of the wrist and hurried inside.

Nazi muscle memory. Schreier puffed his cheeks and entered the large foyer, where two greeters signed in attendees. He gave the name Don Schroeder to a buxom woman with Heidi braids, who ran a finger down several pages on a clipboard. She threw him a questioning look and whispered something to her companion, who studied him a long moment.

Schreier had expected extra scrutiny and had dressed discreetly. His stingy-brimmed fedora topped a suit of charcoal gray, black tie, and pale-pink shirt.

He threw the women a dimpled grin and thrust his arm from the elbow, palm up. "Free America!" he exclaimed in a crisp Berliner accent. The women lit up, handed him a pen, and pointed him to the rally.

In the atrium beyond the lobby, he found a cheerful Schmidt-for-Sheriff booster at a table brimming with campaign merchandise. When he fingered a red button blazoned SCHMIDT ÜBER ALLES, a gray-haired man leaned in and whispered, "I've got some old souvenirs you might find interesting." Schreier nodded.

The man lit up and led Schmidt off the atrium to a room of wainscoted, stuccoed walls and high leaded windows, dominated by a pair of oak tables that stopped him cold. "Got to keep these on the q.t.," he said with a wink. Schreier met the man's smile with forced cheer. "Can't be too careful, you know, with the bad element trying to bring down our sheriff."

On red table runners, black-on-oxblood swastikas festooned every type of souvenir imaginable. Bund flags, buttons, and badges displayed the American variant of the Nazi rune in a yellow starburst. Books and papers were piled everywhere space allowed.

"These are a bit more expensive, but all proceeds go to our campaign, so you'll be doing your part."

Schreier swept his trembling hands across stacks of *Mein Kampf* and *My New Order*, next to yellowed copies of a booklet titled *Awake and Act!*

Schreier had known of the anodyne Bund screed, and now in his hands it seemed invested with menace. It protested the calumnies committed against Germany by Marxists and an unnamed avaricious race, clear as day to any Jew who'd lived under the Third Reich.

His guide observed Schreier's apparent interest. "A real collector's item, that," he said.

Schreier moved on to a larger volume, *The German*

American Comrade Songbook. Flipping through, he found a familiar title. He hummed the melody, growing quiet as the verses registered.

> There will always be an England—with our
>   Nazi pals and chums,
> We will clear the shores of England of the
>   Asiatic bums.
> There will always be an England, for the rank
>   and for the file.
> In the dawn of coming Europe, hail to Hitler
>   and Sieg heil!

Schreier slammed the book shut, scattering buttons and flags before his sputtering guide, and strode from the room. *Fucking krauts.* He absently tugged on his sleeves and climbed the stairs.

Inside a spacious banquet room, tables and chairs arced the stage. Beyond, tall windows made the hall seem to hover above the lake. French doors gave out to a balcony that took in the full sweep of Lake Mennepequa in twilight.

Pitched conversation bounced off of open roof beams. On the platform, an oompah band sprayed scales and arpeggios above red-white-and-blue bunting.

Flags with the sprocketed red *D* on either side of the podium made clear that Schmidt's campaign boosters were as one with the cult that had raised this same standard above Camp Hochland, wrapping German cultural pride around their Nazi worldview.

Schreier queued up for a beer and took in the crowd. Graying men and thick-waisted women stood at a bar crowded with steins. How many had been cogs in the Nazi machine?

A pair of small, hard eyes drew his gaze. The man appraised Schreier and his jaw locked, as though he had found what he sought. Schreier reflexively pulled down the left cuff of his dress shirt.

The man lifted a stein to his lips, and Schreier saw the ring: embossed silver, the raised skull and bones in a wreath of oak leaves. The *Totenkopf*. The death's-head was flanked by a swastika and the twin jagged runes of the *Schutzstaffel*: the SS.

Does he know me from Riga? Schreier recoiled and bumped into a matron, spilling her beer, and apologized. The room seemed to shrink and darken as he stumbled his way to the double doors to stare out at the lake.

He remembered the spring night in '44 when he'd lain with his parents and sister on the floor of the blackened Levetzowstrasse synagogue, squeezed between benches and suitcases. Hearing moans and cries echo all night under the enormous tiled dome of the ruined hall.

In the morning, they'd been stripped of their valuables and sent to the family intake line. He'd given his name, age, health, and skills, and was ordered to proceed to the left.

His mother had cried aloud when the butt of a rifle released his grip on his father's coat. He was ordered out onto the icy street with men and older boys, and then they were marched at gunpoint to the Putlitzstrasse station and made to stand, hands on heads.

One young man broke away and was instantly shot. The SS guard had made them all watch him place his gun at the prostrate boy's temple and fire, the body jerking and erupting in a plume of blood. No one moved or spoke. At last, the boxcars arrived to transport them to the occupied Baltics.

An explosion of applause drew Schreier back to the present. A small man with a postage-stamp mustache stepped to the podium.

"Good evening, *meine Damen und Herren.* It is with great pride that I present to you the man who has safeguarded us for years—Otto Schmidt!" The cheering swelled as the burly, uniformed man hopped onto the stage.

"Welcome friends, fellow Highlanders, and all free Americans!" He snapped his leather sash and spread his arms, basking in the crowd's approval.

"We are here tonight to celebrate a great people with a glorious heritage. Two centuries ago, we Germans first came to the Highlands." Otto grew solemn. "We left behind all that was dear to us for the promise of a better life. We tilled the land and toiled its mines, breaking our backs for the thieving British overlords." Mutters of disapproval circulated the room.

He surveyed the upturned faces. "But did we let our enemies dash our dreams?" He shook his head with vigor. "No! We took up arms as the patriots we are and overthrew their tyranny. We built a new nation midst these green hills, pristine lakes, and fertile valleys, and became proud and prosperous Americans!"

Otto's eyes swept the crowd. "Then came the Great War, and the Jew moneylenders and the press they control waged a campaign of hate against us. President Wilson accused us of divided loyalties, of being...hyphenated Americans!" Otto said with mannered outrage, to a chorus of boos.

"We were called Huns, traitors, and bloodthirsty savages. We were arrested and interned! Tarred, feathered, and lynched! Our German schools, clubs, shops, and newspapers were shuttered, our language and culture all but erased!

"And when the *Armistice* came" —here Otto paused to let the scornful cries crescendo—"and the weapons factories went silent, the iron bosses and war profiteers shut down the Highlands mines and abandoned us. But did we give up then?" He swept open arms over his audience.

"No!" the group shouted.

Otto nodded, face grim, drawing out the drama. "Never! We fought our way back, working in the factories and mills, building boilers and clothing and carpets for the comfortable life we vowed to regain in the Munsee Mountains."

Otto smirked. "Until the bosses shipped our factory jobs south, and the Jew financiers rushed in and bought up our towns, filling them with *Untermensch*. Profiting from our misery!

"And as I speak, they still scheme to seize our jobs, our homes, our women! So now my friends, I ask, on behalf of our forefathers, who sacrificed all for us: *Will we let these parasites erase us from history?*" Otto threw his arms over his head, as if summoning the heavens.

"NOOO!" the crowd roared as one.

Otto shook his fist. "That's right! We will not commit social suicide! But my dear compatriots, for the great task before us, we must act with unity of purpose. And so we must ask: Who is with us, and who against?"

Otto drew out the tension. "In this election, Leopold Brandt is the enemy of our people," he said, pounding the podium. Catcalls and hisses filled the air. "He claims he will represent you, but how can he, when he is one of *them*?" Otto's voice dripped with contempt.

"We cannot allow our cherished Highlands to fall into his hands this November! Brandt itches to tear down every fence and wall in the county, and lay out the welcome mat to degenerates from every hovel! We built this new *Schwarzwald*, we will fight for it, we will renew it, and we will never concede it!"

"Blut und Boden! Blut und Boden! Blut und Boden!" The chant rolled through the crowd, and the oompah band picked up the beat. Otto clapped along.

"Only I can protect you, your families, and our homeland

from this moral inferno. Reelect me, and I will rid us of the troublemakers and bloodsuckers who threaten us all! Together, we will revive our pride and purpose. My fellow patriots, recapture your heritage! Pledge your sacred honor to free the Highlands, and free America!"

Amidst clangorous applause and music, Otto plunged into the crowd to slap backs and pump hands. The band launched into a martial tune, and slowly, steadily, the throng picked up the melody.

> Zum letzten Mal wird Sturmalarm geblasen!
> Zum Kampfe steh'n wir alle schon bereit!
> *For the last time, the call to arms is sounded!*
> *Already, we all stand prepared for the fight!*

Schreier's throat closed up, and he pushed his way outside to the railing before a dim wash of lake and mountain. The hiss of water on the rocks below soothed him, and slowly he felt his body relax.

"Hello, there, young fellow." Schreier turned to see a backlit figure advance on him, and his neck prickled.

"Good evening to you," he said, and edged away.

The man sidled closer. "You new around here?"

Schreier couldn't make out the shadowed face in the fading dusk. "Fairly," he said.

"And where are you living?" the man asked.

"In town," Schreier said curtly, turning his back to his inquisitor.

"I can't recall seeing you around." The man's tone was odd, both casual and urgent.

"We ought to get back—"

As Schreier pivoted from the railing, a forearm pressed against his windpipe, pulling him backward. Something pricked his neck, followed by sudden cold. A cry locked in his throat, and his body went rigid. Strong arms gripped him from behind, and his shoes scraped across wooden planks into darkness.

Sunday August 21st

Stefan Van Hoek and Hans Kaiser munched garlic knots at a table on Sharkey's Pier, throwing occasional glances toward the fuel station at its far end. In the slanting rays of evening, runabouts and ski boats skipped along the lake's shimmering surface, while mahogany cabin cruisers churned seaweed into green soup.

Eddie's evening relief at Marine Gas was late. Balancing one leg on the floating dock, he guided a powerboat to a soft sideways landing. As he juggled the fuel hose, gas cap, and pump lever, a small, dark teenager with slick black hair approached, mumbling apologies.

"About time, Chico!" Eddie spat. He slammed the nozzle into its cradle, threw down his cleaning rag, and ducked into the staff hut. He emerged tugging on a tee, and marched over to his friends.

"Greasy spic does this to me every time," he fumed. The sun gilded his crew cut.

"Looks like you're pretty greased yourself," Stefan said, handing Eddie a napkin, pale blue eyes gesturing to his friend's forehead.

"Job's fuckin' bullshit," Eddie mumbled. He dropped into an aluminum folding chair, shirt taut across his back. Below one rolled sleeve, the name *Karla* sashed a red heart.

"You need a beer, man," Hans said, and waved over a waitress. "Little darlin', would you please bring our grease monkey a Schlitz?" Eddie gave him the finger and a smirk. The beer came fast, and Eddie chugged half before pouring the rest into a glass.

"So what've you lazy shits been up to today?" Eddie asked, eyes drifting to the faces around the pier.

"Pinched the old man for cigarettes. Then I finished detailing the T-Bird and parked it at Shore Road with my number in the back window," Stefan said.

"You selling her?" Eddie asked.

"Yeah, so I can bum rides with jokers like you." Stefan play-punched Eddie in the chest. "I'm trying to get customizing work, blockhead."

"Cocksucker," Eddie responded. He raised his arms in boxing position and landed a right hook on Stefan's left shoulder. They all laughed, then ordered two large pies and a pitcher of beer as the sun torched up the mountain. Stefan stretched his long legs and yawned.

"Hey, man, thanks for getting outa bed today," Eddie said.

Stefan ran his hand over a shock of platinum hair. "Late night at the drive-in."

Eddie snared Stefan's gaze. "Was Karla with you?" he asked.

Stefan turned toward the lake. "Nah, I think she went bowling with her girlfriends."

"Your sister can't hit a tenpin with a wrecking ball. What's the real story?"

Stefan studied Eddie. "It's over, man. Let it go."

"Don't bullshit me, okay?" Eddie snapped.

Stefan let out a sharp breath. "Some guy in an El Camino dropped her home last night around midnight."

"*Some guy?*" Eddie reddened.

Stefan shook his head. "Cool it, man."

"Tell me!" Eddie thumped the aluminum tabletop with his finger.

"*Stop* already." Stefan rubbed the back of his neck and scowled. "It was night, and I didn't get a good look at his face, but I'm pretty sure he wasn't our kind."

Eddie reddened. "Don't hold back on me."

Stefan squeezed his eyes. "Okay. I think it was the mountain man I seen her with before."

"You saying Karla left me for some Jackson White retard?"

Just a week or so before Karla broke it off with Eddie, he'd shown up unannounced at her door with flowers. It had been an I-love-you-I'm-sorry-let's-make-up thing, after the latest fight they'd had about some bullshit or other. When she'd opened the door, Eddie'd seen him standing nearby, acting all protective.

She'd sputtered that the guy was there to fix something, but Eddie never heard what it was over the roaring in his ears that she'd been two-timing him with a wild man. Eddie'd flung the bouquet at her and said some crazy shit, and the guy had stepped between them and pushed him out the door.

Stefan spread his arms. "Hey, man. I told her to break it off, or I'd have to end it myself, for everyone's sake."

"I could pound the shit outa him right now," Eddie growled, bile eating his gut.

"That's your problem in a nutshell," Stefan snapped.

"Fuck you!" Eddie shot back. People were always judging him—bad boy, hothead, a chip on his shoulder. He couldn't abide being told what to do or say.

"No wonder you and Karla ain't together," Stefan said, as if he'd read Eddie's thoughts.

Eddie's stomach flipped. "Oh, what did your little sister tell you?"

Stefan looked like he's just smelled something rotten. "She didn't have to, man. I saw the bruises and cuts for myself."

"What, a week after we split? It's the mountain fucker, not me."

"She has pictures. Says she was afraid you'd hurt her again, and she wanted evidence."

Eddie reddened and downed the rest of his beer. He smacked his lips, rolled his tongue along his teeth. "And what if I told you she started it?"

Stefan's eyes narrowed, and he leaned in to Eddie. "Listen, buddy boy. You want me to fight your battles, you better not bullshit me about my sister. You hear me?"

"Yeah, well, I was saying how the mountain mixbloods are gettin' out of hand, and she starts calling me names, so I lost it! Eddie raised his voice to drown out Stefan's expletives.

Hans chopped the air between his friends. "Hey! We're all on the same team!"

Stefan crossed his arms. "Yeah, sometimes I wonder," he muttered, and looked heavy-lidded at Hans. Hans faked a cough to hide a smile, and Eddie shot him a dirty look.

"You think this is some kinda joke? Like the Man ain't plotting to do it to us again?"

Stefan shook his head. "What 'man'?"

Hans cocked his chin. "Where does he get this stuff?"

"His uncle," Stefan replied.

"Make fun all you want, but it's a war right here in the Highlands," Eddie fumed.

"And your uncle's the Storm-Führer-in-Charge," Stefan mocked.

"You want them mountain men making mud babies with your sisters? Ain't you proud of your skin?"

"Something's got under yours, all right," Hans said.

"You don't see what's going on? Inbreds leaving their shacks in the hills, pushing into *our* Highlands."

"It ain't an invasion, Eddie," Stefan said.

"Call it what you want, if we do nothing, they wipe us out, like the gypsy moths chewing their way through the forest." Eddie's eyes were red. "They already came for Karla."

Hans and Stefan went quiet.

Stefan reached across the table and patted Eddie's hand. "Hey, man. I know how you feel about these lowlifes. We all do," he said, sweeping his gaze around the pier. "And I know the breakup was hard on you. But it ain't worth doing something rash. This is family business now. Let me deal with it."

The knot in Eddie's stomach pulled tighter. "Sorry, man, but this is between me and the mixblood. I need to put him in his place."

"Hold on, buddy. Is this really worth getting fucked up over?" Hans said.

Eddie sputtered. "If I let him get away with this, that just tells the rest of them Jackson Whites to come on in and help themselves! Then who's next?" He looked accusingly at his friends. "No, I got to teach him a lesson."

Stefan stared hard at Eddie. "Not by yourself."

Eddie took it in and slowly nodded. He studied Hans. "You in?"

Hans glowered. "Why you got to drag everybody into your own messes?"

Eddie taunted Hans. "We do nothing, that just makes us all look like pussies."

Hans rolled his eyes. "Maybe it makes you feel like one."

Stefan shot daggers at Eddie. "I will handle this. You lay low until you hear from me, understand?" Eddie pursed his lips and nodded. He looked across at Hans, who rapped his fingers on the table.

Eddie regarded Hans reassuringly. "Hey man, let's see what Stefan says about his little sister first, and then we'll all make a plan, okay? What say, next Wednesday, Lulu's, five o'clock?"

Stefan grunted in assent. Hans wavered. "Listen: If I go in on it, then we're just gonna rough him up a little. I ain't up for no serious trouble, okay?" he said, more plea than demand.

Eddie nodded. "Sure, no big deal," he said, carnage coursing his thoughts.

February 20, 1939

"**E**dward, please hold still." Mama straightens the knot in my tie.

I am seven. I wrinkle my nose. "Why do I have to get all dressed up again? Church was yesterday!"

"We're going to show everyone how much we love America." Mama tousles my hair.

"Why do we have to?" I protest.

She smooths my collar. "Because people say we love Germany more, Liebchen."

Papa crosses the room and takes my hand. "Eddie, everything will be fine. We're going to celebrate George Washington's birthday at Madison Square Garden with Uncle and all of our friends." As always, Papa calms me.

Thirty minutes later, we emerge from the subway at Fiftieth Street. Despite the icy wind off the Hudson, the atmosphere around the Garden is buoyant, electric. Buses, taxis, and cars release a torrent of humanity, and we ride the current along the broad avenue to the wavelike awning of the arena, and jostle our way inside.

A din fills the cavernous hall. Men and women in their Sunday best pack long rows of seats, shaking hands and patting shoulders, while children squirm and squeal. The aisles swarm with uniformed men in separate lines of blue and brown. The mezzanine above us is hemmed with banners that proclaim STOP JEWISH DOMINATION OF CHRISTIAN AMERICANS *and* FREE AMERICA!

Behind the stage hang flags tall as a building, stars and stripes mixed together with yellow swastikas that shoot like Roman candles. Dead center, a towering George Washington in general's topcoat holds a rapier. Flanking the podium, brown-shirted men gaze fiercely around the stage, flashlights like nightsticks in their leather belts. I spot Uncle Otto and wave, and he nods my way.

A color guard moves through the crowd to scattered cries of "Sieg heil!" and "Heil Hitler!" After a pretty blond lady sings "The Star-Spangled Banner," a man takes the microphone, raises his hand for quiet, and begins.

"My fellow Christian Americans!" he thunders, to the roar of twenty thousand throats. For hours, speakers denounce "President Rosenfeld" and "Bolshevik Jewish parasites," and the air throbs with one long cry: "Free America! Free America! Free America!"

Wednesday August 24th

Eddie marched into Lulu's bar and grill trailed by Hans and Stefan and planted himself in the last booth with his back to the wall. The chrome-rimmed Formica tabletop hid Naugahyde upholstery crisscrossed with duct tape.

A heavily made up waitress came over. Her teased blond

hair was brown at the roots, and she wore a skirt too short to hide a delta of blue veins.

"Hello, Eddie. I saw your mom by herself at church on Sunday. Everythin' okay, honey?" Penciled eyebrows pinched with concern.

What she meant was *Why haven't you been at church in six months?* Eddie's eyes burned. "Fine, Mrs. Van Stroop. Three Buds, " he said sharply. That woman always got under his skin. Didn't the ladies at the beauty parlor have anything else to gossip about but Helga Schmidt and her no-good son?

"Anything you need, just ask," she flung over her shoulder, on a plaintive note that said, *That poor woman.*

"Nosy bitch," Eddie hissed. "Okay, men, we're here to plan our moves. We all still in?" The other two nodded.

Eddie looked expectantly to Stefan. "Whatcha find out from Karla?"

Stefan stared daggers at Eddie. "First, you gotta swear that whatever happens, my sister comes to no harm."

Eddie smacked the table with his palm. "I want her back, man. Don't that say my intentions?"

Stefan digested Eddie's response, looking unconvinced. "I'm telling you flat out, if anything happens to her, you're gonna answer to me."

Eddie simmered. He wanted Karla to hurt the way she'd hurt him. But he needed Stefan on board. Eddie buried his frustrations in his beer and gave Stefan a thumbs-up.

"It's cool, okay? So what's the story?" Eddie pawed the floor.

"Well...turns out Silas been meeting Karla by the boat launch near Buzzie's Tackle Shop, and then driving around the mountain. I tailed them on the state road. He pulled off by Sherman's Bridge and took the old mining trail up past the forge and the big water wheel. They disappeared into a beat-up house with two chimneys and a veranda."

"The foreman's mansion?" Hans asked.

Eddie worked his jaw. "So that's the way it is. But not for long," he snorted. He moved his head slowly from side to side. *She's gonna pay.*

"Eddie, what you gonna do?" Hans asked in a reedy voice.

Eddie regarded Hans with contempt. "What you think? A good beating's the only thing these degenerates understand," he said, sneering.

"And Karla?" Hans pressed.

Stefan cut off any reply. "I'll deal with her," he said, bearing down on Eddie. "Everyone got that?" Eddie and Hans studied their beers.

Stefan shunted the tension into present business. "Now, best I can tell, Silas works weekdays at the farm extension service, so Saturday night he should be hot to trot. I'll work out what I can from Karla."

"We go in one car, get to the trail before dark, and stake out the house," Eddie said. "Whose car?" He looked at his two friends. Hans looked at Stefan.

Stefan eyed Eddie with annoyance. "Well, we sure ain't taking your junkheap," he said.

"What if he puts up a fight?" Hans protested.

"It's three against one. He may be half animal, but we can take him down. Pack a blade," Eddie said. His leg banged the table.

"I'll bring my hunting rifle for insurance," Stefan said.

"Now you're talking," Eddie said. "Around six, we meet at the first trailhead up from the bridge, so's we don't attract attention. From there, should be a half hour tops in your T-Bird."

Stefan rubbed his neck and sighed. "We set, then?"

"So long as that big ape don't cross me before Saturday," Eddie said.

"Just don't go looking for trouble," Stefan snapped.

Hans and Stefan took out their wallets, got up, and moved toward the cashier.

Eddie threw his head back and drew the bottle to his lips to suck up the last suds. The bright bay window up front drew his eye to the sunlit mountain it framed. *His* mountain, *his* Highlands. He screwed up his face and stamped his bobbing leg. *"Blood and soil,"* he whispered.

Tony's Falcon bucked and heaved on the rutted road. Through a scrim of dust, he strained to keep Jake's pickup in his sights as he barreled along each hidden fork on the mountain. He was already dreading the drive home.

After half an hour, the route leveled out. Sunlight shot through the trees and pooled in clearings that revealed solitary houses sagging with their burdens, yards full of weathered cars, swing sets, and tricycles. Jake tapped his horn three times at each house, as if signaling friend, not foe.

The human mark on the landscape grew more frequent: PRIVATE PROPERTY signs and crumbling walls; a chassis stripped clean. A hand-painted sign for DeGroat Street. Barking rose above the crackle of gravel.

Jake's pickup turned sharply left, climbed a precipitous driveway, and coasted to a stop. He tapped his horn and got out. Fifty feet behind, the Falcon banged its way up the incline, engine whining. The sedan pulled alongside the pickup and lurched into stillness. Tony's head rode a sea swell.

Jake walked to the Falcon and peered in. "You okay, Tony?"

Tony cracked the door, threw his head into the breach, and heaved.

A large woman walked toward them from the house, wiping hands on a calico apron. She poked her head past Jake's and clucked her tongue.

"Jacob Emery, what have you done to this poor boy?"

Her visage filled Tony's unfocused view. Her eyebrows clenched a caramel brow, and woolly hair spilled from a checkered kerchief tied tight against her head. *The face from the syrup bottle.*

"Jake, help this boy up and get him into a clean shirt!" she ordered.

Jake nodded obediently. "Yes, ma'am," he said.

Tony's clothes were stuck to him. He tried to raise himself up, but the world spun, and he closed his eyes and slumped back. In another instant, something warm and wet lashed his face, and his eyes popped open.

"Sit, Maisie!" Jake commanded, and the coonhound obeyed. "Come on, Tony, let's get you washed up."

"I guess I made a spectacle of myself." Tony attempted a laugh, and managed a coughing fit. He slipped out of the driver's seat, and immediately tripped over his own foot. Jake crouched alongside and slung Tony's arm over his shoulder. They walked haltingly to the stairs, where Tony paused and took in the scene before him.

The wood frame house was girded on two sides with a covered porch brightened by open slats of sky. Its weatherworn railing rested on two-by-fours and a handful of painted balusters. Several attempts to paint the wooden siding had run short of supplies or inspiration.

Patches of linoleum and plywood creaked under their feet as the two men threaded their way to the front door past a couch and a refrigerator. Tony looked charily at Jake.

Jake shrugged. "It's home."

Jake held open the front door, and Tony stepped into the scent of bleach and lavender. The house-wide parlor was spotless. A sofa and two chairs of different styles and colors anchored a brightly patterned carpet on a shiny wood floor.

A knitted throw covered the couch; needlepoint pillows were everywhere. A polished oak table with tooled legs hugged the wall nearest the kitchen, its chairs nicked and weathered. Floral wallpaper glowed in the light of an amber glass chandelier.

"Come wash up," Jake said. He led Tony through the kitchen, where pots bubbled on the stove and the kerchiefed lady bustled about her domain.

"Jacob Emery, you going to set the table? Your brothers ain't home yet." The cadence of her speech reminded Tony of voices from the sketchy streets behind Columbia.

"Yes, ma'am," Jake said.

They doubled back behind the kitchen sink to a white-washed bathroom. Jake handed Tony a towel from an open shelf. "I'll be right back," he said, and left.

Tony tossed his soiled shirt on the linoleum floor. He turned the sink's only handle, splashed his face with icy water, then shook his head in it. He wet his chest and arms, drawing goose bumps in the humid air, and rubbed down with the towel. Instantly, he felt better. He rinsed a rust-stained cup, filled it, and gargled.

"Delivery!" Jake handed him a faded green T-shirt, which he slipped over his head.

"Feel better?" Jake asked.

Tony smiled and rolled his eyes. "Yeah, thanks."

"Guess I should've warned you about the rough ride," Jake said.

And how. "It's okay," he said. Best that he be on good

behavior with this family tonight, Tony thought. The sort of people no one at the lake had a good word to say about.

"Um, Jake? Are your cousins joining us?"

"Brothers," Jake corrected. "They should be here anytime."

"And they know I'm coming?"

"Yes, they've been duly warned to act polite." Jake's wisecrack was sharp around the edges.

Tony decided to show some goodwill. "Jake, I'd like to properly thank the cook for her concern at my arrival. What's her name?"

Jake's expression clouded over. "Just call her Mrs. DenBleyker," he said flatly, and left.

A clangor of shouting and barking came through the windows, and Tony stepped outside to investigate. Jake's three brothers piled out of a metallic-blue El Camino; they looked familiar, Tony thought.

The men headed straight for the flatbed and pulled out three long ropes weighted with rabbits, squirrels, and some kind of long-legged bird. The tallest man had a face like Jake's, except for the auburn hair and brown eyes. Tony approached, and he held out the rope with the squirrels, as if in greeting.

"Euel. And them other two scoundrels makes three Muellers," he said, jerking his thumb toward his companions. "Pleased to meet you. You must be Jake's friend from the new zoo. Mind bringing this out back to the table by the shed?" Euel poked the air with the twisted mess.

"Uh, sure." Tony snatched the rope so hard that it snapped back at him, and a squirrel thumped his chest. He marched off toward the backyard, Maisie shadowing him, the day's catch held far from his body. The smell made Tony's insides contract. With a quick look behind, he dropped the rope on the ground, leaned against the house, and closed his eyes.

What kind of life, what *world* was this? He recalled his

revulsion when Nonno and Nonna described foraging in the hills of Sicily for snails to quell their gnawing hunger. It had seemed to Tony like an old folktale that had nothing to do with real life. Only *this* was happening right here and now in New York, USA.

He spotted the table and steadied himself. He heard snuffling at his feet, opened his eyes, and shooed Maisie away from the kill. He picked up the rope. He sucked in, held his breath, and made for the table, looking up only when he was upon it.

There on a grooved slab of wood sat three severed chicken heads; blood dripped into a plastic bucket below. Flies were everywhere. Maisie looked at him expectantly.

He swallowed hard and flung the new sacrifices onto the heap of gore. Over the dog's whining, he heard the brothers heading his way and sprinted to the far side of the house before they could set another task for him.

Back inside, the dining table had doubled in size and was now covered by a crocheted tablecloth. In the kitchen, platters and pots clattered, and a voice lifted in song.

"*All my trials, Lord, soon be over,*" the cook sang out.

The fragrance of butter, lemon, and garlic wafted through the parlor, and Tony relaxed for the first time since leaving work. He sat down on a lumpy wing chair draped with doilies, and his gaze fell on a sepia picture on a side table.

A bride and groom stared dreamlike before a gauzy, opulent backdrop. The groom was a full head taller than his bride and stood with noble bearing, bony wrists protruding from too-short sleeves. He had Jake's high cheeks, light eyes, and long nose.

He was fair of face, and seemed almost ghostly alongside the deep complexion of his bride. She seemed much younger, the lacy veil and bodice framing dark, glowing eyes. Her hair was set in finger waves tight to her face.

She was the cook in the kitchen. Mrs. DenBleyker. Jake's mother. And aunt.

Tony's pulse quickened. Where he came from, Jake's family was something there was no polite word for. He studied the patterns in the rug as crude words elbowed into his thoughts.

The brothers burst through the door, laughing and ribbing. Mrs. DenBleyker shouted from the kitchen. "Good gracious, you boys be terrible late for dinner! Euel, Malcolm, Silas, get yourselves cleaned up, changed, and back down here afore I feed your dinner to the raccoons, you hear me?"

"Yes, ma'am," they said as one, hustling past Tony, one to the bathroom and the others pounding their way upstairs.

Ten minutes later, Mrs. DenBleyker sat at the head of the table, her four sons surrounding her, hands in their laps. Tony sat at the far end, next to Jake. Before them lay a vast platter of glossy chicken and a gravy boat. Two bowls flanked the platter, one a large mound of mashed sweet potatoes in molasses, the second with cubes of bacon sinking into wilted greens.

Tony made to pass the greens toward Jake's mother, and his knee received a firm hit from Jake. Tony froze and looked sideways at Jake's pinched brow, then up at the matriarch, eyes boring holes into Tony. He returned the bowl to its appointed place.

The—sons? cousins?—clasped their hands before their faces, and Tony mirrored them. The lady of the house closed her eyes and cleared her throat. "Lord God, humble our hearts and make us grateful for this bounty. We thank the Great Spirit for the living things that sacrificed themselves for us today, especially the bear and the chicken."

Tony pressed Jake's leg and shot him a worried look, mouthing *bear?* Jake smiled under knotted fingers.

"Amen," Jake offered, and the others echoed him, Mrs.

DenBleyker adding her own thunder. The brothers took thirsty gulps from their beers.

Tony kept his hands under the table and watched the dance of plates and platters. When it was over, Tony had more food piled on his dish than he could negotiate. He looked Jake's way, but he only smirked and shook his head.

Tony gathered a forkful of greens and bacon and closed his mouth around it, letting it flower on his tongue before swallowing. He moaned a compliment and added, "Mrs. DenBleyker, this is wonderful."

"Why, thank you, Mr. Tony, I—"

"Please call me Tony." He smiled solicitously.

Mrs. DenBleyker's tone sharpened. "As I was saying, *Mister* Tony, I have my boys here"—she nodded at them with pride—"to thank for the special addition to my greens today."

Tony's smile froze. "And that would be—"

"My boys have brung me down from the smokehouse of Old Lady Ten Eyck a most marvelous thing I have not tasted in many a moon: bear bacon!" she boomed.

Tony dropped his fork, which clanged on his plate before clattering to the floor. He ducked under the table to retrieve it, but instead sent it skittering toward the matriarch.

On all fours, he extended one hand as near Mrs. DenBleyker's legs as he dared, locked on his utensil, and rose so fast that he banged his head on the table. He slid back into his seat, all eyes on him. He grabbed his soda glass, took a big gulp, and had a coughing fit.

"Wrong pipe," Tony managed.

Euel, Malcolm, and Silas elbowed and snickered with full mouths until their mother shot them a deadly look.

Euel made to mollify her. "Mama, with what we saved from the hunt, we got enough meat to last through winter. It's still curing with the rest of the stomach down by Ten Eyck's," he said, his poker face slipping. This set off a new round of titters from Malcolm and Silas that they smothered in their beers. Tony squirmed in his seat.

Jake glared at his brothers. "Well, I haven't tasted a finer meal I can recall. Mama, you just proved again you are the best cook in the Munsee Mountains!"

"I do thank you, child," his mother said, with a satisfied look around the table.

Silas blotted his eyes with his sleeve as one last titter escaped him. "Tony, you remember the first time you seen me, Malcolm, and Euel?"

Tony wrinkled his brow. "Before today?"

Silas uncapped another beer and pointed the bottle at Tony, eyes shining with mischief. "I remember you, all right." Silas glanced at Euel and Malcolm, who stifled grins. "Was maybe seven years ago, down at the whirlpool."

Something glimmered in Tony's memory, and he felt his cheeks go hot. "The swimming hole at Wewappo Creek?"

Silas grinned impishly. "You was standing at the clearing with your mouth hung open, staring at us, bare naked on the rocks." Mrs. DenBleyker grunted her disapproval, with no apparent effect on her sons.

"You spooked us so bad, we dove straight into that ice bath!" Euel added.

Now Tony was there again, riveted by their fit, dewy bodies, mortified when they locked eyes with him. "That was you?"

"Sure as we's sitting here," Malcolm chuckled, and tapped bottles with Euel.

Euel fixed Tony with wide eyes. "Oh, we's a wiiild bunch," he rasped. "We only wear clothes for company." He passed Silas a look of mischief.

With two beers in him and a smile near to bursting, Silas

leaned toward Tony and whispered ominously, *"We even eat bear bacon bare naked."*

Their mother slapped the table. "Children, where are your manners? Ain't no proper dinner talk!" Mrs. DenBleyker lectured, while Euel and Malcolm guffawed. Silas was so pleased with his quip, he couldn't help joining them, and when Jake caved, Tony did, too. Mrs. DenBleyker shook her head in reproach, while her bosom heaved of its own accord.

Once they'd all had their fill, the boys cleared the table, and Jake's mom shooed them out of the kitchen and got to work righting the havoc.

Jake motioned Tony to join him outside. They walked to an old barn behind the house. Jake swung the door open, pulled a chain, and lit up the room.

"This is my special place," he said reverently.

Split lumber and heaps of trimmed branches were everywhere; shavings and shards of wood padded the floor. Tools hung from hooks in neat rows. In the center of the room, an old door made a work surface and brace for two vises holding a long stick.

This wasn't Tony's high school woodshop. Handmade bowls, polished and stained, crowded one wall. Carved animals from a primordial dream filled several shelves: beasts with bristling teeth, tusks, and antlers, grazing, stalking, in battle, their flanks worked so finely that Tony could almost feel their furry hides.

Tony ran his fingers over several benches and two expertly tooled chairs. "Promised my mama a new set of dining chairs last Christmas," Jake chuckled. "Still got a ways to go on that."

Tony slowly took in all four walls, blinking helplessly. "You made all these?"

Jake looked at his feet and said, "Mm-hmm."

"They're amazing."

Jake shoved his hands in his pockets and surveyed the room. "When I come here, the spirit's in charge, and I follow. It's just what comes. See that over there?" Jake motioned to the stick in the vises. Tony noticed now that it had some kind of serpent twined around it. "It's a walking stick. A tribute to my grampa.

"He taught me to respect Snake and all the mountain spirits. We used to go for walks in the forest, and he'd keep wild critters safe from our tread by prodding and pounding his cane. Of course, he carved his own. It was something to behold."

"I'm sure he'd be proud of you," Tony said.

Jake's eyes grew liquid. "He would say, 'Remember that Snake is a *Mësingw*'—that's a kind of channel between us and the Creator—'and Snake has the ear of *Kishelëmukong.*'" Jake saw that Tony was lost. "That's our name for the Creator. So if you honor His messenger spirit, you honor Him, too."

Tony's stomach shrank. If he'd suggested to the nuns at school that Adam and Eve's serpent was God's whisperer, they would have bloodied his knuckles. What kind of god was Jake's?

Jake continued. "Gramps carved everything you can think of. I can't remember when he wasn't making bowls, forks, or ladles. One year on my birthday, he gave me a wooden wagon I could sit in, and it rolled around smooth as a fine car."

"Do your brothers carve too?" Tony asked.

Jake shook his head. "Gramps said was only me that got the gift. Was on account of me getting bit by Coyote when I was little."

Tony cringed. "How did that happen?"

"I was out in the woods, gathering Mama's herbs. Coyote was lying by the creek with his flank all mauled, breathing hard. I was too young to know better, so I went over to pet him.

But Coyote was mad with fear and pain, and he clamped his teeth onto my arm. I fell right into the water with him locked onto me.

"It was summer, and the creek ran low. I pinned Coyote to the creek bed with my body. He stared up at me, like he knew what was happening, and then I felt a jolt, like something passed from him to me, and his jaw went slack. I jumped out of the water and ran home in holy terror.

"Grampa dressed the bite, sat me on his lap, and listened to my teary-eyed story. He looked at me real serious and said it wasn't an ordinary coyote, it was a Manitou, a spirit being, that come to be sacrificed.

"'And now,' he said, 'you got the animal spirit in you.' I didn't understand then, but when I got older, he told me he'd had a vision that showed how I'd come to work the wood because of that spirit." Jake's eyes shone.

"When did you know you had this gift?"

"Since I's old enough to chop wood. I'd save the odd pieces and whittle them. Simple things, like turtles and fish. Grampa noticed; he said, 'You got a red haze about your bones.' That I made the wood come alive.

"He taught me to make useful things, like an axe handle or kitchen tools. Later, they got more fancy. I decorated them after what I saw carved and drawed in caves and rock shelters around these parts—beasts with long tusks and huge racks. And patterns in nature. Like these pots."

Jake handed Tony a wooden bowl, about a foot in diameter. The high collar was divided into rectangles and triangles of incised parallel lines, set at contrasting oblique angles. Another vessel had a neck where slits had been made for eyes and a mouth.

Tony examined an oxblood pot. "I've never seen wood this color."

Jake's eyes shone. "I stained it with bloodroot. It's all over these woods."

Tony shook his head and smiled. "Does anyone know what you do here?"

"Besides family? No."

Tony was dumbfounded. "Why not?"

Jake suddenly got bashful. "It's just a hobby."

"I think the things you make would fetch a lot of money in the city." Tony nodded with conviction.

Jake seemed repelled by the idea. "I got enough work between chores and the boss man. I ain't looking for another job."

"Not a *job*. Listen, I know a guy at school—his parents are rich. I visited their place in the city, and they had beautiful things there, hand carved tables, chairs, and sculptures. Your stuff is every bit as good as theirs. And they have a shop selling things like that." Tony looked at Jake expectantly.

Jake waved away Tony's words. "No one's interested in what I make."

"And how would you know, if no one's ever seen them?"

Jake seemed to take offense. "What I do here, I do to honor Grampa and the spirits."

"And what about honoring your gift?"

Jake had no answer for that. Tony shifted his focus again to Jake's creations, pulsing with life and energy. "Could I photograph your work sometime?" he asked.

Jake eyed Tony doubtfully. "What for?"

"Because the things that come from your hands are magic."

Jake flushed. "I don't know. I got to think on it."

Jake led them out into the crisp mountain air, as a cloudbank swallowed the moon.

"Where're we going?"

"Not far," Jake said. "C'mon."

Tony heard a screech, then a snap, and his stomach fluttered. "I can't see a thing," he whined.

"Just stick by me. I got wildcat vision," Jake said with confidence.

They abruptly stopped by a split-rail fence. Jake dropped to the soft earth and leaned against a post, patting the ground next to him. Tony sat cross-legged, and as his eyes adjusted, he could see the vegetable patch and chicken coop in the faint glow of the clouds.

Jake turned to Tony. "So what was it like being a kid at Lake Mennepequa?"

"I didn't make friends easily. It was such a strange, clannish place: all those Nordic Protestants named Helga and Hans and Dieter, with their beer and sausage and Calvin and Luther. Like a piece of the old country frozen in time."

Jake snorted. "Some of them think they're living in their own little Reich."

"Where no one's named Marsala," Tony added. "In all the years we've been here, the neighbors have never invited us to a barbecue. We definitely don't fit in their worldview."

"But then I met Stefan Van Hoek. Two years older, platinum hair, like a Greek god. Unlike most local kids, he was friendly. We'd go exploring in his rowboat, like Jason and the Argonauts, and when he stroked the oars, I missed a lot of the scenery." Tony chortled.

"You little fairy-in-training." Jake's cheek dimpled. He slid closer and set his chin on raised knees. "So what did you do when you got him alone?" he asked breathlessly.

Tony recoiled. "Are you kidding? He was a straight arrow, and the lake colony was too small to risk the fallout." Tony combed acorns from the lawn. "We're not close anymore, but I still stare."

"Don't he live up the street from you?" Jake asked.

Tony nodded. "In that overgrown patch of houses."

"My brother's seeing his sister," Jake said uneasily.

"You mean Silas? How's that working out?"

Jake gave a throaty hum of censure. "I don't see it coming to no good."

Tony pursed his lips. "*Any* good," he said, sotto voce.

"What's with all your grammar lessons?" Jake asked coldly.

Tony blushed. "Oh, it's just that you used a double negative, which is when—"

Jake cut him off. "I *know* what a double negative is. I'm a hillbilly with a high school diploma."

Tony squirmed. "I—sorry. It's…a reflex. My mom was always correcting my English so I'd make a good impression out of the house."

"Who were you impressing?" Jake asked.

"The people who thought that all Italians were like the *goombahs* who never left the old neighborhood, never got ahead, and spoke bad English."

Jake bristled. "You mean like me."

Tony couldn't make himself object. "Sorry," he managed.

"Just saying 'sorry' doesn't acquit you, you know." Jake smirked.

"I…yes. I mean, no, it doesn't." Tony raked the grass in zigzag patterns.

Jake was quiet a moment, and then said, "Just for the record, I can speak proper English—when I need to. I can switch it on or off, like your parents probably did. And I don't judge people by how they talk."

Tony hugged his knees tight. Tony judged people all the time by the way they spoke. At Columbia, it mattered even more. Did Jake embarrass him? Was he attracted to Jake for who he was, or despite it?

Jake sat up. "I guess you don't have a say in how you get

raised. I shouldn't take no offense"—Jake gasped and put a finger on his lip—"excuse me, *any* offense."

Tony rolled his eyes and smiled.

"Back to your charmed life." Jake winked. "Tell me about little Tony in the big city."

"Okay, so my world went as far as the bus. School and church, the pizza shop and the soda fountain. I grew up with kids whose grandparents came over from the old country.

"The grandparents sat on stoops and gossiped in accents thick as gravy, while the kids played under their eye. No one cared how you worshipped or where you came from, because everyone was different one way or another," Tony said, feeling a surge of pride.

"Who's 'everyone'?" Jake asked.

In his mind's eye, Tony could see the photographs of his classmates lined up in neat rows. "Polish, Irish, Jewish, Czech, German, Italian, and Greek."

"So everybody was white," Jake said cooly.

That got Tony's dander up. "I never thought about anybody's color," he said.

Jake chuckled. "Because you had no cause to."

It annoyed him that Jake didn't drop the subject. "Why do you have to make it about color?"

"*I* didn't make it that way." Jake said flatly. "And if I notice it, that's because people around here won't let me forget about my own skin."

"Well, you're not the only outsider, you know. People by the lake called us *dago* and *wop*, and put a cherry bomb in our mailbox," he said.

Jake studied Tony. "Well, that sucks," he said soberly.

Tony let Jake's sympathy settle over him, and his umbrage abated. "So if people around here are always giving you a hard time about your skin color, why would you want to live here?"

"*Want* to? We've been here since before there was an Algonquin County," Jake muttered. "If they ever try to push us out of the Highlands, they's asking for trouble."

"But we all have to get along, or there won't *be* a Highlands."

"It takes two, Tony. I don't mind sharing these mountains. But sharing ain't what these small-time bigots had in mind from the beginning, and they still don't." Jake ripped a fistful of grass and flung it.

Tony thought of his family's frosty reception at the lake. Jake had a point.

"Anyway, people don't get to choose the lives they're born into," Jake said.

Jake's fatalism ground against Tony's heroic family story. "But they can decide what to do with them," he protested.

"You think that I don't get tired of the hunting and chopping and farming for my mama—and then have to deal with all the bullshit in town? Don't you think I've thought of leaving? And then I'd be hating myself for abandoning my family and the land, just like my pa."

Tony suddenly felt the weight of his own family's expectations and his desperate urge to run from them. Toward something that terrified him.

"Sometimes when it got to be too much, I used to drive to the bars in Paterson, or even Greenwich Village, get drunk, try to score, stay out all night. And wake up guilty."

"But you always came back to your family," Tony said.

Jake sighed. "They're my kin, but I don't fit in here. And I don't belong out there neither." He flung out an arm that seemed to take in the whole world.

Tony wanted to say he felt the same, but almost everything about this evening was screaming how different Jake's world was from his. He checked his watch, and thought maybe he'd had enough of it for one night.

"Jake, it got later than I thought, and I still have to find my way down the mountain. Do you mind if I call ahead to let my mom know I'll be getting home late?"

"Sorry, city boy, you'll need to send her a smoke signal. Ain't no phones on the mountain."

Jake's gaze quickly flicked away from Tony, as if expecting his look of shock. A cool curtain of air had dropped over them, and Tony rubbed his shoulders in the sudden chill.

"Come on, let's go back," Jake said.

They joined Euel, Malcolm, and Silas on the porch. Euel pulled a hand-rolled smoke from his pocket, lit it, sucked in, and held the pungent heat, then sent it to Silas, who gave it to Malcolm, who handed it to Jake. Tony passed on it, and the reefer went around the circle again. When it got too small to handle, Euel lit another.

Jake shot a geyser of smoke skyward. A grin spread across his face as he looked over at Silas. "Rumor has it that brother Silas been partaking of forbidden fruit," Jake said. In unison, Silas's brothers let out a whoop.

"Says who?" Silas said with mock innocence.

Jake stuck his tongue into his cheek. "Says a little bird at Lake Mennepequa who flew by Tuesday night whilst you and your lady was going at it in your machine." A salvo of laughter went around the porch.

Silas got red in the ears and shot back, "And was that little bird at the lake cornholing white boys?" The brothers got quiet. Tony fidgeted in his chair.

But Jake wasn't in a fighting mood. He waved the air with his hand. "Hey, man, any port in a storm." He winked at Silas.

Smarting, Silas walked off the porch. A door slammed, an

engine coughed, and two cats'-eye taillights disappeared down the drive.

Tony stared at Euel and Malcolm in the porch light. Their red-brown faces, the stone-hewn cheeks, the strange legacy of the mountains. They all made Tony's blood race.

They weren't of his world. Like Jake.

Like his first caveman.

Summer 1950

The blond boy who lives up the gravel road invites me to ride bikes in the forest with his older friends, "where there are real cavemen," Stefan says excitedly.

Eddie and Hans say bad words and put firecrackers in turtle shells, and Ma says I can't play with them. But I want to be Stefan's friend, and, well, cavemen…

So I sneak away, and the four of us ride bikes up dirt paths deep into the forest, past broken-down houses. The way gets steeper, each pedal stroke lifting us off our seats. We stop abruptly at a house with a roof like a drooping clothesline. It's quiet. Eddie and Hans disappear behind the building. Then I hear sudden squawking.

The ringleaders return, leering at me and Stefan. "If you ride with us, you gotta prove you're brave. Dare you to steal some corn and grab a chicken," Eddie says. Stefan and I look at each other.

"But—but what if we get caught?" I sputter.

"You want the whole lake to know you're sissies?" Hans taunts.

"No! We can do it," Stefan announces shrilly, while I nod a lot.

Me and Stefan go around back and drop our bikes in the long grass. Stefan rattles the catch on the corncrib, and it suddenly gives, cobs pummeling him. I undo the latch on the coop and open the wire gate.

We spin around at a sudden woosh in the grass. A grizzled man stripped to the waist waves a shotgun at us. "What you doin' trespassing?" he rumbles.

It's my first caveman: eyes like glowing coals, dark face, hair like brambles. I freeze, clutching the flapping wing of a chicken. The savage advances on us, squinting over a shotgun.

Stefan backs up until he thumps my chest. "We—we was just riding around," he stammers.

"Honest to God, mister, we didn't mean no harm." I start to blubber.

The caveman springs forward, grabs my shirt, and lifts me off the ground. "You devils never come around with good wishes!" He blows rancid air in my face. "Now get your scrawny hides gone afore I fill them with buckshot!" he commands.

"I promise we'll never come back!" I squeak.

Stefan and I thrash across the overgrown yard, leap onto our bikes and slam the pedals, but the weeds grab our wheels. Blam! Buckshot dings my fender. Blam, blam! I yank the handlebars, screaming, and we scythe a path of abject terror down the mountain.

6

Thursday August 25th

n the shallows, the charcoal jacket splayed outward, shoulders halfway down each arm, as though the wearer were disrobing at the moment death found him. A deep gash ran from the mangled face down the torso. One pant leg was ripped to the hip, the scored flesh draped in seaweed.

Deputy Sheriff DeVrees left the body with his forensic team and radioed his report. "We've got a positive on an adult white male, approximately thirty, business attire, found near sandbar one-quarter mile south of the Old Rhinelander on east shore. Read me, over."

"Read you, DeVrees."

"Bloating suggests submerged several days."

"Do we have ID on deceased?"

"Negative, Sheriff. Too much damage to upper body." The line went silent. "Read me, Sheriff?"

"What kind of damage, DeVrees?"

"Looks like a propeller impact."

"Christ…"

"Sheriff?"

"Any identifying marks?"

"Sir, I'm not sure I—"

"Tattoos, Deputy?"

"One moment, sir…" The line squawked and hummed for twenty seconds. "Uh, yes, sir, my team tells me a blue tattoo on left forearm." A beat of silence. "Sheriff?"

"I read you, Deputy. Six numbers?"

"Why, yes, sir. What made you think of that?" Static filled DeVrees's receiver. "Sir?"

"Let's stick to business, DeVrees. Radio coroner's office, over."

"Roger. We're done here."

"Not quite."

"Sir?"

"It's election season. Let's see what that bastard Brandt makes of this."

Friday August 26th

Jake leaned on his pickup and watched Tony trudge from the house to the open trunk of his car with a welter of gear, losing a thermos and a pillow along the way. Jake scooped them up and tossed them after the rest of Tony's stash. They stared into the Falcon's boot.

"Guess I overprepared," Tony muttered.

"You done prepared for the Lewis and Clark expedition."

Tony hesitated. "I guess it's obvious I'm not a camper," he said, and braced for the backwash.

"Oh, great." Jake slumped against the bumper and shook his head.

"I did help start a fire once at summer camp." He looked to Jake for redemption.

"Hope you didn't burn it down." Jake gave his head a sharp shake. "C'mon, let's make tracks. We've got two hours of daylight to pitch camp."

"Tony! Oh, Tony!" A figure emerged from the hedges. "You've got to hide me from them!" Mrs. VerHogen trilled.

Tony shot a pleading look at Jake that said, *It's not my fault.* "Hello, Mrs. VerHogen. What's the matter now?"

She grew cross, as if Tony were thickheaded. "The Gestapo! They wouldn't leave, and when I said I knew about their airplanes, they threatened to send me to the death camp on the mountain!"

Instantly, Tony's head throbbed. He glanced sidelong at Jake, but he had turned toward the road, heel tapping furiously. Tony set his hands on the old lady's shoulders and tried to reel in her vacant eyes.

"Mrs. VerHogen...there aren't any more death camps. Just ask Mr. VerHogen."

"They already took him!" she cried, slapping her house-dress with outstretched arms like a flightless bird.

Tony had to end this now. "Mrs. VerHogen, tell the soldiers you need a day to get ready, and then...sneak over to our house and call the sheriff."

"The *sheriff?* The sheriff is their *Kommandant!* You can't trust anyone!" She threw up her hands and walked off, reproaching the empty air.

Tony slunk over to Jake. "So sorry. It's hard to reason with her."

"Then don't," Jake said. He pointed to his watch. "Now it's

two minutes less daylight. Let's get out of here before she invites herself *and* the Gestapo along."

Tony followed Jake's pickup as it surfed the shore's dips and rises. The sun pulsed through a green scrim of lakeside estates. In a few miles, the road leaned away from the lake and burrowed under a vault of hemlock, oak, and ash.

Soon Jake veered off the main road without braking and plunged through the forest wall. Tony flinched at the rush of foliage that swallowed them. After a time, the woods opened into a flat patch of loose earth and stone barely enough for both of them to park on. Jake hopped out and nimbly secured his gear to a hiking pack with straps and rope. Tony watched from his car.

"Time to quit the buggy, city boy."

Tony squeezed into the narrow gap Jake had left him, shut his door, and stared wanly into space. "I don't see a trail."

"If you could *see* it, we wouldn't have it to ourselves. Let's get going." Jake clipped his words, each one a pinprick to Tony's chest. He busied himself pulling things from his trunk until he ran out of shoulders, hands, and armpits. He felt quite ridiculous and looked up to see his hunch confirmed in Jake's eyes.

"This ain't revival camp down the shore. Leave the pillows and blankets," Jake said with annoyance.

"Then what do I sleep on?" he whined.

Jake regarded Tony with disbelief. "Whadya think the bedrolls are for?"

"Those thin mats on your pack? Wouldn't we sleep better with comforters?"

"In *August*?" Jake sighed in vexation. "Look, maybe this wasn't such a great idea—"

"No! I'll be fine." Tony pasted a smile over his alarm that convinced neither of them.

"Then stop complaining," Jake snapped.

They started their climb in silence. The path cut through thick stands of oak and maple, and swiftly grew stony and steep. Jake quickened his pace, while a sullen Tony lagged behind.

This was a mistake. Not twenty minutes into the trip, Tony was failing miserably at setting things right with Jake.

Which shouldn't have surprised him, Tony thought, since he'd had little practice navigating the treacherous shoals of friendship. Since junior high, he'd managed to protect his dark secret by never getting too close to anyone. He'd been agreeable company, everyone's pal and no one's best friend. But now he was in deep, and the feelings Jake stirred in him had left Tony bewildered and terrified.

Tony and Jake had walked in silence for nearly forty-five minutes. Jake stopped at a raised rock saddle and sat.

"Time for a canteen break."

They drank in silence. Jake stretched his arms and legs with a satisfied moan. He looked over at Tony, sitting in a tight ball. "You're awful quiet," Jake said.

Tony forced his attention outward and mimicked Jake's relaxed posture. "It's so peaceful here." His voice quavered.

Jake furrowed his brow. "You okay?"

Tony slumped. "I'm sorry."

"What for now?"

"Being a bad camper. Bad company...bad...news."

"You said yourself this was new and scary for you. It's okay, Tony."

"Not really." Tony audibly sighed.

"Something else on your mind?"

Tony swallowed hard. "I guess Wednesday was a lot to take in."

Jake snorted a laugh. "You wouldn't be the first to say my family's intense."

"I guess so." Tony swept his fingers across the veined stone under him.

Jake studied Tony. "And?"

"It's just that...I've never been around people who were...I mean, your mom and dad..." Tony ran out of air.

Jake grunted. "So you saw the wedding photo."

Tony stared into the trees and nodded.

Jake's body hardened. "So what you mean is there ain't a box you can check for my kin. And if you don't know how to label people, then they make you uncomfortable."

Tony's hand flew to his chest. "I didn't say that."

"But you thought it. I could tell your skin was crawling that night."

"Why didn't you just tell me your mom was Negro?" Tony's voice shook.

Jake's tone darkened. "When you have friends over, do you warn them that your folks are Italian?"

"But Italian isn't a race," Tony protested.

"And my family ain't a *race*, neither."

"All I'm saying is it would have been easier for me if I'd known what I was walking into."

"So my kind don't get to just be themselves, first they got to make *you* comfortable." Jake fingered a loose stone, stood up, and fired a fastball into the trees, tearing a hole in the canopy. Tony flinched at the impact. Jake leaned over Tony, breathing hard.

"But that's not the real reason, is it, Tony? You wanted to know all that ahead of time so you could send your regrets, like every goddamn city boy I ever—" Jake choked on his words, and paced the ground.

"Jake, you're a really good guy—"

Jake spun in a fury. "Don't give me your fucking 'Dear John' speech! *Just go!*"

Tony shot to his feet. "Jake, I've never wanted to be with anyone as much as you my whole life!"

Jake froze and stared at Tony, his breathing ragged. In an instant, they were in each other's arms, Tony clinging to Jake so tightly that nothing he doubted or feared could slip between them.

The morning broke hazy and hot. After breakfast, Jake led Tony on a long hike to a favorite swimming hole. A half hour on, earth gave way to rock and the path steepened. Tony soon lost sight of Jake, his breathing labored, sweat stinging his eyes.

After an interminable passage of trips and stumbles, at last he reached Jake, perched on a smooth patch of stone in the shade, as cool and relaxed as if sitting on his front porch.

"I know a cut through this next stretch that's a lot easier." Jake pointed through the trees at a void in the rock. Tony saw only a shadow and looked at Jake in confusion.

"A manway from an old mine. It goes through the rock to a clearing near the crest."

Tony's throat tightened. "But we'll miss the views on the way."

"Plenty of view once we get there." Jake flicked his head toward the stone passage and stood.

Tony sat frozen. "But how will we see?"

Jake reached into his pack and pulled out a flashlight. "Be prepared, Cub Scout. Come on." Jake headed for the tunnel.

Tony got up, his feet stuck in place. "Jake, I—" But Jake was already disappearing into the mouth of the mountain. Tony pulled his leaden legs toward the dark. As he passed from brilliance into blindness, afterimages of the forest floated before him, obscuring Jake's fading silhouette. Tony tried to call out, but the heavy air swallowed his words.

The light swung toward him. "Tony?"

The specter of his night terrors returned, the crushing weight buckling Tony's legs. "I can't...breathe," he wheezed. Jake broke into a trot and reached Tony just as he slid to the ground.

"Hey now," he said, guiding Tony back to the light, onto a fallen log. Shivering, Tony opened his eyes to Jake's face, lined with worry.

"What just happened?" Jake said, tilting his head like a confused puppy.

Tony gulped air. "Um, I don't do well in dark places."

Jake's eyes widened. "If I thought for a minute—"

Tony cut him off with a headshake. "No, really, I'm fine now."

To convince them both, Tony sprang to his feet and almost fell on his face. Electric swirls filled his eyes. He let himself relax into Jake's grip and sat back down.

"It's okay. We'll take the trail," Jake insisted.

They climbed rock spurs, their crevices wedged with scrub and pine. The thick air clung to them, and a growing radiance pulsed through the forest's fissures. Jake told Tony to take his time on the last hard stretch before the crest, and Tony gratefully obliged.

He felt his mind unclench even as his muscles strained. As the trail snaked upward, Tony caught tantalizing glimpses of blue, and adrenaline pushed him higher. Ahead, he heard a whoop.

"What is it?" Tony called.

"It's the promised land!" Jake bellowed in his best country-preacher voice. Tony emerged at the top of the bluff and peered over Jake's shoulder.

"Wow," he managed.

They flopped onto the stone mantle and basked in the sweep of Lake Mennepequa. Shimmering cyan ribbons trailed toy boats. A crumpled green mantle unraveled to the horizon.

The two men shared the canteen, and Tony released a long sigh of satisfaction. When Jake pulled off his sweaty shirt and knotted it around his head, Tony's breath hitched.

"Don't move." Tony reached for his knapsack, unzipped the top, and pulled out his Retina. He knelt behind Jake.

"Say cheese." Jake twisted around, dewy skin catching the sun, and curled his lip.

Tony wrinkled his nose. "Think Rudolph Valentino."

Jake adjusted his head wrap so it flowed down his neck, let his jaw slacken, and gave Tony a wild-eyed, sidelong glance.

"Like this?"

"Flare your nostrils, and you've got it." Tony squinted through the viewfinder and clenched his shaking arms. "That's...perfect." The glass fogged as he fumbled with the settings, and he paused to wipe his face and the camera with his shirt.

"Rudy's losing altitude, man."

"Okay, ready!" He steadied his hands, held a deep breath, and clicked the shutter at the instant Jake shot him a smoldering look.

"Thanks!"

"Just be glad I didn't crack the lens," Jake retorted.

Tony slipped the camera into his pack and sat alongside Jake on the ledge. Shifting warm and cool currents of air brushed their skin and carried the scent of pine and lake.

"I've always loved this spot. Since I could walk, we come up this range to hunt. Got so I knew every rock and tree inside five miles of here." Jake's words came from far away.

Tony dispatched the thought of all those dead animals in Mrs. DenBleyker's stewpot. "It's a long way to hike."

Jake seemed not to hear. "We'd be gone a night or two and hole up in the old shelters. When the hunting was done, I loved picking potsherds and arrowheads from the forest floor. Like we was visiting the ancestors." A smile warmed Jake's face.

"Your people lived up here?"

"Weren't living, exactly. Mining." The glow left his cheeks. "Great-grampa and all the menfolk he knew lived in bare shacks in company towns, and got paid in scrip. Then the owners got back all the workers' pay in rent and provisions from the company store."

Tony pulled up his legs and rested his arms on them. "Sounds like the Middle Ages."

"Another kind of slavery. When you get down to it, only difference between a miner and a cotton picker was if he walked into the master's trap or was born in it. And my people got a double dose of both." Jake shook his head.

Jake's reply didn't satisfy Tony. "Most people in the countryside move to the city for a better life. Why did your relatives end up in the middle of nowhere?"

Tony's words landed with a thud, and Jake shot Tony a withering side-eye.

"I guess that was a bad choice of words," Tony said sheepishly.

Jake chuckled and then swept his arms across the view, as if the majesty of mountains and water spread before them was his reply.

Jake resumed. "Everybody's got his own version of how we wound up in the Highlands. The elders say the Ramapough

Indians retreated to their ancestral mountains when the Dutch and English settled the valleys.

"Mama says her clan escaped the Carolinas on the Underground Railroad. And there be stories about city folks running from trouble, holing up here and never leaving. Like the Castigliolas on the next ridge over from us."

"So where does 'DenBleyker' come from?"

"Pa says he come from rogues, rascals, and scalawags," Jake said with a smirk. "I think back in time, somewhere near here, a randy Dutch patroon plowed one of his slaves." Jake's smile fled. "I reckon I come from violence, not love."

"I'm so sorry."

Jake's face tightened. "Not your fault."

Tony frowned. "But you don't look like—"

"—Tonto? Buckwheat? Peter Stuyvesant?" Jake's grin didn't reach his eyes. "Mountaineers come red, white, black, and everything combined. My family in a nutshell."

His gaze turned inward. "So many mountaineers just had to run from their demons, I guess." He took another swig of the canteen and let Tony finish it off. "Not much different from your family running here from Sicily," he said.

Jake's words hit Tony like a slap in the face, as if equating Jake's history with Tony's somehow diminished him. In the Marsala origin story, his family's drive to succeed had lifted them above the wretched peasants they'd left behind in the old country. *People like the DenBleykers.*

Tony needed to correct the record. "My family wasn't running away from anything. They were tired of slaving in the fields and sulphur mines of Sicily, and they made the brave decision to start a better life for themselves in America."

Jake interrupted. "But they weren't *slaves*, were they?"

Tony's cheeks blazed. He felt at once embarrassed and

offended. Why was Jake intent on cutting Tony down to size? Why did he have to turn everything Tony said into a contest?

"My family suffered a lot," Tony said with hurt in his voice.

Jake's voice softened. "I don't doubt you, Tony. But that don't make them any different or better than anyone else. There's plenty of suffering in this world, and some of us got more than our fair share."

"But it's not a competition!" Tony declared, still unable to let go of the argument.

"*Exactly*. And that means that you should know who you're talking to if you want sympathy for your troubles." The hurt in Jake's eyes touched Tony's own.

"Don't matter who you are or where you're from, we all fight to survive, from first breath to last." Jake searched Tony's eyes.

And look at where you are. Tony's wounded pride still wouldn't let it be. He nodded vigorously to banish his own conflicted feelings.

"Enough of this doom and gloom." Jake bolted to his feet. "Time for our just rewards!" He pulled off the rest of his clothes, and Tony drank in every swell and hollow. Jake stared back in mock indignation.

"Put your eyes back in your head, pretty boy, and lose them clothes. Time for a dunking."

Jake gave instructions as Tony stripped down. "See them two pines back a piece leaning together? Head between them. I'll be right there."

Jake loped over to the nearest bush, planted his feet wide, hands on hips, and relieved himself, while Tony struggled to put his attention on the path. He hobbled off, pebbles and needles stabbing his feet, then heard Jake jog toward him.

"Enough of that hot-coal dance, tenderfoot." Jake bear-hugged Tony from behind and hoisted him, arms and legs wheeling, fifty yards to a ledge jutting over a void. He gave a Tarzan call and cannonballed them both into a rust-red pond.

They blew mists and smacked sheets of water at each other. Jake jerked away from a head dunk, and then Tony felt hands clamp onto his hips, and he shot up on Jake's shoulders, catapulting backward. They fell onto their backs and laughed at the sky.

Tony idly explored the pond, chin grazing its surface. He gazed at the sheltering pines and rock-slab shoreline, absently drawing and spitting out the cool water. He peered past the surface through lilting seaweed, clear down to the pond's stony bed, the sun bathing everything in a coppery glow.

"I've never seen water this color. It looks like what comes out of the tap when we open our house in the spring," Tony said.

"It's the iron in these hills," Jake said, flexing his arms to stay afloat.

Tony made a sour face and spat into the pond. "Is it safe?"

Jake took in a mouthful of water, then shot it out in a long arc at Tony. "Tastes funny, but for all the times I been here, it never did me no harm."

Jake glided to the ledge and sprang up, legs following arms with a gymnast's ease. When Tony couldn't get the timing right, Jake grabbed him under both arms and lifted him straight up from the pond. Tony teetered and grabbed Jake's shoulders to steady himself. Their eyes locked, and they leaned wordlessly into a tight embrace. They stood that way a long moment.

The trees sighed; boats hummed somewhere far below. They were both hard. Tony loosened his arms just enough to hold Jake's gray-blue gaze.

With hungry eyes, Jake gripped Tony's back and slid down to his belly, stubbled lips brushing Tony's slick skin. Tony gasped, and his whole body seized up. Jake squatted on his haunches and looked up at him, but Tony was already numb to his own pounding heart, gone to the airless place where he shut away desire. Jake's arms dropped to his thighs.

Tony padded away from Jake without a word, as if silence might erase what had just happened. Pausing, he looked back to where Jake still knelt, eyes downcast.

Tony sat on the sun-bleached outcropping above Lake Mennepequa and let his legs dangle over the void. He scanned the ethereal brightness, shame and fear rippling through him. Jake approached silently and grabbed his clothes. Tony stood, brushed himself off, and turned away to dress.

On the hike back, Tony's thoughts replayed their embrace, Jake's hunger, his own body's rebellion. He felt revealed, exposed, as if he'd shouted his ruinous secret from the mountaintop. He felt sick.

Jake paused at a clearing, and Tony caught up. He shot Jake a glance; he was unreadable. Was he hurt? Infuriated? Was he done with Tony? Worse, would Jake expose him?

Back at camp, they scraped up a late lunch of franks and beans. Tony had barely finished before Jake was on his feet, rinsing off their utensils in a pot of creek water, and then pouring it over the embers. Tony could no longer stand the howling silence between them.

"Um, Jake. I'm sorry for what happened today." Tony's skin prickled.

Jake paused and stared long and hard at Tony. "Forget it," he said gruffly, snatched a canvas bag from their tent, and began stuffing stray gear into it with sharp stabs of his arm.

"You're breaking camp already?" Tony asked, a touch of panic in his voice.

"Remembered how much I got to do back home," Jake muttered.

Had Tony ruined everything, or misread Jake all along? He swallowed hard. "I'm still attracted to you."

Jake continued moving at a martial pace. "You got a strange way of showing it."

Tony approached Jake. "I didn't mean to push you away. I guess I...I was a tease."

Jake huffed. "Nothing new for me, man."

"I'm sorry if I hurt your feelings."

Jake looked up at Tony, and shook his head. "Hardly matters now, does it?"

"You have every right to be mad," Tony said wanly.

Jake grimaced. "I'm not *mad*."

Tony was desperate to make things right. "Jake, I know we have our differences, but I want you to know that I like you just the way you are." The words sounded tinny; who were they for?

"I don't need your *approval*." Jake pulled a pot and some tools out of the tent, and tossed them into the half-full bag.

Tony's throat tightened. "I'm sorry, I didn't mean it that way, I just don't know how to say how I feel about you," he whimpered.

Jake threw down the bag with a clang that made Tony jump. *"Goddamn it, will you stop apologizing for your life and just live it?"* Jake cried.

And then Tony's mouth was on Jake's, lips scorching lips, sending all thought up in flames. Jake's hand plunged into Tony's jeans, and instantly the familiar, unbearable weight pressed in, smothering his will. He jerked away from Jake's grasp, and from somewhere beyond his numbed senses came the memory of nightsticks cracking skulls.

Saturday May 31, 1959

My hall mates Taft, Courtney, and James have invited me for an evening of macho debauchery, and I'm anxious to prove myself to them.

We climb up from the subway and walk from Sheridan Square to a place called Julius'. We show our Columbia IDs, and plant ourselves on adjacent barstools. A fit bartender winks and fills our glasses.

The room is full of men. Only men. My chest jolts. Is this some kind of manhood test, or are my classmates playing a cruel joke on me?

An older man nursing a martini presses fingertips against his friend's sternum. "Did you hear they busted up Mary's on Eighth Street?" The other strokes his cheek coquettishly. "Oh, officer, I looove when you play rough!"

I glance at my friends; James has his arm around Courtney. Taft is squeezing a stool mate's muscular thigh. Heat blooms in my collar, my belly, my chinos. I try dousing it with a second beer.

Well oiled, my companions lead me to the Grape Vine. We plunge into a room pulsing with Elvis and dozens of writhing men. A blond in a sailor suit grabs my butt, presses his codpiece against me, and his mouth is on my lips, his tongue in mine, and he's swilling me, pushing harder—

The music stops, and ceiling lights flash. Someone hollers "RAID!" and a dozen policemen barrel in, clubs and fists swinging. I take a glancing blow to the head and crash into my sailor.

"Fags—up against the wall! Move it! IDs!" the lead officer barks.

"Skirts, come with me." A female cop leads the transvestites to the bathroom. The police shove the rest of us outside, some pleading, others defiant. Onlookers stop and gape.

Taft implores a cop who clubs him in the face and drags him to a paddy wagon with James and a dozen others packed inside. Courtney and I are left on the street to watch the police fill a second van and drive off, sirens shrieking.

I awaken Sunday in the dorm, head throbbing and cheek swollen. I throw on sweats, tug a sports cap down over my face, and go out for a paper. I take it to a secluded bench in the quad, riffle to the police blotter, and read.

"Hive of Homosexuals at Greenwich Village Bar." A list of the arrested follows, with full names and addresses. James and Taft leap off the page.

Hands shaking, I snap the paper shut, as if my own guilt were about to leap from the page, as if anything could contain my panic. Did James and Taft rat me to the cops?

Two hours later, I'm on a bus for Lake Mennepequa.

His parents' lane came upon Tony too soon. He pulled into the driveway, rolled up the windows, and sat, eyes closed, chest heaving. Collecting himself, he jerked open the door and banged his head on the frame. Electric swirls filled the sky.

He grabbed rucksack and canteen and trudged down the trimmed path to the bungalow. He let himself in through the unlocked door and padded across the living room, where his dad sat hypnotized by the gray screen.

"Did you eat?" his mother called from the bamboo chair under a cone of light, crossword puzzle in her lap.

"An hour ago," Tony called to her.

"What, berries and acorns? *Mangia!*" she exhorted. "Veal cutlets are in the oven."

Tony scarfed down an early dinner and retreated to his room. The door was swollen with the sultry air, and he wedged it shut. He slipped out a slim pocket book from under the magazines on his dresser.

He ogled the cover: two Greek youths wrestling naked in a classical palestra. He'd found it the last week of school on the adult rack of a newsstand in the seedy bus depot next to Pennsylvania Station.

He tossed the paperback onto his bed and flopped down. Across the coverlet lay the *Columbia College Bulletin 1960–61* where he'd left it two days ago. Another year of courses to choose for his classics major. That seemed too much for his crowded thoughts just now.

He pushed the catalogue aside, settled onto a pillow with the novel, and read hungrily. The cheap paper tore as he thumbed through workmanlike prose until he found what the lurid cover promised.

"This damn go-cart is gonna crack my nuts!" Eddie sat wedged sideways between the trunk and the bucket seats of the T-bird, legs practically in his chest.

"He whose wheels are on cinder blocks can walk," Stefan said tartly.

"You gonna pay for my new water pump?" Eddie asked.

"You'd *have* the cash if you didn't blow it all on beer and cigarettes," Stefan snapped.

Eddie punched the back of Stefan's seat. "At least I ain't mooching off my ol' man."

"Fuck you for beating my sister!" Stefan rammed his seat backward into Eddie's shoulder.

Hans smacked the ceiling and bellowed, "Shut the fuck up already!"

They all seethed in quiet for a moment.

"How far we going?" Hans asked, his voice high and edgy.

"Like we agreed, the clearing before the stone furnace," said Stefan through clamped teeth. "From there, we walk to the Reefer Barn. The foreman's mansion isn't far past."

Stefan switched off his headlights and rolled the T-bird behind the roofless stone kiln in the fading light. Stefan and Hans hopped out; Eddie twisted himself through the passenger door, limped a few steps, and pressed a hand into his back to straighten up.

"Ready for action, pops?" Hans snickered.

"Ready to knock Silas *and* you into the next county," Eddie retorted. His leg felt twitchy.

"One more reason you ain't leading this posse," Stefan hissed. "Everybody got a flashlight?"

"Yes, scoutmaster," answered Eddie.

They walked awhile in silence. An image of Silas with his paws all over Karla kept filling the gloom before Eddie.

"Damn, this is a long way to go for some beaver," Hans said, huffing.

"One more fucked-up remark about my sister and I'm gonna perforate your skull!" Stefan barked under his breath. In the warm dusk, a weather-beaten barn abruptly loomed.

"Time for a smoke break," Eddie announced. He let the crowbar slip from his hand, throbbing from his iron grip.

"The Reefer Barn," Stefan whispered reverently.

"Been some crazy shit in this place," Hans said.

Eddie peered through the wide gap where a sliding door once hung. He pulled a hand-roll from his sleeve, lit it, and took a long, slow toke. He offered it to the others; each took a deep drag.

They resumed their climb, and slowly the mountain broadened into a flat expanse, saplings alternating with the broad burled trunks of ancient trees. The outlines of stone foundations and broken walls poked through the undergrowth.

The foreman's mansion emerged from the twilight. It sat on a fractured stone base, its roof missing planks, the walls rough and weathered. The whole structure slumped between two derelict chimneys.

Light seeped from the doorway, and Eddie's chest tightened.

The men switched off their flashlights. Stefan had Hans and Eddie keep to the trees that flanked the building, about twenty-five feet out, while he took an oblique position facing the entrance.

They were close enough to hear murmuring. Stefan cinched the strap of his rifle across his shoulder, barrel down, and flashed his light once under his chin. Eddie and Hans dropped to a crouch and gripped their weapons. Stefan flashed twice and windmilled his free arm, and the three men crept forward.

Eddie heard the voices now, one purring, the other a carnal growl. Rage propelled him forward, crowbar above his head. Something snapped underfoot, and the manse went dark.

"Drop it!" Stefan cried, lunging for Eddie just as Silas emerged on the porch in a crouch, long blade in his outstretched hand.

Stefan shoved Eddie aside and kept moving, with Hans right behind. Stefan skidded on damp mulch, regained his footing, and then momentum propelled him directly at Silas. Stefan struggled to right his gun, and all at once, in a reflex of muscle and fear, Stefan fired and Silas thrust the knife.

Tony must have dozed; the alarm clock said midnight. He was hungry again, and remembered a bag of chips in the car. Outside, the dim streetlight caught movement on the upper road. Cat's-eye taillights slowed before the Van Hoek house. A figure emerged with long hair and unsteady gait. The driver swiftly seized her arm, and they both disappeared into blackness.

Tony retrieved the chips and turned toward the house, when a high wail broke the silence. A stray cat? He put it out of mind, went in, and dropped onto his bed. He tuned his transistor radio to the Dodgers game on the West Coast, and stuffed a fistful of chips into his mouth.

Lifting the book, he scanned bland paragraphs before halting at the passage in the palestra, where the two contestants oiled each other's bodies in the portico before their contest. Cheers rose and faded through the radio static.

Tony's eyes closed and the book dropped from his hand. In the colonnaded courtyard, strong arms enfolded him from behind. The champion pinned Tony to the ground to the swelling roar of the crowd, and somewhere beyond the palestra, tires squealed.

7

Sunday August 28th

The morning air seemed lit from within as Tony settled into a lounger above the shore. White wisps rose from the lake as the sun peeked over the sheltering oak trees. Despite ten hours in bed, he didn't feel rested; his head was stuffed with cotton. He had no designs on the day more taxing than lunch and a swim.

Tony cupped his pocket book inside a magazine. After the wrestling match, the youth and his mentor left the palestra arm in arm and climbed to a nearby promontory above the harbor. The older man gathered his *eromenos* in his arms, and they pledged their mutual undying love and sacred honor.

His Greek lovers brought back memories of ninth grade, when a teacher had introduced Tony to the classical world. He'd decided to write his report for class on the great Roman emperors, and went to research it in the marble halls of the public library on Fifth Avenue.

There, he'd stumbled on a passage in an old tome about

Emperor Hadrian, how he had "bewailed Antinous with unmeasured grief...Now he was Achilles by the corpse of Patroclus, now Alexander by the funeral pile of Hephaestion." In an instant, a whole lineage of men loving men had revealed itself.

That discovery had left him hungry for more. All through his early teens, he'd scoured card catalogues, bookshops, and movie palaces, to no avail. The men Achilles and Alexander loved had been sidelined from Hollywood's *Helen of Troy* and *Alexander the Great*, and seemingly from history itself.

Tony wouldn't be gaslighted. In college, he'd studied Greek and Latin and combed Columbia's archives, and found what his course syllabus wouldn't tell: clear-eyed accounts of male desire.

And this week he'd felt its fevered touch. Tony gazed into the canopy above and then closed his eyes. The press of Jake's skin on his at the red pond and their hungry kisses at camp returned to him.

His neck prickled; someone was watching him. He snapped the magazine shut and sprang up from his lounger, which released him in a clatter of metal. Mrs. VerHogen stood on the knoll above Tony, arms swirling.

"Psst! Tommy!"

A quick glance around him confirmed that they were alone. "It's Tony, Mrs. VerHogen."

Eyes wide with fear, she put finger to lips and approached. "From now on, if anyone asks, my name is *Schmied*. You should change your name, too, or they'll find you."

She tugged Tony farther from the kids playing next door. "They're checking to see who's pure, and who they'll eliminate. Even the children are spying on us." She pressed lips to his ear. "They're listening right now."

Tony heard his mother call from the porch steps and

turned to see her with their neighbor, Mrs. Felter, both waving vehemently. "Okay, then, Mrs.—Schmied. Mum's the word."

He sprinted up the sloping lawn to the two women. Mrs. Felter held a hand to her chest.

"What is it? What's happened?" Tony said, wishing the day would just leave him alone.

"Stefan and Karla Van Hoek were attacked last night!" Mrs. Felter gasped for air.

He scanned the women's faces. "Attacked? What do you mean?"

"Karla went hiking in the woods and was set on by a mountain brute! Stefan, Eddie, and Hans pulled him off of her, but he had a knife, and—and now Stefan's dead!" She began to cry, and his mom handed her a hankie. Tony grabbed the railing behind him. *Stefan's gone?*

Mrs. Felter's voice pitched higher. "To think that Stefan paid with his life! Sweet Jesus, he will surely go to his reward."

Tony remembered the car with the cat's-eye taillights on the upper road last night.

"I'm so sorry to bring this terrible news," Mrs. Felter whimpered, but then her face darkened. "Those disgusting Jackson Whites. We should round them all up and put them in cages like the animals they are!" Her mouth quivered before she could resume. "Eddie Schmidt recognized the attacker. He said his name was Silas."

"Silas? Silas Mueller?" Tony asked, temples throbbing.

"Yes! That's it. The police are still looking for him."

But Jake had said Silas was *dating* Karla. He'd driven her home in his car last night; Tony had seen them get out together. His mind reeled.

"Lock your doors tonight, Antoinette."

The two women prattled on, and Tony excused himself. He pounded to the dock's edge and sat, legs churning small whirlpools in the water. He looked at the mountain, and it filled him with fear.

Nothing's making sense. I've got to talk to Jake.

Monday August 29th

Tony stood in the lot at the park, ten minutes late for his eight a.m. punch-in. He'd felt uneasy from the moment he woke up. He scanned the other vehicles, noticed that Jake's pickup wasn't there, and his gut churned.

He wasn't sure he could concentrate on work today while his old friend Stefan was being laid to rest, and walked into George's office to tell him so. George held the phone to one ear, and a walkie-talkie pressed against the other.

"No, Baby does *not* go to the petting zoo—she's riding with me until I decide otherwise, or you fire me!" He slammed down both receivers and looked up at Tony with a curled lip. "I love my job! How we doing, mate?"

"Not great. I think I've got to go to a funeral today."

George gave Tony a knowing look. "A shame about DenBleyker's brother, ain'it?"

"Um, *what?*" Tony asked.

George's cheeks paled. "They found his brother's body in the woods Sunday. Jake's taking time."

"His brother?" Tony echoed stupidly.

"Lad's name was Silas. Believe the funeral's today."

Silas, the man the police were still looking for. Tony's mind was on fire. "I-I've gotta go, George. You can mark me down as a no-show. I'll make it up on the weekend, I promise."

George grunted his disapproval. "It's Monday. We'll get by.

You do what you think is right. And send sympathies from the crew."

"Thanks, George," Tony shouted over his shoulder, and sprinted out of the office.

Tony gunned his car up the mountain and tried to make sense of everything. It seemed impossible that Silas Mueller and Stefan Van Hoek could be gone in the space of twenty-four hours.

At dinner on Wednesday, Silas had seemed like a good-hearted guy; why would he attack the girl he was dating *and* her brother? Tony had never known Stefan to pick a fight; how had he wound up on the wrong end of Silas's knife?

Tony pushed the Falcon so hard on the washboard road, his skull rattled. Something else bothered him about Mrs. Felter's story. How had all the players found themselves together in the vastness of these mountains? And if Silas was dead, why were people saying he got away?

Tony pulled up the drive to utter stillness at the DenBleyker house. He knocked on the front door to no avail, and then walked over to Jake's woodworking barn. He pushed the door open; dust danced in bright shafts that streamed through the windows. Shards of wood lay across the work-table, and the vise still gripped Jake's walking stick.

Jake's prodigious spirit suffused the room, filled the shelves of his magical creatures, damping Tony's dark thoughts. He took a moment to breathe it all in and calm his racing mind.

Jake's whole family must be at the funeral. Where to look for them? He remembered the smokehouse of Old Lady Ten Eyck; he would go ask there. *Down by Ten Eyck's*, Euel had said.

Tony bounced the Falcon backward down the drive and spun rubber downhill, peering up every side trail. Then the road took a sharp bend left, and up ahead on Tony's right a sign nailed to a fence declared TEN EYCK — FINE SMOKE MEAT.

A chain looped across the drive. The border fence was more marker than barrier; brush obscured the property. Tony honked three times like Jake had, inciting furious barking that grew louder as two dark forms rose and fell in the foliage.

Three large dogs crashed against the Falcon's window, paws up, teeth bared. Tony quickly rolled the glass shut and pounded the door lock. A boy no more than twelve appeared at the gate, shotgun pointed in his direction. Tony raised his hands to his head, palms out.

"Go on, git over here! Heel!" the boy hollered.

The dogs retreated to the boy's side and sat. Only now did Tony get a good look at them: tall and bony with tented ears, patches of fur missing from their brown-black coats.

The boy lowered the barrel and commanded, "What you want here?"

Tony cracked the passenger window. "I wanted to ask Mrs. Ten Eyck—"

"She's a 'miss.' And she ain't here."

Tony smiled. "You're a good house guard." A faint grin flashed across the boy's face.

"She my gramma, and I be protectin' my kin," he said.

"That's only right," Tony said, nodding energetically. The boy nodded back. "I came by to ask if Miss Ten Eyck knows where I can find the DenBleykers. I understand there's been a death in the family."

"That's right. Gramma gone to the funeral for Silas. She be there now."

"And how would I get there?"

The boy squinted a long moment at Tony. "Go downhill a

ways to the next fork and take the road to the right. Pass three *housen* afore the old stone furnace. Go right after that, uphill past the waterwheel, to a clearing. That's the path to the cemetery."

Tony tipped an imaginary hat. "I am grateful—what's your name?"

"Jeb. Like my grampa." The boy straightened as he invoked his elder.

Tony soon found some thirty people gathered around a mound of earth amid irregular rows of grave markers: flaking tombstones, limestone panels flush with the ground, painted wooden crosses.

He moved slowly toward the crowd and snapped a twig. Heads turned. Jake strode over, face drawn, eyes flinty.

"Jake, I'm so sorry for your loss." Tony extended his hand, but Jake ignored the gesture.

"What are you doing here?" Jake rasped.

"I was upset about Silas, and worried about you."

Jake's cheeks reddened. "Were you?" Jake's eyes hardened. "Too late for Silas, ain't it?"

Why was Jake throwing his sympathies back in his face? "I don't understand—"

"Look, Tony, you don't belong here. If we wanted outsiders, we'd've invited them." Jake turned heel and walked back to his family.

Outsiders. Them. Tony felt gut punched.

He stumbled away, the midday sun layering the woods in scorching white and blackness. He sped down the mountain, heedless of the banging and scraping of the forest.

Why did Jake push me away?

What is he hiding?

Eddie Schmidt pulled to a stop behind the funeral cortege. He got out of the El Camino and studied it, spattered and dusty except for the sparkling passenger door.

When he'd parked it at home Saturday night, he'd switched on the dome light and found Karla's bloody handprints everywhere. He'd scrubbed the seat and dash, sprayed and wiped the smeared window and door inside and out before burning the soiled rags in the firepit back of the house.

Now Silas's borrowed car seemed to mock him. Why hadn't he gone to the car wash by Mount Zindel? How could he be stupid enough to drive it to the funeral? He turned away and hurried through the cemetery gates.

Reaching the hearse, Eddie watched as six men in shades and black suits emerged, lowered the tailgate, and hoisted onto their shoulders the brass-trimmed box carrying his friend.

Eddie had knelt on the forest floor, held Stefan's head, spoken useless words like *everything's okay* while his friend gargled his own blood. And now he was gone, and nothing was okay.

The men in black stepped slowly to a freshly dug grave by a bed of shriveled hydrangeas. They positioned the load over two heavy straps and gently set it down alongside the cavity.

Eddie stepped next to Karla and laid his hand on her back. She flinched, and he pressed harder, leg jiggling. She shrugged him off and stepped between her parents, who eyed him fiercely. Eddie fell back to the crowd's perimeter. His gaze drifted to Hans, who caught it and flicked it away.

There were more folks here than Eddie had ever seen in one place in Iron Run. Some were familiar: shopkeepers and teachers; high school classmates. The county sheriff, in full uniform, shifted among clumps of mourners, positioning himself to be seen. Wasn't that just like Uncle in an election year, Eddie thought. Most faces were dry-eyed and darker than grief.

The minister addressed them. "To all gathered here today: take heart that we knew a man like Stefan Van Hoek. He embodied all the good in us: Family. Faith. Freedom. Pride in our heritage. And a willingness to honor, defend, and preserve our values against those who would defile them.

"Let us vow to bring Stefan's killer to justice, through faith in our Lord God and savior, Jesus Christ. Amen." The crowd's echo pierced the air like a battle cry.

Karla and her parents each took a rose from the coffin's lid and stood stiffly, eyes hooded. The six silent helpers grasped the straps and slid the box over the aperture, then let out slack, and the metal case, its floral sprays shuddering, slipped into the earth.

As the Van Hoeks tossed their flowers into the pit, the sheriff muscled his way through the tight graveside cordon and held the mourning mother's hand. Then he grasped Mr. Van Hoek's shoulder and spoke into his ear, Mr. Van Hoek nodding as the sheriff pounded the air with his fist.

The Van Hoeks walked off, Karla lingering to receive condolences. Eddie intercepted her as she turned toward the cemetery gates. She covered her throat with her hand and, with effort, lifted her face to him.

Gone was the blush in her cheek, and the white-gold hair that usually flowed to her shoulders was pulled back in a tight ponytail. Through her sunglasses, he saw what makeup couldn't hide and felt sick.

"Karla, I—I'm here for you," Eddie stammered.

Karla's red-rimmed eyes turned fierce, and she made to leave. He squeezed her shoulder hard, but she squirmed free and pounded toward the gates. He sprinted ahead to block her path and pulled her to him. She turned her cheek away and squeezed her eyes tight.

"You're not getting away from me again."

"Leave me alone!"

"We're a team to the end, Karla. How could you ever forget what I done for you?" Eddie's grasp tightened, and she gasped.

"For me, or to me?" she asked shrilly.

Eddie felt other eyes on him and stepped back from her. "Don't think you can just walk away now, scot-free."

Karla threw back her shoulders. "Watch me," she said, and joined the crowd.

Eddie tailed her. "You owe me," he growled in her ear.

Karla stepped up her pace. "You ruined my life, and now I owe you?"

"Just shut up and listen," Eddie hissed. He ran a hand over his bristling hair and snorted sharply to throttle his racing mind. "If you do what I say, your big secret is safe with me," he said, nostrils flared.

"You *bastard*!" she sneered, and wobbled on her feet.

Mrs. Van Hoek approached. "Darling, is everything all right?" she said stonily, staring at Eddie.

"Everything's fine, Mrs. Van Hoek. Karla and I just need a minute." He made to stroke Karla's neck, and thought better of it.

Mrs. Van Hoek's eyes bored holes into Eddie. "Karla, we're leaving," she barked, extending her hand like a command. Karla took it and strode off with her.

"I'll be watching," Eddie spat after Karla.

From out of nowhere, his neighbor Mrs. Felter collared him. "Eddie, you are a such a hero—defending Stefan, rest his soul, and rescuing his sister from that brute."

He gave Mrs. Felter a tight smile and started walking away,

but she clasped his hand between hers and continued. "I shudder to think of that killer on the loose. You got a good look at him, didn't you?" His leg twitched.

From over his shoulder, Eddie heard a whoop. "Hey! That's Eddie Schmidt, the big hero!" A knot of people gathered around him and patted his shoulder, thumped his back, pumped his arm.

"Eddie, how'd you take him down?" a young kid in Sunday suit and bow tie chirped, pulling on his father's arm.

"I'm sure the savage fought tooth and claw," declared the butcher Mr. Franck, apple cheeks flushing. I say it's open season on all of them!"

A guy from Eddie's high school gang clasped him on the neck. "I heard that dick got his paws on your girl. Just let me at him, I'll cut off his balls!"

Eddie felt dizzy, every outburst tightening the knot around his throat. He turned to leave and almost collided with the minister's wife.

She patted his chest, and smiled sweetly. "Eddie, don't you worry. I just know with your uncle in charge that this Jackson White will be locked up in no time. Sheriff Schmidt's been our rock, ever since Camp Hochland." She grew wistful. "Don't you miss those times?"

Eddie stared into the haze. "'Scuse me, ma'am," he said, and bolted.

On the street, he stopped short of the El Camino. Hans and Karla stood paces apart, staring at it. Eddie saw the fear in Hans's eyes, and his own gaze shot to the spotless passenger window, and Karla's reflection in it. For an instant, their eyes met in the glass.

"You *monster*," the image hissed, and vanished from the frame.

Hans watched Karla go, then muttered to Eddie, "What do we do now?"

Eddie sprinted to the cab and was gone in a burst of acrid smoke.

The DenBleyker table was a groaning board of casseroles, roasts, and pies. Jake and his mother and brothers exchanged nods and hushed words with their relatives and neighbors on Blackman's Ridge, and others who'd come from as far as Breakneck Mountain and Anthony's Nose.

Gideon DenBleyker was there to mourn his son, his first appearance since the rupture with Delfinia. In a subtle dance, they welcomed each well-wisher while avoiding each other. Everyone talked about the big storm expected late the next day.

Old Lady Ten Eyck sat in a wing chair, holding herself upright with a cane, and nodded to everyone. Euel and Malcolm made the rounds, thanking all who filled the house. On the couch, two women flanked a sniffling Delfinia and held her hands.

They bore considerable resemblance to the grieving mother. One was sandy haired with skin like creamed coffee; the other had a deep brown complexion and teased black curls. Jake crouched next to the fair-haired woman, who patted his arm. Malcolm leaned in from the other side of the couch, and Euel came over and stood behind it.

Betty was telling an old chestnut about Big Mama. "When she and Papa was courting, she cleaned rooms in the fancy inns on Lake Mennepequa where white city folks came up weekends. So one day, she bats her eyes at Papa and says, 'Oh, that must make for a lovely honeymoon.'" Jake nodded and smiled.

"So Papa goes down to the fanciest hotel and books the Queen Victoria suite. They made no fuss about it, being Papa was fair enough to pass.

"Come their wedding night, they get to the hotel in all their finery, and this little pink man with a twitchy eye takes one look at Big Mama, claps his book shut, and points to a sign that says NO NEGROES OR ITALIANS." The smile left Jake's eyes.

Malcolm asked his customary question. "What did they do then?"

"Big Mama looks at the man, draws herself up on her high satin shoes, and says, 'Well, we certainly won't be staying where the help is so *rude!*'" Euel and Malcolm managed a chuckle. Jake rose silently from a squat, hands in pockets, and stared into the afternoon light.

Malcolm walked over to Betty. "Gramma was a formidable woman," he said.

Betty squeezed his arm. "As God is my witness, child."

Euel came to his aunt and kissed her cheek. "Aunt Betty, thanks for coming."

She dropped her head in a prayerful gesture. "Child, I'd give my right arm if it would bring back your brother."

Euel started to speak, then clamped his mouth shut. His eyes watered. "Auntie, Silas's passing will not be in vain. Whoever done this, we're gonna bring them to justice."

Malcolm's hands clenched and released as his brother spoke. "They will pay," he said. The two brothers looked to Jake for consensus, but his mind was elsewhere.

Aunt Betty laid her hand softly on Malcolm's fist. "Child, you mind your old auntie: there is a proper season for every-thing, and today is for honoring Silas with your kinfolk.

There'll be plenty of time to talk justice. God's will be done." Malcolm dipped his head with reverence, but his eyes were fire.

Jake slipped out to the porch and scanned the brightness. Soon, Malcolm stood alongside him.

"Something I got to tell you, Jake. That girl they said Silas attacked? Well, he told me somebody threatened him over her."

Jake studied Malcolm.

"Wednesday night he goes to see her, and this tough is waiting in the street. He tells Silas to get out of his neighborhood. So Silas says, 'Who's gonna make me?' and the guy threatens to smash his head in."

Something snapped into place in Jake's mind. "Silas told you this, and you didn't say nothing till now?" Jake said sharply.

Malcolm shrugged. "I didn't think nothing of it at the time. You know these local boys—they talk big to feel better about their sorry lives and small dicks. Then when Silas died, it all just went out of my head. Until now."

Jake clutched his brother's shoulder. "Malcolm, we gotta tell the sheriff."

Malcolm shrugged him off. "For what? Law's only good for keepin' us in our place."

The rage under his brother's words was Jake's, too. "So what you meaning to say?" he asked, in dread of the answer that burned in his chest.

"We want justice, we take it in our own hands," Malcolm intoned, like a mortal decree.

Jake pushed down the fire in him, desperate to convince them both that the truth his brother spoke was folly.

"And after you kill a white boy, they gonna send a lynch mob up here for you. Mama just lost one son—it'd kill her to lose another. For her sake, we got to talk to the police," Jake said, dreading that this would only defer an inevitable reckoning.

Malcolm looked away and shook his head. "One chance. That's all they get. Then we go out and make some serious trouble for these white boys." Jake could see tragedy coming for them like a slow-motion train wreck and felt utterly powerless to stop it.

Despite the sunshine, a gloom hung over Sharkey's Pier. Eddie ran his eye along a row of tables. He saw a few faces from the morning funeral. Hans studied his beer.

"Whatcha do after the cemetery?" Eddie asked.

"Worked on the truck. You?" Hans appraised Eddie.

Eddie stared at the empty chair across from him. "Ah, fuck does it matter." His leg jiggled.

Rubber crunched gravel in the parking lot. Eddie turned toward the sound from habit, then winced. He wished Stefan were here now. He squeezed an empty can and flung it to the deck.

Hans's face collapsed. "What are we gonna do?" he whimpered.

"Just shut up, okay?" Eddie shook off threatening tears.

The silence stretched out between them. They ordered more beers. A sudden squeal of laughter affronted him, and he wheeled around to find its source.

A stranger at the next table had his arm around Olga, the girl who'd once cockteased him all afternoon at one of Stefan's barbecues. It pissed him off thinking about it. This guy was powerfully built, Eddie's age; a black Elvis cut and blue eyes set off his brown complexion. The smiling man studied Eddie, unblinking.

"What you lookin' at, boy?" Eddie barked. Hans's eyes snapped onto Eddie.

The stranger's genial expression flipped like a switch. "What did you call me?" He leaned forward, elbows on the table, showcasing meaty fists.

Eddie sensed things were going south but couldn't help himself. "Something nicer than you deserve." A guffaw punctuated his words.

The man stiffened, smashed his fist on the metal tabletop, and a cup went flying. All chatter on the pier abruptly halted.

Eddie ignored Hans's mute protests and pushed back his chair. "You got a problem with that?"

"I got a problem with what you and your posse did on Blackman's Ridge Saturday night." The man shot up from his seat to a fearsome height and flexed his neck and shoulders.

"I got no idea what you talkin' about."

"*All* they talkin' about on the mountain, white man."

Eddie jerked to his feet, knocking over his chair.

"Cliff don't," Olga pleaded.

Without taking his eyes off Eddie, Cliff shushed his date, and then took two steps toward his adversary. "Your kind been starting trouble with us for too long. Time we finished it."

Eddie rolled his shoulders. "What's finished is your little party right here." He hid his jumpy leg in a boxer's shuffle.

Cliff's face was stone. "You need to say right now, 'I'm sorry, sir, I shouldn't'a called you that,'" he said, as to a child.

Hans looked open-jawed at Eddie. Eddie papered over fear with a smirk, swept his gaze across the silent, staring patrons, and mouthed a laugh. Then he looked at Olga with pity and said, "Go on, sweetheart, take your ape back to his cave."

In one fluid move, Cliff sprang forward and landed a fist on Eddie's jaw. Eddie staggered back a few steps and rubbed his face. "Fuckin' inbred," he muttered.

He came back at Cliff with a roundhouse punch at the temple that threw the man off balance, but Cliff quickly righted himself and pummeled Eddie in the gut, chest, and face. Blood spurted from Eddie's nose, and Hans finally leaped to his feet, swiveled around Cliff, and wrestled the man's arms backward.

As Cliff struggled to free his hands, Eddie put his full force into a gut punch. Cliff twisted his body away from Eddie and doubled over, and Eddie brought him to his knees with a double-fisted strike to the temples. Now Eddie went to town on Cliff until his head lolled and he collapsed onto his back. Chest heaving, Eddie thrust his fists into the air in a show of bravado he knew he hadn't earned. Someone clapped.

Olga crouched over Cliff's limp body and patted his cheeks in a futile effort to stir him, as a crowd silently circled. Someone spat in Cliff's direction. A long moment passed.

A whining siren drew all eyes to a squad car that screeched to a stop in the parking lot. Two officers jumped out, hands on holsters. Otto strode straight to Eddie, back in his chair, one leg on the table, blotting his nose on his shirt.

"Eddie, what the hell happened here?" the officer asked.

Eddie snapped upright, his swagger deserting him. "Just a friendly fight, Unc—Sheriff."

"Who started this?"

Eddie nodded at the ground. "That would be this wild man here. He was slobbering over that *fraulein*, sir."

Otto turned to the crowd. "Anyone else got something to say about this?" he barked, more threat than invitation. Nobody spoke.

Olga whirled toward the onlookers. "What is wrong with you? You all saw what he did to Cliff!" she rasped.

The sheriff stared down at Olga, a sneer curling his mouth. "Olga, would you like to come down to headquarters and make a statement? Of course, being you're underage for this liquor establishment, your folks will have to meet us there," he said, voice filled with enmity.

She glared at him. He signaled his partner, who pulled Cliff to his feet, cuffed him, and dragged him to the back of the cruiser.

"All right, folks, enjoy your afternoon." The crowd began to disperse, and Otto signaled Eddie to follow him. They walked past the squad car to the back of a utility shed. Otto turned to Eddie and stood nose to nose with him.

"Did the bastard disrespect her?" he asked.

"Sure did," Eddie said, leg spasming.

Otto's face roiled like a storm cloud. "Good, then. A lesson to these halfbreeds."

Eddie sniffled more blood, which trailed down his jaw. Sheriff Schmidt wrinkled his nose and handed Eddie a hand-kerchief.

"But there's something you keep forgetting, Eddie."

His sharp tone sent Eddie into a protective crouch. "Uncle?"

Otto bared his teeth. "*Choose your battles.* You coulda got your head handed to you out there. Keep control or you'll get into a mess you can't get out of. Do I make myself clear?"

Like always, Uncle's scolding made Eddie feel five years old. "Yes, Uncle."

"And another thing. Rumors been circulating since Sunday that some kid from town killed a mixblood on the mountain Saturday night, not far from where the Van Hoek boy died."

Eddie's ears went hot. "Who says?"

Otto crumpled the collar of Eddie's T-shirt in his fist. "Don't bullshit me, son. Why haven't I heard a word from you about it?"

"Well I—I didn't think..."

"Think *what*, Eddie? That a story like this wouldn't just go away, like some school prank? I have my hands full with a murder case you're a witness to, and you're avoiding my calls. I need you at HQ tomorrow to tell me what you know about Karla and Stefan's attackers. Got it?"

Eddie trembled all over. "Um, yes."

"Yes, what?" Otto wrenched his closed fist, yanking Eddie along with his shirt.

Eddie shielded his eyes from Uncle's searing stare. "Yes, sir!"

Otto released Eddie and marched off, barking orders to his officer. Eddie bent over, spat red, and then stomped toward the pier, fists straining his pockets.

Tuesday August 30th

Eddie shot up from his pillow, blinking into darkness, grasping after the threads of a nightmare. He and Karla were gliding in a rowboat, and out of nowhere, a speedboat reared above them, Silas at the bow, and then the world ripped apart.

He shivered and then stretched, sending a jolt of pain from jaw to temple. He glanced at the nightstand through puffy eyes. The clock read five. Four more hours till his reckoning with Uncle.

It seemed like just yesterday life was good: wheels, girl, job, Mama's drinking under control. And no shit from Uncle, not for a while. How had everything gotten out of hand so fast?

Back at the start with Karla, they had been all over each other. He'd show up like a puppy on her doorstep almost every day after work. Once they were going steady, he'd gone back to seeing his old buddies and working on his car. But she'd nagged him to be with her all the time, and needed constant reassurance that he loved her.

The breakup kept playing in his head. Eddie had complained to Karla about the Jackson Whites fishing on the lake and hanging around town. He'd said it wasn't the Highlands he grew up in, the one Uncle campaigned for, where everyone knew their place.

Karla had shot back that Otto was a two-bit Hitler, and if Eddie really believed all that, he was no better. She was so mad, he'd gotten crazy-scared that she didn't love him anymore, and he didn't know what to do to set things right. And that was when he'd lost it.

The bile rose to his throat. He wished he could take back everything, go back to how things were, before the bruises and the breakup, before Saturday night.

What a fuckup, Eddie thought. *A little dictator,* Karla's mom had said, when she thought he couldn't hear. But then Mrs. Van Hoek had always thought him a bad influence on her children.

Truth be told, he'd been a wild teenager. When grownups tried to lay down the law, he'd seen red. Christ, who wouldn't be pissed off at the people in charge, after what they'd done to Papa and his whole family?

His first year in the Highlands at age fourteen, Crystal City was a raw wound. Papa had been gone five years, presumed dead in the war. *That life is finished. You should be grateful for your uncle's protection,* his mother had scolded. And Eddie was just supposed to wall up his feelings.

So he'd lashed out at the world, making a mission of every sin in the Sunday sermon: drinking, reefers, lying, brawling, stealing. And when his mom couldn't take any more, he'd get the crap beat out of him by his Nazi uncle. The more Uncle had bullied him, the more trouble he'd made, in a carousel of rebellion and punishment.

But Uncle had been the only one who seemed to care what Eddie did. The longer his dad was gone, the more Uncle's influence had grown, until his harangues and beliefs had lodged in Eddie's mind. But they'd never felt quite like his own; more like they owned him.

That first fall at Munsee High, Eddie'd been an unwilling refugee in this dull outpost in the woods. He'd longed for Yorkville's bustling streets, the clatter of trains, buses, and trolleys that quickened his blood. The sounds of home.

Rootless, cynical, and aggrieved, Eddie had hungered to be a part of something again. Find others who understood him, shared his scorn for the world's injustice and hypocrisy.

And then, leaving school that September day, he'd seen a pack of older boys in the student parking lot with their bomber jackets and Brando sass. He'd heard that they raced souped-up cars and went all the way with girls. They met the world with a leer, and nobody messed with them.

Eddie'd felt the prickle of their attention, heard the sharp crunch of gravel closing on him. He'd wanted to bolt for the bus, but wouldn't be branded a sissy. So he'd frozen.

The gang had surrounded him. A guy with a high pompadour in a brown leather jacket had stepped forward and gotten a hair's breadth from Eddie. "Hey there, little boy, what's your rush?"

Trembling, Eddie had tipped up his chin. "I'm not in a rush."

"Good thing, 'cause you ain't going nowhere." The boy had shoved Eddie backward into the arms of a second boy, who'd pushed Eddie to the next, until they'd each had their turn. They'd howled like hyenas.

They'd begun to pummel him. Eddie had blocked the blows as best he could, and as the jeering crescendoed, something in him had given way. Eddie had roared and flailed with his fists. He'd felt the sting of his knuckles hitting bone and saw one boy stagger.

"You little shit!" the boy had yowled. Jeers had given way to hoots of encouragement. Then a muscular youth with a flat nose in black leather and chains had slashed the air with his arm, and the group quieted. He'd circled Eddie, eyes scouring his face, chest, and shoulders.

"Not bad, for a kid." From the breast pocket of his jacket, the muscleman had drawn a chrome lighter and a finger of paper, lit one end, and made it red hot with one long breath. He'd handed the joint to Eddie, lips in a smirk, and said, "Come on, little man, have a drag."

He'd looked each of them in the eye, sucked on the joint, and gagged. The group had erupted in laughter, and the muscleman slapped Eddie on the back. His chest had burned and his eyes watered, but he'd willed himself to toke again.

"Easy, kid," said a pale guy with a blond ducktail. "So what's your name?"

"Eddie." His voice had come out raspy and low.

The blond had snickered. "Do you have a last name, Eddie-boy?"

"Schhhhmidt." Eddie'd giggled. He'd felt oddly euphoric.

"Our kind. Good." The pale blond had play-punched Eddie's arm. "We go up the mountain tonight. If you want to run with us, be back here at eight thirty. Dig?"

"Dig, daddy-o!" Eddie had managed, before doubling over in laughter.

That night, Eddie had lain blindfolded on the ground in a drafty barn somewhere in the woods, stoned out of his mind. He'd felt no grief for Papa or shame over Crystal City, only comfort for the company of guys like him with a burning desire to stick it to a world that had cast them out.

Eddie started from his reverie and squinted at the brightness pooling around his bedroom curtains. That same thirst for revenge all those years ago had undone him on Saturday. If the whole story came out, could Uncle save him? Eddie lifted his head from damp sheets and slipped out of bed.

8

Eddie sat shivering before Uncle's massive desk in the sweltering office. The sheriff's secretary Margarete positioned herself alongside him, pen poised above her steno pad.

Sheriff Schmidt looked askance at his nephew for a long moment, picked up a pen, and scribbled something on a clipboard. "Let's start at the beginning. In your own words, Mr. Schmidt."

"Well, Uncle—"

Otto Schmidt looked at Margarete, who suppressed a smile. "This is a criminal investigation, and you will address me as Sheriff," he intoned, stone-faced.

"Yes, sir. Sheriff, sir," Eddie called out, like a boot camp recruit.

"Begin your testimony," Otto said with annoyance.

"Well, so Stefan and Hans and me went up the mountain Saturday night to hang out at the Reefer Barn—"

Otto tapped the clipboard with his pen. "Eddie, you're not helping yourself. Rephrase your statement."

Eddie gave Otto a sour look. Did he want his version or Eddie's? "Okay, then, so we was going to a hideaway we knew in the woods."

Otto grunted approval. "Go on."

"Then we heard a girl screaming—and all three of us ran up to this old miner's house, and this Jackson White retard was pawin' Karla—"

"A mountain man was assaulting Karla Van Hoek?" Otto said, voice curdling with impatience.

Why didn't Uncle just write his damn lines for him? "Sir, yes, sir," Eddie mocked.

"Yes, *what?*" Otto said through clenched teeth.

"The fucker was *molesting* her!" Eddie nearly shouted.

Uncle slapped the clipboard. "Watch your tongue!" he boomed. After a tense moment, Otto motioned to Eddie. "Continue, please."

Eddie's leg bounced furiously. "W-we started beating on the monkey—"

"You attempted to rescue Karla Van Hoek from her assailant," Otto reinterpreted.

Eddie leaped to his feet. "You know, I'll say whatever you want, but I'm proud I pounded the shit outa the scumbag who stabbed Stefan!" He stomped on his jumpy leg for emphasis.

Otto's lips pulled back in a snarl. He shot up from his desk and throttled Eddie with one meaty paw. Margarete gasped as Eddie sputtered for breath. Otto shoved him into his seat, clutching his throat and coughing.

Otto proceeded as if nothing had happened. "And so you attempted to stop the assault against Stefan Van Hoek."

Eddie sat slumped, ashamed of himself. No matter how old he got, Uncle gutted him. "Um, yeah." His voice was high and shaky.

Otto studied his nephew with distain. "And who was this man with the knife?"

He stared straight ahead. "Silas Mueller," he intoned.

Otto carved checkmarks down the clipboard. "And how did you identify him in the dark?" he asked.

Eddie stared glassy eyed at Otto's slashing pen. "I knew him from town."

Otto rubbed his eyes and forehead as if soothing a bad headache. "You shone your flashlight on him." It wasn't a question. When Eddie paused a moment too long, Otto snapped his fingers.

Eddie stiffened. "I wasn't thinking about no flashlight, okay? I was too busy keeping me and my buddies alive," he said defiantly.

Otto's face purpled. "You shone your flashlight in his face," he dictated to Margarete.

Eddie shrugged. "Whatever you say."

Otto's eyes shot fire. "And *then* what happened, Eddie?"

Eddie threw up his hands. "He escaped?"

Otto stayed his secretary's fingers with a slashing hand. "Do you hear how pathetic you sound? A single assailant molests your girl, and then escapes *three* armed men? What kind of *man* lets that happen?" Otto said with contempt.

Uncle always knew just where to stick the knife. Eddie's eyes grew moist, and he looked at the floor. Otto seemed to soften.

"Think carefully now, son: doesn't the killer's escape make much more sense if there was a second attacker? With those odds, you're the hero." Otto bounced back in his leather armchair, a treacly smile on his face.

Eddie knew Uncle was playing him, and felt helpless to resist. "Yes, sir. Two attackers makes much more sense."

With brisk cheer, Otto waved for Margarete to resume. "And they both escaped," Otto said with assurance.

The spasm in Eddie's leg had grown to a charley horse. "The two attackers escaped," he said robotically.

"And then what happened to Stefan and Karla Van Hoek?" Otto asked.

Eddie squeezed his errant thigh with both hands. "We, uuh...we got Karla and Stefan down to where we parked. We laid Stefan in the T-Bird, and Hans drove him to Saint Gertrude's."

"And how was Miss Van Hoek?"

"Um, she was shook up pretty bad," Eddie's words ended in a whimper.

Otto looked up from his pad. "And her appearance?"

Eddie saw her battered face, the terror in her eyes. "Her hair was mussed...she had a cut on her cheek, and"—he made a sound like a strangled cry—"she had bruises around her neck, and her clothes were all ripped. There was blood everywhere." Eddie felt nauseated.

Otto's gaze hardened. "Continue," he said.

"That's how I found her when I got back...I mean, when I got there." He looked at Otto and Margarete and saw in their eyes the monster that he was. "God's honest truth!" he pleaded. The secretary looked from Eddie to the sheriff.

"No one's saying otherwise, son. Anyone in your shoes would be just as upset as you are right now." Otto pushed on, all business. "What did you do after helping Stefan?"

Eddie scoured the ceiling. "Karla, uh, asked me to drive her home." Was there a shred of honesty left in him?

"And how did you get there?" Otto asked.

Eddie kneaded his leg. "Uh, well...there was another car up there, so I stole it, and—"

"You borrowed the nearest available vehicle in an emergency to get Miss Van Hoek to safety."

The dead man's. "Yeah." Eddie stared blankly at Margarete's dancing fingers.

"And then?" Otto coaxed.

"I drove her home and made sure she got up to her room okay." Eddie took his next cue from Otto's windmilling hand.

"And then I went home," Eddie said in a monotone. He was a complete sham.

Sheriff Schmidt finished scribbling and pushed back from his desk. "Thank you for your cooperation, Mr. Schmidt." He waggled his pen and ran down his notes.

"Let the record show that this statement is herewith concluded at nine thirty-eight a.m." Otto thrust his clipboard and a pen toward Eddie, and pointed to the bottom of the top sheet.

"Sign here." Eddie obeyed. Otto seemed pleased at how the interview had gone. He nodded at Margarete, who smiled and left the room. Otto shut the door and stood over Eddie.

"Eddie, *what* car did you drive Karla home in?" Otto demanded.

Eddie looked up at Uncle, wide-eyed. "An El Camino." Otto nodded for more. "M-metallic blue," he stuttered. "Custom."

"Me-tal-lic blue." Each syllable seemed to offend Otto. "Custom, as in one of a kind. And where is it now?"

"My driveway," Eddie said quietly. The worst possible place for the trouble he was in.

Otto's voice dropped to a rumble. "Go home right now and move it behind the house. Find some tarp or canvas and cover it. We'll talk more about this later." Otto stood, and Eddie sprang to his feet obligingly. "Be sure Hans squares his story with yours."

"Yes, sir," he said meekly, his will to resist Uncle in tatters.

Otto held Eddie's gaze. "And what will you do about Karla?"

"I told her she'd better come see you today, if she knows what's good for her," he said, the swagger of the words belied by his quavering voice.

Otto kept pressing Eddie's hand. "Don't lay it on too thick, Eddie. We need to keep her on our side," he chided.

"Things between us is gonna be different now. I'll keep her in line," Eddie said, hoping to holy hell he knew how.

Otto sat back down at his desk, and swiveled left and right, his fingertips pressed together. Eddie faced him, head down, a dog not sure of treat or trouble.

A grin rippled across Otto's jowls. He looked past Eddie and barked triumphantly. "We're gonna make this mountain trash regret they ever looked crosswise at our women. And soon enough, Brandt'll get his comeuppance, too."

His eyes were wrath wrapped in delight, and Eddie searched them for a sign that he'd pleased his master, that it might be the last time Uncle humiliated him.

Otto tapped pen on paperwork, then frowned at Eddie. "Son, those fingernail marks on your cheek: cover them up."

Eddie held tight to his moment of grace. "Oh, it ain't nothing." He smiled until it hurt, willing Uncle to favor him. Uncle grew red, and Eddie's eyes dropped to Otto's balled fists. Eddie knew the feel of them, smashing bone and flesh.

The sheriff spoke so slow and quiet, Eddie had to lean in. "I said *cover them up*. It don't look good for our case."

Eddie pulled himself to attention as if yanked by an invisible chain. "Okay, sir."

Nothing with Uncle would ever change. He was a bastard, like the schoolyard bullies in Yorkville, and the men who'd dragged him off to Crystal City. Eddie nodded and looked at his shoes. His head pounded and his thigh ached.

"Good boy. Now run along," Uncle said. "And don't get yourself into any more trouble before I close this case. For your father's sake, rest his soul."

If only Papa was here to wrap Eddie in his arms and tell him that everything would be all right, Eddie thought, just like he always had before their lives were ripped apart.

August 1942

The radio, schoolyards, and streets of Yorkville buzz with talk of raids and arrests. At the market this week, someone called Mama a kraut and a Nazi.

She cleans up after dinner; I sit in Papa's lap on the sofa, listening to happy-ever-after stories. A faint rumble swells into pounding feet on the stairs, and a fist batters our door.

"Police! Open up!" Papa looks calmly at me, puts a finger to his lips. Mama rushes to his side. After a long moment of muffled words in the hall, the door gives way with a huge crack, splinters flying, and four uniformed men burst in, guns raised, barking orders. Papa calmly sets me on my feet and stands erect, his hand trembling on my shoulder. Mama clutches his arm.

One man wrenches Papa's wrists and handcuffs him. Mama wraps his overcoat around his shoulders, the door slams, and Mama and I are alone with the sound of fading footfalls.

After an eternity, a letter comes. Papa is at an alien enemy detention facility in Texas. Nothing Mama can say allays my fears. I dream of Papa before a firing squad.

On a cold January morning at school, I am called to the princi-

pal's office where two men in dark suits are waiting for me. "No questions," one orders. "Come with us."

I remember a speeding car, a gray building. Harsh light, loud questions about summer camp, Nazis, the Bund. Then: A dark platform, a train with blacked-out windows. A carriage of smoke, sweat, and fear, packed with boys and men, German and Italian and Japanese, and soldiers with rifles.

Two days later, I'm on a bus bouncing through fields of spinach and rocks, to towers and steel fences. "Keep it moving!" MPs shout as I stumble through gates and line up in the punishing sun for next orders alongside mothers, fathers, and children.

I wait, hurry, then wait on another line, where the intake officer hands me a packet marked 9-32 and nods toward my destination. I dodge crowds, tear down a dusty street to a wood and steel box with my number, shadowed by a high metal fence.

Squealing with anticipation, I push through the doorway to a sweltering room where a bare table and two chairs sit under a bright window. My heart leaps at the scrape of shoes on cement behind me.

"Papa!" I shout, and spin around.

Uncle Otto stands at the threshold, face drawn, shoulders slumped.

My chest pounds. "Where's Papa?"

Uncle swallows hard. "Your father has been...sent back to Germany," he rasps.

I am one long, piercing scream.

"That's quite a yarn." Otto smiled stiffly. The three brothers stood against mahogany paneling and glowered at Sheriff Schmidt. He sized up his visitors, turning his pen end over end.

"Where's your evidence, boys? I got sworn statements from one victim and two witnesses who say otherwise."

Euel pressed a palm against Malcolm's back, and he stepped forward. "I got proof," he said. The sheriff leaned forward, head cocked, hands folded on his blotter.

Malcolm flexed his hands like a boxer before a fight. "Silas told me he was seeing Karla Van Hoek, and that her ex-boyfriend didn't want him to."

The sheriff splayed his fingers. "Anything else?" he said.

Malcolm's mouth clamped down on puffed cheeks, like he was containing an explosion. Jake put a hand on his shoulder and stepped forward. "That would be your nephew, Eddie Schmidt."

The sheriff thrust his chin forward and locked eyes with Jake. "Haven't heard anything so far that sounds remotely like a crime."

Malcolm's chest squeezed and spread like a bellows. "Well, how 'bout this? Silas shows up at Karla's house, and Eddie's waiting for him in the street, holding a baseball bat and a melon. He tells Silas to get out of his neighborhood.

"So Silas says, 'Who's gonna make me?' and the guy heaves the melon, smashes it to pieces with the bat"—Malcolm smacked his knuckles in his open palm—"and says, 'That's gonna be your head.'"

The sheriff shrugged. "A boy got mad and took it out on a piece of fruit. Is that your case?"

Malcolm snarled, and Jake put himself between his brother and Otto. "Eddie killed Silas! I found my brother's body at the bottom of a ravine Sunday morning." Jake's voice throbbed.

Doubt flickered on the sheriff's face, and he scowled. "You boys know better than I do that a whole lot of drinking goes on in these mountains on a Saturday night. Sounds like your brother did a little celebrating after his crimes, got himself pissed, and walked off a cliff."

Jake wasn't having it. "His head was *crushed,*" he shot back.

"Exactly what happens when bone meets rock."

"I saw the damage." Jake's voice faltered. "On the side of his head *away* from the rock."

Otto stiffened. "And just what are you suggesting?"

Jake laid his open palms on the great wooden desk and leaned into Otto, who smelled like a cornered animal. "Silas didn't die by accident, and you know it!" Jake's temples drummed.

Otto leaned back in his chair, fingers linked behind his head. "Boy, I got no crime sheet, hospital record, or autopsy report. You are accusing a man of murder, when he has two eyewitnesses who say it ain't so. Where is your proof? Where is the *body*?"

Euel and Malcolm looked at Jake. "Funeral was yesterday," Jake said.

Otto's chair snapped forward. "That so? Makes me wonder why you were so quick to bury your *proof.*" Otto surveyed the three men. "Now, your mama could request an exhumation. Of course, we'd need her to come in to formally identify her son's remains."

Jake turned to his brothers, faces gone pale. He muttered under his breath, shot a look at the sheriff, and shook his head.

Otto leaned in and spread his hands wide. "Well then, *this case is closed*," he declared, luxuriating in the words.

Jake turned heel and strode to the door. He paused, shoulders arched, and wheeled around. "Somehow, some way, we gonna make you and your nephew pay for this," he said, whipping his finger at Otto like a revolver.

Otto leaped to his feet, propelling his chair into the wall behind him. "Are you threatening an officer of the law?" His cheeks reddened. "Now you listen to me, and listen good. One of you was with your littermate at the crime scene."

He locked eyes with Jake. "And you just distinguished

yourself on my list of suspects. So be damned careful what you do and say from here on, *boy*." Otto spat the word.

Jake stormed out, his brothers trailing him. Two slamming doors rocked the pickup. Euel turned to Jake. "*Now* what you think of the white man's law?"

Jake simmered; he tried to focus. His brothers had been right: he was a fool to believe in Highlands justice. He turned the key and slammed the pedal in a screech of rubber on asphalt.

Boy, the sheriff had called him. A warning not to forget his place. Like the world had been reminding him every day since he left the mountain for kindergarten.

Pa had marched him up the steps of the brick schoolhouse on Broadway. Three girls had ogled him rudely, and then began to chant, *"Miney! Miney! Miney!"*

Jake had looked blankly at them. "What's *miney*, Pa?"

"Pay no mind to that pack of brats," his father had hissed, tugging him along to his classroom. He'd handed Jake his lunchbox, and Jake had stepped into the brightness as pitched voices hushed. The room had been a Dick and Jane book come to life: eggshell faces, fair hair, blue eyes.

A pleated gray curtain had towered over him. Above it, a stiff smile anchored two beady eyes.

"You must be Jacob. You're late," the woman had snapped. "I am Miss Epperhardt. Now, go sit down and be quiet until you're spoken to." She'd pointed to an empty seat and turned to the chalkboard.

As Jake had sat down, a *psst* came from behind. "Hey, you live in a cave?" Monkey sounds had erupted nearby, and a banana peel landed on his desk from over his shoulder.

"Stop it!" Jake had grabbed his lunchbox, turned, and whacked the offender, who howled in pain. The teacher then had swept up the aisle, lifted Jake by his ear, and marched him to the hall.

"Straight to the principal's office with you, and no back talk!"

"But I didn't start it—" A thunderclap had jolted Jake's cheek. He'd scurried off, wailing, Miss Epperhardt's voice echoing down the tiled hall. *"You Jackson Whites are nothing but trouble!"*

Jake's pickup scraped against the driveway's upgrade, snapping him back to the present, and he eased up on the gas. He ground the gearshift and rocked to a halt. Euel and Malcolm swore under their breath. Maisie popped up her head from the front porch.

Jake marched to the edge of the yard and kicked a shriveled corncob into the forest.

Coroner Leo Brandt blotted his forehead and landed hard on his office chair. It was only 5:30 Tuesday afternoon, and already a frantic week, with the pressure for forensics before the Van Hoek boy's funeral yesterday. But it had been a clean wound and a straightforward cause of death.

He knew that the aftershocks from that death, and the claims of the three white witnesses in the case, would reverberate to the far corners of the Highlands. There was nothing just now that his office could do or say to satisfy the mountain folk or the old guard of Iron Run, each still mourning their own and nursing lifetimes of grievance.

He knew how it was playing in both worlds, because both were his. In the twenties, his papa, Hermann Brandt, had started the Happy Breezes Beer Garden on a shady patch of rock overlooking Lake Mennepequa.

As coffers had allowed, he'd expanded until it had become a lakeside mainstay. After the Great War, he'd weathered the anti-German sentiment with stars-and-stripes bunting, Fourth-of-July fireworks, and an all-American menu alongside the wurst and schnitzel.

The day the beer garden's painted billboard went up, a ruddy-faced *mädchen*, fine of feature, had walked right past the construction signs and barriers and told Papa he should hire her. He'd been impressed with her pluck and beautiful smile, and agreed on the spot.

When she'd disclosed in her first week waiting tables that her folks were from the mountains, it had only added to her allure for Papa. Like himself, he saw in her the bootstrapping outsider with the optimism and drive to succeed in the land of freedom and opportunity. Within six months, she had advanced from server to fiancée.

Leo Brandt was the product of that union of strivers, and he'd absorbed his parents' ethos. Ambition had taken him from after-school busboy in the family business to college honors in the physical sciences.

A summer internship in a forensic crime lab had given him the bug that eventually led to his present post, and lately, a first try at electoral politics, running for county sheriff on his crowd-pleasing family name.

Right now, Brandt needed to give himself fully to the Schreier case. He stroked the stubble peppering his chin; the missus would be sure to comment tonight on his usual shoddy appearance, if he made it home before her bedtime for once.

He sighed. Frieda put up with a lot, living with a short-handed coroner with a shoestring election campaign. Maybe more than he deserved.

Schreier's autopsy report still bothered him; if a boat propeller was the cause of death, there ought to be heavy bleeding proximal to the lacerations. And there was no systemic dilution of the bloodstream with lake water, consistent with drowning.

So death likely occurred before the body entered the lake—making foul play more likely than accident or suicide.

When he'd first skimmed the sheriff's findings the previous Friday, Brandt had found it strangely lacking in detail. So he had exercised his discretion to order a battery of toxicology tests for alcohol, drugs, and common poisons.

The victim's tattoo and jacket had given him all he needed for an ID: a Holocaust survivor with a Schmidt campaign button in his pocket. With a little checking, Brandt found several staff and rallygoers at the Old Rhinelander who placed someone fitting Schreier's description at the Saturday event; none had seen him leave.

So Brandt had taken it upon himself to speak with Schreier's colleagues at the *Mountain Observer*. Snooping for a cause of death didn't legally overstep his authority; but he had probed deeper than a coroner with full confidence in his sheriff had reason to.

Editor Tom Langer had volunteered that Schreier was obsessed with the unsavory side of the region's past. He'd assured Brandt that had he known Schreier was poking into the sheriff's personal history, he would have squelched the project.

Schreier's two fellow stringers had agreed to speak with Brandt, but only after hours, away from the office. That caution had instantly kinked Brandt's eyebrow. They separately confided their surprise that Langer had given Schreier the green light to go undercover for the *Observer* at a Schmidt fundraiser.

Langer, each confirmed, was one of the sheriff's biggest boosters, and stories affecting the sheriff's office usually got run past Otto Schmidt before they went to press—often heavily edited.

The two reporters had learned quite a bit about the voluble Schreier in the eight months since he'd arrived in Algonquin County. Schreier was as American now as he'd once been German, but he carried a torch for the Berlin life Hitler had snuffed out.

The Nazis had decimated Schreier's family, and the trauma had shaped his choices since his arrival in New York in '46. Schreier was a man on a mission: a Zionist fighting anti-Semitism and hunting Nazis. It was no fluke that he'd left a good job with B'nai B'rith in New York to work for a paper in Podunk.

The two newsmen confided to Brandt that Schreier had made Otto Schmidt his personal cause, and that going under-cover at the sheriff's rally was part of that crusade. When Brandt's interview was done, the reporter named Emil had slipped him a large packet of Schreier's research on Schmidt.

Brandt fingered a ring and slid a small steel key into the side drawer of his desk. He removed a brown envelope, unwound its binding, and drew out the contents. He fastened his reading glasses and began.

Case originated at: NEW YORK, NY

File No. 27-197

Report made at: NEW YORK, NY

Date when made: 9-30-41

Period for which made: 9-1-41 to 9-30-41

Report made by: [Redacted]

Title: GERMAN AMERICAN BUND (GAB)

Character of Case: VOORHIS ACT

Being set forth at this point information furnished to

the Bureau by Confidential Informant [redacted], which information informant obtained while in attendance at closed meeting of the Bund on September 21, 1941, at Camp Hochland, Munsee Mountain Fire Road #6, Algonquin County, New York. Informant advised twenty members, all male, present, and OTTO SCHMIDT, GAB chapter leader, presided.

Informant stated SCHMIDT introduced topic of Lend-Lease Act; spoke angrily of President Rosenfeld [*sic*]'s efforts to supply Britain with warships and planes, calling this "tantamount to war against Germany. Comrades," he said, "we are now in enemy territory."

Informant stated SCHMIDT declared it was of "utmost importance to defeat Rosenfeld, his Jewish servants, and Churchill." Attendees spontaneously chanted "Sieg heil!"

SCHMIDT proclaimed, "democracy is on its last legs." SCHMIDT further said that "a new Veltanshung" [sp?] would soon take its place, and Third Reich would "overrun America." Informant stated that this inspired table pounding and foot stomping.

Boycott Committee chair MANFRED GRUNNWALD reported on Jewish-owned businesses in Newburgh, Monroe, and New Paltz, and it was agreed by voice vote to recommend to Yorkville [Bund HQ] these shops be added to official "Jew boycott."

Informant stated SCHMIDT closed meeting in usual fashion with Bund motto: "To a free, Gentile-ruled United States, and to our fighting movement of awakened Aryan Americans. Free America!"

Brandt returned the report to its folder and placed the

packet at the bottom of the drawer. Sheriff Schmidt certainly had motive to silence this snoop Schreier. But that was a long way from proving murder.

Wednesday August 31st

The toxicology results were waiting for Brandt—a minor miracle, even with the rush he'd put on them. He wriggled his compact, wiry frame out of his jacket and riffled through the thin sheaf.

The first battery of tests for the Schreier autopsy had left Brandt unsatisfied. It had ruled out alcohol, drugs, and common poisons, but couldn't explain the signs that death preceded the body's submersion. So he had ordered a second round, this time including barbiturates and other central nervous system depressants.

Brandt fingered each line of the report summary, then poked the page. He sprang from his desk, strode to the hallway separating offices from holding cells, and entered a room with a locked refrigerator. He flipped through the ring on his belt, slipped in a key, opened the door, and zeroed in on a cardboard crate with a torn wrapper.

He eyeballed the empty spot where several vials should have been, then resecured the fridge. He walked over to a steel wall cabinet, unlocked that, and surveyed three long rows of hanging keys. One hook was bare; next to it, a label read MED FRIDGE.

Brandt grabbed a clipboard that hung from a hook next to a hand sink. He ran his fingers down two pages of entries. He found what he was looking for and walked back to his office.

Truth serum was a versatile drug in a sheriff's department:

useful to sedate an agitated prisoner or extract a confession. But it was dangerous business: administer too much, and muscles go limp, breathing slows, the brain starves, and you induce heart failure.

The missing vials added up to twelve times more sodium amytal than anyone in his right mind would administer to the most violent detainee. Brandt pressed a button and spoke into his intercom. "Get me judge's chambers at the courthouse. Tell the switchboard we need search warrants ASAP in the Schreier case. It's now a murder investigation."

As he waited to be patched through, Brandt's gaze fell on the sheriff's report for the Van Hoek murder-assault. How remarkable that the three witnesses' sworn versions of events aligned perfectly, despite their different vantage points in the woods. In the dark.

He reflected on the grievous events and shook his head. Mendacity and hubris had their limits, even in Algonquin County.

Karla lay in bed, in dread of the world she woke to. The last three days had been an unending nightmare, and today seemed utterly formless. Silas was gone, and she had no big brother to squabble with. Or protect her from Eddie.

In their early days, she'd taken comfort knowing that no matter how wild Eddie got, her brother was there to rein him in. That seemed like another lifetime, before the bruises and the breakup, before the day Silas appeared on her doorstep with a truck full of cordwood.

They'd shared a few awkward words, but Silas's gentle way had stayed with her. When they'd crossed paths again at the farm stand on Mount Zindel two weeks later, they'd chatted about corn and cabbage and the weather. Silas's voice was like a warm embrace. When they'd run out of small talk, neither made to leave.

Being it's a pretty day, I was fixing to go for a hike to Jennings Ridge. View of the lake's something special. I could show you, if you like.

Karla had smiled in reply. Silas's patience and courtesy on the climb had put her at ease. So different from Eddie, who smothered her like a parent, cop, and bodyguard rolled into one. Then at the top of the ridge with Silas, Karla had been wholly seduced by the freedom she'd felt seeing the speck of her town in the vastness spread beneath them.

But since Saturday night, she was alone with her fears again. And Eddie'd made it clear at the funeral that he was taking back what he said was his.

Late that same day he'd come by, bruised, bloody, and so belligerent he'd scared her into telling the sheriff Eddie's version of Saturday night. To deny what she had seen with her own eyes. Betray Stefan and Silas. And herself. Her stomach hurt.

Karla had been raised in a pious Calvinist sect steeped in victimhood and injustice, Saint Bartholomew's Day its proof of an evil world to be shunned. Father forbade fun on the Lord's Day, and Karla dreaded summer Sundays, when she'd be in a hot church all morning and again late in the day.

In between, while her friends played in the lake, she'd sit on a lawn chair and stew. Karla couldn't see how enjoying summer was a sin, and her parents' drunken fights weren't exactly keeping the Fourth Commandment.

From an early age, she'd stopped taking the world on faith. She was the skeptic in school debates about Joseph McCarthy and civil rights. On a field trip about the Huguenots—her own ancestral martyrs—Karla interrupted their red-faced teacher repeatedly until he conceded that those pious pioneers had filled their stone cellars with human property alongside the potatoes.

Karla had forsworn the pastel whirl of proms and lettermen that led inexorably from high school to marriage and keeping house, fueling her mother's pestering about her future. At Easter dinner this year, her mom had tried to fix her up with the scrawny, pimply son of a church elder she'd seen eyeing Karla as they'd left the sanctuary that morning.

At that, she'd announced she was going to college. Instantly, all activity at the table had stopped. Her dad looked at her as if she'd just insulted the Redeemer.

"No man wants a wife smarter than him," he said.

Her mother studied her lap. "But dear, by the time you graduate, you'll be an old maid."

"Only to the boys I wouldn't have anyway," she shot back.

"Don't be sassing your mother," her father snapped.

Karla scowled at him. "I learned how from you."

Stefan shot Karla a look that said, *Quit before there's trouble.* Then he chuckled and said, "Come on, sis, the only degree a girl needs is an *M-R-S*."

"If you want to marry your mother, that's your goddamn business," Karla sneered. Her mother bit her lip.

Her father's glass hit the table with a clang. "Young lady, there'll be no sputting in this house!" Her pastor's funny word for insulting the Lord. Karla's dad had no clue how much church kids went around sputting when the adults weren't around, and she suspected the adults did as much.

She laughed at his naivete. "Marriage is a life sentence I refuse to serve."

Her mother reached across the table and slapped her hard.

That day had only driven Karla to stay out after school and weekends. She'd swapped her poodle skirt for clamdiggers, and spent time up the street with the Kaiser boy and his friend Eddie, smoking behind Hans's broken-down garage.

Eddie was ten years older, and a rebel like her. He had seemed so experienced, coming from a big city like New York. Wry and funny, too, but wounded inside those wild eyes.

She had fallen fast. Eddie had pushed right past the strictures of her upbringing, and she'd found herself in way over her head. But she had weathered that storm, and later the breakup, and come out the other side stronger, more confident.

But that was before Saturday night.

Karla looked at the time, and her heart lurched. She was already late. She rose, walked unsteadily to the bathroom, and braced herself on the lip of the sink. She lifted her eyes to the mirror and watched the image slowly contort, like a party mask thrown on the fire. Nothing she could tell Sheriff Schmidt today would change the fact that Eddie now utterly owned her.

Tony's mind was a battlefield. Everything he'd learned about the awful events on the mountain led inexorably back to Jake. Tony had to know the truth. After scouring the park for him all day, Tony finally spied Jake rushing from the locker room and hastened after him. He had the motor running when Tony caught up and grabbed hold of the open driver's window.

Jake stared far away as if Tony weren't there. He desperately needed to plumb the gray-blue depths of those eyes. "Jake, we have to talk," Tony managed.

"What's there to talk about?" Jake's voice was hard, expressionless.

"The newspaper's reporting that two mountain men attacked four of my neighbors last Saturday."

Jake turned burning eyes on Tony. "Two against four's pretty bad odds for a couple of inbreds, don't you think?"

"So you don't believe Eddie Schmidt's story?"

Jake laughed mirthlessly. "What difference does it make what I believe? The word of ten mountaineers don't matter a damn against one white boy's."

The words landed like a slap in the face. "Bullshit! This isn't *Mississippi*—"

"What do you know about justice, behind your hedges and Keep Out signs?"

"I know my neighbors for most of my life, and they would *never*—"

"—lynch a mountain boy for violating a white girl?" Jake fired back.

"If you're so sure of yourself, then why haven't you gone to the sheriff?"

Jake laughed bitterly. "I told your sheriff the truth, and he threatened to arrest me for murder!" he spat. "No, Tony, it don't matter if it's Mississippi or the Highlands, the law's a mad dog to sick on my kind to protect you from us!"

Tony felt the truck shudder as Jake revved the engine. Tony was panicked that there was no going back if they parted like this. "Jake, you've got to believe—"

Jake cut him off. "I'll tell you something I *used* to believe. Every day from kindergarten to high school, I put my hand on my heart, and said, 'justice for all.' But I found out it didn't matter how many times I pledged allegiance, justice was for someone else, not me. So no, I don't believe Eddie, and I don't believe *you*."

The truck lurched backward, and Tony's desperation curdled into rage. "Why won't you say you're innocent?" Tony demanded. The truck kept rolling, Tony holding on. "Because the second mountain man with Silas that night was you, wasn't it? *Wasn't it, Jake?*"

Jake grimaced. "You damned whiteys are all the same!"

Instantly, Tony felt their congruities fall away, and all he felt was revulsion. "Then go! Go back to the inbreds on your trash heap of a mountain!" Tony bellowed, as the pickup disappeared in a cloud of dust.

He jumped into the Falcon and rolled up the windows despite the stifling heat. His head dropped to the steering wheel.

It was over with Jake.

He gunned it down the county road and was home in ten minutes. He jogged straight to the dock and into his boat. The air was dense, metallic; the promised storm was near. He slipped off the moorings, spun the wheel, and headed out.

He eyed the gas gauge, swore out loud, and swung the wheel to starboard, speeding straight for Sharkey's. Tony's mind churned with Jake's angry words. Low clouds scudded across the wind-whipped lake, eerily deserted.

He steered the boat sideways, and it met the floating gas pump with a squeal, bucking in the restless waters. The slack-shouldered attendant, head downturned, steadied the boat with his sneaker.

Then the man lifted his face, and in the fleeting instant Tony's gaze met Eddie's, Tony saw his dread and doubt, and then it was gone, leaving them transfixed in the pummeling wind.

"Hi, Eddie. Regular, please." His words trembled with his pounding pulse. *What if Jake was right?*

Eddie's jaw worked his cheeks. "Mm-hmm." He unscrewed the fuel cap on the bow deck and inserted the nozzle, squatting close to Tony. Unease swirled about them.

Tony struggled to be heard in the stiff wind. "Sorry about Stefan," he called out.

Eddie's eyes shot daggers. "Well, it ain't my fault!" he shouted. The swelling gale blew the words back in his face. The nozzle seemed to fight Eddie for control, and he yanked it from the reservoir, splattering fuel across the deck.

"Six bucks," Eddie said, and before Tony could dig out his money, Eddie had thrown a knapsack over his shoulder and yanked a baseball cap from his back pocket, tugging it low over his face, like a hunted man in a hurry.

Tony paid and rode off, mind reeling.

9

Jake sped recklessly down the county road. He should have seen it coming with Tony. He was just like all the rest: an electric look, the breathless words, a hungry kiss, every last one of them looking for a toy to use and throw away before morning. How was it he hadn't learned his lesson, after what happened to Elias Donck?

Jake had been fourteen, wandering the old miners' camp in the woods, when he'd spied the hazel eyes, auburn hair, and salt-and-pepper goatee. They'd both known why they were there. He'd been gentle with Jake, held him when he'd shivered with delight and shed long-held tears.

Months later, near Paterson's falls, Jake had found himself at a steel door on a dead-end street of blacked-out factory windows. He'd knocked, and a whole world had opened.

Jake had barely warmed a barstool when his shoulder got a squeeze from the man from the miners' camp. He'd introduced himself proper this time, ordered a round, and then two more.

Elias had talked about the men at the port of San Francisco in the war, the Defense Department job he'd lost in the

Lavender Scare, the sugar daddy in New York who'd left him well fixed. And how he lived now in his late mother's mountain house, between trips to Morocco and Amsterdam, Fire Island and Provincetown.

Jake had said he couldn't imagine that kind of life. "Make your dreams your reality," Elias had replied, hand warm on Jake's thigh. "Why don't we take this conversation someplace else?"

They'd woken up in a motel on Route 46, threadbare sheets smelling of musk and bleach. Elias had sat on a hard chair and watched Jake dress before sun-fired curtains.

"You're beautiful," he'd said. Like you'd say the sky is blue.

Jake's chest tightened. "Elias...this was real nice, but..."

Elias had nodded and said, "I know, Jake. Makes this all the sweeter." Jake had blushed, and let himself out.

By summer, Elias had company on the mountain. Elias introduced him as *my new handyman,* a built blond boy with a baseball cap always pulled down over his face.

But on Labor Day, screeching tires had sent Jake sprinting to the road. The blond kid was whaling in Elias's station wagon, the stain on his T-shirt an odd shade of crimson. Jake took off at a run for Elias's house, past the swinging door, upended chairs, drawers flung from cabinets.

He'd taken the stairs by twos and found Elias, limbs tied to bedposts, eyes dull, blood fanning from his throat. And on the wall above, scrawled in red fingerpaint: HALFBREED HOMO.

The El Camino hairpinned up the lake's western rim, cloaked in storm clouds. A fist squeezed Eddie's chest. He felt like he'd been called to the *Vorsteher*'s office at Camp Hochland all over again. Uncle wouldn't ever let him live that down, and Eddie was sure that today he would find a way to remind him.

What was this about? Another lecture on his duty to the Master Race? It was Uncle's goddamned religion; Eddie only half believed that crap. As a teenager, he'd been commanded up here too many times to keep the faith with Otto and his Bund cronies in their leather sashes and boots. Protecting Germans from God knows what.

They would all stand and recite the Bund pledge, hand over heart, the other thrust toward stars and stripes and swastikas. Then would come debates on the New Order, diatribes about *Juden* plots, and readings from Nazi scripture that made Eddie's eyes glaze over.

Finally, the men would raise steins and sing "Horst Wessel." Pretty stupid, Eddie thought, after they got their asses kicked in the war.

Before they adjourned, Uncle would vow to never give up the struggle to take back this country from the world's degraded peoples.

Uncle had never deviated from that script. And Eddie had to admit that this kind of talk made him feel...less anxious. More righteous. He shouldn't have to watch his back or defend his turf from outsiders moving in on them. Defiling their women. Eddie's stomach hurt.

If only Uncle would stop running Eddie's life like he was his dad. Because he had a dad, even if he was sixteen years gone. Eddie thumped his palm against the wheel. He swerved to avoid a skunk and her three kits, then almost skidded through the last curve before the Berghof. He wiped his nose on his sleeve.

Eddie rocked to a stop at a steel gate before an imposing chalet clad in massive logs. He honked, and the gate slid open.

He followed the drive to the house's opposite face, concealed by the forest.

A flagpole at the end of the drive flew a wreathed swastika, a black eagle perched atop it, stylized wings spread perpendicular to its body, signaling that Uncle was in residence at his phony Eagle's Nest.

Eddie parked the blue flatbed next to Uncle's Mercedes. He trudged up the flagstone steps to where Otto waited, cigar in hand, regarding his nephew with gimlet eyes.

"You're late," he spat. Putting Eddie in his place before he'd even stepped inside. He was twenty-eight, goddammit; how much longer was he gonna put up with this shit?

Inside, large windows that faced the lake lit the broad knotty-pine room, divided at its center by an enormous stone hearth. On its mantel, painted steins propped a dog-eared library: *The Forced War, Protocols of the Elders of Zion, The International Jew, Mein Kampf.*

Above the mantel hung a poster framed by gilded oak leaves. A glowering Adolf Hitler held high the sacred *Blutfahne* and led a throng through an alpine valley. A battle cry shimmered beneath the scene: *Es lebe Deutschland!*

Otto waved Eddie to an armchair and sat facing him. He puffed, let out a stream of smoke, and crooked his cigar between thumb and forefinger. Eddie studied Uncle with apprehension.

"Eddie, I've been saving your ass since before your dad was taken. I expected you would eventually shape up, but I'm running out of patience. There are limits to what I can do when you screw up. The brawl at Sharkey's was one thing. Two dead boys is something else."

"But I didn't kill nobody!" Eddie stammered.

Otto arched an eyebrow. "I didn't say you did." He aimed

the stogie at Eddie and peered at him through the smoke. "Eddie, what are you still doing with that El Camino?"

Eddie squirmed in his seat. "I told you, I drove Karla home."

"That was last Saturday. How long did you mean to keep it?"

"Well, I ain't got wheels just now, and I had to get to work, and then…things came up, so I kept it a couple more days."

"The dead boy's car." Otto rose and paced before the fireplace. "Do you have any idea how this looks? Mueller's brothers say they found him Sunday with his head bashed in, and meanwhile, you're cruising around in his car. Do you want your whole life to unravel over this?"

Eddie wanted to bolt from the room, but he knew that the only way out was to play Uncle's stooge. The man was never satisfied until he had Eddie on his knees. "No, sir," he said through gritted teeth.

Otto gripped the mantel and drew up his powerful frame. "Your father would turn in his grave to see his only son punished for standing up to a mixblood." Otto's hand tightened to a fist, and he pounded the wooden shelf with each word: "Get rid of the evidence!"

Eddie gave Uncle his best shit-eating lament. "I'm real sorry, Uncle. I shoulda been more careful. I promise, I'll take care of it."

Otto stiffened, as if Eddie hadn't sufficiently groveled. "Oh, you will, my boy. That car will stay right here, and you have one hour to clean every damn inch of it, starting now.

"Then I will take you home. At sunset, the Kaiser boy will drive you back up here. You will put on a pair of gloves and take the El Camino back to where you found it last Saturday. Your friend will drive you straight home, and you will stay there until morning.

"I've already spoken with Hans and both of your mothers. All they know is that you two are helping me bring the Van Hoek assailants to justice. Is it absolutely clear what you have to do, boy?"

Eddie sprang to his feet. "Yes, Uncle Otto." *You fatheaded bastard.*

"Don't fail me again, son, or this case will be out of my control. Do you understand me?"

"Yes, sir." Eddie stared scorch marks into the floor.

Otto crossed the room and clasped Eddie's shoulders, and he braced for one final salvo. Otto's tone was grave. "Our Yorkville life, our dignity, our birthright as *deutsche Volk*, they were all stolen from us. We must make sure no one ever has that power over us again."

Eddie nodded gravely. *You mean like the Allies who still occupy Berlin?*

Otto walked to a closet near the entrance and pulled out a wooden box with chamois cloths, cleaners, scrub brushes, and gloves. He thrust the box at Eddie. "I have a meeting at HQ with my officers in less than ninety minutes, so get to work, *mach schnell!*"

Eddie marched outside, stewing in bile. He set a tub of sudsy water alongside the passenger door. He opened it and his eye instantly found a trail of red where the door met the hinge. He must have missed it when he scrubbed off Silas's blood before the funeral. He plunged the brush into the tub and got to work.

His mind flooded with images of Stefan on his back, mouth streaming blood; Silas clutching his stomach, staggering toward Eddie, blade out. Eddie's crowbar landing hard on bone, and Karla pummeling him. Eddie knocking her down, dragging Silas to the ledge, rolling him until the ground gave way. And after scary quiet, a thud.

Tony tried to fit Jake's fury and Eddie's fear with the facts. Rain needled the lake, and he struggled to steer against buffeting winds. He pushed the throttle, and the boat slapped a whitecap and breached, engine snarling. The hull slammed the next trough, shaking loose an image from late Saturday night.

The cat's-eye taillights on the upper road. Silas's car.

But he wasn't in it, because he was already dead.

The storm pulled Tony's attention back to the wheel. Nearing his dock, he gunned the engine in reverse, but the lake was a boiling pot, and the boat smacked wood.

Tony's mind sparked and spun like fireworks as a new picture of the players and the plot came into focus. With fresh urgency, he snapped on the canvas cover, leaped onto the boards, and raced inside.

Completely soaked, Tony pulled the porch door shut and stood for a moment, dripping on the doormat. He grabbed a beach towel from a wall hook and roughly rubbed himself dry. Then he sprinted inside to face his mother, hands on hips.

"Anthony Dominic, *what* were you doing out on the lake on a day like this?" She pouted. "I was nearly mad from worry!"

Tony felt the familiar tug of her feints. "Ma, I was perfectly safe in the boat. I just didn't expect the weather to change this fast."

She sensed an opening and dug in. "You mean to tell me you didn't know there was a hurricane coming?" she scolded, eyes flashing. "Did you once think about me?" Her lip quivered.

Like a thousand times before, her tears cowed him. "Sorry," Tony mumbled through clenched teeth, furious that she still treated him like a child, and at himself for letting her.

She took a moment of comfort from his apology, sighed

theatrically, and was on to her next worry. "Your father's still at the scrapyard, preparing for the worst.

"Thank God the handyman came and secured everything against the storm, or you'd be running around in the rain all evening catching your death. Now go change your clothes, and come have supper," she commanded.

"Be right there, Ma," he fumed. *Two more years and I'm out of here for good.*

Tony's thoughts turned to Jake as he pulled on a fresh shirt and shorts. How was he faring on the mountain? He raked his damp hair in the bedroom mirror and startled at the worry in his eyes.

He marched to his seat at the table, grabbed a fork, lopped off a chunk of meatloaf, and stuffed it into his mouth. He splashed grape soda into a glass and chugged it.

His mother huffed and slapped the table. "Will you slow down before you give yourself indigestion?"

Tony glared at her and chewed a little slower. The wind flung rain against the windowpane, filling up the silence between them.

He felt like a fool. Jake had been right about everything; Eddie's guilt was written on his face. How would Jake clear his name now? Would Eddie ever see justice for what he'd done, when his puppet master of an uncle knew how to play these Highlanders until they screamed for mountain blood?

His mother's prattling pierced his troubled thoughts. "That poor Van Hoek family. I wonder how they are getting along. Such nice people. Do you remember the birthday party we had for you and Karla?"

What if Jake went after Eddie? And if he killed a Schmidt in this county...

His mom got louder. "I'm sure she could use a friend right now. Why don't you see about her?"

Tony needed to warn Jake off before he went too far. He couldn't pick up the phone; he had to get to Jake now.

Antoinette Marsala stared at her son. "Are you listening to me at all? Your eyes are shooting around your head like the Fourth of July. What is the matter with you tonight?" She wore the same pained expression she affected during the final act of the Metropolitan Opera's Saturday radio broadcasts.

"Nothing." He needed to do something right now, before everything spun out of control.

"This is a night you should curl up with a good book," she said.

Tony'd had enough of her meddling. He bolted upright, knocking over his chair. "I should see if the neighbors need help before the storm," he declared.

"But Tony, it's already here," said Mrs. Marsala on a rising note.

Tony set the chair upright, avoiding her eyes. "I'll be fine, Ma," he said firmly.

"Oh, well, then, pay a call on Karla. You know, she was always sweet on you."

Tony exploded. "You don't get it, Ma. You just don't get me at all!" He strode to the entrance and dug through a rack of foul-weather gear.

Mrs. Marsala rose, arms beseeching the empty air, like her favorite soprano in a scene-stealing aria. "What is it I don't get? Tony!"

He pulled on a plastic poncho, grabbed his keys from the entry table, and hurried outside. The screen door banged behind him, ricocheting twice more in the surging tempest.

Sheriff Schmidt swiveled to face a gallery of grim faces. In his hand was the day's edition of the *Mountain Observer*. He threw it on his desk. "Van Hoek Murder Still Unsolved," the headline brayed.

The sheriff surveyed his officers. "The paper's asking why it's been four days without an arrest. Bad press is the last thing I need two months before an election, with our coroner waiting to pounce.

"Men, Leo Brandt hasn't shown himself to be particularly loyal to the people of this county. He's expressed his...suspicions about what some of us did here before the war."

The wall of uniforms rustled, but no one spoke. Their sheriff pressed tongue to cheek. "A Sheriff Brandt with the power of subpoena might go digging for dirt." Drumming rain filled the silence. "Ask yourselves, gentlemen: Will you be remembered as heroes by your people, or the cowards who sold us out to the mixbloods?

"Tonight is our best chance for a successful collar. This herd can be difficult to track, but on a night like this, we can surprise them in their hovels." He shot a look at each drawn face before him. "I want someone in cuffs before the papers go to press tomorrow. Do I make myself clear?" His officers looked like he'd just canceled Christmas.

"I never promised you a nine-to-five job. So we're gonna earn our overtime tonight and make the citizens of this county proud of our department."

His deputy cleared his throat. "Sir, you're talking half the county, and a good part of the next. With our numbers, how we gonna drop a dragnet big enough to catch these guys?"

"Simple, Deputy. We're gonna use our heads," Otto said with growing impatience.

"Meaning?"

Otto regarded DeVrees as he might an impertinent child. "Silas Mueller is implicated, and we know where his clan lives. One of them, name of Jake DenBleyker, was here yesterday with a tall tale about Mueller, and making threats against law enforcement. Which makes him my second suspect," Otto trumpeted. Heads nodded.

"They live uphill a piece from the murder scene. So we're gonna do ourselves a good old-fashioned ambush. We take two vehicles and go in pairs. Two approaches to the homestead give us the advance and backup we need to flush 'em out."

Officer Wygant raised a finger, and Otto granted the interruption. "Sheriff, some parts of town are already flooded out—"

"—and that's why we're making this collar *tonight*, officer, while these mountain scum got worse odds of getting away than a Jew has getting into heaven," Schmidt said tartly.

Wygant muttered under his breath.

"Deputy DeVrees rides with me, and Officers Wygant and Buehler, second car. We take the last turnoff before the mountain pass, and you'll take the first after. Now let's get a move on. We ain't seen the worst of this storm."

Tony sped toward Blackman's Ridge, blood pounding in his ears. Rain exploded on the windshield, turning the road into a bleeding watercolor. He scanned the local hangouts for Jake's pickup, but there was no sign of him.

He almost missed the turnoff, half hidden behind a screaming rig that pushed the Falcon sideways from the force of its airstream. He struggled to get traction in the slurry that flowed off the mountain.

Sunset wasn't for another thirty minutes, but the feeble light that penetrated the woods was no better than dusk. Tony turned on his headlights, and fog instantly blotted out the way forward. He switched them back off and resumed his crawl up the mountain. His hopes sank that he'd make it to Jake before dark.

Sheets of rain made every fork inscrutable. He tried to remember the twist and grade of the route he'd taken to Jake's house on Monday, but each tree and clearing blended into the rest. His chest vised.

After just missing a huge boulder, Tony lurched to a stop. He fumbled in the glove compartment for a flashlight. He clasped its shaft and slid the switch: nothing. *Shit.* He secured the snaps of his poncho and shoved the door open with a groan.

The mountain thundered like a mighty waterfall. The tempest pelted from every direction and threw shrouds of steam into Tony's path. Tree limbs thick as telephone poles flailed wildly against the sky.

He stumbled to the car's trunk, flung it open, and grabbed a ski pole. He felt his way forward one footfall at a time, the incline guiding him. The storm soon snuffed out the sky, and the forest lashed him unawares. He wished he'd worn more rugged gear. He found few firm footholds; mud slicked his sneakers and spattered his poncho.

Worry and dread pulled him uphill, legs and lungs burning. He squeezed his eyes and opened them, but there was nothing to focus his sights. His gut spasmed with fear.

"Jake? Anybody? Can you hear me?" In the deafening chaos around him, he heard a sound like cracking timber. Suddenly the ground beneath him gave way, and he keeled into empty space.

Tony ran fingers over sightless eyes. He lay on his side, cold and wet. He shifted his weight, and fire shot up his shin. The heavy air swallowed his cry of pain.

He noticed a *bwop bwop bwop* and reached toward the sound with one leaden arm. He let it drop, and it splashed up to the wrist. Tony started, and his body seized with pain again. His head thudded against rock. A cold sweat enveloped him, and he started to shake.

How was this happening? How long had he been here? He remembered a slamming impact. He hugged himself and closed his eyes. His felt his chest exploding. He began to sob and pressed himself against the sweaty stone. Water over-topped his shoes.

"Help me! Heeeelp!"

He rose on all fours, pain razoring the injured leg, and dragged himself through the muddy current.

"You have a death wish? Slow the hell down!" Malcolm hollered.

Jake grappled the wheel of his shimmying pickup and vaulted it up the steep drive, the three brothers grazing their heads on the ceiling. Jake threw on the handbrake and marched from the cab without a word, Euel muttering curses behind him.

The three brothers sloshed through pooling waters toward Delfinia, who stood in the doorway and thrust towels at them.

"Take off those clothes right here and dry yourselves," she ordered, eyes bright with pride. "You done a kindness helping Old Lady Ten Eyck afore the storm."

"*In* the storm," Euel corrected.

"Let your mama give you all a kiss." They each dropped their sopping laundry at the door, toweled down, and offered a cheek.

The aroma of dinner drew them inside. Euel followed his nose to the bubbling stew on the stove, and his mother was right behind him, smacking his back. "Get now, you get! You'll have yours soon as you're cleaned up and into dry clothes."

Malcolm and Euel marched upstairs. Jake rubbed a shoulder and wheeled his arm. His mother looked at him with concern.

"You hurt, Jacob?"

"No, Mama, just sore from all the moving and sawing and nailing the old lady wanted done." He looked past his mother with hollow eyes.

"I thought you was getting yourselves in for a heap of work. That woman can squeeze blood from a turnip." Her eyes twinkled. "You stay right here. I got something for them aches."

Delfinia reached into the oven and removed a rolled cloth that smelled of earth and vinegar. "Now you just sit right here and press this to your shoulder long as you can stand."

She placed the hot cloth on Jake's skin, and he winced.

She frowned. "That's right. Only stings a minute. Then the heat does its work. You remember how much good it done your toothaches?"

"Yes, Mama. But right now I'm appreciating it more than my shoulder do," Jake said, his brows squeezing the bridge of his nose.

Jake rose and paced the floor, clutching the poultice to his skin. The wind wailed in the walls and fluttered the lace curtains of the parlor, lit by six scattered hurricane lamps. He strode to the glass and peered into blackness.

He felt weary to his bones. Too much had unraveled too fast. For an instant, Jake envied Silas, released from the enmity that swirled around the mountain, that had Jake in a chokehold.

Jake tasted the bitter certainty that the break with Tony had been inevitable. Defying his own painful experience, he'd played it by Tony's rules, blown through all the warning signs, and been spurned like always.

How had he fooled himself yet again?

He'd thought Tony had seen that he was another lonely soul like him, wanting what he wanted. But in the end, it hadn't been enough. How could it?

Tony moved unhindered through his world; how could he understand how it feels when the world fences you in and never lets up, and you're so weary for a way out, you let the world dash your dreams?

What were dreams anyway, but a tease, a dangerous distraction from survival? Once and for all, he had to accept that there was no place he could be completely himself.

Except...

At the red pond. The secret cove. The lake in moonlight.

With Tony.

Jake's eyes stung. He tried to shake off the heretical thought.

No! He'd pushed Tony away because he didn't, *couldn't* understand Jake, just like all the other men—no, *every*one—off the mountain. And on it. Even his own family.

Because he'd buried who he really was.

He'd spent years at the bars playing a parody of himself, a goddamn gay Li'l Abner, and then rejected Tony because he couldn't deal with the hillbilly inside.

His shoulders heaved, and he cried for all the hurt and fear and distain that dogged him every day, that he'd visited on

Tony, that had compounded his own suffering. Pain he felt powerless to undo.

A hand squeezed his shoulder. He turned to find Euel looking at him with concern. "I know how you feel, Jake. Like someone cut off your arm." Euel's eyes were hard. "Ain't no justice for us but what we bring ourselves."

Jake wiped his damp cheeks. "And then what? Where does it end, Euel?"

Euel released Jake's shoulder. "That's up to God. A man must act or hang his head in shame." His face flamed.

Jake thought about his brothers, his mother, the Van Hoeks and Schmidts, and everyone who grieved or feared them, and the Highlands suddenly seemed to him like a cauldron of misery. He felt a lacerating dread that the bloodlust over Silas would only consume his clan and smother him alive if he didn't find a way out.

Thoughts of Tony brought waves of desire and remorse. He pushed out to the porch and cut through the grass to the barn in the downpour. Jake threw open the door, eyes raking the room. He strode to his worktable and ran his fingertips over the vised walking stick, felt the snake's smooth body coiled around the shaft.

He gripped the cane, squeezed his eyes shut, and moaned. He grew dizzy from the blackness churning inside him. How could he possibly make right all that had gone wrong?

Grampa, help me find the way.

From the chaos of his thoughts, the familiar voice came.

Honor the Manitou in you, and you honor the Creator.

He'd taken it on faith from Grampa that Coyote's spirit was in him, but he'd never fully understood what that meant. Could it mend Jake's fractured soul?

You possess all that you need to fulfill the Creator's plan.

But it's never been enough, Jake protested.

Enough to be something you are not?

Jake chafed at the notion. *What other choice do I have?*

The choice you believe in.

Jake fought down the hot fear that rose from his belly. *Then what do I do?*

Be who you are.

It's too hard! A sob pried its way past Jake's pressed lips.

Harder than it was for Coyote?

A child's hot tears coursed his cheek to the line of his jaw. *It wasn't my fault he died!*

No, not anyone's fault; it was a choice. Coyote's choice. He commended his spirit to you so you could become who you are meant to be.

But who is that? Jake keened through gritted teeth and rocked the unyielding cane until the whole worktable shook.

You will not find answers with more questions. There is power in choosing. Begin, and you will know your path.

Jake petulantly stamped his foot. *But* what *path—?*

Look inside yourself!

"But how—?" Jake's voice landed in empty silence. His hands and arms were on fire; he released Grampa's cane.

He'd never felt so alone. Grampa had made it clear no one else could help him. Look inside? Choose? Begin? What did he mean?

He batted away his own questions.

No more buts.

He wouldn't waste Coyote's gift. He would do right by him, by his Creator, be true to himself, let that truth guide him. Maybe that was the only answer he needed. Maybe that was the path.

Jake found his brother brooding on the porch. "Euel, there's somewhere I got to go."

Euel squinted. "Ain't no place a sane man got to go on this night, brother."

"Just tell Mama I'll eat when I get home."

Euel studied Jake. "Steer clear of trouble. Dark spirits be riding this storm." Jake turned away, grabbed a raincoat, and headed into the night.

He leaned hard on the gas pedal, wipers churning, and felt his way down the mountain's muddy gullies. Finally, the pickup bounced hard and waggled as it hit pavement on the county road, gaining traction, the crackle of rain on the cab drowning out all else.

After a dip, the road rose to meet a pair of high beams, low to the ground, rushing at Jake, followed by two distinct blasts of steam. Jake's eyes darted to his rear mirror. Taillights flickered. He braked hard, screeched to a halt at the shoulder's edge, and hunched over the wheel.

Two vehicles. One pair of cats-eye taillights.

Jake swung the pickup around and sped after them. He had too much ground to make up in the smothering storm; he'd have to go on instinct. He flipped open the glove compartment and checked for bullets. Then he felt the floor behind him for the shaft of his rifle.

Jake wrenched the wheel and skidded into a blind breach in the trees. The truck chewed mud and gravel, branches thrashing metal as the chassis plunged through walls of foliage. The mountain could put nothing in Jake's way.

Abruptly, the forest parted at a crossroads, and Jake slammed the brakes before a blinding white barrier in the darkness.

Tony's car.

Jake grabbed a flashlight, leaped from his pickup, and sprinted to the Falcon. A feeble light seeped from the windows. He yanked a door, saw the open glove compartment. He reached across the seat to check behind; nothing. He walked to the trunk, lid ajar, and found a jack, jumper cables, and a single ski pole.

Tony had left here in a hurry. Why was he out here in this whirlwind?

Jake took the ski pole and probed his way uphill. After an interminable climb, the pole suddenly dipped. He squatted by an opening and felt with his hand. The dirt fell away with a light touch. A fresh sinkhole.

Jake wasn't surprised; in mine country, where shafts and tunnels spread in every direction, a big storm could saturate and collapse the roof of the underworld without warning. He'd easily find a few breaches on this night.

As he rose, his pole clanged. He shot his light onto a glint of metal at the edge of the pit. He gasped; it was a match for the shaft in Jake's hand.

"Tony! Can you hear me? Tony, it's Jake!" Jake dropped to his belly and felt his weight sink into the oozing earth. He thrust his flashlight down and swung it around. Rain speared through the light and vanished soundlessly.

Jake edged forward and aimed the light straight down. His stomach lurched. Far below, he saw a surging current. "Hold on, Tony! I'm coming!" Jake scrambled to his feet and resumed his ascent.

Though Jake knew the mountain well, he'd lost his bearings many times in its maze of twisting corridors and sheer plunges; they would quickly overwhelm Tony, he thought, heart battering his chest.

He had to find the closest way in. He swept his flashlight, straining to register a familiar landmark through the slashing rain.

The ruins of the Munsee ironworks emerged from the blackness like phantasms: a waterwheel, wood rims peeling from towering metal hoops; a shattered stone furnace; the tumbled walls of a stable or smithy. A roofless barn loomed to his left.

A few more twists along the brush-choked path, and he saw it: a truss of beams and rods high and wide enough for a horse team and a hopper.

The mine entrance opened from a broad rock face like the gable of a buried mansion. Its iron grate had been repaired too many times, and Jake easily found a point of weakness. With a roar and a wrench of his shoulders, he broke a piece of it open, sending himself flying backward. He heaved the severed bars off his chest and staggered to his feet.

Jake torqued his torso through the hole he'd made, one shoulder at a time. He reached back and grabbed the ski pole and flashlight, and started moving.

Eddie and Hans rolled their vehicles to a stop at dusk in the same clearing they'd left the night of the rumble. Eddie double-checked the El Camino's cab front and back. He felt cold metal crammed under the driver's seat and gasped. If he'd missed Stefan's rifle, Uncle would've put him in the hospital. *But that's never gonna happen again.*

Eddie grabbed the gun, took one last look around, and whacked the door shut behind him. Instantly, he plunged into a swirling deluge. Hans got halfway out of his car and called out to Eddie, who seemed not to hear.

Eddie moved aimlessly in the wind-driven rain. He heard a door slam, Hans cursing.

"We done what your uncle sent us here for! Where the fuck you going?" he protested.

Eddie kept meandering. The shifting storm cloaked each

landmark until he was upon it. All at once, the ruined forge emerged, breathing iron and sulfur like a living thing, stoking the sky. Eddie felt himself shudder before its power, and the feeling brought with it Uncle's image.

There was something besides Uncle's stupid mission he needed to do tonight, something that had been needling him for too long. He had to prove that he was done being the dog on Uncle's leash. He had to stop setting the same trap for himself and waiting for Uncle's blows to land. He had to act like he was his own man, and if he didn't do it right now, he was going to explode.

He hadn't noticed Hans following him, and his voice startled Eddie. "I don't like this place," Hans said. "Why are we still here?"

Eddie's words broke through a cinch of fear. "I got to find the mountain fucker."

"What the—?" Hans raised his voice in agitation. "We're already soaked to our nuts!"

Eddie frantically swatted the air at Hans.

"What?" Hans's voice shook.

"Shh! I heard something." A voice. He tightened his grip on Stefan's hunting rifle.

"C'mon, man, let's get outa here," Hans pleaded. Eddie shone his flashlight into Hans's eyes to compel his silence, and saw his own alarm reflected there.

Eddie clenched his heaving chest. "This is our chance, Hans." he said, with a confidence he barely recognized.

"For what?"

"Could only be an ape-man out in this storm, and if it's the other ape who attacked Stefan, we got to take him out, on our honor." Eddie had practiced Uncle's lie so many times, it had become his. Eddie clenched his leg hard but couldn't keep it still.

Eddie followed the sound as it moved, and lifted the rifle to his shoulder, the metal handle cold in his hand.

"We're *going*, man, " Hans cried out.

What was Eddie doing?

Who was this for?

What do I do, Papa?

10

The roar of the storm quickly ceded to Jake's echoing footfalls. Almost instantly, the tunnel declined, and he steadied himself, one hand against the wall. It felt tacky and moist. He panned his light across the rock, coated in a gray paste, water tracing its surface. He reflexively hunched his shoulders and looked up into a bower of bats.

Jake froze. He had few qualms about the natural world, but he'd always hated bats, maybe because they unfailingly appeared in the sky at the moment evening stole the light, the most melancholy time for Jake, when the day's promise had been denied him again.

Hope was what he needed most just now. He snorted out the stench, gritted his teeth, and sprinted to the tunnel's first crossroads. Straight ahead was a moist pile of stone and earth. The path to his right dropped precipitously and sounded like a filling bathtub.

On the wall's edge to his left, his light caught a chiseled arrow, pointing left. Years ago, hiking through the mines, he had followed similar blazes to the surface, like generations of miners who came before, he'd thought. He let himself relax.

Jake headed left into a ferrous draft. The denser underground air was feeding the storm at the surface. This might help him hear Tony; but the wind would swallow his own calls.

He had to try. "Tony! It's Jake! Can you hear me?" Jake banged the ski pole against rock. He paused and heard only rushing air and the gurgle of water. What if the fall had knocked him out, or worse?

As he moved, the tunnel sloped away from his feet, and soon his boots splashed water.

"Tony, I'm coming!" he hollered. Jake tripped on rubble, and his head made hard contact with the wall. His temple throbbed.

He rubbed the pain with his palm, and his hand came up sticky. He wiped the blood on his pants. He shoved the light into his pocket, yanked off his T-shirt, and wrapped it around his head. He felt for the pole, hitched it through his belt, and steadied himself. The water was now up to his ankles.

"Tony, make a sound! Let me know you're okay!"

Each new shaft and byway seemed to stretch time; Jake struggled for his bearings. He swung his light wildly, throwing sepulchral images across the rock, and the sudden thought of Tony entombed here stole his breath. Only tricks of the light, he assured himself.

Except that the light now caught a body poking above a pool, straight ahead.

"Oh, shit! *Shit!*"

He thrashed toward Tony, and lifted his head. When Jake patted his cheeks, water dribbled from the corner of his mouth. Tony's pulse was weak; his eyelids briefly fluttered.

Jake pressed Tony against his heaving chest, lifted him

under the shoulders, and dragged him out of the muck. Jake grunted and swore as his skin grazed stone. He groped for the flashlight and swung it around them. Three maws trailed off into black.

The blood sang in Jake's ears. Which way out? He struggled to feel the press of air, the pitch and dip of the earth. He hoisted Tony onto his shoulder, and lurched through the nearest opening, calves straining up an incline. But water continued pouring over his feet, and soon the rise leveled out.

His elders had taught him to respect the mines, to never wander them alone, come equipped for anything, and always mark the path out. Now, with Tony's life on the line, he'd thrown out caution. Had he made a fatal choice?

Panic and Tony's dead weight made progress agony. The water soon covered Jake's knees and continued to rise. After an endless interval, the air grew liquid, and he heard a sibilance.

An exit. The closer they came, the more the pool churned around them. Without warning, Jake's feet left the ground, and he was treading water, struggling to keep Tony's face above it.

The force of the current spun him, and he lost his bearings. He sensed something collapsing below, pulling them in. Jake roared and propelled them to the outer rim of the vortex.

Under the surface, something snagged his shoulder, and he shot out his free hand and seized it: a root. He caught his breath, rain spattering his face. And now he grasped the extent of their peril.

The same force that had opened the mountain's flank had pummeled its way to the tunnel's floor—a second sinkhole inside the first, sucking everything toward it. The water swiftly dropped below Jake's handhold, which slipped from his grasp.

There was no time to lose. Jake maneuvered Tony, arm over shoulder in an iron grip. With his free hand, Jake felt the sodden earth above him for a rock or root, as patches of earth gave way.

Panting, he moved at a maddening crawl, muscles screaming, until finally he felt the lip of an opening. And then, whispering "sweet Jesus," he clenched his whole body and sprang them both over the edge in a howl of agony.

Jake laid Tony flat and felt the side of his neck. *Fuck!* He pressed Tony's chest three times and put an ear to his lips: nothing. He felt inside Tony's mouth and scooped out something thick and muddy. He pumped Tony's chest again, then tilted Tony's head back. He clamped Tony's nose and lips and pumped air, faster and faster, chest, mouth, chest.

Winded, Jake shook Tony's torso and keened wildly. "Fight for me, Tony! Breathe! *Now!*"

Tony's body convulsed, and water poured from his mouth. He wheezed air and coughed violently. Jake set his arm under Tony, tilted his chest forward, and smacked his back. More liquid trickled from his lips.

The coughing finally subsided. Jake held Tony to him, felt him breathe and shiver, and stroked his hair. He felt Tony tense, and his leg jerked.

"Oh, thank God!"

Sudden bolts of light stabbed Jake's eyes, and he threw himself over Tony. Moving just his arm, he reached behind to where he'd fastened his pole, swiped empty air, and swore to himself. Through bright, overlapping halos, Jake made out a figure, gun drawn, opposite three other silhouettes.

"My, my, if it isn't Jake DenBleyker. What a happy coincidence." The voice was sickeningly familiar.

"What do you want?" Jake heaved his words from burning lungs.

"Ain't you heard, boy? There's a killer on the loose. And fact is, you fit him to a *T*. If I were you, I'd put both hands where I can see them, nice and slow. Don't make me have to use this," Sheriff Otto Schmidt said, waggling his revolver at Jake.

Jake released his grip on Tony with effort, and raised both hands over his head.

"Now *get up*." Schmidt snarled.

Jake's gaze shot from Otto to Tony. "He near drowned, and his leg's hurt. Help him!"

"I'm giving the orders here," Otto snapped. "Deputy DeVrees, cuff this man on probable cause for the Van Hoek crimes." DeVrees swung Jake's hands down and behind him, securing them with a sharp steel click.

Anger and pain throttled Jake's words. "I done nothing wrong!"

The butt of Otto Schmidt's revolver slammed Jake's nose, and it gushed blood. "Boy, I'd advise you to cooperate," he snarled.

Pain bloomed across Jake's face as he slid to the ground. "You got...no proof...I got...rights."

Otto Schmidt laughed. "What rights does a killer have?"

Jake snorted blood, chest heaving. "Tony Marsala...please... help..." His tongue grew thick, and each word knifed between his eyes. "Car...downhill..."

"Wygant and Buehler, ride Marsala to the hospital in your cruiser, and Deputy DeVrees, hitch a ride with them to Marsala's car, and follow them down. I want status on the boy in the morning. Understood?" His officers nodded.

"All right, men. See you back at HQ. I'm taking this one down for booking." The three officers scattered. Otto wiped the rain from his sights, wrenched Jake by the shoulder, and started for his cruiser. Splashing footsteps stopped him short. Before him, Eddie and Hans emerged from the forest.

"Uncle?" Eddie's face dropped like a curtain.

"Why aren't you both home?" Otto barked. Hans looked at Eddie.

Eddie felt his newfound resolve buckle. "Well, we brought the El Camino, just like you said, and then we heard someone in the woods, and I thought it might be the killer, so we went after him," Eddie said, patting the rifle slung on his shoulder.

"And here you are, accomplishing nothing, as usual." Eddie stiffened. The sheriff forced Jake upright and spun him around to face Eddie. Hans took two steps back.

"So now you have him, Eddie, right where you want him!"

Eddie looked at Jake, his face and chest a spreading delta of blood, like the image of Stefan seared in his mind. His leg twitched.

"For Chrissakes, Eddie, show some balls!" Otto bellowed.

With a yelp, Eddie thrust his boot into Jake's groin, doubling him over. His eyes reflexively shot to Otto, looking contemptuous, and fury ignited in Eddie's chest. Otto dragged Jake to the patrol car, heels raking damp leaves. He stuffed Jake into the back seat, the storm pelting him through the open door.

Eddie stood hunched against the thrashing wind, his body tensed for Uncle's next command or rebuke. Otto turned into the storm to speak.

"Listen good, Eddie. You and Hans are in my office at opening tomorrow to make a statement, and the facts will fit the arrest," he said, shouting out each word as if Jake weren't three feet away. "Understood?"

Eddie knew the script, but his tongue refused to follow Uncle's command. Rain drummed metal. A gale of emotions buffeted Eddie. He was done groveling, no more *Yes sir, sorry sir, it-won't-goddamn-happen-again sir*. Water coursed his jaw.

Otto frowned. "Lost your tongue, boy?"

"I'm not your *boy*."

Otto went for Eddie and grabbed his shoulder. "Until you start cleaning up your own shit, you will do as I say, *boy*," he spat.

Eddie's hand tightened around the rifle handle. "This is the last time. Then I'm *done*."

Otto whispered, "You're done when I say you are." He threw his weight into the cruiser and gunned it, splattering Eddie and Hans in mud.

Thursday September 1st

Karla's hands shook so hard she could barely button her blouse. She studied the bruised face in the mirror. Today, she would forgo the heavy makeup she'd worn since Sunday. She had to set the record straight.

The story she'd given the sheriff yesterday was eating her up. Karla had told her mother the truth last night, and she had responded with disbelief, insisting that the trauma of events had Karla confused.

Then Karla's secrets had all tumbled out in a stream of tears. Krista Van Hoek had hugged Karla and whispered, *"Leave it be or things could get ugly."*

But it was too late for that. She braced herself against the sink, examined the angry marks around her eyes and cheeks, the cut on her forehead. Could the way forward be any clearer?

She saw now that desperation to escape her small-town fate had made her blind to everything wrong with Eddie. It had led directly to the trash-choked street in Jersey City, the unmarked door with three locks, the sharp-nosed man with darting eyes who had thrust cold steel inside her and excised her illusions.

After the abortion, she and Eddie had fought even more than before. He'd used their secret to cow her. And she had stayed with him, longer than she should have, afraid he would ruin her.

No more. Grim resolve stared back from the glass. Eddie had blackmailed her. Time, then, for a reckoning.

Krista and Karla Van Hoek were waiting for Otto at his office at half past eight. He entered, turned to them, and snapped on a smile. Karla's cheek twitched, and her mother stared stonily ahead.

"Krista, you have my condolences." She squeezed her eyes against Otto's bromide. He shifted his attention to Karla. "I know this has been a difficult week for you—"

"Your case is a big lie!" Karla blurted out.

Otto shot a look at DeVrees, who arched an eyebrow. "Ladies, would you please follow me to my office?"

The hall door buzzed open, and the two women followed three steps behind Otto. He guided them to seats before his office desk. Everyone cleared their throats; Mrs. Van Hoek folded and unfolded her hands in her lap.

Otto knitted his brows and laced his steely gaze with concern. "There's been a break in the case. We apprehended Jake DenBleyker last night, and he's confessed to the crimes."

"That's impossible!" Karla glared at the sheriff.

Krista clutched Karla's hand, but her daughter shook her off, curling her fingers into fists. Krista looked at her with a mix of pride and dread.

Otto leaned in, eyes sharp. "Is there some...detail you would like to add to your previous signed statement?" He lingered on the final two words.

Karla reddened. "It's Eddie's fault Stefan and Silas are dead."

Otto's neck reddened. "What are you saying?" he asked, riding his ire.

"It didn't happen the way he said." Karla held her breath a long moment and then burst out, "Eddie beat Silas to death!"

"Don't tell us you didn't know about your own nephew," Krista snapped.

Otto clucked his tongue and threw a knowing glance at her. "She's been through so much. And we know how trauma can play tricks with memory."

"I know what I saw, Mr. Schmidt," Karla declared. "It's the truth."

Otto stood abruptly, sending loose papers flying from his desk. "And just what is the truth? Is it the story you gave me yesterday, your imaginings today, or what you'll concoct tomorrow?"

Karla sprang to her feet to meet Otto's blazing eyes and pulled off her large sunglasses, revealing the cut over one eye and purple, yellow, and oxblood welts on the other, down to her cheekbone. "I didn't make this up!" she snapped. "Eddie did it!"

Otto Schmidt leapt up and slammed the door shut. His words were biting. "Miss Van Hoek, we have taken testimony from two eyewitnesses corroborating the signed statement that you yourself gave us. Are you saying that Eddie Schmidt and Hans Kaiser were lying, and so were you? Do you think that will go over well in court?"

"Eddie made me say what I said before. He said that if I

didn't cooperate"—Karla shot a look at her mother—"he would ruin me." Her voice shook.

Otto Schmidt looked sharply at Mrs. Van Hoek. "The events of this week have clearly affected your daughter's reason. A terrible blow, especially after her lost pregnancy, hmm?" Otto said, voice steeped in menace. Krista's lip quivered.

Karla scowled and leaned in close. "I'm not afraid of you." She tossed her hair from her face and tipped up her chin. "You're just like Eddie. A little boy's idea of a man." Her voice was low, assured.

Veins popped out on Otto's neck. "Watch your tongue, miss," he hissed.

Karla turned heel, threw open the door, and faced the corridor. "I know about that Nazi camp of yours, and what happened after," she trumpeted to anyone in earshot. With that, she strode to the outer office, her mother in tow. A seated couple watched wide-eyed as the women marched out.

Otto Schmidt slammed the door to his office and detoured around his desk to a credenza. His hand shook as he poured himself a glass of whiskey. He pinched the bridge of his nose and seemed to shake away some private torment. "Damned dike-jumpers. We crushed you in *five days*," he hissed.

The voice came from far away. "Tony, darling, we're here." Tony blinked rapidly until the smudges resolved into two faces. He answered with a throaty rumble.

"Honey, you've had quite an ordeal," said Antoinette Marsala.

"Try not to talk, son," his father added.

"Wha...time...?" Tony slurred his words.

His mom shushed him. "It's morning. They gave you something for pain, and you're woozy."

"Doctors say nothing's broken, and you'll be home before dinner," Mr. Marsala added.

A chair scraped closer on the other side of the bed. He turned toward the sound, and pain shot through him. He winced, and a warm hand covered his own. He looked up into hooded blue eyes framed in blond hair.

"Karla?" he managed.

Her drawn face crumbled. "Tony...I'm so sorry."

Tony squeezed her hand. "It's not your fault."

"What happened to you?" Karla squeaked.

Tony wrestled with his clouded thoughts, and shrugged.

"Where's...Jake?" He strained to sit up, eyes scanning the room.

Karla didn't meet his gaze. No one spoke for a long moment.

"Tony, I need to talk to you about last Saturday." Karla's voice wobbled.

"Karla, not now," Krista Van Hoek chided.

Karla spoke over her. "The sheriff's lying about what happened. He's arranged it so Eddie gets off scot-free."

Krista straightened the edges of her dress. "I think Tony needs his rest," she said firmly.

Karla addressed the room. "I need to talk to Tony now. Alone, if that's okay with you, Mr. and Mrs. Marsala."

Antoinette looked at her husband and sighed. "It's been a long night. We should probably get a nap at home before they discharge you later. If it's all right with you, dear."

"Fine, Ma," Tony managed.

"Oh." Sal dug a set of keys from his pants pocket, and placed them on Tony's nightstand. "The police told us they'd left your car here in the hospital lot."

Antoinette leaned forward and kissed Tony's forehead. "We love you," she said.

"Be strong, son." His dad squeezed Tony's arm, and he flinched.

"We'll speak soon, Krista," Tony's mom said, and got up.

"Well then, I guess I'll be going, too," Krista said. "Karla, call when you're done, and Dad will come get you. She gave her daughter a tight smile.

"I won't need a ride, Mother," Karla said firmly. She turned to the Marsalas. "If it's okay with you, I'll stay with Tony, and I can drive him home in his car." She gave her mother a defiant look. "I've got my license now, so I'm legal," she said, directing her cheer to Tony's parents.

Sal and Antoinette looked at each other, then Krista. "If it's not any *trouble*," Antoinette said, as if she meant, *Is it safe?*

Krista Van Hoek shot her daughter a look that said *We'll discuss this later, young lady*, gave Tony's parents a pursed smile, and said, "We're happy to help." All three parents left, and Karla closed the door and sat on the edge of Tony's bed.

She surveyed the bruises and cuts covering Tony's head and neck and winced. "How do you feel?"

Tony pushed out his words like boulders. "Everything hurts."

Karla nodded nervously, then seemed to summon all her strength. "Tony, about last Saturday...it's not what you think." She gulped down tears. "Stefan died by accident, and Eddie beat Silas unconscious." Karla gasped for air.

"Raise bed...please," he said. Karla fumbled for the lift button.

"So you're the...only one...telling the truth," Tony said. He studied Karla's quivering mouth, felt her damp hand on his, and braced for worse.

"But that's the thing. Eddie threatened to ruin me over

something in my past. And I panicked." Karla teared up, and it all came rushing out. "So I told the sheriff that Silas and another mountain man attacked me and murdered Stefan and got away. I said exactly what the sheriff wanted to hear, same as Eddie, same as Hans. All lies!"

Another mountain man. Tony was suddenly, painfully alert. "You told the sheriff the second attacker was *Jake*?"

Karla's eyes brimmed. "I gave the sheriff what he needed to arrest Jake for murder!"

Tony's mind raced as everything he believed about justice seemed to collapse like a house of cards. He struggled to speak. "Where is he now?"

"In a holding cell. I went to the sheriff this morning to tell him the truth. He said that Jake confessed to murder. And he made it clear that if I testify against Eddie, he'll say I lied to the police. And he knows things about me he can use to make my life a living hell. But I'm not giving up without a fight."

Tony fidgeted with the tubes coiling his arms. "So how do we save Jake?"

"I think Otto Schmidt's more worried about his reelection than his nephew."

Tony shook his head in confusion. "But what does that have to do with—"

"Tony, the sheriff's hiding something bad." Karla leaned in. "He got sent to a prison camp in World War II. Eddie, too. He told me all about it."

Tony's mouth was a perfect *O*. "So the sheriff protects Eddie to protect himself."

Karla nodded. "And Silas and Jake get framed for murder…"

"…because it's easy to convince a Highlands jury that two mountaineers did it."

"But I made it clear to Otto this morning that I've got his number."

Tony pouted in confusion. "But if it's your word against his, and he calls you a liar, why would anyone believe what you say about him?"

For the first time since Karla got to his room, Tony saw her smile. "Because I know where the proof is."

***

Otto Schmidt switched off the tape recorder and nodded from across the table at his two witnesses. "Well, gentlemen, you can now feel proud that your statements will keep a murderer behind bars." The sheriff looked at his watch, and eyed Hans. "Son, please wait in the outer office."

The sheriff closed the door and turned to Eddie. "We've got a problem with that bigmouth girlfriend of yours." His lips flattened in a hard line.

Heat climbed Eddie's neck. "What do you mean?"

"She's telling people you beat her up, and that you killed Mueller." He spread his arms wide as if to say, *How could you let your little bitch get the best of you?*

Eddie's leg shuddered. "I gave you my word, I'm gonna take care of her!"

Otto fixed his nephew with a leaden stare. "It seems your word means *nothing*," Otto snapped. "This girl has her own ideas. Is she telling the truth, Eddie?"

"She was my girl, and he was screwing her. They both had it coming!" he replied defiantly.

"This isn't just another of your juvenile brawls. We're talking assault and murder, not bloody noses. You didn't think to mention this before now?"

"He stabbed Stefan, and I was defending him, so I didn't think—"

"You didn't *think*. That's your whole problem, isn't it? Didn't you *think* that there would be a body?"

"I hid it real good."

"Not good enough for Mueller's brothers, who know the mountain like you know *nothing*!" Otto smashed his fist on the desk, and it was 1941 all over again, Eddie standing before the *Vorsteher*'s desk.

Uncle knew just how to riddle him with doubt. "I'm sorry, Uncle." Eddie fumed.

Uncle pulled back at his show of contrition. "The story of your sorry life," Otto muttered. "That's not even the worst of it. This morning Karla hinted that she knows about Camp Hochland and Crystal City. What does she know, Eddie?"

She would never. Not with what I got on her...

Uncle's flaming eyes incinerated his thoughts. "*What does she know, dammit?*" he bellowed.

"She started it! She said your voters were Nazis. So I said Roosevelt was worse than Hitler, and she just laughed, so I—I told her about the FBI and Crystal City."

For the briefest of moments, fear scudded across Uncle's face. "You *what*?"

"I was defending us!"

"And now our story is all over the Highlands," Otto said in a gravelly whisper.

"I told her it was a secret," Eddie said from behind gritted teeth.

"Nineteen years after I put you in German camp to make a man of you, here you are, still thinking like a child!" Otto seethed. "Have you forgotten what happened when we came back to Yorkville after the war? Every door slammed in our faces! And you trusted our *secret* with your little Dutch treat?"

Eddie stiffened. "Karla's not like that."

"Fool! Sooner or later, everyone betrays you! And now that

slut has you right where she wants you. You haven't learned your lesson since shitting your pants at camp."

Eddie bolted upright at the umpteenth mention of his mark of shame. "You think you can just bully me forever? You don't think I see who you are under all your hot air? You're terrified I'll go rogue with all of your secrets."

Otto's face purpled. "Make your goddamn Barbie doll shut her trap, and get it right, Eddie, because there won't be another chance!"

"I'm done taking Führer's orders," Eddie said, matching Uncle's tone. He strode out of Otto's office, and as he pushed through the secure door to reception, Mrs. VerHogen barreled past.

"Where's the sheriff? I've got to see him!"

Otto Schmidt looked up from his desk to see Margarete hot on her heels. "I'm sorry, Sheriff—she just barged right in."

"It's all right, Marge." Otto cracked his neck and straightened his tie. "What may I do for you today, Mrs. VerHogen?"

She planted herself in front of his desk. "It's *Schmied*!" Otto shot Marge a look. "They buried secrets under my house. Send men with shovels right away!"

"*Madam,*" he barked, "there's been a hurricane. We've got rockslides, washed-out roads, trees down, and sunk boats, so your problem will have to wait. Marge, escort her out."

Mrs. VerHogen jerked her arm away from Marge's guiding hand and swept her gaze around the room. She smiled bitterly and fixed Otto with beady eyes. "Oh *you're* responsible. Well, you listen to me, *Kommandant.* You'll get your just rewards!"

"Come along now, Mrs. VerHogen," said Marge, encircling the old lady's waist with one arm and pulling her forcefully.

Mrs. VerHogen stabbed the air with a crooked finger as she was led away. "Your! Just! Rewards!" she shrilled.

Sheriff Schmidt slammed the door after her and sank into

his chair. He looked down at the day's paper, swore, and swept it from his desk. From the floor, its headline mocked him: "Unsolved Deaths Dog Schmidt Reelection Bid."

Karla watched an orderly wheel Tony into the lobby, a bag of belongings in his lap.

"The royal treatment," Tony said, rolling his eyes.

Karla smiled. "Better to rest that leg. We'll wheel you to the car."

Once Karla had Tony settled in the front seat, she started the engine and reached for the gear shift. Tony put his hand over hers and squeezed.

"I remembered more about last night. I only made it out alive because of Jake." He explained what he could to Karla. "And now I'm safe and he's in jail, because he saved me instead of himself," Tony choked out.

Karla shushed him. "Let's get you home so you can recuperate."

"I want to go to the sheriff's department," Tony said, his gaze hard and steady.

Karla looked askance. "Are you sure you're ready for this?"

"I've got to get Jake out of there."

Fifteen minutes later, they walked up the steps of the station house, Tony leaning on Karla's elbow. They were barely in the door before Deputy DeVrees disappeared down the hall.

Behind the counter sat a thick matron in a floral dress. Her hair, braided and pinned high on her head, reminded Tony of a cruller. She looked up, and her blank face grew pained.

"Karla, we're all so sad about your brother. How is your mother doing?"

Karla ignored her question. "We're here to see Jake DenBleyker."

The woman pulled her glasses down her nose. "Oh, my dear, only legal counsel and next of kin can visit that— him," she said, wrinkling her nose like she'd just smelled something foul. "Is there anything else I can help you with?" she asked with a treacly smile.

"Please tell Sheriff Schmidt that Karla Van Hoek and Tony Marsala are here to see him," Karla replied curtly.

Before the woman could respond, Sheriff Schmidt strode to the counter and smacked two meaty paws on top of it. "Good day, Miss Van Hoek. Mr. Marsala, I'm glad to see you are on the mend. What can we do for you today?"

"Release Jake DenBleyker," Tony said, more command than request, drugs and ire stilting his speech.

Otto drew himself up and chuckled. "That's not how I run my department."

"We need to see him," Karla said flatly.

His smile mocked her. "A confessed killer forfeits his right to chitchat with friends." He studied Karla. "Frankly, young lady, you shouldn't be involved with that element."

Karla bristled. "What 'element' is that? People not *white* enough for you?"

Otto's expression soured. "Watch your mouth, little lady, or I'll have something to say about you to the Jersey City police."

Karla made a strangled sound and lurched forward, nails swiping at Otto, who stood safely beyond her reach, lips thinning into a smile.

"In any event, we've taken DenBleyker's signed statement," he said matter-of-factly.

"You *monster*," Karla growled.

"You mean you beat it out of him," Tony said, rage sharpening his senses, "because I know Jake would never do that."

Otto drew closer. "Boy, I think you know this Jake a little *too* well. In fact, I'd say he's had an unwholesome influence on you."

Tony's skin prickled. *What else did he beat out of Jake?*

Otto got nose to nose with Tony, his stale breath hot on Tony's face. "How terrible it would be for your family to see your name on my police blotter," he mocked. "For *vice.*"

The flashing lights, the crack of baton on bone, the terror and the shame, it all came rushing back. How much longer would Tony knuckle under?

His voice came ragged. "You've got more to lose than me, so don't push your luck."

Otto bared his teeth. "Oh, is that right? Tell me: What did your father do in the war?"

"He built ships in New Orleans," Tony shot back.

"So that's the soap he sold you?" Otto chuckled cruelly. "Your father didn't build ships. He got locked up for working for *il Duce.* He double-crossed his country."

Tony felt the blood drain from his face. "You're lying!" he shouted. Tears threatened at the edge of sight.

"Your father is a *traitor,*" Otto spat.

The room seemed to tilt, and Tony staggered. "He loves his country. You and your Nazi friends are the real traitors!"

Otto's eyes were BBs. "You try to smear me, boy, and I will ruin your family."

Tony threw an unsteady punch at the sheriff, who swiftly grabbed Tony's arm at the wrist and slammed it palm up against the counter. Tony whimpered in pain.

"One more stunt like that, and you are behind bars in a heartbeat," Otto said, and released him. "I'll be watching, Marsala. No more free passes." He stepped back and smoothed his uniform. "Now, if you'll both excuse me, I have a murder case to wrap up." A slamming door swallowed the clack of bootheels on tile.

Karla paced Tony out into the parking lot.

"There's no way Jake confessed to that bastard," Tony said.

They slipped into Tony's car, and Karla turned to Tony. "Sheriff Schmidt will take us seriously if we have proof that he worked for Hitler."

"*Worked* for him?"

"Before the war, Eddie went to a sleepaway camp near here that his uncle ran. They told everybody it was for German kids to learn about their culture and heritage. But the camp's real purpose was to turn them into little Nazis.

"The FBI shut it down in the war, but they never found the camp records. Eddie said Otto hid them there before the raid. That could be all the evidence we need."

"So you mean...there's proof that Otto collaborated with Hitler?" Karla pressed her lips and nodded. "But how would we even begin to look for this?"

"Eddie took me up there once. I know where it is."

"Then we'll go first thing tomorrow."

Karla squinted at Tony. "With your leg?"

"That's nothing compared to what Jake's going through," he said.

Karla looked dubious. "Are you sure you're up to it?"

"As sure as the sheriff is going to pay for this," he said, and stared unblinking into the late-day haze.

Karla audibly gulped. "Okay, then. We're on a mission."

"Come hell or high water!" Tony cried.

Karla regarded him with amusement and awe. "Well, high water didn't stop you."

Tony closed his eyes and filled his lungs with resolve before his doubts could crowd it out.

The wheels of justice had spun faster than Leo Brandt thought possible. The courier's envelope had arrived that afternoon, the day before Labor Day weekend; he had his search warrants. Lucky he'd caught Judge Flannery in chambers. He'd encouraged Brandt's run against Schmidt and hadn't questioned the coroner's new tack in the Schreier inquiry.

Reopening the Mueller case was more problematic. He knew the DenBleyker family wouldn't allow an exhumation, and Brandt needed more to go on than the word of the victim's incarcerated brother. He'd need three eyewitnesses to recant signed police statements. Inconsistent testimony and no forensics wasn't a winning formula.

Leaving Brandt with the Schreier case, the one charge against Eddie that might stick. Brandt could argue murder one. Even if the charge got bargained down, sending Eddie away for a long time for that crime would more than compensate for passing on a lesser punishment in Mueller's death. But Brandt also was betting that the Schreier evidence led directly to the sheriff's office—which just might reopen the Mueller case.

Now he had to produce proof: the murder weapon, a coconspirator, a new witness. The first likely lay at the bottom of the lake. He knew where his search for the rest began.

Brandt grabbed his warrant and drove up the last street in Iron Run to a white clapboard house, its sky-blue window boxes spilling with geraniums. A gray-haired woman wearing a long-sleeved, ankle-length dress and a tight smile welcomed Brandt in and waved him over to a pastel blue wingback chair. She perched opposite on a matching couch, her bony hands tightly folded.

"Mrs. Kleiber, I do appreciate your cooperation with this vital investigation."

Schmidt-for-Sheriff campaign secretary Marthe Kleiber ran her eyes over the warrant Brandt handed her. Her lips twitched as she studied him a long moment, chest rising and falling. Finally, her whole body seemed to unclench, and she nodded with assurance.

"Anything I can do to help!" she trumpeted. She sprang up, crossed the room to a mahogany secretary, drew out a folder, and cheerfully handed it over to Brandt. Maybe Team Schmidt wasn't in lockstep after all.

"Much appreciated, ma'am," he said, rising. He dug into his jacket pocket and retrieved his card. "If you think of anything that might be relevant to this case, anything at all, don't hesitate to call me, day or night." Mrs. Kleiber nodded gravely, and Brandt took his leave.

"God bless you!" he heard her call after him.

Back in his office, Brandt positioned his lamp over the attendance sheets for the Old Rhinelander rally and thumbed through ten pages of signatures. A reminder that Otto Schmidt held much of the county by the short hairs.

Amazingly, Mrs. Kleiber had taken the trouble to alphabetize the list and staple her typed pages to the signature sheets. Prussian discipline, he mused. Brandt pinned the list to his desk with an index finger. Scheibl, Scheidgen, Schmidt. First name, Eddie. His adrenaline rose. He'd placed Eddie at the scene of the murder: good, but not enough.

He paged back through the alphabet, and something else snagged his eye. It stuck out like spaghetti and meatballs at Oktoberfest. Marsala, Salvatore. The owner of the scrapyard in town. A savvy businessman, backing the winning horse? Brandt frowned.

The sign-in sheets hit his desk with a smack, and Brandt blew air at the ceiling. A Jewish reporter sleuthing around a de facto Bund reunion meant trouble for everyone in the room. All beholden to this sheriff, each at risk should Otto fall from grace. But which of them was ruthless enough to silence Schreier?

Eddie propelled himself out the door and tried to keep up with his racing thoughts. *Get it right, Eddie, because there won't be another chance.* He stopped at the hedge, blood throbbing in his ears, and considered his predicament.

He hadn't told Uncle that Karla knew about the camp records. Would she, *could* she even dredge up all that? He had to make her understand that he could match her threats, that spilling secrets could destroy all of them.

But he had to keep her on his side, and not just to save his own skin. He didn't know what he would do if she didn't want him anymore.

Eddie slipped past the hedge and padded across the lawn like it was a minefield. He stepped up to the tiny wooden stoop, stood at the rust-red door, and stared at the wooden plaque that proclaimed JeSUS iS Lord in jumpy brushstrokes.

Eyes closed, he positioned his fist before him, took a breath, and knocked. He felt the boards under him tremble with footsteps, heard the creak of the door. He opened his eyes to see Mrs. Van Hoek peering from the gap. "What is it, Eddie?"

"Hello, Mrs. Van Hoek. I need to talk with Karla." The stoop groaned under Eddie's shifting weight.

She eyed him warily. "She's...not well."

"It's okay, Mom." Karla stepped forward, and her mother shrugged and retreated.

"Can we talk someplace?" Eddie extended his hand, and Karla retreated in equal measure.

She crossed her arms and stood on her back foot. "Here is good."

Eddie put weight on his unsteady leg. "So, um, I've been thinking about you...How're you doing?" He tapped a fist against his palm over and over, like a catcher waiting for a pitch.

Karla tossed the blond mane from her face and studied him coldly a long moment. "Eddie, why are you here?"

His fist now made a smacking sound. "Karla...I know you're real upset with me right now—"

"Since when do you care how I feel?" Her words throbbed with anger.

"Baby—I'm sorry about Saturday. And, well...everything. And I—I need you to know how much I still love you." Eddie grabbed his pounding fist and held it in a white-knuckled grip.

Karla exploded in bitter laughter. "Do you really think that after everything, I'd take you back?" She made to close the door, but Eddie threw his shoulder into the gap, and she gasped.

"Listen, Karla. I know you hate my uncle, and you're mad at me now, but...you can't go digging up the past. A lot of people could get hurt."

"More than you and Otto have already hurt?" She pushed against the door, but Eddie gave no ground.

"Please, Karla. Promise you'll stay away from the camp. 'Cause if you go there, I don't know what might happen...to us," Eddie said, his tone beseeching. He released the door, and his shoulders slumped. He suddenly felt very small. He reached out his arms across the impossible gulf between them.

"It was never *us*!" she shouted. "It was always what *you* needed, what *you* wanted! To control everything I did, who I could talk to...my own body..." Karla's face twisted with contempt. "Well, you can't anymore!"

"Don't make me tell everyone about Jersey City." He snorted like an angry bull and threw his weight against the door.

"You don't own me now!" Karla pushed hard against Eddie, squealing from effort.

The tremor returned to Eddie's leg, racking his whole body, and his shoulder slipped from the door. He knew what he couldn't accept, and his anger and despair combusted into rage.

"You are finished, you baby-killing bitch—"

The slam of the door felt like the end of everything.

11

Eddie found Hans in his driveway, head buried deep in the engine well of his truck.

"Hans, we got a problem with Karla," he said to his friend's backside.

Hans grunted in time with the rise and fall of his elbow, and then paused. "I thought she was *your* problem," he said.

Eddie shuffled around the grille to face him. "She wants revenge for what happened on the mountain, and that means trouble for both of us."

"But she gave the sheriff the same story we did." Hans's voice was muffled, distant.

"She's got something on my uncle."

Hans wrestled a socket wrench. "What you talking about?" he said, his voice sharp.

Eddie ran a hand over his crown, looked all around, and leaned into the well. "I never told you."

Hans picked up a machinist's hammer and banged metal with short, sharp blows.

"Would you stop that shit and fuckin' listen?" Eddie shouted.

Groaning, Hans extracted himself from the truck. He wiped his forehead and hands with a dirty rag and looked askance at Eddie.

Eddie swallowed hard. "My whole family had big problems during the war."

"And who cares now?" Hans asked.

Eddie saw in Hans's doubting eyes the world's ignorance of his past, and he was eager to explain what it was like to be an innocent kid interned for years, and then pretend it never happened.

"You have no idea," Eddie said, his voice trailing off.

"Try me," Hans taunted.

Eddie told him about Crystal City, and Hans stared at Eddie a long moment.

"I thought you spent the war in Yorkville."

The bile rose in Eddie's throat. "That was our cover story. The FBI swore us to secrecy about the prison camp, or else they'd deport us."

Hans slammed shut the hood of his truck and regarded his friend soberly. "Karla knows all this?"

Eddie nodded. "Uncle thinks she'll go public as payback for Silas Mueller."

Hans kinked an eyebrow. "But your uncle told us we had an open-and-shut case."

"That was before Karla told him she knew what went down at Camp Hochland. I know what she can get her hands on, and it's still up there."

Hans frowned. "After twenty-five years? Rotting in the woods?"

"Hidden in strongboxes under the camp headquarters. Uncle calls it 'our insurance policy.' And he's been watching over it ever since."

Hans squinted. "But why should anyone care if Karla digs up this shit?"

"Because it's enough evidence to ruin a lot of lives in this county, including Uncle's. And *he's* the only thing keeping us out of big trouble with the law."

"You mean keeping *you* out of trouble," Hans said, cocking his head defiantly.

Heat filled Eddie's cheeks. "I ain't going down alone, man. It's my word against yours," he said, more panicked than cocky.

"Against mine *and* Karla's," Hans said, poker faced.

Eddie's throat went dry. He stepped forward, forced a grin, and gave Hans's shoulder a punch. "Hey, man, that ain't never gonna happen, long as we're a team, right?" Eddie's voice wobbled. "We just got to beat Karla to the goods."

Hans crossed his arms and gave Eddie a sour look. "And just how do we get to this buried treasure?"

"Alst' we got to do is slip under the floor of the building and get to the vault, under a big flat stone. A couple crowbars should do the job."

Hans rolled his eyes. "As easy as all that."

Eddie had only ever heard Uncle talk about the vault, but he wasn't giving Hans an out. He squared his shoulders. "First thing tomorrow, we get what we need at Uncle's Berghof and go. You in?" Eddie feigned a left-right boxing combination inches from Hans's jaw.

Hans didn't flinch, and gave Eddie a dirty look. "Do I have a choice?"

Eddie nodded to the truck. "Not if you'd rather bang on that junk heap than rot in jail." No one laughed.

"Like your Uncle would ever let that happen," Hans said.

Doubt needled Eddie. What if Uncle couldn't stop that kind of shit anymore?

Leo Brandt stood over Fritz Weber's shoulder and peered into a glowing red tray. A watery image captured a cluster of suited men and women in dowdy dresses holding steins. Just behind were a server dressed Bavarian style, and to his left, French doors dissolving into white.

Marthe Kleiber had called Brandt late in the day with the tip that a guest at the Schmidt rally had taken lots of snapshots. She'd said that shortly after the sheriff's speech, campaign co-chair Klaus Holtz spotted Weber and made him put away his camera.

Brandt had known that this meant another late night. He sensed the momentum now building in this case could very well carry him right through the long holiday weekend with barely time to shave, but he wasn't going to think about the consequences for his domestic life or election campaign just now.

He noticed a wavy blur, left of the server. It seemed to lead toward an exit to a terrace. Brandt stared at the patch of gray in the fixing bath, grunted, and returned his attention to the same image on Weber's first contact sheet.

He moved the magnifying glass to the next thumbnail print, and the blur became a forearm opening a door. It belonged to a man of average height, light build, in a dark fedora and suit. Weber's image captured a rear view.

Brandt glided the magnifier across another row of images and then backtracked. A second figure headed for the doors. The next shot was clearer: a short, muscular man with a crew cut, in striped short-sleeved shirt and jeans. He looked through the glass door in a way that would conceal him from anyone outside.

Odd. The natural impulse would be to admire the lake views, but the angle of the second man's attention suggested he was focused on something nearer. Next frame: the lagging foot, a work boot perhaps; a denim pant leg; and the door, closing. Then a row of prints with no movement in or out of those doors.

Brandt's focus began to waver halfway through the second contact sheet, when he slapped the magnifier on the counter. "An enlargement of this one, please." A man almost glowing in a white suit and pinstriped shirt, no hat, bald spot, light tennis shoes. Hand on the terrace doorknob.

That made three men out, and none back.

Brandt snatched up the first sheet again, found his place, and put his eye and the magnifier right up to the glowing man. He seemed to study something through a long glass pane, but the man's face bled into the bright view.

The back of the suit jacket seemed to ride up on something beneath it. Brandt moved among the images for a better view of that bulge, but no luck. He circled the two shots of the bright white man.

"I need your best blowup of the figure in these two as well," Brandt said. Weber nodded and got to work. Ten more minutes, and Brandt had his prints. He reached for his jacket, paused, and turned back to the photographer.

"Didn't you say you shot three rolls?"

Weber looked up. "Oh, yes, sorry. I got interrupted before I pulled the third sheet off the drying rack." He reached behind him, and plucked it from clothespins. "There you go."

Brandt took a cursory glance at the sheet and looked at Weber. "Is this the last roll you shot, or the first?"

Weber took the paper from Brandt, studied it a moment, and handed it back. "The first."

Brandt grabbed the magnifier and worked his way slowly backward through the shifting patterns of men and women, then stopped and stared.

"This as well."

No one else seemed interested in the million-dollar views. Brandt left Weber ten minutes later with four eight-by-ten glossies and hurried back to his office.

Friday September 2nd

Tony lay awake in bed, leg aching. His mind had churned through the night with the sheriff's damning words about his father.

His dad had always been tight-lipped about the war. When he'd come home after the Japanese surrender, Tony had been breathless with questions about the great warships his father had built, and Sal had given him a look that said, *Don't ever ask me that again.* What was the truth?

He remembered his father's annoyance at Sunday dinner whenever Tony's dotty Nonno, who'd idolized Mussolini for breaking the Mafia, would mumble the Fascist motto in Italian. Everyone else at the table would have a laugh; Why had it bothered Sal so much?

And something about his dad's business now drew his scrutiny. A few years after his parents bought the lake house, his dad had closed the scrapyard in the city and started over in the Highlands. That meant that during the school year, his dad had made the long commute from home in New York City to Iron Run. Why had he put himself through all that?

Then in '55, there had been the "incident." Dad came home all bandaged up, bruises and scrapes on his face. He closed the business for a week—*For a little R and R*, he said. Tony knew not to ask for explanations, but eventually, he pieced it together.

City thugs had caught up with Dad in the Highlands to collect on some IOU. But nothing bad had happened since, and Tony had thought little more of it. Until now.

Life between the wars had been tough for his parents' generation. Late evenings from Tony's bedroom off of the kitchen, he'd heard the Marsala men talk about earning respect with their fists growing up, and how hard it had been to make it in America when the headlines made all Italians seem like mobsters, bombers, and assassins.

Tony had eventually understood that for strivers like the Marsalas, there was no success without the loan sharks and protection racketeers. Had the Mob punished his dad? Was that somehow connected to Otto Schmidt's innuendo about his father?

Tony put weight on the bruised leg; the pain was bearable. He splashed water on his face, dressed, and tiptoed to the kitchen to stuff a sandwich, soda, and two apples into his backpack.

He edged the front door open and listened for the catch behind him. Leaves shimmered in the day's dim glow. As he walked toward the gate, the Marsala name plate on the fence-post snagged his eye.

Something seemed off; walking up to it, he saw that the last three letters of the family name had been snapped off. Above what remained, the words GO BACK TO had been scrawled in red.

His gut twisted. He spun around and probed the morning air for the malice he sensed around him. His comfortable life, his elite education, his cultivated speech and looks and manners, all that suddenly seemed irrelevant. Here he was just another greasy wop, like his parents and grandparents before him.

Was he crazy trying to take down this sheriff?

His bad leg shook as he approached the car. He lowered himself into the driver's seat and closed the door softly. He let the Falcon roll to the street before starting the engine. The pick and shovel in the trunk clanged as he took the corner.

From the edge of her yard, Karla strode over and slid in next to Tony.

"Are we ready for this?" Tony asked.

Karla flicked Tony a troubled look. "Start driving before I lose my nerve."

They swung around the far side of the lake and took the gravel lane as Karla instructed. After a mile or so, his gaze briefly caught on a gated chalet, a Nazi guard framed in a window. He chalked up the image to drowsiness and an over-active imagination. He needed to keep a cool head.

The path abruptly narrowed, branches stroking the car, and Tony slowed to a stop.

He turned to Karla. "Now what?"

"It's just a little farther to the clearing. There'll be a sign on a tree," she assured him.

The morning lit the mountain taupe and olive. Ahead, the colors intensified, and with one last slap on the windshield, the forest's gloom gave way to a celadon glow.

Tony nosed the car to the center of the open lot, shot through with weeds and saplings thin as his arm. The doors closed like gunshot in the mountain's still. Tony and Karla traded worried looks. From the trunk, Tony retrieved a length of rope, wrapped it around his waist and cinched it, then grabbed his pick and knapsack. He handed Karla a shovel.

"There it is," Karla said, gesturing toward a faded gray

square tacked to a tree. As they got closer, the image emerged: a sprocket, the year *1939*, and above it, the letters *DAB*.

"The camp welcome sign." Karla's smile dimpled with irony.

They walked in silence past roofless cabins and rubble. After ten minutes, a well of light drew them to a large pond choked with algae and bordered by smooth stones. They rested at the water's edge, the stillness punctuated by the rumble of bullfrogs. Tony offered Karla an apple.

"Eddie and I came here when we started dating. Before things went bad." Karla sighed.

Morning thermals climbed the hillside, rustling the trees. Tony and Karla tossed the apple remains into the pond, and a pair of ducks pedaled their way, bills scooping and chattering.

"I wonder who else besides the Schmidts have worked to keep this past buried," Tony said.

Karla considered Tony's words. "The answer to that probably explains a lot about this screwed-up county."

Tony nodded. "Think of it: a Nazi camp, right here, less than twenty years ago. Somebody led the campers, cooked the meals, did the laundry. I wonder if those people still live around here."

Karla dismissed all doubt with a puff of air through pressed lips. "Most people born in this pit never make it out."

Tony grew solemn. "I think a lot of people don't want us to find these records."

They heard a snap in the forest nearby. The ducks cocked their heads. Tony and Karla turned toward the sound and then each other. "We'd better get going," Karla said, in a breathless whisper.

"They beat your dumb ass up here," Otto hissed.

It was only eight o'clock when a bleary-eyed Eddie and Hans got out of Hans's old Chevy and made their way unsteadily to where Otto stood at the door in his absurd Bund regalia, crowbars and rifle in hand, eyes blazing.

"Marsala's car went by at seven thirty. Your little bitch was with him," Otto said.

Eddie stiffened. "Just give me the damn tools and let me worry about the job." Hans toed the gravel. A brittle silence ensued.

With a growl, Otto flung the bars at Eddie's feet and then launched the long gun at his head. In a defensive reflex, Eddie threw up his arm and snagged the barrel midair, scowling. "What the hell?"

"Get up there and *eliminate* them!" Otto boomed.

Eddie snapped wide-awake, senses humming, and looked from the rifle in his hand to Otto, his gaze sharp, unyielding. "I decide what needs to be done," he spat.

"You will do everything that it takes to stop those *Untermenschen!*" Uncle thundered.

Eddie let Uncle's storm blow past him, slipped the rifle over one shoulder, then straightened. "It's 1960, Uncle. Time to wake up from your Nazi fantasies." For the first time he could remember, he matched Uncle's fire and rancor.

"You little punk," Otto sneered, and reached for Eddie's throat, but Eddie was quicker on his feet and dodged him. He grabbed the crowbars, pounded his way to Hans's car, flung the trunk open, and threw in his equipment. Then he got in the driver's side and revved the engine until it belched out a black cloud.

"Eddie, what're you doing?" Hans exclaimed over the din, and jogged toward the car.

Eddie wasn't taking anyone's shit anymore. He had to get

off this merry-go-round, be his own man, no matter what came next. He left Hans and Uncle behind in a spray of gravel and dirt and hurtled around switchbacks toward that cursed place where his life had gone off the rails.

———

July 1941

"Willkommen *to Camp Hochland's 1941 summer season!"*

A teenage boy in a brown uniform with a big yellow X on his armband thrusts his arm out and salutes me at the bunkhouse door. He studies a clipboard.

"I am HausFührer Kurt. You are Edward Schmidt, from Yorkville, age nine, yes?" I nod. "Your first time, I see." Kurt coolly appraises me. "We're not the Boy Scouts. Here, we are molding the future leaders of the Aryan race.

"You'll learn all about Lebensraum *and the Thousand Year Reich, but brains are useless without brawn. In all things, you will compete, sometimes with your fists." I blanch.*

"You'll get the hang of it." Kurt winks. "You might not make friends here, but you'll need allies."

My eyes scout the room for trouble. "Thank you, Ha-haus-furrier."

"Stow your things below bunk twelve, bottom, and get to bed early. Reveille is at five thirty. Be at the parade ground six o'clock sharp for morning ceremonies."

In bed, I toss and turn, heart pounding. Finally, I hear an amiable voice from above. "You must be new here. My name's Günter. Don't feel bad, my first night I just wanted to go home," he chuckles.

My insides unclench for the first time in hours. "It's so different here."

"Like the planet Mongo. But I got used to it. You will, too," Günter assures me. *"Come on, let's get out of here. Lots of stars tonight."* He scrambles down the ladder with his balled-up blanket. I follow my first ally at camp, past the latrines and woods to an open field. He spreads the blanket, and we lie on our backs, staring into the void, insects screaming all around us.

"Bet that's more stars than in all of New York City," Günter says.

But they're too far and feeble, the sky huge and formless, and I am lost in it. I want my room, our block, fences and streets and side-walks. I start to cry.

"What's wrong?" Günter asks.

"I'm scared!" I wrap my arms around Günter and blubber.

"Get off of me!" He shoves me away, grabs the blanket, and jumps up.

"Don't leave me here!" I plead, clutching at his ankles.

"Stay away from me, faggot!" Günter shouts, and hurries off.

At breakfast, Kurt taps my shoulder. *"You're wanted at camp HQ."* My heart skips a beat. Kurt leads me past the drill field and inside a dormered farmhouse. He speaks to a matron, who smiles and shepherds me to a large room labeled VORSTEHER - CAMP DIRECTOR.

Inside, a large, bull-chested man sits at a massive desk, eyes bearing down on me. My jaw drops. *"Uncle Otto! Why didn't Mama and Papa tell me you were in charge?"*

"Because then you would run to me with every problem. And it seems you already have one on your first day at camp." He appraises me sourly. *"Another boy has claimed that you are unfit."*

The word thrusts knives into my belly. *"It wasn't my fault!"*

"Then why did you not confront him? Will you let a misguided moment between boys brand you a degenerate? There is no place in the New Order for weaklings!" Otto's eyes are fierce.

He seizes some invisible prize with his hand. *"Think of it, Eddie:*

to awaken your true nature, subdue your enemies without mercy, have dominion over a debased world...”

It hits me all at once: allies, not friends. compete with your fists. subdue without mercy. “Please, Uncle, I want to go home!” Tears stream down my cheeks, and then I soil myself.

“I will not rescue you again. You will complete your Jugendschaft *training, and you will leave this camp a man. Is that clear?” I nod mechanically. “Now go change your clothes, and do your duty for* Deutschtum*!”*

A tinny broadcast hounds me all the way to the latrines. “A youth will grow up before which the world will tremble...brutal, domineering, fearless, cruel...The free, splendid beast of prey must once again flash from its eyes!”

Eddie jerked the wheel, tires in shrill protest, and barely missed a stone post. He stomped the brake pedal, heart battering his chest. That damn camp had taught him jackshit about life, and set in motion every bad thing that had ever happened to him. He had to silence the loudspeaker in his head. He needed those strongboxes.

Leo Brandt landed on his desk chair at 8:30 and regarded the thick pile of documents he'd swept aside at 6 o'clock the previous day. He'd been working on the Schreier case when two unexpected visitors altered the trajectory of his evening.

It had meant another campaign event postponed, another late dinner of reheated leftovers while Frieda snored. He'd make it up to her, he swore.

With all the roadblocks in his capital cases weighing on

Brandt, he listened with burgeoning interest as his visitors described what they'd found in the woods. Brandt fingered the pages of his cases; so much work with so little to show for it.

But just maybe, at this very moment, in a ditch on a mountain, Otto's tinpot Reich was coming undone, and with it the last obstacles to justice for three grieving families.

Karla moved carefully across the forest floor, ten steps ahead of Tony. He kept his focus on the path between them, as if a false step might spring him into a ghostly trap. He came to a fallen log and paused, insides fluttering.

"Karla! Come look!"

She backtracked and followed his gaze to a decaying wooden rod. He squatted and brushed aside the dirt until he'd exposed the shaft to its end: a pole, and beneath it a crossbeam lying askew. A rotted guy line was threaded through one end and across the transverse shaft.

Tony clawed and swiped the loam and leaves to expose a rope that led to a faded swath of fabric. He shook the panel free of the dirt, held it taut, and gasped at a ringed swastika.

His fingers recoiled as if the flag had seared them. He leaped to his feet, rubbing his hands, and stood alongside Karla. For a moment, they both stared at the ground in silence.

"This makes it pretty hard to deny the truth," Tony said.

Karla shrugged. "Otto hasn't been hiding it all that well. That big log house we passed at the start of the camp road? Eddie says that's his shrine to Hitler, with a big Nazi flag around back. And it's his lookout for snoops like us."

Fear sizzled under Tony's skin. The Nazi he'd seen in the chalet window hadn't been a ghost. "So why has no one stopped us yet?" he asked. The sigh and rustle of the forest only amplified his unease.

Karla locked eyes with him. "The sooner we get the strong-boxes, the better."

They pushed through dense woodland that thinned to saplings and then a clearing of toppled structures and weed-choked gravel. In its center stood a hulking mansion, gambrel roof partly collapsed, empty dormers watching over the ruins.

They advanced to the mansion's porch; the entry door lay across it like a gangway. Tony conjured row upon row of stormtroopers goosestepping out of the building's shadows, clattering across these broken planks, grinding his world to dust.

He shivered. "If Hitler had made it to New York, everyone from this place would have been there throwing rose petals."

They clambered over the fallen door and peered inside an open vestibule. "This is where Otto ran the whole show," Karla said.

"A twisted boot camp," Tony said, scanning the murky recesses.

Karla looked at Tony. "Are we ready?"

Tony swallowed hard. "For Stefan and Silas," he said.

"And Jake," Karla added. Tony tightened against a flood of feelings and nodded.

Past the entry, shattered beams and shingles lay every-where. Woodwork dangled overhead. Tony motioned for Karla to stay back and searched for firm footing. He inched his way forward in the half-light until finally vanishing from view.

Karla peered into the gloom. "Maybe this wasn't such a good idea. Tony?" she called from the doorway.

"We have to try," Tony replied, not at all convinced of his own urging. He pricked his ears; the building sighed and groaned like a ship at sea. He felt a malicious presence and girded himself against the instinct to bolt.

He thought of Jake in a prison cell, his life in the hands of the man he'd come here to thwart.

Jake, I swear I will make you believe in justice again.

Tony filled his belly with resolve and unhitched the pick from his belt. Grasping the head, he probed the floor with the butt, wood splintering and cracking with each tap. Then the tool's shaft plunged right through the floorboards, and a snapped plank landed beneath him with a muffled thud.

"Tony!" Karla cried from the threshold.

A few creaking steps, and he reappeared in the foyer. "It's not safe."

"No, it sure ain't." A sharp click followed the familiar voice.

Tony and Karla turned to find Eddie, rifle in hand. "What are you doing here?" he demanded.

"I think you know, Eddie," Karla said.

"I need those papers. And then, I'm—I'm through with Uncle and all his bullshit."

"You don't get to devastate two families and then just walk away," Tony said.

"We have to stop Otto once and for all," Karla said, her voice hard.

"Karla, those files will destroy me," Eddie said.

"What more could they do to you that you haven't already done to yourself?"

Eddie tilted the rifle down. He panned his sights across the rubble-strewn fields, then squeezed his eyes against them. "This camp...it turned me into one of *them*. They beat the kid outa me. And everyone ever since been telling me that my troubles is all my own fault." Eddie's face contorted.

Karla felt a twinge of compassion for the lost boy in Eddie, but it quickly withered before her resolve to see both Schmidts held accountable.

"You're just afraid that if we get those papers, you'll lose your protector," Karla snapped. "You knew all along what he was hiding. Did you really think he could keep it from the world forever? That he would always be there to rescue you?" Karla's eyes flamed.

Eddie wiped his nose on his wrist. "Baby, take all the papers and do what you want to my uncle, just say you love me again." Sweat and tears trickled down Eddie's face.

Karla studied him, unmoved. "We can't change what's happened, Eddie. All we can do is try to make amends and move on."

"It's not too late for amends!" Eddie pleaded, eyes wide.

Karla thrust her bruised cheeks at Eddie. "I told my parents about Jersey City, and I told the police what you really did on the mountain. And now I'm going away to college. I'm moving on, Eddie."

The rifle wavered. "Karla, I love you more than Silas ever did."

Karla shut her eyes against his grief, her regret. "I stopped loving you long before Silas," she said, and wrapped her arms around herself.

Eddie visibly flinched, then snapped to shooting stance like a toy soldier and aimed Uncle's rifle at Karla.

Tony thrust a splayed hand toward the gun barrel. "Eddie, you can still help us—"

"Help you destroy me?" Eddie snorted like a bull. His trigger hand shook as he lowered one eye to the rifle scope and trained the barrel on Karla. The forest seemed to hold its breath.

"Eddie, this won't change anything," Karla said. Tony cordoned her with his arms.

"I warned you, babe—if I go down, I take you with me," Eddie said woodenly.

"You have no hold on me anymore, Eddie!" Karla shot back.

For a long moment, everything slowed and blurred. Tony grabbed Karla's arm and stumbled back into the building. Eddie pressed the trigger, and the world knocked back, flashing, screaming, cracking, tumbling.

Otto drummed the desk and gazed at the alpine view in the filtered morning light. After Eddie had gone rogue to the camp, he'd sent Hans home in a taxi, rather than take him to join his nephew in Otto's custom Mercedes 300d that every Highlander knew on sight. Not in the thick of this bumpy re-election campaign.

Otto was steamed but not entirely surprised by this week's unflattering news headlines. He had no illusions about the loyalty of that news hack Langer. He was like all the other weak-minded men in the county who'd knuckled under to Otto with the "promise" of protection from their past lives: their fealty was entirely transactional.

Otto knew Langer would gladly run a damning story about him in his rag if he thought it was enough to get Otto off of his back for good. And sell papers doing it, the swine.

Otto's focus narrowed to a glass paperweight on the desk. He held the sphere aloft and gazed at the dark eagle that floated within it. He let his view distance, and the globe dissolved into the mountain and sky beyond his window, leaving the raptor suspended above his domain.

Now Otto cursed himself for entrusting today's dirty work to that idiot spawn of his brother's seed. Time was running out for Eddie to redeem himself. Otto's grip on the globe tightened, and it shot from his hand to the floor, smashing into a hundred shards.

He swore, then strode to his liquor cabinet, grinding bits of glass. He poured himself a large snifter of *Kirschwasser*. The clear liquid quaked in the glass as he lifted it to his lips. He inhaled its bitter, nutty astringence, clenched his brow, and gulped. Through watering eyes, he glanced at the hearth, a pyre of logs carefully readied for the contents of the camp strongboxes.

Soon, it will all be smoke and ash.

His sights drifted upward to a music box with an intarsia of contrasting woods in a braided floral pattern. Atop it sat a family portrait: a woman in brimmed hat tied with a bow, arms encircling two boys in sailor suits.

A flinty-eyed man in a crisp linen jacket stood stiffly alongside. The older boy held a salt-and-pepper schnauzer, blurred tongue licking his cheek. The boy squinted and smiled.

Schatzi had been Otto's shadow. Curled up with him in a window seat or on long walks in the Grunewald, he'd been Otto's solace through the uncertain years of war and the upheaval that followed.

He recalled the day in 1921 when his family's reduced circumstances forced them to move from leafy Wilmersdorf to a scruffy tenement in Wedding. Otto had searched vainly for Schatzi midst the chaos of heaped belongings and boxes, then run to his father, who was emptying the library shelves.

"Papa, I can't find Schatzi anywhere!" he shrilled.

Heinrich Schmidt straightened a stack of books with precision before replying. "Dogs are not permitted in our new home," he said flatly. "I brought him to the shelter."

Otto's stomach twisted. "You had Schatzi *killed*?"

Heinrich scowled at his son. "Edward, every German family must sacrifice now for the good of our country, and many are far less fortunate than we. So until you can fend for yourself, be grateful for what you have!"

"I am *not* grateful, Papa, and I promise I will never rely on you or anyone else!"

Otto walked for an hour to Schatzi's favorite spot on the Grunewaldsee and wept.

The strongman of Algonquin County pushed down the lump in his throat and took the photo and box to his desk. He sprang the catch, and Schumann's "Slumber Song" played, just like a thousand nights in his Wilmersdorf bedroom.

Otto cradled his glass and stared with liquid eyes at the humorless man in the picture. He snapped the lid shut, and pressed a shaky hand to his forehead.

I kept my promise, Papa. Aren't you proud?

The muffled sound of rifle blasts shattered his reverie.

As Eddie pulled the trigger, an arm locked around his neck and another tore the rifle from his grasp. He clawed wildly at the open air, struggling for breath, until a blow to his head from behind sent him sprawling to the ground.

The two strangers crouched over Eddie's stilled body. One checked his pulse and nodded to the other. Karla stood above them, shell-shocked.

"Are you hurt, miss?" one asked.

Karla startled from her trance and gasped. She struggled to form words, stabbing the air toward the doorway behind her. "Tony!"

The pair raced inside. Karla heard grunts of effort and the scrape of shoes on wood, and after an interminable moment, three men walked across the threshold.

Tony sat hard on a fallen joist, chest laboring. Karla knelt next to him and stroked his back, as though assuring herself that he really was alive.

"Tony! But I saw— I heard—"

"I'm okay," Tony ventured. "The floor gave way, and my guide rope must've caught on a sturdy board. I was hanging by my waist when these guys pulled me up." He smiled wearily.

"Thank God," Karla exclaimed. She rose to face her rescuers, hands on cheeks. "Thank you for saving our lives," she said softly.

"Was our duty. To Silas, and to Jake," said the taller one, with auburn hair and brown eyes.

She studied the two men, and her brow furrowed. "Do I know you?"

They both nodded gravely. "Euel and Malcolm. Silas's other brothers. Never had the pleasure, miss," Malcolm said.

Karla's eyes went wide. "Oh! Silas and I— I'm so sorry."

Euel stopped her. "Love's never wrong," he said with fierce eyes.

"If I'd known it would come to this—"

"None of us ever know, and that's a blessing. How could you start in to lovin' someone if you already knew how it was gonna end?" asked Malcolm.

Euel clasped one of Karla's hands between his own. "At least we all loved Silas in his time on this earth."

Karla swiped both cheeks. She took a long, unsteady breath and studied the brothers with a puzzled look. "But...why are you here?"

"Same reason you are, I reckon," Malcolm said.

Euel finished his thought. "We just didn't think to find *you* here."

Meaning dawned on Tony. "So you knew—"

"About the strongboxes. For years," said Euel. "Folks in

town don't appreciate mountaineers know every inch of the Highlands." He gave a shy smile.

Malcolm elaborated. "We was kids hunting for buried treasure when we found the boxes here. But instead of doubloons, it was papers and pictures and film, so we let it all be," Malcolm said.

Karla pursed her lips. "So you came back for it now—"

"To find justice for Silas," Euel said.

"But how did you connect the sheriff to the strongboxes?" Tony asked.

"We went to see Coroner Brandt yesterday," Malcolm said.

"He told us all about the sheriff and his nephew," Euel added, his tone darkening.

Tony squinted. "After all the law's done to your family, you trusted the coroner?"

"Cousin Leo? No big secret. Since the election campaign started, sheriff's been using Leo's mountain family against him," Malcolm said.

Euel clarified. "His mom was sister to our Grampa Mueller."

"Whoa," Karla said, eyes wide with wonder.

Tony nodded with satisfaction. "So here we all are, partners in crime—"

"—partners to *solve* crime," Karla corrected. She looked expectantly at Tony and nodded to Malcolm and Euel.

Euel studied the other three faces. "So what do you say we get those records?"

Karla shot a worried look at the crumpled body lying before them. "What about Eddie?"

Malcolm exchanged glances with Euel. "He'll keep," Malcolm said. "First things first."

"Okay then, down the hatch," said Euel, and grinned.

Brandt studied the avalanche of papers, reels, and photographs on his desk and beamed at the four faces before him.

"Incredible. For years, many in this county suspected that proof existed of Otto Schmidt's dark past. Now you've brought me enough to interest an army of prosecutors, and acted just in time to save it. Great work!"

Karla, Euel, and Malcolm smiled at the coroner. Tony frowned. "I don't understand why Otto Schmidt didn't destroy all this years ago."

Brandt pushed back in his armchair, hands cradling his head. "Because it was useful to him. Many people key to his political success are likely implicated by this information. The specter of ruin was a powerful motivator to do the sheriff's bidding. I would go so far as to say that these boxes secured his hold on power."

"So what does all of this add up to?" Euel asked.

"Proof of local involvement in a pro-Nazi camp and its national movement. My friends, Otto Schmidt betrayed his country. And the word for that is treason." The room went silent.

Karla frowned, then looked at Brandt. "Eddie complained to me that there were Communists and Jews in the government, the banks, and the press who conspired against his family."

Brandt frowned. "A convenient self-deception," he said.

"The thing is, Eddie really did go through so much in the war, and I felt bad for him. But he couldn't take responsibility for his troubles afterward—it was *always* someone else's fault. And he got that from his horrible uncle." Karla studied her lap.

Brandt leaned forward and spread his hands on his desk.

"Miss Van Hoek, it may be that you rightly judge the Schmidts. But their lives also offer another lesson worth heeding.

"In their shoes, any of us might have followed Eddie's path, or his uncle's. Who hasn't wanted to blame someone else for what we can't make right in our lives?

"It seems that whenever people are frightened and aggrieved, a demagogue appears to seduce us with stories of usurpers and their noble victims, like a fairy tale enchants a child. For his acolytes, Otto spun the grand illusion of a glorious past and a new world order to recapture their stolen supremacy. A myth to vindicate him and galvanize his followers."

Tony looked at Karla. "With a sociopath for a role model, it's no wonder Eddie turned out like he did. And you got caught up in his fantasy world."

Brandt's eyes probed Karla's, hooded in grief. "Miss Van Hoek, I'm sorry that you had to learn the whole truth about Eddie and Otto at such a cost to yourself and your loved ones."

Karla sniffled, and Tony put his arm around her. He cleared his throat. "Mr. Brandt, what happens now to Jake DenBleyker?" he asked.

"Today I will see to his release and strike his alleged confession from the record."

Karla's brow wrinkled. "*You* will? But...isn't Otto Schmidt still sheriff?" she asked.

"Not for long," Brandt said, and raised from his desk an eight-by-ten photograph labeled BERLIN 1936 for all to see: a smiling Fritz Kuhn, German-American *BundesFührer*, shaking hands with a grim Adolf Hitler, and behind them, dead center, Otto Schmidt beaming at the camera.

Tony shook his head. "That says it all, doesn't it?"

"Know a man by the company he keeps," Brandt said.

"So he learned from the masters how to demonize and

destroy people. But when you pull aside the curtain, you see that he's just projecting his own twisted soul on the world," Tony said.

Euel shook his head. "No way now that sunuvabitch's gonna gaslight a judge and jury."

"Or anyone in this county ever again," Malcolm growled.

Brandt pressed his lips in a tight line, and under the gaze of these brave young people, felt the full weight of his duty to secure justice for them and their loved ones. Then he glanced at the blinking light on his phone and nodded at his visitors. "If you will excuse me, my friends."

12

The sun torched the tops of the trees as Eddie staggered past the gates of the Berghof, bruised and dirty. He limped down the drive and banged his fist on the great oak door.

"Uncle Otto! Open up!"

Otto swung the door open and grimaced, hands on hips, imperial pistol in his belt. "God almighty. What happened?"

Eddie puffed out his chest and tried to stand erect, but a wobbly leg betrayed his brave front, and he staggered one step back. "I got ambushed."

"Get in here and explain yourself."

Eddie stumbled to the center of the great room, head bowed, drained of resolve. Otto paced before the fireplace, flexing his hands into fists, the tools of coercion Eddie knew too well.

"Where are the strongboxes, Eddie?"

"I tried to convince Karla that we could have a fresh start if she'd just let me have the files—"

Otto exploded. "If she *let* you? You bargained for our future with that snatch?"

Eddie's head pounded. "I gave her an ultimatum, and she refused, so I...used the gun."

Otto's face contracted. "Jesus, Eddie...you *shot her*?"

"I guess I might've." Eddie felt shaky all over. "Or else Tony Marsala."

"You *might* have just killed someone?" Otto shouted.

Eddie's voice quavered. "The gun went off, and then I got attacked from behind and I blacked out. When I came to, I went straight for the stash, but...it was gone."

"You had one thing to get right today, and you *slept* through it!" Otto advanced on Eddie.

Eddie braced for Uncle's full fury. "How did I know I'd get ambushed?" Eddie cried.

Otto snorted like a mad bull. "You are spineless, just like your father!" In one swift motion, Otto swiped a ceramic stein from the mantel and launched it at Eddie's head.

Eddie ducked, and the stein hit the polished plank floor, shattering into fragments. The sudden violence tripped the memory of Uncle's beatings, and Eddie ran at Otto, fists flying. But he managed only one blow before Otto had him pressed against the mantel, arm twisted behind his back.

"Y-you dragged Papa into the Bund, and *destroyed* him! *You ruined my life!*" Eddie sputtered.

"I am not why you have no father," Otto sneered. "And now you will know the truth." He spun Eddie around and shoved him backward into the hard hearth.

Eddie's spine exploded in pain. "Spare me your us-against-the-world speech!" he howled. Eddie pushed his way toward the panoramic windows, Otto on his heels.

Otto addressed Eddie's turned back. "I will tell you the kind of man your father was," he said, voice thick with contempt. "Haven't you wondered why your father was deported from Crystal City, but not us?" Eddie whirled around, body clenched as if bracing for a blow.

"The prisoners would try to bribe the duty guards to escape, but few could make it worth their while. Your father was determined, so he bartered himself to two MPs."

Eddie twisted free of Otto's grip. "What do you mean, 'bartered'?"

"The guards had their way with him and then turned him in. Your father was deported to Germany for treason, bribery, and *acts of sodomy*."

"That's a load of bull," Eddie said hoarsely.

"Is it?" Otto laughed cruelly. "Your father kept so many secrets from you. He sold his body by the hour on the streets of Berlin! I took him to America to save him from himself."

"Papa was kind and loving...and a better man than you'll ever be."

"Franz was a dissolute fool."

Eddie exploded. *"What kind of monster smears his own brother?"*

"*Dummkopf!* He smeared you and his entire family!"

Eddie's face was a knot of revulsion. "Is there anyone you won't slander, Uncle? You want the people to vote for you, but you despise them all!"

"Because this is a county of cowards!" Otto thundered.

Eddie shook his head slowly. "You never gave a shit about me. The threats, the beatings—they weren't for *me*. You just needed to show me—and everyone else in the Highlands— that you have power over us!"

Otto bared his teeth. "Power is the only language the world understands, and without it, you are *nothing*!"

Uncle wheeled at the sudden pounding at the door. Eddie saw the doubt in his eyes, and felt a strange relief. The door burst open, and a phalanx of uniformed men in FBI vests encircled them, weapons aimed. Leo Brandt stood framed in the doorway.

"Hands over heads, both of you!" Brandt commanded.

Eddie did as he was told, but Uncle squared his chin with a swagger, hand resting on his gun. "And what would be your business here, Coroner?"

"Otto Schmidt, you are under arrest for abuse of public office."

A throaty sound, part laugh, part cry, burst from Otto. "You're dreaming."

"Conspiracy, bribery, intimidation, falsifying evidence, coerced confessions, excessive force, torture: no, not dreams, Otto—facts." Otto surveyed his audience, all eyes on him.

Otto snickered. "Now, really, this is all a bit silly."

Brandt continued. "As it happens, it was quite easy to confirm your malfeasance. Besides sloppy attempts to conceal your recent crimes, others in this county have been quite forthcoming about your past. It seems your strong-arm tactics have made you many enemies during your time in office."

"*My* office, Brandt. You have no power or authority here." Otto took a step forward, and the agents responded in kind.

"If you'd bothered to read the statutes, Otto, you'd know that in New York State, a coroner has the power to arrest," Brandt admonished.

"Fool! I only have to pick up the phone, and subpoenas, prosecutors, and grand juries are all over you for libel and exceeding authority!"

Brandt frowned. "Do your worst, Otto. As you see, I am working with the FBI, which I expect soon will open an investigation of your seditious activities before and during the war—including a trove of new revelations concerning your so-called summer camp.

"We are transcribing the camp records as I speak," he said briskly. "The strongboxes arrived at my office a short while ago."

"You swine of my brother's sow!" Otto spat at Eddie, who regarded his uncle, unblinking.

"Don't blame him, Otto. The boxes were recovered by those who are most aggrieved by your acts of injustice: Tony Marsala, Karla Van Hoek, and Silas Mueller's brothers. It is your own misdeeds that have led you to this present humiliation."

"*Verräter!*"

"German insults won't help you in a court of law." Brandt nodded to his FBI support. "Enough talk. Time to face the truth."

Otto's eyes flitted from one agent to the next. "Are you going to let this crook steal an election with his outrageous charges? He's the one who belongs in jail!" Eddie watched in wonder at the spectacle of his tormentor afraid and out of control.

The group advanced on Otto. He snapped erect, lifted the Luger from its holster to his temple, and shouted, "*Für die Neuordnung!*"

"Uncle, don't—" Eddie gasped.

As the gun discharged, an agent seized Otto's firing arm and pinned it, while a second locked him in a head vise. Red rivulets flowed from Otto's temple, and his body slackened. A third agent cuffed him, and the three officers dragged him across wide planks smeared with his own blood.

Tony made it to the sheriff's office right before closing time. He pushed inside to reception and gasped. A bowed figure sat alone, face battered and swollen, his clothes torn and caked in mud. Tony knelt and hugged him tight.

Jake grunted. "I'm a little sore."

"Oh! Sorry." Tony released his grip.

Jake pulled him in and pressed his face against Tony's cheek. "Don't be," he said.

Tony felt Jake's ribs rack against his own, and he welled up. "Schmidt will pay for this," Tony rasped.

"Both of them," Jake whispered. They released one long breath. Tony held Jake at arm's length, swiped a muddy tear creeping down his jaw, and nodded fiercely. Jake managed a faint smile.

"Come on, let's get you out of here," Tony said.

Jake laid hands on Tony's outstretched arms and lifted himself from the chair. They made their way slowly past the reception counter, Tony's eyes shooting fire at the frowning receptionist.

They hobbled out to his car, and Tony settled Jake into his seat, then got in and started the engine. He shifted into drive, paused, and pushed the gear stick back into park. The car gently rocked and hummed.

Jake looked quizzically at Tony, and Tony's gaze bounced from Jake's eyes to somewhere beyond the hood of the car. "I'm ashamed of the hateful things I said to you." His voice trembled.

Jake wiped his nose on a mud-caked sleeve. "Me too."

Tony faced Jake, his face burnished by the western sky. "I should have known that you would never—"

Jake squeezed Tony's thigh. "Don't be too hard on yourself. I started it."

Tony tipped his head back, but the tears spilled anyway. "I kept replaying Silas's funeral, trying to work out what I did wrong."

"Nothing you could have done to make it right. I was mad at the world and everyone in it." Jake stared at the dashboard. "And seeing you made me think, if they killed Silas for loving Karla, what good could come of us?"

None, because I'm not supposed to be like this, hissed a voice in Tony's head. Tony thumped the wheel with the heel of his hand. "Why is it so damn hard to be happy?" The question hung in the air.

Jake took Tony's hand, still stinging from the impact, rubbed it between his palms, and then pressed it to his chest. Tony felt it pounding.

Jake tapped the rhythm inside of himself on the back of Tony's hand with two fingers. "I guess I quit trying a while ago." His eyes brimmed.

"I don't want to live that way anymore!" Tony wailed.

Jake gently shushed him with a wet kiss, and Tony raked Jake's matted hair and swept his hands over Jake's battered body. Jake purred, letting Tony hold him in his arms until he audibly groaned from the pain, and leaned back in his seat.

"Your people and mine been getting their hearts broke forever," Jake said. "And still we climb mountains, cross oceans, and go out in the storm for love. We find a way."

Jake took in Tony's watery eyes and gently brushed the tears away. Then he smiled as much as his bruises allowed.

Tony flexed an eyebrow. "What?"

"I just gave you two shiners," Jake said, chuckling.

Tony ran his fingers under his eyes and they came up brown, and he tittered. "Okay, it's time to get you into a hot bath." Tony put the car back into drive and they headed out.

Soon they were rolling on the county road, shadow and light racing over the windshield, as a dozen questions jostled for Tony's attention.

"How bad was jail?" Tony asked gingerly.

"Sheriff roughed me up some. Kept threatening that I'd fry if I didn't cooperate."

"That monster!"

"I wasn't worried. Told him I wouldn't fry so easy without all of his blubber." Jake's laughter made him wince.

"And the conditions?"

"No food or shower. A dirty mattress and a bucket to crap in." Jake blew air at the ceiling.

"Oh! I almost forgot." Tony reached behind him and pulled out a brown bag. "You must be starving."

"Understatement," Jake said, and bit open the plastic wrapper on a sandwich.

"Did Otto make you..."

"If you want to know if I confessed, no, I never did," Jake managed between mouthfuls.

"I knew the bastard was lying," Tony huffed.

They arrived at the DenBleyker house as the sun slipped below the trees. Delfinia outran her boys to the car. Her eyes went wide at the sight of her son.

"Lord in heaven! What did they do to my baby?" She reached through the open window and stroked Jake's hair.

"It's okay, Mama. Let me get out so I can give you a hug," said Jake, grinning weakly. Tensing against his aches, he released the door and lifted himself with a groan to embrace her. Delfinia's keening ended in a tongue click.

She drew back and set her jaw. "I ought to tan your hide for running out in the storm! You got any idea what heartache you caused your mother these nights?"

Jake bowed his head. "Yes, ma'am. I'm sorry for what I done." He winked sideways at Tony, who suppressed a grin.

Delfinia swatted the air. "And if you hadn't risked your life to save your friend, would he be delivering my baby back to me now?" The corners of her mouth tugged at her frown.

Jake smiled. "No, ma'am."

Eyes glistening, Delfinia turned to Tony. He shifted his weight and blinked fast. She held her hands tight to her bosom. "Mr. Tony—*Tony,* that is—I see why Jake sets great store by your friendship." Euel and Malcolm nodded.

Tony's face went hot. Delfinia's arms hovered a moment before she stepped forward and pressed Tony to her. Tony eyed Jake, his mouth forming a tiny *O* of surprise.

"I am thankful he...has you." She sniffled and tipped up her chin. "Now you *will* stay for dinner, and no backtalk," she commanded.

Tony's gaze clouded, and she chuckled. "Don't worry yourself child, ain't no bear bacon on the menu tonight." With that, everyone broke up, and all the brothers exchanged hugs, Tony getting his share, too.

Otto sat on a hard bench and stared at the flickering tube above him. His temples throbbed. Glorious death hadn't come; the bullet had only grazed his temple. He'd been handcuffed to a gurney and bandaged at the ER in Monroe, and then whisked away to his own sheriff's lockup.

He would have his revenge with the scum who'd taken him down. He'd already begun plotting his comeback in the ambulance, life ebbing away, whispering orders that Eddie bring him a jackknife in prison as soon as he was allowed visitors.

Brandt has no clue who he's messing with.

He would never surrender his badge to that snake, never give the coroner's legion of half-breeds, those Van Hoek whores, and the faggot Marsala the satisfaction of his dishonor. Otto dug fingernails into the worn wood beneath him, the bile in his throat dredging up his first betrayal.

He'd enlisted in the Kaiser's army in March 1918, spirits high, Russia newly vanquished and his company advancing on Paris, only to see his country capitulate by November. Back in Berlin, he'd found the bitter reward for his sacrifice: a nation extorted and stolen by enemies and profiteers, Allied and German, and his family reduced to squalor.

He'd exchanged his infantry boots for the polished shoes of a hotel doorman, bowed and scraped to carpetbaggers, then spent all his daily pay on food. He saw in the greed and depravity and lawlessness all around him that Germany's national creed had become survival at any cost.

As he'd struggled to get through each day, Otto had warmed to the National Socialists' platform to end war reparations, create jobs, nationalize industry, and start land reform. For those promises, Otto could overlook all of the groups they vilified.

He and Papa, a devoted Weimar functionary, had fought bitterly over politics. Papa decried *that brown-shirted madman* and counseled patience. Otto protested that he was at the breaking point, with the price of bread higher every morning and his cash wages filling an army rucksack each afternoon.

By autumn of 1923, he'd had enough. Otto stood in their dingy tenement hall with his younger brother Franz, their possessions on their backs, sights set for America. Papa's parting words to Otto were like iron.

Your spite and grievance toward the world will only turn men against you.

The gate to the holding area clanged, and shortly the duty guard's face appeared at Otto's cell door. Dieter Bremer was the son of an old Bund comrade; Otto had hired him to keep the boy's family beholden. Now was the time to trade on that favor.

Dieter bowed deferentially. "Good evening, Sheriff. Your nephew is here to see you."

"Dieter! It seems like only yesterday your father confided to me your dream to be a policeman. And without hesitation, I said, 'Bring him in! I'm happy to help such a fine boy.'"

Dieter rubbed the back of his neck. "Uh, Sheriff, if I could—"

Otto ran right over him. "And look at you now! Whip-smart, and a credit to this office."

Dieter blushed. "Why thank you sir, I—"

"Of course, of course, no need." Otto locked eyes with him and smiled magnanimously. "Now, you won't mind if I have a bit of privacy with my nephew, will you?"

"Well, sir"—he strained to clear his throat—"like you taught me, I've got to be present during visits to prisoners…"

Otto's eyes narrowed. "But seeing how I'm your sheriff… who gave you a leg up when you needed it…"

Dieter shifted uneasily. "You did, sir, and I'm grateful. It's just that—"

Otto nodded gravely, lips pressed, the slightest flare of a nostril betraying his irritation. "Absolutely, Officer Bremer, I completely understand your position. You're a man of integrity, and I will not forget that in your annual review. Now that we're clear on all that, why don't you show Eddie in, and I'll rap on the door when we're done."

Dieter opened his mouth, then clamped it shut and dipped his chin. "Okay, then, but…I'll have to lock you both in. If that's all right."

"Oh yes, of course. Do your duty, officer," Otto encouraged, an ill-fitting grin on his face.

Dieter gave a tight smile and retreated down the hall. He led Eddie through the gate to Otto's cell, unlocked the steel door, and swung it open. "Well, then, enjoy your visit," Dieter said, and decorously waived Eddie in.

Through the door's steel-mesh window, nephew and uncle watched Otto's flustered minion fumble with the keys and lock the door. He threw Otto a sheepish last look, and padded away.

Otto heard the outer door close, and his face hardened. "Where is it?" Eddie pulled the knife from his pocket.

"Good." Otto weighed the blade in his hand. "And no one saw you with this?"

"No!" Eddie's leg jiggled. "Well, maybe my mom."

Otto's brow pressed against his eyes. "What does that mean?"

"Well, I was making to leave, and she got in my face, so we struggled, and...the knife fell out my pocket. She started hollering, and I...hit her."

"*What?*"

"And she fell and...hit her head, and then I panicked and ran out." Eddie's chest heaved.

"Christ, Eddie—"

"I didn't mean to hurt her, I just wanted her to get out of my way!"

Otto paced the cell from door to cot and back. "Christ, Eddie. Do you have any idea how this looks?"

"How it *looks*?"

Otto pressed Eddie against the metal door with the heel of his hand. "I have no time for your family drama. You've jeopardized my plans!"

Eddie saw red. "Me and Mama are never part of your plans, except when you need to remind voters you're a great family man!"

"If you want to save your sorry ass, shut up and do as I say!" Otto said.

"It's *your* ass you want to save. You'd rather die than lose this election."

"Boy, do exactly what I tell you right now, or you will go to Sing Sing for a long, long time!" Otto said, his voice trembling strangely, like he wasn't quite in command.

Eddie saw clearly Uncle's naked need to subdue a world he couldn't control, and an odd feeling came over him: pity.

"Go on," Eddie said abruptly. "Let's save both our asses."

Doubt scudded across Otto's face, and he released Eddie. Otto eyed the clock. "The shift changes at ten, and I need everything in place before then. You will bring me three things. Take the key from the envelope in my top desk drawer at the Berghof and unlock the cabinet behind the fireplace.

"Inside is a false wall; slide it to the right, and you'll find a canvas bag with my *Karabiner* and ammo. Second, bring me the Bible on the mantel; it contains my sheriff's keys. And lastly, grab a stack of newspapers from the pile near the back door.

"When you get back here, place the gun bag in the trash bin behind this building, and cover it with newspapers. Then present yourself to the night duty guard, and insist that you hand the Bible directly to me."

Eddie looked dubiously at Otto. "And if I get caught, who bails me out this time?"

"If Brandt succeeds in court, we're finished. Take a stand, Eddie, if only to save your own skin!" Otto pulled Eddie away from the small cell window and hailed Dieter.

Eddie barreled up the road to the Berghof, the long shadows of evening passing over Hans's borrowed Chevy. His heart banged his ribs like a trapped animal. He was more convinced than ever that Uncle's fevered plans wouldn't put him back in power, and with Brandt now in charge, he was probably already in the coroner's crosshairs. But he had something to prove, and the proof had to be in Uncle's goddamn command center.

Eddie found the ordnance, Bible, and newspapers right away and set them by the door. He then started in on Otto's files, strewn across the great room where the FBI had left them. Eddie raked through the papers for ten, fifteen minutes, his agitation building.

He scanned several cabinets, locks broken and contents emptied, and a safe dragged from somewhere, cracked and cleaned out.

Think! Where would Uncle hide something personal? He returned to the gun cabinet, slid the false wall open, and reached deeper; he touched not plaster or stone, but another panel. He groped his way along it, fingers finally finding a groove, and the thin board shifted.

He shoved an arm into the farther cavity and felt something leathery, thick, and pliant. Then another. He flung each behind him, until six bound books lay in a heap on the floor.

He scuttled backward and examined the bindings, each inscribed with a date: 1918, 1919, all the way to 1923, the year the Schmidt brothers had left Germany. He flipped through that latest book, handwriting filling almost every page and margin.

Eddie scrambled across the room with it, landing hard on Uncle's desk chair. He swept loose files and papers from the desktop, planted his elbows on the desk, and with shaking hands opened the volume. He started halfway through, riffling pages in a frenzy, tattering his way to November, the month of Papa's departure with Uncle.

8 November

I leave the Hotel Adlon and scurry up Unter den Linden toward the Berliner Dom and the Stadtschloss. I turn north on Friedrichstrasse, thankful there are no rioters today, only the hedonists, like schools of gaudy fish, tacking from theater marquees to supper clubs.

I tug up my collar against the icy wind and shrug my rucksack higher on my shoulder, berating myself for not going straight from payroll to the stores during lunch to spend this load of banknotes before prices rose again this evening.

I cross the Spree and head up Chauseestrasse, where the nightly circus begins. Young girls made up like Clara Bow and Mary Pickford, and older flappers with rouged knees flirt with fur-collared men in limousines. Hustlers lead johns and janes from bars up fire escapes. The street stinks of puke and beer.

Approaching Wedding's new U-Bahn station, I see three hookers in spike heels and short skirts prospecting. They are tall, strong jawed, wobbly on their feet. I lock eyes with the pretty blonde, and her mouth goes slack.

She dashes into the station, and I race after her down a flight of stairs. One of her heels gives out, and I catch her. I spin her around and slap her hard; she staggers, and her blond locks fall to the platform.

"Franz, what the hell are you doing?" I manage between gulps of air.

My brother's mascaraed eyes are fierce. "Putting food on the table for Mama and Papa!"

"You have the gall to justify this? Arschficker!" I say.

"I'll make your entire week's pay tonight, so get out of my way and let me earn it!"

I stand frozen as this twisted creature sashays past me. He is right - we survive on the wages of his sins. I burn with shame. I bolt up the stairs and heave in the street.

We have become a nation of whores, pimped by our own depravity.

Eddie's head was splitting apart. He flung the book to the floor. Who was this freak of nature pouring off these pages?

Papa had been his rock, salved his hurt and fear, made the ugly, angry world all right. And when Eddie had lost him for good, he'd never really felt safe again. Tears coursed his cheeks.

Twisted? Whore? *Arschficker*? Eddie pushed against the sordid words.

Maybe Papa had made bad choices to survive a world beyond his control; hadn't Eddie?

Was he to blame? Was Papa?

Hadn't Uncle done worse?

Otto had no qualms about who he hurt to get ahead. Eddie

had the scars inside to prove it: starting from Camp Hochland, Uncle had drummed his dark vision of life into Eddie and so riddled him with doubt, he hadn't known what to believe.

But that didn't have to be his destiny. He could recapture the Eddie Papa had loved. If the father he'd idolized had risen from the gutters of Berlin, that gave him hope that he could redeem himself.

Take a stand, Eddie.

Eddie scanned the roomful of books and photos and banners that reeked of Uncle's malice, and finally knew what he had to do.

Soon, sticky with sweat, he'd returned from Uncle's garage, grappling the drums of fuel he'd found there. He dragged one into the deep hearth, where an enormous woodpile sat untouched.

Eddie knelt, tilted the barrel, and grimaced, struggling to control its great weight, as gasoline gushed over the logs, making him light-headed. Acrid rivulets sluiced across the floor, and as he rose to dodge them, his grip on the barrel slipped and a wave of fuel splashed at his feet. Eddie inhaled the sweet pungency filling the great room and grew giddy on the fumes.

A wild growl sprang from his depths. He picked up a smaller jug and flung its contents into the air with wide sweeps of his arm, splashing furniture, walls, and the big picture window. With a final effort, Eddie heaved the last of the fuel all over the mantel, where Hitler's dour image rippled in the wash.

Choking on his own laughter, Eddie lurched at the mantel shelf and grabbed a lighter shaped like a metal stein. He thumbed the igniter at its top and tossed the lit tankard onto the logs. With a great bang and *whoosh*, the hearth exploded in flame, throwing Eddie to the floor. A line of fire scuttled across the room in a zigzag dance.

Eddie scrambled to his feet, staggering from the heat and smoke. He felt a piercing pain in his hand and looked down to find the spent jug still in his grip, fire circling its handle. His hand unclenched, but something hot wouldn't let go.

With a throaty roar, bright, angry tongues shot up the mantel and climbed the gilt-framed poster. They licked Eddie's arm, then his chest, and rose to his cheek. He swung his body wildly before the sullen man and his faceless throng in the high mountain valley, as their Valhalla turned to ash.

***

Brandt nursed his fourth cup of coffee. It was already eight pm, and he still had a stack of pressing business to go through for the Van Hoek and Schreier cases. The report on Otto's arrest would just have to wait.

He fanned the photos before him like a winning poker hand. Alongside lay images of Schreier's body at the recovery site, and the headshot that the *Mountain Observer* had run with his obituary.

Brandt had placed Schreier on the balcony where he was last seen alive, along with two men who appeared to have little in common. One was Eddie Schmidt. Who was the second?

The final image he'd seen at Weber's had caught a face and collar. He was sure he'd seen the balding man, but couldn't pull in the missing piece of the picture. The guy was dressed differently from the other patrons, too sharp for this stodgy Highlands crowd.

White suit, in a sea of gray and navy. Tennis shoes, not clodhoppers. His presence certainly would have drawn attention from that tight-knit club. Why hadn't any of them been able to ID him to Brandt?

The answer came quickly: they were simply unwilling. Which suggested that this putative outsider was in tight with this cult, and his special status could only have been bestowed by its leader, Otto Schmidt.

Brandt tapped his pointer finger insistently on the oak desktop, then yanked a clipboard from the middle of his case stack. He flipped through to the M's, and there it was, that inapt name that had snagged his eye. He'd put it out of mind when it hadn't fit with his blinkered focus on Eddie Schmidt, but now it leaped from the page: *Marsala, Salvatore*.

Was it the clue he needed? All Brandt knew for sure was that now he would have to find the answers himself. After he'd put the sheriff in jail, Otto Schmidt's squad of loyalists wouldn't have Brandt's back. And he'd have to haul in Eddie Schmidt for more questioning, without backup. He would stop by Eddie's house for a little chat tonight before heading home.

Brandt slipped a holster over his shoulder, and filled it with a revolver from a locked desk drawer. He considered his decision to go it alone in this probe, with all of Otto's officers likely arrayed against Brandt's authority, and decided to add a scoped rifle to his battery.

He headed out to the officers' lot, stopped short of his cruiser, and swore. The words JACKSON WHITE were spray-painted across the windshield, and all four tires were flat.

Brandt procured a spare squad car and sped down to the Schmidt house. The door swayed and creaked; the dirt drive was empty. Brandt got out, hand on his revolver, and scurried to the near corner of the house. He crouched beneath the shrubs that hugged it and crept toward the threshold. Springing onto the stoop, he swung his weapon left to right through the open doorway.

"Police!" he boomed.

Silence.

Brandt stepped in and moved methodically through the neat, cramped parlor, one eye on the darkened hall beyond, and trawled for something askew in the furniture, the table-tops, the pictures on the wall. His gaze dropped to the carpet and traced its border of floral garlands past one corner, then two, and stopped at a break in the pattern.

Splayed legs protruded from behind an armchair. He threaded his way over to find a middle-aged woman in a housedress lying face up, unmoving.

Brandt dropped down to feel her jugular and check her breathing; she would be okay. He snapped on his walkie-talkie and called for backup and an ambulance. Then he shut the front door, sprinted through weeds to his car, and spun rubber.

Nothing he'd just seen suggested the work of an intruder. He could only guess it was Eddie. Had he flung his mother to the floor like a broken doll? The boy had little self-control; his behavior this morning, as Brandt's cousins and their friends had described it, made that clear.

Eddie was a loose cannon who endangered Otto's standing in the county, and so he'd kept Eddie on a short leash. Now Eddie was speeding down a one-way street to calamity without the brakes his uncle usually applied. Still, that didn't fully explain Eddie's actions tonight.

The answer lay with the uncle and his secrets. Otto had bailed out his nephew repeatedly; the boy's loose lips in a courtroom could be bad for Otto. Now, with Brandt in charge, all bets were off. Eddie would be terrified, expecting no immunity for past misdeeds that Otto had squelched.

Otto likely assumed that Brandt would interview all the blackmailed, compulsory members of Schmidt's fan club, tongues suddenly untied. And that Brandt would revisit his nephew's case files, review old testimony, and gather new statements—especially from witnesses to the deaths on the mountain. Those people could be a big problem for Otto.

Unless there were none.

And with the stakes intolerably high for his career, Otto would leave nothing to chance to make that happen. Even behind bars, Brandt thought, the man was a present danger. If Schmidt could no longer crush threats to his authority by force of law, Brandt had little doubt that he'd employ any means necessary—including his bumbling nephew.

Brandt pushed the squad car hard up the stony road to Otto's Berghof. About midway in the climb, something harsh in the air tickled his throat and made his eyes water, and by the last bend in the road it had become an acrid fog.

He rolled to a stop, covered his mouth with a handkerchief, and leaped from the car into a storm of smoke and flame. The air shifted, and the compound emerged from the roiling heat, stopping Brandt in his tracks.

Flames licked window frames, and an orange geyser shot into the sky, collapsing the roof. Brandt called in the fire, raced through the open gate, and followed the driveway to the back of the building, halting short of the entrance. The sight confirmed what he already knew in his gut: there was no possibility of search or rescue.

Billowing clouds smothered the grand house of the man who had long compelled awe and fear from his visitors. Now, above the sundered roof, Brandt saw the last flicker of Otto's fief, a flag of an eagle clutching a swastika in its talons. It flapped wildly over the inferno, like a panicked bird in the jaws of death, before it, too, vanished in a growing circle of flame.

Otto watched the wall clock; two minutes to ten. Where the hell was Eddie? He heard the outer gate creak open, and a halting gait. He thrust his face up against the barred window of his cell door, and it was presently filled by the night officer, Phil Mullin.

He'd been hired by Otto's predecessor, so Otto had nothing on him or his family. But the man was in his last months on the force and a bit complacent.

"Evening, Sheriff. Mr. Schmidt. Otto." Mullin chuckled. "Confusing situation we got here, ay?"

"Strange times, Phil."

"Truer words…" Mullin trailed off, shaking his head. He eyed Otto and clucked his tongue.

"If not for friends like you, Phil, a man might lose hope." Otto pressed his lips gravely. "How's about a smoke for old times, officer?" he asked.

Mullin rubbed his front pockets, then struggled to reach past the billy club and pistol on his hips to pat his backside. "Musta left the smokes at my desk." He gave Otto a sheepish smile and lumbered off to his duty station.

Mullin returned several long minutes later with the lighter and two cigarettes. Mullin lit the first, took a couple of puffs, and then made to do the same with Otto's.

"Uh, Phil, if you don't mind, I'd like to light mine," Otto said.

"I, uh, sir, wish the two of us was just sittin' at the bar, but here I got my duty to consider," Mullin said without much conviction.

Otto probed it. "Oh, Phil…You know how good that first puff can be after a hard day." Otto shrugged and tensed his right arm, felt stiff metal slide between wrist and sleeve. "And this one's hard as any I ever had in my whole career."

Mullin's unease had him swaying. "Well, now, I suppose there's no harm in it. Of course, I can't just hand you the lighter like that, you being on the wrong side of the bars." Mullin chuckled nervously.

Otto smiled, eyes on Mullin's hands. "Of course not, Phil. You always played it by the book." He slid the tensed arm behind him.

Mullin's chest puffed out a bit, inflating his gut. "Thank you, sir. I'm looking forward to handing in my badge this fall."

"And your retirement's well earned, Phil, well earned, indeed," Otto brayed, a sharp shake of his shoulder sending the steel shank into his hidden palm.

Mullin dipped his head in gratitude and said sprightly, "Just so, just so." He squared his chin and said, seemingly to himself, "All right, then, all right." He lifted a ring of keys from his belt, and on the third try, unlocked the cell door. Mullin stepped in and handed Otto his smoke.

Otto planted it between his lips while his other hand closed on the hilt. "In just a few weeks, you'll pass the torch, Phil. Come, light the flame for old time's sake!" he urged with hungry eyes.

"For old time's sake!" Mullin parroted back.

Otto's right arm swiveled to his side, then tensed. "To the man who always answered the call of duty!"

Mullin stepped forward and sparked the lighter, then waved its flame under the tip of his boss's cigarette as Otto thrust the knife upward, just below the sternum.

"Oh." Eyes wide, Mullin clutched at the air, then dropped to the floor with a meaty thud.

Otto squatted and yanked the service revolver from the dying man's holster. "Faith in mankind can get a man killed," he mocked, lips to Mullin's ear. He turned the knife ninety degrees, then yanked it from Mullin's gurgling, spasming body.

"Such a waste of a badge and uniform," Otto sneered. He stepped over his prey and sprinted through open doors into the night.

13

Tony sat with Jake on the porch after dinner, unsure how to navigate Labor Day weekend. He felt the familiar ache of endings: the last hot sunrise and long swim, the final boat ride and dazzling sunset. The summer colony busy drydocking boats, draining pipes, and shuttering bungalows.

With all the turbulence of the past four weeks, it seemed as if he and Jake had barely gotten started. Tony tried to enjoy this moment together, fog wisping from the warm earth, but the future kept intruding.

"Jake, we need to talk," Tony said.

"I know." Jake's urgency made Tony's eyes sting.

The porch door snapped shut after scraping boots, and Malcolm and Euel came into view, beers in hand, ribbing each other, something about their prowess with a mountain girl.

Tony whispered to Jake, "Can we go someplace more private?"

"My thoughts exactly. Be right back." Jake squeezed Tony's shoulder and hobbled off, returning shortly with a knapsack and two flashlights. Tony's eyes went from the bulging bag to Jake, who smiled and shrugged.

"Might as well be comfortable." Jake winked, and Tony's chest fluttered. They made for the porch steps.

Euel pointed his bottle to Jake. "Hey!" he called. "Where you nighthawks off to?"

"Someplace quieter than this saloon," Jake answered with a smirk.

Malcolm waggled his finger like a mad preacher. "No carousing with the nightlife, you letches," he said, breaking up.

Jake tipped an imaginary hat toward his brothers and grinned. "The wildlife's more sensible than you drunk fools."

Jake and Tony rode fifteen minutes in the pickup to a blind turnoff. They set out on foot, Tony for once pacing Jake. As the terrain steepened, Jake grunted with each footfall but pressed on.

A strange sound rose above the chitter and hiss of the night, something like a moan. The sound grew as Tony pushed his way up the pitched trail, his thoughts jumpy. The trail twisted, and Tony found himself in a small clearing dominated by a boulder big as a shed.

Jake stood still but for his heaving chest, and cocked his head. Tony placed a steadying hand under his elbow. Jake gently declined help by slipping his hand into Tony's.

"Jake, what is—"

"*Shhh.*" Jake squeezed Tony's hand. "Listen."

As if in response, a keening from the rock enveloped them, and then just as suddenly the sound ebbed and died.

Tony released his grip and rubbed his prickled arms. "That sounded almost...human."

"The elders say powerful spirits live in these great stones. This one's called Black Mag. They say she rides on stormy nights, making mischief."

Tony harrumphed. "I've had enough mischief lately, thank you. Please tell her to leave us alone and get back in her rock."

Jake stared thoughtfully at Black Mag. "Grampa used to say she comes out when there's a score needs settling."

Otto parked Phil Mullin's cruiser at a small clearing where the miner's camp began on DenBleyker's side of the mountain. He stuffed the dead man's revolver into the belt of his Bund uniform, and looped on one shoulder a satchel of ammo he'd hidden at HQ in the dead case files closet. Intended for all possible contingencies. Including a coup by his coroner.

Now everything Otto had done to keep his sycophants in line and the world out of his business was at risk, thanks to his goddamn nephew. At least he had more than enough bullets for what he'd come up here to do tonight.

Before leaving HQ, he'd used his spare sheriff's keys to fortify himself with an open *Kruke* of Steinhäger from his office liquor cabinet. A little juniper gin went a long way, and he had a long night ahead, he'd thought, as the bottle went bottoms-up. It had only stoked his burning desire for vengeance.

He stood and listened. He heard a crunch, then another, and turned toward the source. Otto walked uphill and felt for the gun.

Tony heard rustling, then looked at Jake with alarm.

"There are too many strange sounds around here," he protested.

Jake chuckled. "You lake folks only know these woods from a sunny summer stroll, when it's sleeping off the heat. The forest wakes up after dark," he said, "and that's nothing to be afraid of."

"With everything that's happened lately, it's hard to take that on faith," Tony said, his neck prickling.

Jake put a hand on Tony's shoulder. "I can spot a wildcat at a hundred paces."

"It's not the wildlife I'm worried about," Tony said. "It's the human kind."

Jake stroked Tony's back. "Cousin Leo's got things under control, so relax."

"In the dark, with no one to know if we live or die." Tony huffed.

"Okay, city boy. Time we got to my safe house," he said, and plunged back under the mountain canopy. Soon the woods gave onto a meadow, and right after a sharp turn in the path, Jake's light struck a looming wall of wood.

"The Reefer Barn," Jake announced. "Every bad boy's favorite hangout."

"No more run-ins with bad boys, please," Tony whined. "Let's get out of— "

The unmistakable crunch of boots on the forest floor jolted them, and they sprinted like spooked deer.

Brandt made it to Sherman's Bridge in fifteen minutes. He shut off his siren as he sped through the last stop sign after the Old Rhinelander Inn, three miles short of the mountain turnoff.

The fire across the lake had rung all the alarm bells. There was nothing measured or reasoned in what Brandt had witnessed. Eddie had means and opportunity to torch his uncle's chalet, with a lifelong grievance toward his uncle the likely motive.

With Otto and the power of his office off the battlefield, Eddie was spinning out of control, waging his own kind of war, and Brandt feared Eddie would now turn his attention to the people who threatened his alibis in two Highlands murders. He could cause carnage if Brandt didn't get to him first.

At the turnoff, Brandt downshifted and switched off his headlights, keeping the search spot low to the ground. His radio receiver squawked to life.

"Coroner Brandt, read me, over," came a familiar voice.

Brandt leaned into the dash, eyes scouring the road. "Yes, DeVrees, over," he barked.

The reply broke into clumps of words. "First responders... human remains...Schmidt compound."

Brandt grappled the wheel, and a new reality. "Christ...Any ID, Deputy?"

A long pause. "I thought that was your department."

Brandt suppressed a profanity. "I need immediate follow-up and a report back to me within the hour." Brandt punched his words.

Static, then nothing. The chassis bucked from a hard impact, and Brandt's head banged the ceiling. He swore and directed his ire to the deputy.

"Is that understood, officer?"

"Yes, Coroner. If that's all, the fellas and I are gonna go take our regulation break, and then we'll see to those *urgent* matters..." DeVrees's mocking tone cut through the static. Brandt didn't take the bait but filed away the man's insolence for later.

"Negative, DeVrees. I need to know who's on night shift at HQ."

"Phil Mullin." The reply was slow and indifferent.

Mullin on watch with Otto was the hen guarding the fox, and that shifted Brandt's thoughts.

"Mullin hasn't been on regular rotation for months. How did he get assigned to solo lockup duty, tonight of all nights?"

"A *sheriff* would know that holiday weekends, the department makes do with the back bench." Brandt thought he heard a chorus of guffaws over the screeching signal.

Brandt nearly bit off his mike. "Goddammit, DeVrees, if you value your job, if you have to piss your pants, you will switch on your siren right now and drive full throttle to HQ. I want a report in fifteen minutes on the prisoner's status."

"Is that an order?" DeVrees seemed indignant.

"For Chrissake, *now*, DeVrees!" Brandt shouted, and gunned the cruiser.

Jake and Tony skirted the barn and headed uphill, pausing to listen for footsteps, but heard only rustling overhead. Soon they stood before a long, squat structure that leaned left onto a chimney, all joints out of kilter.

A row of small windows punctuated its facing wall, and on the building's short end, an open door hung open, one step up from the ground. The chamber was pitch black on this overcast night.

"Where are we?" Tony asked.

"They say it was a dormitory for workmen in the old iron village. Probably goes back a hundred years or more. Been rumors it was used as a safe house for runaway slaves, too. But we always called this place the Italian Shanty," Jake said, and fished a flashlight out of his bag.

Tony scanned the moldering hovel with distaste. "It's hard to picture anyone living here, Italian or not."

He gave Tony's arm a squeeze, and flipped on his light. "Come on."

They carefully made their way inside. It was longer and deeper than Tony expected, bigger than his parents' sizeable lake house.

Jake walked to the center of the undivided space near the rear long wall, where the flooring was still relatively intact. He pulled a large blanket and a thick candle out of his knapsack and snapped the blanket over worn planks. He set the candle down, lit it, and shut off the flashlight.

"Country comfort," Jake said, a smile dimpling his cheek. They sat and stared into the flame, Tony leaning against Jake.

Jake broke the silence. "I reckon the Germans and Irish who first came here called this bunkhouse 'Italian' as shorthand for 'shabby,'" he said, shaking his head. "People always putting others down to feel better about themselves, y'know?"

"And it makes no difference if you're from Sicily or the Highlands."

"Still convincing yourself we're the same." Jake sighed.

Why did Tony need Jake to be wrong? Did their differences make it all too clear to Tony that his infatuation with Jake couldn't last past Monday?

"But we both like *Li'l Abner,* and lake swims, and pepperoni pizza with root beer…" Tony's shoulders began to shake.

Jake shushed Tony and steadied him with strong arms. "Hey, hey, Tony. Don't you get me? *Me*—not the made-up version in your head." Jake's voice quivered.

Tony wiped his eyes. "I guess I'm just scared. Next week, everything changes. School…life. Us."

"And you think once you're back at school, you'll finally see we're too different, and that this"—Jake gently rocked Tony—"was just a summer fling." Jake's eyes were bottomless pools.

Tony felt stripped naked, but also relieved that Jake had read his thoughts. "Maybe I need to convince myself that's not true." He paused, wishing Jake would supply the words to make him feel sure.

Jake nuzzled Tony's neck. "Don't you think it's better to stop fighting against how things are?"

They both left Jake's question suspended in the room, and watched the weathered walls dance in shifting candlelight. Jake stretched out his legs and peered beyond the room.

His voice lightened. "I used to come here to be alone."

Tony glanced around the decaying space and shuddered. "Or disappear."

Jake laughed. "I made out here with a boy from high school."

"My favorite school fantasy was—"

Jake cut him off with a hard, wet kiss. "Time to stop daydreaming."

That slowed Tony's racing mind, but not his tongue. "You know...last year, I was in a bar in Greenwich Village for the first time. It was packed with men, and they were fearless. To be themselves, to hold another man—and for a little while, I felt this freedom, and joy..."

Jake squeezed Tony tight. "It can be that way if you want it." He kissed Tony's ear and sighed. "That night in bed, holding you, I could tell how much pain you were in. And that stayed with me. Because I'm a guy who stuffs it down, too."

Tony craned his neck to look at Jake. "Another way we're alike?" he asked.

Jake conceded with a smile. "You know, I was actually relieved when we had angry words. Because then I didn't have to deal with this whole mess we're in," Jake said.

Eyebrows knotted, Tony gave the slightest nod, and kissed the black eye, the bruises on Jake's brow. Maybe what he and Jake had in common was enough to make their differences the spice in the recipe, like the *peperoncino* in his mom's gravy. The heat that fired his senses, like how he felt right now. Jake's unanswered questions came to him.

You've never let your hands go where they wanted? Let your body be in charge?

Then Tony burrowed his face under Jake's shirt and his mouth went everywhere. Jake growled, his hands reaching down Tony's belly to his shorts, unbuttoning them, probing the thicket inside.

For a while, they fed on each other, murmuring, tugging, shedding clothes. Then Jake lowered Tony onto his back and gently entered him. They drew breath from each other like drowning men, bucking and riding wave after wave, like Hylas with Herakles on the *Argo*, then Alexander and Hephaestion coursing the sea, until the final swell broke on a distant shore.

Tony lay harbored in Jake's arms, drifting in mythical times, until he was wrenched back to the present by the click of a gun.

Brandt's car climbed the drive to the DenBleyker house, headlights bouncing off treetops. Euel and Malcolm looked over from where they sat on the porch, littered with beer bottles. Rifle on his shoulder, Brandt hit the ground at a jog and wheeled an arm toward the house.

His cousins wobbled to their feet, grinning. "Cousin Leo!" Malcolm exclaimed.

Euel solemnly saluted. "The new county *Führer!*" They bent at the waist, snorting laughter.

"Get inside!" Brandt barked. "Euel—gather the family weapons. Malcolm, draw the curtains all around. And tell Jake to join us in the parlor."

Euel and Malcolm sobered to their orders. "Well, Jake—" Euel began.

Brandt bounded up the porch steps. *"Go!"*

The brothers loped across the porch and followed their cousin into the house.

Delfinia looked up from her reading at the commotion heading her way. "Boys, what in— My word! Cousin Leo!"

Brandt came straight over and held her offered hand. "Delfinia, listen carefully. There's a shooter on the mountain, and your family may be in danger."

She clapped a hand over her mouth and squelched a cry. "But who...why...?"

"I don't have all the answers just now. But I am using all means at my disposal to protect you. I've contacted law enforcement from the next county and the state police for backup."

Euel spilled boxes of buckshot and bullets onto the dining table, while Malcolm pushed the large breakfront against the front door. Delfinia's gaze shot to the near window and she began to wail.

Brandt followed her eyes. "Delfinia, what is it?"

"My baby! Jacob..." She clutched her cousin's arm.

Brandt's eyes widened. "Jake? Where is he?"

"Jake and his friend, they went out," Euel said. "More'n two hours ago."

Brandt's chest hitched. For Delfinia's sake, he needed to believe Jake had the advantage on the mountain at night over a lone gunman from town. "Delfinia, look at me." He squeezed her hands. "If this family stays calm and acts together, we will be all right."

Brandt bobbed his head until Delfinia nodded. She swallowed hard, rose, and balled her hands into fists. Her eyes were slits.

"They take another son of mine over my dead body." She strode to the breakfront, slid a panel, and pulled open a drawer. Removing a .44 Magnum revolver, she walked back to her chair, and sat with great dignity.

Her eyes flashed toward her sons. "Euel, baby, bring me a box of bullets."

"Uh, yes, ma'am." Euel traded looks with Malcolm, and did her bidding.

Face drawn, Delfinia calmly opened the chamber and began loading. Eyes on the door, she snapped the chamber closed with the ball of her hand, propped the gun on an armrest, and aimed.

Brandt regarded her with wonder and smiled faintly. "They had better think twice before tangling with you."

He thought of the Highland's great web of complicity in Otto Schmidt's ruthless reign, how Brandt's cases for Silas and Schreier threatened that entrenched order, and realized with a jolt to the gut that all his assurances to Delfinia were bunk.

At the first crack, Jake contracted into a fetal coil. Tony dove and snuffed the candle. Hot wax splashed his wrist, and he bit down on his lip to keep from crying out, then clamped a hand on Jake's side. Five more shots ricocheted off the walls.

Sudden silence, and the shooter growled. Then, a ratcheting sound, six times. Tony tensed to flee, but the gunman blocked the only way out, and Jake was in no condition to run for it. They were fish in a barrel. Tony's mind froze. Jake murmured.

"What?" Tony pressed his ear to Jake's mouth.

"Trap...door."

"What—where?"

"Fire...place."

Tony grabbed Jake's shoulders and pulled him toward the far end of the shanty.

Click.

Four shots raked the air. Tony shook violently. Two left.

Tony dragged Jake nearer the chimney, but he struggled to shield him while fumbling for the hatch. His thoughts hectored that he was leaving Jake a sitting duck.

Which is what they both were, unless they found a way out.

Tony girded himself, released Jake, and got on his belly, sweeping the boards with both hands. Nothing but grit and leaves and raw wood.

A fifth shot sailed over his head.

Tony reached a wall. Where was the hearth? He fingered cracked plaster and bare lath, mind screaming that this was not a plan, it was suicide.

The sixth shot scattered sawdust near his head. Tony kept moving. He felt something smooth and cool: the fireplace.

Jake's breathing grew labored. Tony's panic unleashed a torrent of thoughts: he couldn't save them; Jake was dying; Tony was a coward.

Click, click, click. More swearing.

Tony frantically clawed the floor in widening arcs. He bit his lip to keep from crying out at the stabbing splinters. Then he scratched something hard and round, flush to the floor: a metal ring. He slid a finger in, and it swiveled. He wrenched it, and a piece of the floor, as wide as his shoulders, came up with it.

A gunshot resounded across the shack, bouncing off stone.

No! Not when we're so close!

Tony roared and let the heavy panel slam open. He ducked his head into the blackness.

Shot number two sang past his back.

He ignored it and groped the void below. His hand brushed wood, zigzagging away.

He scuttled over to Jake just as something cold and hard poked his bare chest.

"Nice try, Marsala." Otto Schmidt's voice was flat, cold. "How do you like your Eye-talian Shanty? Remind you of home?" Tony could smell the alcohol on him.

Tony shielded Jake's body with his own. "Otto, don't—"

"Get out of my way, faggot, or I'll finish you, too!"

His body and mind seized up. He was out of options. It was over.

"Okay, then, have it your way," Schmidt said. The next blast sparked off of something metal on the hatch panel, and then another flew past Tony into the darkness.

"Where's my goddamn flashlight," Otto muttered to himself. Tony heard the short scuff of a shoe, as if the man was off-balance.

"Now, I've got you," Otto gloated, and Tony was suddenly blinded by Otto's light. Shielding his sights, Tony could just make out Otto's restless eyes, the clenched jaw, a twisted brow slick with sweat. The mask of a man out of control. Which could compromise his judgment, make him careless. And that made him weak.

Tony linked his hands and rushed forward, punching upward on Otto's wrists. The gun discharged above them, and the flashlight smashed into the wall and went dark.

"You little shit!"

Otto grunted and swore, as if wrestling for control of the gun, and it sent a bullet into the floor. Tony head-butted Otto in the stomach, and Otto gripped Tony's skull and threw him against the hearth with a frightening crack. He slid to the ground and moaned.

"I think you'll keep while I finish what I came here for,"
Otto snarled. His scraping steps seemed headed for Jake.

Tony's head was a blast furnace.

Otto pulled the trigger.

Click. Click, click, click.

He hadn't counted.

Tony thrust himself to his feet through exploding pain and
groped for Jake, grabbed his shoulders, and hoisted him
through the gap in the floor. He held on to Jake and took the
steep steps on faith until the earthy air signaled he'd cleared
the floor of the shanty. Then he slammed the panel after him,
almost losing his balance and Jake.

He prayed there was some moving part on the door's
underside; he fumbled for one, his hold on Jake slipping. He
leaned face down into the steps and gathered his strength.

Scratching sounds came from directly over his head.

Tony tightened one hand on Jake, shot his free hand over
his head, and banged a knuckle on the moving part. He
clutched it, and with a grunt made it turn. He felt Jake's weight
shift, and shaking with effort, Tony wrestled Jake's limp arm.

Were they safe? He thrust his head against the unyielding
panel; Otto was locked out. But Tony still heard his footfalls
above them. He had to get them both to safety before Otto shot
the floor full of holes.

Tony thudded his way down the crude stairs until his toes
touched bottom. Annihilating darkness surrounded him, and
like a phantom from his past, the familiar, crushing weight
pressed down, stole air from his lungs, and then he was gone.

Minutes? hours? later, Tony felt his stomach clench like a fist,
and he threw up. He rose to his haunches and hovered there

until his groans of pain subsided. Then he felt for Jake and pulled him upright, just barely, arms slung around Tony's neck. Where were they?

His senses worked overtime in the blind underground, and he wished now for Jake's abandoned flashlight. He slapped the hard ground with one foot, and the sound echoed crisply around him. He smelled stone and iron. The air hitting his sweat was cool, and the cool brushed his skin.

A current. *A passage.*

He recalled his nakedness and stepped forward gingerly, feeling the rough earth under his bare soles. Every few steps, Tony freed one hand to feel the walls. Some parts were rough, damp, and crumbling, others smooth masonry.

Every now and again, the walls would bow outward, and he'd feel a seam where the roughness was filled in, as though a channel had been sealed. Now the floor felt like cobblestone. Through it all, the path kept tending downward.

What is this place?

Then Tony remembered what Jake had said about safe houses and fugitives. How many had passed this way? Had they known what lay ahead, or, like Tony and Jake, only the hell they'd left behind?

Euel pushed out of his chair and paced. "We can't just do nothing," he fumed.

"Oh, Leo, my heart can't take much more waiting and wondering," Delfinia whimpered.

Malcolm peered through the parlor curtains and slapped the window frame in assent. "Jake and Tony been gone three hours already. We gotta *do* something!"

Brandt was livid. None of his requested backup from other

jurisdictions had materialized. He'd underestimated Otto's powers of influence. Now his restlessness told him to act.

He waved Euel over to Malcolm's post and huddled with his young cousins. "You said Jake and Tony went out—where?" he asked gravely.

"They didn't say, exactly," Malcolm mumbled.

Brandt pressed his lips together. "This is your brother we're talking about. Where is the likeliest place for him to go around here at night?"

Malcolm looked at Euel, who blew air at the ceiling. "Well...could be the Reefer Barn," Euel said. "It was a high school hangout."

"Or the Italian Shanty," Malcolm added. "That's someplace you go when you don't want no one to bother you."

"Maybe the whirlpool?" said Euel, more question than lead.

"On Wewappo Creek," Malcolm clarified. "That's secluded, too."

Leo Brandt rubbed his scalp, head cocked, seeming to query the ceiling. Finally, he turned to the two men and chopped the air with his hand.

"Okay. How do I find this...shanty?"

Malcolm drew the route on the windowpane with his finger. "Three miles down, look for a break on your left. Straight back over the trees, the old furnace pokes out. It's a short ways uphill from there."

He studied his cousins. "Now, gentlemen, listen up." Brandt's words came in martial scansion. "Until my return, I hereby deputize you as officers of the law. Your duties are strictly defensive, but do not hesitate to use your weapons to protect yourselves and your mother."

His gaze fixed on Delfinia, lips moving, eyes pressed tight. He'd be damned to see her or her surviving children come to harm. Brandt turned to the two young men, grasped their shoulders, and walked them toward the barricaded door.

"I want you both to swear to me that you will do your utmost to avoid a shoot-out," he said under his breath. "And do not approach the gunman. We are dealing with a desperate, dangerous man." The boys nodded uncertainly.

"Promise me!" Brandt commanded.

"Promise," the brothers said with one voice.

"But who is it, Cousin Leo?" asked Euel.

Brandt paused, pursed his lips, and whispered, "Otto Schmidt."

For a moment, his cousins were stunned to silence.

"On my honor, that lying bastard come anywhere near, Silas gonna be avenged," Euel hissed.

Malcolm assented. "Sure as I'm standing here—"

"Remember your oaths!" Brandt snapped. He scraped the breakfront aside and slipped into the night.

Tony felt Jake shiver. His blood was sticky on Tony's back; it was just a matter of time before Jake lost consciousness.

"Just a little longer," Tony said, unsure of who needed more consoling. He was bone tired, and they'd made only halting progress. Without warning, Jake slumped, Tony's legs buckled, and together they dropped to the ground.

Jake's gasp of pain lacerated Tony. He pressed numb hands to his face and moaned. *This is how it ends.* Tears filled his sightless eyes, and a long, keening wail burst from him.

As if in reply, he heard Jake's voice in his head.

What do you want?

What does it matter, when the whole fucking world is against me? his thoughts shot back.

People been getting their hearts broke forever, and still we find a way, the voice replied.

Jake had so many reasons to give up on the world, on Tony, and still he'd stuck it out, dared Tony to want. Want something enough to stop making excuses, and grab it with both hands.

Maybe it wasn't the world standing in Tony's way.

Maybe it was him.

Telling himself that he wasn't *supposed* to be this way, wasn't *allowed* to have what he wanted. Believing that life was a choice between happiness and survival.

Which was no choice at all.

I have to get out of my own way.

Fight his own battles, be the hero of his story. Like Alexander at Arbela. Macedonia's fifty thousand, against a million Persians with their war elephants and blades of death. The Greek king and Hephaestion had rent the Persian line like scythes through wheat. And Alexander had borne his wounded lover from battle.

In Tony's dream life, he had always been the rescued, but now only he could save himself and what he wanted most.

With a roar, Tony hoisted Jake onto his back and broke into a run. Instantly, his limbs were on fire, and still he pumped, thudding down the tunnel, growling as he grazed the curving walls, until his whole body heaved and he slowed to a stop.

He sensed a lightness in the air. Rustling. Hissing.

He let the slope of the tunnel pull him forward. He gasped, built to a jog, and...sprinted. The roof of the underworld vanished, infinity above, pine breezes on his skin.

Tony dropped to his knees on the cool earth, exhausted and exhilarated. He cradled and rocked Jake. The clouds had thinned enough to cast a faint moonglow on Jake: eyes closed, face pale and sweaty. Tony stroked Jake's cheek, and he made a faint sound.

Fresh tears stung Tony to think how few moments of intimacy they'd managed midst all the defenses and delusions they'd put between them. To protect themselves from a world that made them doubt their own beating hearts.

And still they'd persisted and reconciled, if only for these past hours. How precious time seemed now, as Jake slipped away with it. He wanted to tell him so many things, how grateful he was that they'd met, that Jake hadn't given up on him, had taught him so much about himself.

"Jake?"

Jake gave no sign of hearing him. Exhaustion was pulling Tony under. He yearned to simply close his eyes, forget their danger for just one blessed, peaceful moment...

No!

Jake had risked his life to save Tony, and he'd be damned if he'd hand Otto victory now.

He strained for a sign in the stew of sounds: rhythmic ratchets in the branches, shivering leaves. Then, faint beneath them, a whoosh: flowing water. Tony willed it to be Jake's creek, their highway home. He pushed off the forest floor, slid on slick leaves, and planted both feet on the ground.

"Okay, Jake. Time to go home," he whispered.

Tony lifted Jake's bloody, pallid body, and his legs wobbled and jackknifed. On his knees, he closed his eyes and gulped the night air. He clenched every muscle and sprang forward, Jake against his back. He trotted toward the sibilance, branches and leaves slapping his face and shoulders.

Tony took the downward slope of the land to where the ground grew damp. He reached out for a handhold in the trees. He gasped and kept moving. Soon the sound ahead swelled to a roar, and then the woods opened into a volume of space.

A waterfall. *The whirlpool.* Tony knew it so well, he didn't need the dim moon to find the steps in the rock that delivered him to the wide shelf dividing the cascade.

The plangent falls transfixed Tony. He shivered in its spray, dizziness pressing in. He slipped Jake from his shoulders and lowered himself to slick stone. Cradling Jake's head in his lap, he closed his eyes and bargained with weariness. *Just a moment, and we'll be on our way.*

He was parched; the falls called to him. He'd be stronger for the hike ahead if he drew a deep draft of water; yes, he needed to, he must do it for both of them.

Tony silently begged indulgence from Jake and laid his head on soft moss. Tony crawled to the shelf's edge and grabbed it with both hands. He let himself hang in space, and plunged his face into the current. He opened his mouth wide to take his cool, quenching relief, just as an explosion ripped through the trees.

Tony scrambled to right himself. Footsteps crunched nearby.

"Fancy meeting you again," Otto called from the opposite bank.

Before Tony could react, Otto bridged the gap between shore and shelf. He swayed, gun poised, and Tony scrambled to shield Jake with his body.

"You can't do this," Tony said, breathing hard.

Otto crept forward. "I have no quarrel with you, Marsala. Give me the mongrel and you won't get hurt."

Tony struggled to pull Jake farther from Otto while keeping himself between Jake and the gun. He eyed the woods beyond the ledge, hopelessly far away.

"But I have no qualms about taking you out, too, so get out of my way, you little cocksucker!"

Tony pondered the swirling waters below. He'd dived into

them from this rock many times, but he'd never heard the whirlpool this wild and angry. It sounded as though it was running high enough to submerge its scattered boulders, making them a deadly danger. Surviving the plunge would be a crap shoot for a strong swimmer, and he didn't dare risk it with Jake.

"*Now*, Marsala!" Otto fired at Tony's feet, and Tony threw his whole body over Jake's. Instantly, a loud crack resounded downstream. The blast showered them with bits of the forest. Otto swung toward the sound and fired back.

"Police! Drop your weapon!" The voice was Brandt's.

Tony scrambled to protect Jake from this new threat and strained to discern the source of the answering shot. Otto exploited his distraction to close in and bring down the butt of his gun on Tony's head.

Blinding pain shot through Tony, and he lost his grip on Jake. Then he felt himself lifted by powerful hands and shoved backward. Tony skidded before stumbling to the ground between the stone saddle and the trees flanking it, his body a crucible of pain.

"Nooo!" Tony howled, clawing the air for Jake.

A rising light found Tony. "Mr. Marsala! Where's Jake?" Brandt called.

Giddy laughter drew the cop's light some fifteen feet to Otto, hunched over Jake, blade to his neck, while Otto aimed his revolver toward his armed adversary.

"Drop the gun!" Brandt demanded.

"You'll follow *my* orders, Brandt, or you and your kin are history." Otto flicked a glance at Tony. "Looks like your plan didn't go so well, Marsala," Otto trumpeted. "And this would-be sheriff thought he'd outsmart me. But I've got both monkeys by the tail now, don't I?" He giggled at his own epithet.

"Otto, hands over your head!" Brandt boomed, and his searchlight went dark.

The afterimage of Jake and the knife pulsed behind Tony's eyes. Two more gun blasts rang out and pumped new life into Tony. He sprinted for Otto, dropped down, and locked onto his shins, throwing him off-balance.

Something went skittering, and Otto lunged for it. Tony raced to Jake and enveloped him, and then watched spellbound as Otto skidded on slick stone toward the sheer drop and slipped over. Otto's arms windmilled, and he caught the ledge with a forearm, the rest of him out of sight.

"*Help me!*" he roared.

Brandt's light drew closer as Tony frantically urged life into Jake. After an agonizing interval, Jake groaned, and Tony put his face to Jake's.

"Jake, stay awake!" Jake gave a gravelly rumble. "That's it! Keep talking!"

"Pull me up Marsala, or *I will destroy your family!*" Otto bellowed above the roaring falls, and Tony turned to see eight fingers at the lip of the ledge in Brandt's searchlight.

"Thirsty..." Jake's reedy voice lanced Tony.

"Jesus, somebody help me!" Otto shrieked.

"Tony, stay with Jake until I get up there!" Brandt called from below.

Otto was about to drown.

Jake's would-be executioner.

Tony's mind churned. Two men were in peril. Could he simply let one of them die?

Heeding no one and nothing but his own thudding heart, Tony hurried toward Otto and stopped at the shelf edge inches from the pleading man's grasping fingers, scooped a handful of water, scuttled back to Jake, and slowly funneled it to his lips.

Brandt emerged from the woods onto the shelf and barked,

"Schmidt, grab my arm!" As he reached down, Otto's spotlit fingers slipped away, and a thump and a whoosh swallowed his howl of terror.

As Brandt gave commands into his walkie-talkie, he took in Tony, naked and battered. "Mr. Marsala, what happened to you and Jake tonight?" he asked, wide-eyed.

Tony grinned. "We won."

Filling his hands with water again, he dripped it slowly past Jake's lips. Then Tony dropped down and enfolded Jake from behind, palms pressed to Jake's chest, skin to skin, hearts pacing quaver for quaver.

14

Saturday September 3rd

From Jake's hospital room, Tony watched the morning sun dissolve in the haze. It was three days before the start of his junior year, and life seemed suspended between endings and beginnings.

They'd both arrived at the ER in the small hours. Jake had been whisked off to surgery, leaving Tony on his gurney to be patched, prodded and hydrated. Then he'd sat for hours in a hospital gown on a hall chair, his cut and blistered feet swaddled in bandages, left to wonder if Jake would pull through. He hadn't slept a wink.

Now he studied Jake's bruised face, purple giving way to yellow.

"Where am I?" Jake croaked, eyes roaming the room.

Tony squeezed his hand. "Right here, with me."

Jake's brow wrinkled. "But how...?"

Tony leaned in close and stroked Jake's temple. "It's over, and you're safe," he murmured.

Footsteps approached, and the two men turned to find Leo Brandt in the doorway, shopping bag in one hand, eyebrow arched over an equivocal smile.

"Cousin Leo," Jake managed, wincing. Tony and Brandt shared a look of concern.

Brandt offered the bag to Tony. "I thought you two might need these."

Tony saw it contained a bundle of clothing, and blushed to recall how Brandt and a legion of paramedics and hospital workers had found him and Jake in their natural state last night.

"Mr. Brandt, thank you for your thoughtfulness"—Tony released a shaky breath—"and for everything last night."

Brandt stood above Tony and squeezed his shoulder, lips pressed against his own welling feelings. He appraised his cousin, extended his hand toward the blanket, and met Jake's eyes. "May I?" Jake nodded.

Brandt lifted the covers to reveal Jake's battered, bound up body, and he flinched. He covered up his cousin and took a long moment to compose himself.

"Glad to see you on the mend." He forced a smile.

A grin flickered on Jake's face. "Glad to see you and not the sheriff. Him and his nephew finally gonna stand trial for Silas?"

Brandt's brow furrowed, and he shot Tony a querying look. Tony gave a quick, sharp shake of his head.

"Jake, do you remember what happened last night?" Tony asked.

"Waterfalls. And bad dreams." Jake's eyes seemed to scan his memory.

"Mr. Brandt saved our lives," Tony said reverently.

"Your friend is too modest," Brandt objected. "*He* saved both of you. I was merely an accessory to his heroism," he said, shooting Tony a look of gentle approbation.

Jake looked at Cousin Leo and Tony with wonderment.

"No one could've just stood by while Otto..." Tony bit his lip.

Brandt snorted in protest. "I came armed for battle, but you, without even the clothes on your back, stood up to a ruthless killer! That's bravery far beyond what duty called me to do," he said, voice throbbing.

Tony grew thoughtful. "Everything got real clear staring down the barrel of a gun. I saw what I stood to lose." Blinking fast, Tony locked eyes with Jake.

Jake's voice seemed far away. "I remember now." His face crumpled, and he whimpered. Tony stroked Jake's hair until he had spilled his grief.

Brandt appraised Jake, and pursed his lips. "Jake, I want you to hear this from me. After the medics came for you last night, I went back up the mountain to check on your family, hoping to find the extra police protection I'd requested."

Brandt's lips disappeared, and after a pause, he continued. "What I found instead was a burning cross on your lawn." Another pause. "And next to it, a handmade sign on a stake that read FROM NEW YORK'S FINEST."

Jake sat straight up and cried out, "What did they do to my family?"

"Everyone's safe. I spoke to your mom and brothers, and they are understandably shaken, but unharmed."

"Who would do this?" Tony exclaimed.

Brandt breathed a heavy sigh. "My guess is a few hardcore Schmidt loyalists on the force who were enraged by his arrest. They knew where Jake lived because Otto was executing a police sting on Jake's house at the time of Jake's arrest at the sinkhole during the storm."

"They did that before the sheriff died. Just wait until *this* news hits the fan," Jake said.

"I'm afraid it's already in this morning's paper. My advice to the both of you: stay vigilant. Some of our neighbors in the Highlands marched in white hoods alongside Otto's old Bund comrades."

Cousin Leo turned his attention to Jake. "I am doing all that I can to safeguard your family. I've arranged for a trusted friend with phone service who lives near your highway turnoff to watch the mountain traffic. He'll report anything suspicious to my direct line at HQ. And your brothers know they can go to our watchful friend anytime and reach me, night or day."

"But that's no guarantee." Jake wrestled with his bed covers. "I've got to go help protect them."

His cousin restrained Jake with a hand to his chest. "The best way you can help your kin right now is to heal yourself, or you won't be good for anything."

"You know he's right, Jake," Tony added. Jake stared back glumly, and stayed silent.

Brandt looked at his palms and cleared his throat. "Tony, may I have a word in private, please? It's about your father."

"I'd rather be here just now." Brandt looked askance. "Go ahead, you can tell me," Tony said, cupping Jake's hand to anchor himself.

Brandt scratched his head and frowned. He looked toward the open door, got up, closed it, and pulled up a chair. He looked steadily at Tony for a long moment and then began. "Tony, we have detained your father as a suspect in the death of the newspaper reporter."

Tony's mouth went slack. The words hung in the air, not quite cohering. He traded looks with Jake.

"My father. A suspect?" His eyes drifted to Brandt, who nodded. Tony scoured his memory for anything that might link his dad with the terrible murder that had been in the local paper for nearly a week.

Tony's eyes hardened. "This has something to do with Otto Schmidt, doesn't it?"

Brandt looked down and gave an unvoiced sigh. "Yes, it does. Your father's relationship with Otto…"

"Were they close?" Tony shot back, hoping Brandt would quash the sickening notion.

"That I cannot say," Brandt replied. "But in this instance, I believe Schmidt coerced him to conspire to commit murder."

"But how could Otto possibly make my dad…" Tony wrinkled his nose.

Brandt shrugged. "I would be speculating at this point. What we do know is that Otto was providing protection for your father's business."

"Protection? From what?"

As the words left his mouth, Tony knew.

The goons from the city. The incident.

Otto was the reason Dad's scrapyard had been spared more trouble. And if Tony had learned anything about Otto, it was that every favor required a sacrifice. So what had he wanted from Dad?

"From a repeat of the attack five years ago—"

"On my dad, and his business. Yes, I know. But what does that have to do with this reporter?" Tony asked impatiently.

"This protection seems to have been the key to their whole relationship. And it was why your father became one of Otto's biggest boosters. That was the price he paid to keep a roof over your head."

My dad, in bed with the man who wanted Jake dead? Tony's throat burned. He fought against Brandt's inexorable logic. "But that doesn't prove my father killed anyone!"

Brandt continued. "Your father and Dan Schreier attended Otto's election rally at the Old Rhinelander two weeks ago. Schreier was never seen alive again."

Tony squirmed in his seat. "Weren't a lot of other people there, too? Why aren't you going after any of *them*?" he protested.

Brandt gently raised his palms toward Tony. "Tony, someone at the rally took photographs. Eddie Schmidt pursued Schreier from the banquet hall to a balcony, and then your father followed Eddie out of the room. Schreier never came back."

Tony sat on a bench in the small park alongside the jail, digesting the talk he'd just had with his father. From across the visitor's table in the sickly light, Sal had admitted his guilt. What was Tony supposed to do with that?

His dad had described the whole arc of his business struggles in Iron Run: building a clientele from scratch in these clannish Highlands, naming his new scrapyard Patriot Metal to conceal his Italian ancestry.

How he'd made the rounds of the church bazaars, Steuben Day celebrations, and Oktoberfests, sponsored Little League and charity drives. And allied himself with the county's powerful sheriff.

But then Otto had called in a stunning favor: rub out a meddlesome reporter.

His dad's soul baring had triggered still more questions from Tony. Why hadn't Sal said no? What sort of man does that? What kind of *father*?

Sal had remonstrated through anguished tears that if he'd made bad choices, it was so his own family could avoid the struggles of his immigrant parents. Seeing his dad defeated and humbled, Tony had felt remorse that he'd stood in judgment of him, and taken for granted his own comfortable life, unaware that it had all come with an enormous cost to his father.

Rage and sorrow battered him. Why had his dad's dreams of happiness and security come so hard, and been so cruelly snatched away?

And Tony saw all at once the unstoppable sweep of suffering, in his own life and Jake's, for his parents and Silas and the reporter and too many others in the Highlands, that its threads were woven into every life and clan and tribe, generations of Sicilians and Ramapoughs, Germans and Jews, of migrants and slaves, in steerage and exile, captivity and flight, in camps and mines and cotton fields, their dreams snuffed and rekindled in endless cycles of anguish and yearning, reaching and grasping, having and lacking. Tony swiped away hot tears.

And still Otto Schmidt's words gnawed at him. *Your father is a traitor.* They didn't fit the contrite man in a prison cell. Tony needed the whole truth about his father and the war. He wiped his eyes and looked at his watch; time to check on Jake.

He headed for the visitor's parking area, where a glittering spot of asphalt alongside his car drew his gaze. He jogged toward it and stopped before a circle of shattered glass on the ground, an empty rear window frame, and on the seat beyond it, a brick wrapped in paper.

With shaking hands, Tony tore off the note, and read its scrawled message: FREE AMERICA FROM GUINEAS! He spun around the empty lot, but there was no one.

Otto was only hours gone, and the retribution had begun.

Leo Brandt sat in his office, pondering the wreckage of his cases. Eddie's talent for wreaking havoc had survived him. Brandt had to admit, with some bitterness, that his cousins would never get their day in court with Silas's killer—though Eddie's self-destruction seemed justice enough.

That left the Schreier murder and what to do about Salvatore Marsala. Under questioning, the man had spilled everything. Marsala had told Otto Schmidt that the city thugs who'd messed him up would make far better hit men than he, but Schmidt had let Sal know that his refusal to help would not be good for business.

So they had struck a compromise: Eddie would jab Schreier with the truth serum and dump the body in the lake; Marsala's presence would ensure that the deed was done right.

But in the event, a panicky Eddie had dropped the needle between the deck's planks, and it was Sal who'd drawn from his pocket the backup syringe, which became the murder weapon that Eddie soon after flung far from shore.

Eddie had unraveled when the body didn't sink as expected. He stole a cabin cruiser from the Old Rhinelander's docks during the celebrations inside, and then repeatedly ran the boat over Schreier's body until it disappeared.

Brandt felt in his bones that Marsala was telling the whole story, down to the details of the pilfered truth serum. All Brandt lacked to tie up the case with a bow was the murder weapon, but short of sending in divers to scour the deep, weed-choked lake bottom, chances of finding it were zero.

So now he had to decide: With all of Marsala's cooperation and mitigating circumstances, would he recommend that the DA take him to trial for conspiracy to murder, when he was the only living witness to the crime? Did Brandt want his first high-profile case as sheriff to be a legal circus?

Could he so easily dismiss justice for the Schreier family?

In Brandt's shadow investigation, he had contacted the closest kin of the victim he could find. It turned out that Schreier's father was the only relative to survive the death camps. When he'd informed Abraham Schreier that his son Dan's death was a homicide, the man had teared up and wanted to talk.

Abraham had described his family's German life before Hitler, their wartime ordeal in the death camps, and after V-E Day, searching the displaced persons camps for Dan. From the time they'd reunited, he'd told Brandt, he and his son had remained close.

Together, they had stood watch against the family's extinction, refusing to give up the search for other loved ones. Abraham still made regular inquiries to the Jewish Agency.

It had gotten Brandt thinking about Schreier and his killer, such natural antagonists and polar opposites. And yet their lives had similar contours. Christ, their parents might have been neighbors in Berlin.

An ocean apart, Dan and Eddie had been raised in hardship and upheaval, their childhoods stolen, both sent to live behind barbed wire. Each boy had lost a parent to the war, each betrayed by his own country.

And Schmidt and Schreier would have emerged from those betrayals burning to right the wrongs done to them, their families, and their people. Maybe their earliest impulses had been righteous; but in the end, blind loyalty to a just cause had driven both Eddie Schmidt and Dan Schreier to their encounter, with consequences devastatingly unjust.

So what could justice look like in this three-way tragedy? Yes, Sal Marsala had conspired with Otto and Eddie in Schreier's death, but under threat of ruin. It was clear to Brandt that Marsala was tormented by his own conduct. And Sal's own son had recently stared down death; hadn't his family already been through enough?

Algonquin County these past weeks had seen tragedy enough for ten summers. Brandt's choices could fuel still more.

Would another human sacrifice console a grieving father? Would it help the Highlands heal?

The groundskeeper at the Old Rhinelander Inn was juiced this last summer Saturday. He'd had a long lunch and a few rounds at his favorite dive in Iron Run. What the hell, he'd worked hard all year to satisfy that taskmaster Grunnwald.

Time to ease off the pedal. He was halfway done already, with plenty of time to catch stray leaves and groom the grounds to perfection.

He trimmed and edged the sweeping lawn, then grabbed hand rakes and worked his way along the building's underbelly, a crawl space hidden by latticework, combing the flowerbeds as he went.

At the building's south face, near the cliff edge, the man leaned into the shade of the balcony, flicking tines of dead matter from the shadows in a steady rhythm. Just inside the lattice, a slender silver rod glinted.

All manner of treasures would regularly turn up in the weeds from a beery Saturday night at the Old Rhinelander, like shells on a beach after a storm. The best prizes never made it to the lost-and-found drawer of his skinflint boss, who wasn't exactly generous with job perks. So this glorified servant had no qualms about helping himself to one of the job's few dividends.

He twisted his head away from the shiny prize to extend his shoulder and arm under the wood strips and inched his fingers forward. At last, he folded the thing into his palm, and instantly recoiled from a jabbing pain.

"Sonuvabitch!" He yanked his hand into the light to find a small bead of blood where the needle had broken his skin.

Sunday September 4th

Unshaven and still in Saturday's clothes, Brandt held the syringe up to the early light in a gloved hand. Sometimes, he mused, help comes from where you least expect it. Good thing he'd taken Frieda to celebrate their tenth anniversary at the Old Rhinelander last year.

The event had cemented a personal bond with Manny Grunnwald, an old Schmidt ally who seemed lately to have stuck a wet finger in the air and adjusted to the change in the weather. Brandt scratched his neck and smiled. You never knew when old-fashioned goodwill would pay off.

For a brief moment, he recalled the candlelight, the flaming desserts, the band in lederhosen, the devoted look on his wife's face. And that delivered him right back to his desk, regretting how little of her he'd seen since the Van Hoek autopsy six days ago.

Time to make amends; he made a note to call Manny for a Labor Day window table with a sunset view, hoping the missus would still be speaking to him by then.

Brandt had called in some hefty favors on Labor Day Saturday and gotten his test results delivered by five o'clock. The trace contents of the syringe were positive for the formulation of sodium amytal found in Schreier's bloodstream and the sheriff's refrigerator. As expected, prints had come up positive for the inn's groundskeeper and Eddie Schmidt, but not Salvatore Marsala.

Brandt returned the needle to its bag, placed it inside his top desk drawer, and paused. Next to the hypodermic sat a leather datebook embossed with the Algonquin County seal.

Brandt opened it, scanned last week's entries, and pressed his lips.

There was the date of Schreier's murder, in black and white. Cocky as ever, Otto had failed to cover his own tracks. Brandt returned the book to the drawer and snapped off his gloves.

He strode down the short corridor to the holding cells and unlocked the main door. He turned to his left and stepped up to the glass. Salvatore Marsala stared back, Saturday's *Mountain Observer* in his lap.

Marsala studied him. "Seems Otto Schmidt drowned Friday night. Your thoughts, Sheriff?"

Brandt shared a knowing smile. "I can't close a case without a body, though I know a brave eyewitness who can corroborate that story," he replied.

Marsala beamed, and Brandt winked. Not a decorous exchange for an acting sheriff and a prisoner, perhaps, but then, it had been a helluva week for both of them, and it seemed the decent thing to do.

Brandt briskly set a key in the cell lock, and twisted. The cylinder released the bolt with a short, sharp click. Sal Marsala snapped to his feet, the newspaper scattering on the cement floor.

"Mr. Marsala, it is the judgment of this department that you shall be released to home confinement until contacted by the DA's office. Bail is waived." He threw open the cell door and gestured for the prisoner to leave. "In the meantime, enjoy what's left of the weekend with your family. I'll call you a car," he added softly.

Salvatore Marsala acknowledged Brandt's reprieve with a knowing smile. He extended his hand to this new sheriff, who met his own firmly, signaling to Sal that perhaps for the first time in years, justice in the Highlands would be done without prejudice or favor.

Jake's valise stood by the door next to Tony's sleeping bag. Jake emerged from the shower, stood on his towel before a wall mirror, and surveyed the week's toll.

"I look like the loser in a bear-rasslin' contest," he humphed.

Tony quickly glanced to the hall, then approached from behind and stroked Jake's back. He flinched and patted the large gauze bandage at his side.

"They sewed me up good. Said if the bullet had hit an inch different, I wouldn't be here talking about it." Sober eyes met in the mirror.

Tony guided Jake toward the bed and drew the privacy curtain around them before he gingerly wrapped Jake in his arms and kissed his neck. They stood for several moments in mingled warmth.

Despite qualms about his family's safety, Jake had agreed to convalesce by the lake for a day before facing his mother. Euel had readily concurred after seeing Jake at the hospital late Saturday, while Malcolm kept watch at home against further mischief. Euel had promised Jake to tell their mother the fib that he'd be discharged Monday.

Tony lightly traced Jake's shoulders, neck, and jaw with his lips. "What do you say we get this bare-naked bear rassler into a lounger by the lake?" he whispered, feeling Jake's cheek stretch into a smile.

Tony maneuvered the hospital wheelchair to his car, the damaged rear window covered with cardboard and duct tape. Jake eyed it askance.

"Did my drunk brothers smash their way into your car for beer Friday?" he said with little humor.

"No...um, someone delivered a message tied to a brick."

Jake studied Tony with alarm. "What message?"

"*Free America from guineas*," Tony said, grimacing.

"Whoa," Jake said. "Otto's cult got a score to settle."

On the drive to his house, Tony's thoughts turned to his parents. Since seeing his dad in jail the day before, he'd had little time to digest all that he'd learned about him. He had barely seen his mother since Thursday; she must be going through hell right now, which didn't begin to describe his dad's predicament. Worry and guilt needled him.

He decided that after lunch with his mom, he'd set up Jake with a blanket and chair in the sun and take his mother to see his dad in jail. He was sure there was nothing to be done for his case until the long holiday weekend had passed.

When Tony's own life would either change completely or not at all. He sighed. In the long hours he'd watched Jake sleep off surgery, he'd thought of little else but what the end of summer meant for both of them.

Tony's senses hummed. The reckoning at the whirlpool had clarified the stakes, sharpened choices. For maybe the first time in his life, he'd ignored the flashing lights and sirens and put everything on the line for what *he* wanted. But in the cold light of day, could he sustain that?

There was school to consider. He had worked hard to get into Columbia and make his family proud—Ma and Dad and Nonno and Nonna, who'd mortgaged their lives for a dream Tony could redeem. Didn't he owe that to them?

Except there was no place in their dream for two faggots.

He frowned at how easily he heaped scorn on himself, aped the prejudice he's been weaned on, and it occurred that this same unwitting contempt had almost broken Tony and Jake apart. Just as it had ruined lives in the Highlands these several weeks. It was the air they all breathed. Tony felt an overwhelming sadness.

We're all victims, and we're all guilty.

Tony glanced over at Jake, eyes closed, exhausted: this strong, proud man, wounded and wary, who loved him despite all the ways Tony had hurt him.

He wanted to do something, anything, to salve all the pain, but what could one person do?

Forgive.

Forgive himself for disparaging Jake. For caring what others thought. For exiling his own affections. Time wasted, time he could have spent loving this lonely soul from another world, who loved and wanted *him*. Tony's eyes stung, and the road and trees and sky bled together.

In the fractured light of the pines, the Falcon rode Mount Zindel's swells, dipping and weaving like a runabout. They soon came to a long, straight stretch of roadway, where a small rectangle appeared in the distance.

The familiar billboard came clearer: a smiling Leo Brandt, large letters alongside his face that spelled JUSTICE FOR ALL. A reminder that Tony's choices at the whirlpool last Friday had rewritten the story of an election.

As the campaign ad loomed before him, he was jolted from his reverie by a swastika slashed across the word *justice*, and a pair of jumpy words scrawled over Brandt's face: CHERRY NIGR.

Maybe the sheriff had changed, Tony thought, but not people's hearts. Gradually, the road declined, and he tapped the brakes as home and hard choices loomed.

Antoinette Marsala hugged her son at the door, then clucked her tongue at Jake. *"O, Dio!"* She cupped Jake's bruised cheeks, and he smiled through the pain. "Straight to the porch and off your feet!" she ordered.

Tony led Jake toward the light and abruptly halted. A slim silhouette bled into the brightness. Tony squinted and blinked, and the figure filled in.

"Dad?"

Sal stepped forward and kissed his son, stubble sanding Tony's cheek.

Tony's brow knotted. "But why...how...?"

"Sheriff Brandt released me on my own recognizance this morning."

"But you...*confessed*." Tony frowned.

Sal studied his son a moment. "Yes, Tony, I confessed to being Eddie's handler for the killing, and I thought that Brandt might well charge me with murder. I can only assume that the weight of the evidence convinced him that I was accomplice, but not executioner."

"So Brandt didn't exonerate you, but he still let you go?" Tony said.

"Until I am presented with formal charges after Labor Day. I think he felt that my cooperation warranted home confinement until then."

Tony's frown held firm. "So you're still guilty," His eyes glinted reproachfully.

Sal's measured facade broke, and he sighed deeply. "I don't expect that anything I've just said acquits me in your eyes."

"I guess I'm just...disappointed," Tony said, fingernails scoring his palms.

Sal's eyes dropped, and he nodded to himself. "I'm disappointed in me, too, son. The test of a man's character comes when the chips are down, and I failed. I can live with that black mark, but not the reproof I see in your eyes.

"Otto Schmidt gave me a Hobson's choice, and I chose the well-being of you and your mother over my honor. So I ask you: Will you forgive me?" Sal stretched out his arms, and before Tony could think, he filled them, sniffling. He knew what it was like to fall short in his own eyes. And he felt grateful that he had never been tested like his father.

Tony held his father at arm's length, and smiled. "Dad...you don't need my forgiveness." He wiped his cheeks. "I guess we could all be more forgiving. And not judge people so harshly for just being...human."

"The monsignor calls that grace," Sal said. "Time to start acting with the grace of God." He beamed at his son. "You know, Tony, I don't say often enough how proud I am of you. Since you were a kid, and most especially, for what you did Friday."

Tony's eyes darted to his mom, a smile blooming from quivering lips.

Sal continued. "You've taught this old man something about heroism."

Tony studied his dad with a bemused grin. "But how—"

"Leo Brandt told me all about your naked courage," Sal said with a wink, and Tony blushed.

Sal grew more serious. "There's something else I want to say, son. About your friend."

Tony gestured toward Jake and stood aside. "Why don't you tell him yourself?"

"Yes, I think I will." Sal studied Jake, who squared his jaw. "Mr. DenBleyker, you saved my son's life, and for that you have my undying gratitude."

Tony and Jake shared a smile.

"Now...my wife tells me"—he glanced at her, and she

nodded—"that I put you on the spot with my remarks about your people. I hope you'll accept an apology from this Italian yokel." Sal extended his hand. Jake paused a beat and then grasped it, jaw set.

"Dad, there's something else that's been on my mind," Tony said.

"Sure, son, anything." Sal spread his hands solicitously.

Tony wet his lips. "The Delta Shipping Company."

Sal Marsala frowned. He looked to his wife, wagging pressed fingers close to his chest.

"I guess it's time to come clean on everything," he said, sounding almost eager.

They all sat down to the kind of meal usually reserved for a feast day, and Sal Marsala held forth for half an hour. Tony insisted Jake sit while he helped his mother with the dishes. Sal continued to put it away like a starving man.

"Beats jail food," he said, working on another mound of veal cutlets and baked eggplant. Jake quietly kept Sal company, though it seemed Jake's propped elbows were all that were keeping him from sliding under the table. Tony set down the dish towel, sat next to Jake, protectively wrapped one arm around him, and laid his head on Jake's chest.

The gesture did not escape his parents' notice. Tony looked up and saw the shock and dawn of understanding in their eyes. Tony steadied his sights and dared himself not to flinch at his mom's familiar look of reproach. He felt Jake's warm skin pulsing against his cheek.

And he saw the rightness of this moment and this man, of owning his love for him here where they sat. He lifted his head and regarded Jake with a tenderness that he returned.

Tony directed his burgeoning happiness to his parents, who seemed to startle at its radiance. "Ma, Dad, excuse us, please. Jake's had a rough couple of days. We're going to go sit down by the water," Tony said.

The cheer infected his father, and he stabbed the air with his fork. "It's a fine day to be out in the sun," he said sprightly.

"Oh, Tony?" his mother said. "You had a message yesterday. I kept it here in the drawer." Tony motioned for Jake to go on ahead of him.

Mrs. Marsala smoothed out the note and squinted. "A Mr. Harford. He says he got your package. And to please call right away to set up a meeting. Do you know what this is about?"

Tony smiled and slipped the note into his pocket. "Thanks, Ma."

Tony caught up with Jake at the shore. Boats stirred the lake to foam, waves overtopping one another in a spirited dance. Tony grabbed cushions from a shed and pulled two loungers into the sun.

They sank into their chairs. A crisp breeze tousled Tony's hair, reminding him of autumn. Sunlight winked through withering leaves.

He shot a stream of air from his lungs. "I would never have guessed that my dad and Otto Schmidt had a past."

Jake chuckled. "Two Americans in a Texas war camp? *Stalag 17* meets *The Twilight Zone*."

"I can't believe they put my father away for three years on the word of a mafioso." Tony slapped the aluminum arms of his chaise lounge.

Jake studied Tony through one squinty eye. "On the bright side, he *was* framed."

"And Otto lied," Tony huffed.

"That M.O. didn't work out too well for the bastard, did it?"

A smile flickered on Tony's face. "God, my dad carried that secret for fifteen years."

Jake looked past Tony to the shadowed mountain. "Seems we all got our cross to bear."

A wave slapped the bulkhead and plumed. Tony turned toward the sound just as a second wave struck, and the wind carried it to them. They both jackknifed from the shock. Tony scrambled for beach blankets, and they toweled off the chill.

No matter how hard Tony rubbed, his goose bumps stubbornly persisted. Something inside wanted out. He had been through too much and come too close to happiness these past four weeks not to claim it for himself. He inched out to the edge of the high board, closed his eyes, and dove in.

"Jake, I can't go on pretending anymore."

Jake swiveled toward Tony, the alarm in his eyes stirring Tony's own.

"My whole life, I've been the golden boy, and where has it gotten me?"

Jake looked doubtful. "All the way to Columbia."

"Where I live under cover, because I'm scared that one slipup could ruin me, like it ruined my friends." His eyes welled.

Jake regarded Tony with urgency. "Tony. Since I met you, you risked your life *three* times. You beat the toughest man in Algonquin County. And I noticed you weren't under cover in front of your parents. You are *brave*, Tony."

Tony sat up, shimmied his chair against Jake's, and leaned in. "If I am, that's because you made me see that some things are worth fighting for, no matter what the world thinks!" Tony's eyes were torches.

Jake seemed untouched by Tony's zeal. "Just don't expect the world to change because you do."

"But nothing changes if *I* don't." Tony abruptly stood and

swept his gaze all around, taking in every window and porch and dock inside of one hundred feet. He eyed the tacking sailboats and runabouts, the skiers and swimmers, imagined every eye on him, and then slid onto Jake's lounger and gently wrapped himself around him. Jake reflexively tensed at Tony's bold transgression, then eased against him.

"I'll tell you a secret: I haven't even looked at my college course catalogue," Tony said.

Jake's breath hitched. "Tony, don't throw away your schooling."

"I'm not. But things are going to be different. For starters, I'm dropping my major. I think I was never in love with the classics. They were just a place to park my fantasies." He pulled back from Jake enough to study his eyes. "Because it's clear to me now, it's you that I want."

Jake kinked an eyebrow. "So *I'm* your fantasy?"

"No, you're the real thing." Jake squirmed at their public embrace.

Tony swung himself off of Jake's chaise and crouched before him. "And so is your art. Jake, you have to bring your carvings to the city. You have so much to show the world."

"Why would I, when the world's never shown no kindly interest in me?"

"Sharing your gift with the world is the kindest thing you could do for yourself."

Jake gave him the side-eye. "Where are you going with this?"

Tony's lips disappeared in a coy smile. "You remember that couple with the crafts shop in the city?"

Jake narrowed his eyes. "What about them?"

"Well, I sent them some snapshots of your work—"

Jake rocked the lounger. "You *what?*"

"—and now they want to meet you!"

Jake frowned. "You had no right—"

"Okay, maybe I should've asked first. But I knew you'd say no." Tony's eyes twinkled.

"And you just figured I'd give in anyways."

"Well, yeah, once I proved to you that you're talented."

"Says you," Jake harrumphed.

"Says two Manhattan art dealers who sell fine design to a lot of rich people. Which reminds me—" Tony pulled the folded slip of paper from his pocket, and handed it to Jake. "A message for you." Jake studied the note, jaw grinding.

"Jake, they *want* you," Tony said in a spirited whisper.

Jake's brow furrowed. "What are you trying to do?"

"Make you see who you really are," Tony said.

Jake stiffened, and crossed his arms. "How did you manage to get those pictures?"

"I stopped at your house Monday on my way to Silas's funeral and shot them with my new instant Polaroid Highlander." Tony's eyes twinkled.

Jake probed Tony's face a long moment. "Tony, all your scheming isn't really about my carvings, is it?"

Jake had caught him out, and suddenly, he felt the old fear.

Time to get out of my own way.

He steadied himself, and began. "Jake, I'm taking a furnished apartment in Greenwich Village for the school year. Will you come live with me?" Tony's heart was in his throat.

Jake's eyes pinballed across Tony's. "My life is on the mountain." His voice was barely audible.

"But you've said that you can't really be yourself there. Jake, you made me confront what was missing from my life, so now it's *my* turn to ask your question: What do *you* want?"

The color drained from Jake's face, and he clutched Tony's arm. "Don't leave me," he rasped.

"I won't have to, if we leave this place together."

Jake's eyes grew distant. "I can't walk out on my family while they're grieving Silas. And now people threatening their lives..."

"Otto's gone, and your cousin's in charge."

"And the people who worshipped Schmidt ain't going nowhere. I seen what they wrote on Cousin Leo's billboard. And that ain't the end of it."

"Could there be a clearer sign that it's time to leave the mountain?"

"What makes you think my life would be any easier in New York City?"

"The Village is a place where everyone comes to be themselves."

"I been with those city boys more than you, Tony. They make nice in the bars, but they don't want to know me on the streets, same as here. Only difference in the city is they're too polite to say what they really think."

"But you'd be with me."

"Tony, this is still America, where your family's the wrong kind of white, and you're an impostor at school, and everywhere I go, I'm a freak or a threat."

Tony had no comeback for all of that. He felt completely deflated.

"I care about you, Tony. But this world won't let us have the kind of life you want."

Jake began to shiver as the breeze grew chill. Tony tenderly laid another beach blanket over him and gently stroked his shoulders.

"Jake, I'm leaving for school Tuesday. Please...take the bus with me to the city, and see about your carvings. And then come stay the night at my apartment."

Jake sat up and pressed himself to Tony's chest, the touch as electric as any moment they'd ever shared.

"Okay. But I'm not in any kind of state to see your fancy shopkeepers just now."

"All right," Tony whispered.

Jake pulled back and studied Tony. "And I want to see my family before I go, and I gotta come back the next morning. We all need to heal together."

Tony swallowed hard. "I know."

"I'm sorry, but right now, I just can't see—" Jake clamped his mouth shut and took two shaky breaths. He began again. "If there was some way..." Jake's words dissolved in a whimper. The two men searched each other's eyes for an answer that eluded them.

"Shhhh. We have today." Tony's chest ached.

The sun breached the clouds, throwing bolts of brightness over a quicksilver lake. Steps approached on the lawn, and they both turned from the luminous spectacle to find Mrs. VerHogen, wide-eyed and smiling.

"The Gestapo and the Luftwaffe left today with all their planes and lists! Isn't that wonderful?"

"That's great, um, Mrs. Schmied?" Tony asked.

Her face crumpled in confusion. "Who's that?"

Tony and Jake's laughter shook loose a torrent of tears, and Mrs. VerHogen nodded knowingly.

"There, there, you just let it all out. It's been a long, hard summer. We won this time, but stay vigilant! The enemy is still out there."

They nodded soberly, and she gave them a warm smile. Then she shielded her eyes with one hand, scanned the sky for trouble, and disappeared behind a hedge.

END

AUTHOR'S NOTE

The characters and main locale of this story are fictional, but much else is drawn from the historical record. The American Nazi movement of the 1930s, its youth camps, and its 1939 rally at Madison Square Garden were real, as was the Crystal City, Texas detention camp for American citizens of Japanese, German, and Italian descent during WWII.

The mountaineers in this story are the Ramapo (aka Ramapough) Munsee Lunaape Nation, a Native American tribe living in the Ramapo Mountains of New York and New Jersey. This people has a history documented by European settlers as far back as America's colonial beginnings, and that is perhaps 10,000 years old in the archaeological record.

I have no cause (or right) to contradict this tribe's Native American identity, heritage, and ancestry, and yet these aspects remain unsettled in the (mostly non-native) historical record, as well as in ethnographic studies, journalism, and other works of non-fiction.

In this novel, I have made the perhaps controversial choice to consider the Ramapoughs' ancestry expansively, to include the oft-cited theory that many Ramapough are bi- and multi-racial. I beg the pardon of anyone I may offend with this choice. My intent is not to diminish in any way this people's deeply held American Indian identity.

In my childhood summers spent in the Ramapo Mountains, non-natives who spoke of the mountain people used an epithet that many consider on par with the N-word. I made the decision to employ that slur in the mouths of my white characters to reflect the truth of those times, and underscore its racism. My sincere apologies to those whom that choice offends.

ACKNOWLEDGMENTS

The long, episodic aborning of this book has had a number of indispensable midwives.

I brought my earliest drafts of *Blood and Soil* to the 92nd Street Y's Fiction Writing Workshop. Getting to work my critical faculties with a great teacher and a roomful of sharp, thoughtful writers was invaluable to better my craft.

Caroline Leavitt, my developmental editor, was the tow-truck operator who helped pull my creaking jalopy of a story out of the ditch and down the highway. I am grateful for her superhuman capacity to convey glowingly upbeat assessments of my most execrable attempts at storytelling.

Renee Cafiero has frightening superpowers of copyediting. She can hunt down and kill without mercy every last atrocity of grammar, syntax, fact, or chronology that might escape lesser mortals.

My circle of readers has kept me grounded and full of cogent advice as I wallowed in my story's alternate reality. Indispensable are you, Susan Alexander, Marcy Feller, Richard Lishner, Fran Weick, and others whose insights have made this a far better book.

Certain authors deserve mention for helping me authentically render the people, places, and history touched on in this book. I'm grateful to Jan Jarboe Russell for *The Train to Crystal City*; CUNY Professor Mark D. Van Ellis, on the history of the German-American Bund; Edward J. Lenik, for his studies on

Ramapough ethnography; Arnie Bernstein's *Swastika Nation*; Otto Friedrich's rich portrait of Berlin in the 1920s, *Before the Deluge*; and *Angels Make Their Hope Here*, Breena Clarke's imagining of the Ramapoughs in 19th-century America.

Finally, I am thankful for my forbearing husband Steve, who gave me the freedom to write when I should have been holding up my half of our lives, and after it all will still have me. Lucky me!

ABOUT THE AUTHOR

Vinny Cusenza cowrote his first novel, *The Adventures of Pen and Pencil*, in fourth grade with his best friend Steve Drayzen. It was so little noticed, they wrote a sequel. In addition to novels, he writes personal and travel essays, memoir, and epistolary meditations on his place in the world.

He has won awards for his travel and journalism photography. He founded a small New England inn recognized by the *New York Times* and the Michelin travel guides. His favorite onstage moment was singing with Liza Minnelli in Central Park. He was Bugs Bunny for pay at a theme park, and he's herded rhinos.

A native New Yorker, Vinny lives in Park Slope, Brooklyn, with husband Steve and Neko, their transsexual Russian Blue cat, who sometimes puts up with him. He loves to photograph his city, walk its boroughs, attend the lively arts, and travel the world.

www.vinnycusenza.com

www.ingramcontent.com/pod-product-compliance
Lightning Source LLC
Chambersburg PA
CBHW021024310726
48969CB00006B/1526